MORGAN'S
HUNTER

BOOK ONE IN THE *BODYGUARDS OF L.A. COUNTY* SERIES

CATE
BEAUMAN

DEDICATION

For my boys, Brian, Joel, and Connor, whose love and support made all of this possible.

ACKNOWLEDGMENTS

A big thank you to my amazing husband, my number one fan, for your love and support during this exciting journey. I couldn't do this without you!

To my Critique Circle crew – Melissa Mayberry, Rachelle Ayala, Dawn Wimbish Prather, Joel Muranelli, Susan Elsworth, Aminah Grefer, and Angela Quarles. Thank you for helping me shape my story into something I can be proud of.

‍❦ CHAPTER ONE ❧

September 2010
Helmand Province, Afghanistan

G UNNERY SERGEANT HUNTER PHILLIPS AND HIS MEN drove toward their target: the hideout of Al-Qaeda's number three. Satellite imagery confirmed Abbas Muhammad Muhammad Tayi was holed up in a small village ten miles away, but a source warned they had the wrong man. Hunter and his Force Recon unit were about to find out. After a year of searching, tracking, hunting, they would substantiate the evidence either way. Bringing the fucker to justice thirty days before they departed this godforsaken land would be the perfect end to their tour.

The caravan of two up-armored Humvees moved swiftly down the endless, dusty road, dodging enormous blast holes created by Soviet mines years before. They came past the blackened remains of a truck three Marines died in yesterday. Like a mascot of death, the burned vehicle welcomed the recon unit to "The Danger Zone." In the last month alone, ten soldiers had lost their lives along the eternal stretch of dirt.

Rocky terrain laden with caves and deep crevices surrounded the Humvees. Insurgents roamed the area, ever eager to take their shot at US forces. Although the route clearance team had driven by twenty minutes ago, ten pairs of eyes scanned the road and dirt beyond, watchful for mounds of sand and small rocks—telltale signs of IEDs.

"And as we drive through the valley of the shadow of death, I would like to remind you all that God is good, men. Keep Him with you today," Hunter said into his radio.

Nine "Amens" answered back.

Tension hung thick and the vehicles were silent except for the hum of motors and the constant click of Carson, Hunter's gunner above, moving in half circles in his mechanical seat. The unit had gone a year without a casualty—a miracle in direct action warfare. But the law of averages told them they were due, and they all knew it.

Somewhere during the last mile, the AC had petered out. Hunter, sweat soaked and miserable, tugged at his collar, trying to ignore the one hundred degree heat and baking sun boring through the windshield, zapping energy from him and his men like a furnace straight from hell. Perspiration trapped by camouflage fabric and bulletproof vests mixed with sand, chafing, burning, only adding to the wretched conditions.

As the truck plowed ahead, Hunter's shoulder blades itched and his stomach pitched. His eyes narrowed and his focus sharpened as he searched the rocks beyond. Something wasn't right. His gut instinct was never wrong, and his men didn't question it. "Men, I've got the itch. Stay alert. I repeat, stay alert."

"Still glad you picked this route, Gunny?" Jake Johnson said from truck two.

Despite the situation, a small smile ghosted Hunter's mouth. "Don't be a pussy, Johnson." He lurched to the right as the driver swerved around another blast hole. "The fastest route isn't always the safest. That's why I'm lead truck. I'll keep you safe, honey."

Jake chuckled. "Fuck you, man."

Hunter grinned, forever scrutinizing their surroundings.

"You'll be tucked in with your blankey before—"

The massive explosion cut him off, shaking his vehicle with its deafening boom. "What the *fuck*?" He glanced in his rearview mirror as smoke plumed from truck two. *Oh God—Jake.*

Bullets pinged against the armored trucks as the unit took on fire.

"Return fire! Return fire!" Hunter instructed, peering back at Jake's vehicle. "Truck two, do you copy?"

Static crackled in his earpiece as his heart pounded—in his chest, in his throat. His body revved from the swift flow of adrenaline and fear coursing through his veins. He radioed back to camp, struggling to remain calm. "Thunder Main, this is Patriot Zulu. We have IED detonation—one truck hit. We're taking fire. I need fire support now and casualty evacuation on standby!"

"Patriot Zulu, this is Thunder Main. That's a good copy of last transmission. Scout weapons team is inbound. ETA ninety seconds."

With help on the way, Hunter tried Jake's Humvee again. "Vehicle two, do you copy?"

"Hunter, this is truck two. We're smoking and rattled, but we're—" Another explosion roared, cutting them off as a rocket-propelled grenade hit Humvee two. Metal smashed and scattered through the air as Jake's vehicle rolled twice.

"Shit! Shit! Fire support, what is your location, goddammit? Carson," he hollered to his gunman, "suppress that fire so I can move toward those rocks." He had to get to Jake's truck.

Carson gave him a nod, pummeling fifty caliber rounds into the boulders, decimating rock and anything behind them.

Hunter opened his door, crouching next to the wheel well, assessing the unit's dire situation. Help was still sixty seconds away, and they were surrounded by insurgents. Truck two lay on its side four hundred yards back as heavy black smoke plumed from the twist of metal. Hot rubber and burning electrical equipment choked the air.

A movement in the rocks caught Hunter's eye. He fired his weapon, watching a man fall to the ground.

"Let's do this," he said to the three soldiers waiting for his command. The men took his place at the wheel well as he ran for the boulders in the distance. "Clarke, Tanger, I need an update on truck two. Move forward."

Carson continued shooting from the Humvee roof while Hunter and Sergeant Smith laid down fire, providing cover as the soldiers ran. Halfway to the vehicle, bullets rained down from an unknown area in the rocks above. Clarke and Tanger stumbled, falling to the ground.

"No! Cover me, Smith." Without a second thought, Hunter sprinted toward his fallen men as the rhythmic thump of chopper blades echoed closer.

A Kiowa Warrior soared overhead, dropping missiles among the crevices and caves, obliterating large chunks of mountainous terrain. The helicopter banked right as the next aircraft flew in, repeating the same procedure.

Fire support vanished as quickly as it had appeared, and the air fell silent. The heavy breathing of his soldiers filled Hunter's ear. The firefight was over. For the moment they were clear of danger, and a weight lifted off his shoulders, leaving him lightheaded with relief.

Sergeant Tanger groaned as a chunk of dangling metal fell from truck two with a deafening crash, and reality rushed back like a punch to the gut.

Hunter ran to his men, who were shot and bleeding, as Carson continued with precautionary fire into the mountainside. "Smith, get the truck over here!" Hunter dug into Clarke's medical pack and applied a tourniquet to the unconscious man's arm. As he twisted the black fabric tight, the flow of blood ceased.

With Clarke as stable as he could make him, Hunter crawled to Tanger, ripping Tanger's pant leg, exposing three bullet wounds. He glanced at Jake's truck, desperate to get to him. Distracting flashes of their childhood played through his mind, and he ruthlessly squashed the memories. "Shit, man, you're a mess," he said to Tanger, attempting to keep his soldier lucid and himself calm.

"It hurts like—shit!" Tanger tensed as Hunter packed his first wound.

Sergeant Smith backed the Humvee closer and crouched next to Hunter, waiting for orders.

"Smith, finish this. Get them secured. I'm heading for truck two." With his gun to his shoulder, he peered through the sight, moving toward Jake's vehicle. It had only been five minutes since the attack began, but it felt as if it had been hours. "Truck two, do you copy?" The air remained dead, and panic rose from his depths. Everything he'd learned as a Force Recon escaped him. All the training on procedure vanished as he thought of Jake and the other four men. "Jake. Jake, do you copy? Can you hear me?"

"Hunter," Jake answered, coughing.

"Oh, thank God. You scared the sh—"

"I'm hit, Hunt. I'm hit." Jake wheezed, coughing again. "And they're all dead, man."

Pain sliced his heart as he yelled into his radio once more. "We need casualty evac, ASAP! Get them here now! I have four confirmed KIAs and three wounded." Hunter whirled when footsteps approached from behind. Sergeant Smith's face lined up in the crosshairs of his scope.

"Clarke and Tanger are secure."

"Let's go then," Hunter said, running to what was left of the vehicle. "Jake, I'm here."

Jake gasped for air, coughing violently.

Hunter climbed to the top of the heap, burning and cutting his hands, peering down at Jake's battered face. Gashes riddled his cheeks, dribbling blood. He glanced at the remains of his four other men, burying the fisting pain deep. Jake was all that mattered now—the only one he could help.

Hunter locked his legs around mangled metal, anchoring himself. He reached his arms through the opening, grabbing hold of Jake. "Come on, man, I'm going to get you out of here. Evac's on its way."

Jake tried to sit up on the console and yelled out. "I can't do it. I can't get up."

"Yes, you can. I don't know how long we have before they fire on us again."

Taking a deep breath, Jake hollered, clenching his fists as he sat up.

Hunter hoisted him up, and Jake screamed. "I'm sorry, man. Almost there."

With Jake's head and torso freed from the wreckage, Sergeant Smith climbed up, grabbing hold of Jake's legs, helping Hunter lay him on the ground.

"Sergeant, get me a kit," Hunter said, assessing Jake's injuries as Smith ran for their truck. Blood saturated Jake's plated vest, and sweat covered his face as he grew pale with every heartbeat. Hunter ripped through his friend's armor and cloth to the wound, fighting to steady his breathing, horrified by the injuries. He applied pressure to the gaping hole in Jake's abdomen as blood pooled over his fingers. Helplessness consumed him and desperation clawed at his throat as he yelled into his radio, "We need casualty evac now, goddammit! Do you hear me? Right now!"

Sergeant Smith hustled back with a kit, but there was nothing among the first aid supplies that would help. The medics on their team were dead or gravely injured, and Jake's entire midsection was full of shrapnel.

"I'm not going to make it," Jake gasped.

"Don't you fucking say that!"

He coughed again, violently. "I'm not. Take care of them. Take care of Sarah and the baby."

Hunter pressed harder as blood oozed over his fingers, pooling in the sand. "No, you're going to take care of them. They're coming." The rhythmic sound of chopper blades echoed off the mountains. "Listen, they're almost here."

Jake's body shook. "Promise me. Promise me, goddammit." Tears streamed from his brown eyes. "Tell them I love them, that I'll always be with them."

"I promise, Jake." It was too late. There was nothing the medics could do.

White as a sheet, Jake convulsed, even as Sergeant Smith tried to help keep him still. "Kiss Kylee for me." His voice grew weaker. "Tell her it's from her daddy. I never got to...I never got to hold her. Tell her about me."

"I will. I will." Hunter was losing him. Life seeped from his best friend, his brother. "I love you, Jake. I'll take care of them."

"I love...take care of..." Jake stopped moving, stopped breathing.

"God, no! No!" Desperately, Hunter started chest compressions. "Don't you leave me!"

The chopper landed in the distance, and gunfire broke out. Heat seared through Hunter's left shoulder.

Bullets sprayed from Sergeant Smith's weapon. "I got him, Hunter. I got the fucking bastard." Smith's brow furrowed as he crouched behind the rocks. "Shit, you're shot."

Hunter sat in the sand and dust with Jake while blood dripped down his arm.

———◆———

After a miserable week in West Germany's Landstuhl Regional Medical Center, followed by four days at Walter Reed, Hunter landed in Los Angeles. If he never saw another doctor again, it would be too soon. The constant poking and prodding had been enough to drive any sane man crazy, and he couldn't be certain he was sane any longer. The nightmares he woke from left him in panicked sweats for hours. Loud sounds spooked him, and at the strangest times, he swore he could hear Jake calling out to him. He was a mess—

his life a disaster.

The plane taxied to the gate, and he reached for his bag, jostling his stiff shoulder. On a sharp intake of breath, he clenched his jaw and closed his eyes, waiting for the twinge to pass. The nagging throb wouldn't allow him to forget he had physical therapy tomorrow. He would have preferred another gunshot wound over the twisting and turning, the bending and stretching that left his shoulder radiating with pain and aching worse than the bullet had itself. The sadistic bastards were relentless with their sunny smiles and encouragement. With every agonizing movement, they reminded him that his hard work would be well worth the time he put in when he achieved full range of motion.

At this point, he didn't give two fucks about his range of motion—or much of anything else, for that matter. He could've sat in the hospital bed indefinitely, letting the morphine drip into his veins, inviting the drug-induced fog to take away all of the memories. He didn't want to remember anymore. He didn't really care to live, but he'd made Jake a promise. And it was one he intended to keep.

Hunter stared at the palm trees flashing by and the churning waves of the Pacific as the cab traveled Highway 1 to the Palisades. He rolled down the window, breathing in the salty sea. It smelled like home. He wanted to be happy he was here, to feel *something,* but he couldn't shake the empty numbness that had consumed him since the casualty evacuation chopper flew him back to base. He'd stared at six body bags, the remains of his unit—his family—while medics worked on him and his two fellow men.

He came to attention, shaking the images away as the cab pulled up to the curb in the upscale neighborhood. He stepped from the car, handing the cabbie a fifty, muttering his thanks as a door closed behind him. Hunter peered over his shoulder, staring into Sarah's grief-shattered blue eyes as she stood on the entryway steps, surrounded by concrete planters thriving with sunny pink pansies. The creamy white of the ranch-style house looked exactly the same, but everything would be forever different.

Despite the heat of the day, Sarah hugged herself tight in one of Jake's thick, gray sweatshirts. Hunter turned, taking a step forward, and she ran to him with tears streaming down her cheeks. "Oh my God, Hunter. Hunter," she sobbed, collapsing into his arms, holding on tight.

He freed his arm from the sling and picked her up, ignoring the dull pain radiating through his shoulder as he brought her inside. "I'm sorry, Sarah. I'm so sorry," he repeated over and over as he sat down, gripping her against him on the couch. Twinges of loss and grief attempted to surface as he glanced around the living room. He'd spent countless hours within these walls, watching games with Jake and Ethan, unwrapping presents under a prettily decorated tree. Life had happened here, had been taken for granted. At twenty-eight, time seemed endless—until it unexpectedly ran out.

Jake would never sit in this room again. No more yells of objection at poor referee decisions. No more infectious laughter from one of Ethan's crude jokes. How would he move past the silence? How would he go on? His thoughts threatened to overwhelm him as he pressed his cheek against Sarah's hair, hugging her closer, grabbing hold of something real.

A picture caught his eye—one of many hanging on the wall. Tuxedo clad and grinning, he and Jake gave a thumbs-up. He remembered the flash in time, a special moment he could never have back.

"I'm getting married, man. The photographer wants one more picture before the I-dos."

"This is your last chance to escape," Hunter joked.

"I don't want to run. When you find someone amazing,

you grab them up before they get away."

Hunter studied the men in the picture—the twins, as his mother had always called them. A smile touched his mouth as he scrutinized Jake's classic Italian features and tall, leanly muscled frame—a stark contrast to his honey-blond hair, shocking blue eyes, and tough athletic build. Nothing about the two had ever been twin-like. They'd just been best friends...forever. As another layer of despair overshadowed life's light, Sarah looked at him, sniffling, and he once again remembered his promise.

"I can't believe... I can't believe he's really gone."

"I wish it'd been me. I would give anything for him to be here with you."

Sarah gripped his hand, shaking her head. "No, don't say that. As much as I want Jake back, I could never wish you gone."

Breathy whimpers echoed through the baby monitor, turning into lusty cries.

"Can I—can I get her?" He put Sarah on the couch cushion and stood.

"Yes, of course."

He walked down the hallway to the screaming infant, turning into her pink and pale yellow room, where another framed photograph of Jake hung next to the crib. Looking down, he stared at Jake's newborn daughter as grief invaded him, choking him, consuming him. The night before Jake died, they'd sat before a computer screen, watching via Skype as Sarah pushed Kylee into the world.

Hunter picked her up carefully, awkwardly, tucking her into the crook of his good arm. Kylee's crying turned to whimpers as her baby blues stared up at him. She had Jake's ears and his long, slender fingers. She was so tiny, so soft. He kissed her forehead, hugging her gently against him. "Your dad couldn't be here. He asked me to do that. I'm supposed to—" His voice broke. Taking a deep breath, he tried again. "He wanted me to tell you he loves you and he'll always be with you. I'm going to say that a lot." Tears raced down his cheeks as he glanced up at Sarah standing in the doorway.

Kylee fussed and started crying again.

"She's hungry. Let's bring her out to the living room."

He nodded, wiping at his damp face, wincing when he wrenched his aching shoulder.

They huddled on the couch while Sarah fed Kylee. Hunter draped an arm around her, holding on, taking comfort as he gave it. This was supposed to be Jake's moment. He would have it for him. Hunter told them both what Jake had wanted them to hear, choking on his sobs. When the baby fell back to sleep, he and Sarah cried together, holding each other close.

☞ CHAPTER TWO ☜

May 2012

MORGAN TAYLOR WALKED THROUGH THE PARK-ing garage as fast as her legs would carry her. She whipped out her cell phone and dialed Shelly's number, eager to give her the news. Waiting for her friend to pick up, Morgan pushed the button on her key fob, unlocking her silver sports convertible.

"Hello?"

"Hey, Shell. We got the assignment." She sat behind the wheel, started the sweet little Mercedes, and backed out of her spot with a squeal of tires.

"We did?"

"Yup. We leave Friday." She pressed on the accelerator, gunning her way out of the garage and into DC's rush-hour traffic.

"*What*? This Friday?"

"Afraid so. We're on the first flight out. Do you want to call the guys and tell them?"

"Sure, I can do that."

"Great." She shifted into third, holding the phone to her ear with her shoulder. The man in the Lexus behind her laid on his horn when she cut him off. "Oops. Sorry, mister," she murmured.

"Morgan, are you driving right now? Your driving sucks

when you give it your *full* attention."

She grinned, used to the jokes about her less-than-stellar skills behind the wheel. "I should've waited until I got home, but we don't have a lot of time. I'll be quick. This assignment will be a little different. Half of us are going to Yellowstone and the rest to Maine."

"Aw, but this is my final stint in the field. I wanted one last hurrah before I leave. Can't your dad arrange it?"

"No, he can't," she scolded, uncomfortable with the idea of her father playing favorites. "It'll be weird not having the six of us together, but that's how The Bureau's handling it. Are you sure you want to head up research in smog-choked LA?"

"Yes, Morgan, I do."

The warning tone rang through in her friend's voice, and she blew out a breath. "I know this is something you've wanted for a long time. I'm happy for you, Shell. Let's see if everyone wants to get together tomorrow, and we'll figure out who's going where. How about we meet at your place? We can help you pack."

"Oh, I don't know."

She ignored her hesitation. Shelly had barely begun to get her apartment together. "I'll grab a bunch of food—that'll keep the guys happy. If everything's in order before we go on assignment, we'll be able to concentrate on your goodbye party when we get back. I'll book us a day at Claude's—the works—and we'll plan away."

"What an excellent idea." Shelly's voice brightened. "I'll make the calls now. Oh, by the way, I'm officially electing you to decide who's going where. I have too much to do already without worrying about that."

"Fine," she said with a playful huff as she breezed through a yellow light. "I'm always the heavy."

"Yes, and you do it so well. I'll talk to you tomorrow morning. Crap. My relaxing week just got extremely hectic."

Morgan turned on Connecticut Avenue, heading northwest toward her parents' home in Chevy Chase. "Better get packing, Shell. Talk to you later." She pressed *end* as her speedometer hit sixty-five in a fifty.

———◆———

The team of six rested on the floor of Shelly's one-bedroom apartment. A dozen pizza boxes lay on cardboard boxes stacked and scattered about the room.

"Well, Shell, I can't technically call you a hoarder, but it's close." Ian Ledderbeck sat leaning against the wall, his paper plate heaped with pizza.

"Hey, I don't have that much stuff." She nibbled her veggie-loaded slice.

"Damn, girl, are you *kidding*? I mean look at all this shit." Dave Andrews dabbed at the sweat on his handsome ebony face as he gave the box closest to his foot a slight nudge.

Dave's identical twin, Jim, laughed, and Morgan grinned, elbowing him.

"Leave her alone, guys." Tom Smithson pushed his thick glasses up the bridge of his nose. "You don't have a lot of stuff, Shelly."

"You say that tomorrow, Skinny Man, when your muscles are screaming," Jim said as he laughed again.

Morgan wadded her napkin and put it on her plate. "All right. Now that we've had fun at Shelly's expense, let's talk about this assignment and figure out who's going where."

"We're tagging and tracking a lynx; we don't have to make this into a big thing." Ian stood, grabbing more pizza. "Tom, Shelly, and I'll take Yellowstone, and the Bobbsey twins will go with you to Maine. Now, let's grab a drink at Club Rave."

"I can get behind that." Dave fist bumped Ian, then Jim.

Smiling, Morgan rolled her eyes. "Does anyone object to Ian's oh-so-professional business proposal?" She glanced around at shaking heads. "Okay, everyone go home and change. We'll meet at Rave in an hour."

———◆———

Flashes of bright light pulsed throughout the dimly lit club in time with the heavy bass of the song currently playing. A waitress delivered pretty mixed drinks to the team's table.

"Oh, good. Let's do a toast," Morgan yelled over the deafening music. "To three of the best damn years of our lives. We're going to miss you like crazy, Shell." They clinked glasses, and Morgan sipped the creamy coconut of her piña colada, then enveloped Shelly in a huge hug.

Shelly's eyes watered. "You're going to make me cry."

"No crying tonight." Morgan gave Shelly a final squeeze and stepped back. "We're here for fun. Let's dance."

Everyone in the group jumped up except for one.

Morgan grabbed Tom's hand. "Come on, Tom."

His brown eyes, magnified by his prescription lenses, stared into hers as he tightened the knot in his bright orange tie. "I don't dance, Morgan. I strictly came because this is Shelly's last assignment." He shoved at his glasses for the umpteenth time, and her heart melted. She had a soft spot for Tom—always had. He exemplified the classic geek, and she couldn't help but adore him.

"Well, I guess we better have some fun then." Morgan pulled him into the mob on the dance floor. "Move those hips, Tom." She grinned as his gangly body moved in tight, jerky circles. "The night's still young. You'll get there."

Ian, known for his inner party animal, didn't have any trouble getting into the spirit of things as he spun Morgan away. "I couldn't bear to witness that for a moment longer. I was embarrassed for you. Is he hula hooping or dancing?"

Laughing, she gave Ian's broad shoulder a solid smack. "Stop. He's trying his best."

He pulled her closer. "I've been watching the men around here staring at the hot lady in the little red dress dancing with the nerd. You can tell they're wondering how the hell that happened."

She smacked him harder.

He grinned. "I'm playing. You know I think the guy's brilliant. He just can't dance." Ian's blue eyes darted in Tom's direction, and he winced. "*Really* can't dance." He met Morgan's gaze and took her hand, tugging her petite body to his, then away in a quick spin, then back to him. "So, I can't believe this is it—the end of the six musketeers. It's been a hell of a run." He bopped her hip and smiled, accentuating his handsome face.

"Yeah," she said on a wistful sigh. "I'm going to miss you guys this month. It'll be weird having everyone separated." She spun away and back. "You know, I'm not sure I'm happy with the way our teams were picked. I think I might change the groups around. I should take Yellowstone. And it would be better—"

"It's fine," Ian interrupted. "Everyone's in agreement, so let it go. Besides, how can I talk Shelly into staying if you mess everything up?" He wiggled his eyebrows and smiled. "LA's got nothing on the five of us."

"You've been after her for three years. Maybe you'll finally get lucky—although I wouldn't count on it." She gave his cheek a gentle pat and danced away to help poor, awkward Tom.

An hour later, Morgan sipped her water as Tom removed his ugly tie, swinging the silk fabric like a lasso.

"Good for you, Tommy Boy. See, Morgan? I told you he'd loosen up. He just needed a little liquid courage," said Dave.

"Yes, you did. Hopefully you and your brother will be driving him home." She frowned. "Where is Jim anyway?" She scanned the crowd, spotting the well-muscled man surrounded by several women and shook her head. "Your brother's making time with a pack of ladies."

"Typical." Grinning, Dave took her hand. "Let's join Tommy Boy before he hurts himself."

Jim finally joined the party on the floor, and they all teased him about his pocketful of phone numbers. Six good friends laughed and danced into the early hours of the morning, enjoying their final night together as a group.

———◆———

Morgan walked into her hotel room, filthy, exhausted, and more than glad her team of three had come back for their bi-weekly supply run. She hit the lights and dropped her heavy pack, looking around. The small, stuffy space was far from luxurious, with its burnt-orange bedspread, matching curtains, and décor straight out of the seventies, but it was clean, and more importantly, it had a mattress and shower.

She sat on the bed and sighed, closing her eyes as she pulled off her hiking boots, relishing the feel of something other than cold, hard ground beneath her ass. It was tempting to lay back against the soft, ugly bedding and let sleep pull her under, but she had too much to do. Her father would be expecting her to check in and fax her initial reports for the Environmental Protection Agency, even though she had little information to share since they hadn't found anything yet. Hopefully the Yellowstone crew had stumbled into more luck than she, Dave, and Jim. But faxes would have to wait. Her date with hot water and soap came first.

She stood and walked to the bathroom, casting a wistful glance over her shoulder. One more hour of work and she would be snuggled under the covers of her temporary bed. She faced the vanity mirror and grimaced at her dimly lit reflection. "Yikes. You've seen better days, Taylor." She flicked on the light. "Definitely worse than I thought."

She pulled the elastic from her messy ponytail and chuckled. Claude was going to freak when she stepped into his spa fourteen days from now. He always did after she returned from an assignment. The city's top stylist would cluck his tongue and scold her in fluent French while he yanked her to a salon chair as if her life hung in the balance. A flute of champagne would be thrust into her hand as a team of hair and skincare specialists descended on her like doctors and nurses responding to a stat call.

Cosmetologists would brush green goop on her face, and stylists would fuss and coo over her neglected mane while Claude continued on, outraged. "Beautiful skin should be treasured, no?" or "How can Morgan Taylor of *the* DC Taylors allow herself to fall apart like this every time she leaves town? Disgraceful!" And let's not forget, "What would your *grandmother*, the former *senator*, think if she happened to pass you on the street—like *this*—looking as though you just crawled out of the gutter? Scandalous!"

She shook her head, rolling her eyes as she brushed a hand through her dull hair. She had to admit, a good douse of Claude's special hydrating treatment couldn't hurt. Silky brown locks hid among the tangled mess hanging at her shoulders...somewhere. She swiped at the purple smudges under her dark green eyes, noting her broken fingernails, and shrugged. Vanity and the wilderness just didn't mix. But as soon as she got home, she and Shelly were spending the day with Claude. The appointments were already booked. God knew they deserved it. A month of trouncing through backcountry definitely warranted six hours of pampering, fun, and catching up. While two masseurs kneaded away knots of tension, Shelly would finally fill her in on the details of their last hurried conversation as they parted ways at Reagan International.

"*Morgan, I know this isn't a good time—that we're leaving—but I need to tell you something.*"

"*Okay.*"

"*Ian came to my place last night. We got into an argument—*"

"*Wait, what were you and Ian doing together? Weren't you both getting ready for the trip?*"

"It's a long story. I'll explain everything when we get back, but he kissed me—I mean really kissed me. He said we're going to have a serious conversation in Montana. He thinks he loves me, and he has a lot to say before I just get up and walk out of his life."

"Wow. I—"

"What am I supposed to do? I leave for LA in five weeks."

"I—Jesus, Shell, I'm still trying to catch up here. I had no idea anything was going on between you two. Do you love him?"

"I don't know. I—damn. That's my boarding call."

"We'll talk when you get back."

Oh, they would talk all right. Being left to dangle with small tidbits of a surprising turn of events was its own form of torture. Not knowing what had gone on between her best friend and Ian was unbearable. If she hurried with her shower and phone call to her father, she might catch Shelly alone at the ranger station—if they weren't out in backcountry.

With a shrug, she snapped the shower curtain open and turned the lever to hot, smiling when the spray spit from the head. "I am so ready for this." Steam plumed, fogging the mirror, filling the room with warm, moist heat, and a grin spread across her lips as she unbuttoned the flannel she wore over her t-shirt. This was the best part of her entire trip—real soap, hot water, the feel of soft cotton against her skin.

A faint knock sounded at the door, and she swore. "I was so *close*." She turned off the nozzle with a bad tempered twist and buttoned the grimy shirt she'd almost undone. "Just a minute." Peeking through the peephole, she frowned at the staff member in the hall, then plastered on a polite smile and opened the door. "Yes, can I help you?"

The perky blond beamed. "Ms. Morgan Taylor?"

"That's me."

"Hi, I'm Judy, the night manager. I tried calling up to your room, but I kept getting a busy signal."

Morgan glanced at the phone she'd taken off the hook in hopes of avoiding the habitual and foolish prank calls Dave and Jim were so fond of whenever the team checked into a motel.

"You had an urgent message waiting for you. Someone called a couple of days ago. The guy said you would be staying here. I saw that you'd just checked in, so I thought I should bring this up."

Frowning, she took the pink piece of paper, and unease roiled in her belly as she unfolded the note.

EXTREMELY URGENT! CALL IMMEDIATELY!

Dad

The words were underlined three times. "Thank you, Judy," she murmured, shutting the door and racing to her cell phone, which she hadn't powered on in two weeks. She dialed her parents' house number, listening to it ring incessantly as the coils of tension tightened in her stomach. Why didn't the voicemail pick up? She tried her father's cell next, dialing with unsteady fingers, pacing back and forth while her heart galloped wildly in her chest.

"Hel—"

"Dad, what's wrong? Where are you? Is Mom all right?"

"Thank God, Morgan. I've been waiting for your call. Yes, Mom's fine. I'm at the office."

She sunk to the bed with a sigh of relief. "Okay, good. What's going on?"

"Morgan."

She stood again as nerves skittered down her spine, recognizing the traces of sorrow in her father's voice.

"I have some hard news. I'm not sure how to tell you this."

"Go ahead, Dad. Please."

"Shelly, Ian, and Tom...they—"

"What? What's wrong with them?" She gripped the phone until her knuckles whitened as she moved about the room, unable to be still.

"They're—they're gone, honey."

Morgan stopped in her tracks. "What do you mean they're gone? What does that mean? They're missing? How long? The guys and I'll be on the first plane—"

"No, honey. They're dead."

She stared at the ugly curtains half opened to the fading light, unable to grasp her father's words.

When she didn't respond, he spoke again. "Your team is dead, Morgan."

Wispy fog threatened to dull her thoughts, but she shook it away. "That's ridiculous. There must be some mistake."

"I'm afraid not."

"This can't be true. How can they be dead?"

"We're still waiting for all of the details. I received word forty-eight hours ago."

"No," she whispered.

"Yes, Morgan. Their families went out to identify their bodies, honey. Dean flew out with them to lend any support The Bureau could offer. I should've gone myself, but he wanted to do this."

Her friends were dead? She couldn't get a handle on it. "Was it...a fall, or a bear?"

"No, Love. They were found shot."

Nothing could have prepared her for that. Nothing. She leaned against the dingy yellowed wall for support as her legs gave out and she slid to the floor. "Oh Daddy, I don't understand. Shot?"

"I wish there was some way to spare you all of this."

"I—I can't believe this." Her voice wavered as nausea churned.

"I've been having a hard time believing it myself."

She closed her eyes. "What happened?"

"Why don't we discuss everything tomorrow?"

She was tempted to agree and wait for the horrid details of their accident, but how did three people accidentally get shot? This wasn't happening. It couldn't be. She clenched her fists as her body shook, attempting to gain control over her racking shudders. She wanted to hang up, to go find Dave and Jim and forget the whole thing. Then she could pretend her father's call was some sort of mistake. But she wasn't made that way. "No. Tell me."

He sighed. "They were found shot in the head out in backcountry. We hadn't received any transmission signals from their tracking systems for a couple of days." Her father took another deep breath and continued. "Shelly's transmitter suddenly came on the day before the rangers found them. They think she must've turned it on when she figured out they were in trouble. At this point, we know they walked about a mile before the signal stopped moving. That's where they found their bodies, honey."

She shook her head. "I can't—" Her voice broke as her heart crumbled and tears rolled down her cheeks. Taking an unsteady breath, she stood, even as her legs threatened to buckle. "Dad, I have to tell Dave and Jim. What should I say? How do I explain that our friends—" She pressed her lips in a firm line, choking back more tears.

"I can talk to them, honey."

"No," she said, shaking her head again. "Shelly and I were in charge of this team."

"That's my girl. We'll put the assignment on hold. Helen will book your flights back for late tomorrow afternoon. That should give you plenty of time to drive to Portland. The tickets will be at the counter."

"Of course, but I want to depart in the morning. We'll leave early. I need to get back and find out what's going on." She stared at the cheap lighthouse painting hanging just off-center across the room, struggling to take everything in. "Who did this to them? Why?"

"We don't know. Perhaps I'll have more information when I pick the three of you up. I'll see you tomorrow, Peanut."

"Love you, Daddy. Bye."

"Bye."

Morgan's racking sobs echoed off the walls of the shower until the water ran cold. She wrapped herself in a towel, clutching the cotton tight, seeking warmth. Her friends were dead—had been dead for two days. While she, Dave, and Jim joked and gambled for marshmallows by the light of their campfire, their pals had been murdered. She didn't want to believe it.

Memories of the team's night out played through her mind. She never would've imagined it to be their last. Six people—all as different as could be, from all walks of life—had grown into such a close unit, a family. Now half of them were gone.

Morgan dressed quickly in jeans and a t-shirt, desperate to be in the company of her two remaining colleagues—her friends.

⟋ CHAPTER THREE ⟍

"**D**AD, I'M GOING." MORGAN PACED THE LENGTH OF the spacious office, making flinty eye contact with her father at every turn.

"Damn it, Morgan!" Stanley slammed his hand on his desk. "You aren't traipsing through backcountry by yourself. Not while the team's killer is still at large! I won't allow it."

"Let me remind you that I'm twenty-six." She glared at him as she turned toward the massive windows of The Bureau's presidential suite and stared out at the triangular tip of the Washington Monument in the distance, trying to find some semblance of control over her shaky emotions. For days, she'd ridden Hell's rollercoaster, fighting the waves of turmoil death always left in its wake. At moments she'd fly high, finding sweet relief in numbness and disbelief, allowing herself—for just a moment—to deny that the worst had really happened. But newspaper articles or unwanted conversations brought everything to the surface, and she coasted into tunnels of grief so deep, so dark, so intense she often wondered if she would find her way back to the other side.

The anger coursing through her veins demanded action, forcing her to set into motion the plan she'd come up with while lying awake and restless night after night. She refused to spend another day waiting for news and explanations that would make sense out of a senseless tragedy. Her friends' case grew colder with every passing hour. Relying on others had proved fruitless, so she would act on her own. Answers waited for her in Yellowstone. She wouldn't stop until she had them. Steady again, finding her resolve, she turned, facing her livid father. "Dad, you don't understand—"

"I understand perfectly, but I refuse—"

"Morgan, if I may." Dean Jenkins, Chairman of the Trustees and longtime family friend, sat in his chair sipping herbal tea, the calm eye in a frenzied storm. "I must admit I agree with your father. Although well intended, your idea is too dangerous. You haven't thought this through."

She whirled, facing the ever-composed Dean in his tidy navy blue suit. "I see you two plan to stand firm on this. Well, so do I." She rushed toward the door. "I don't give a damn what either of you think."

Stanley shot out of his seat. "Morgan Elizabeth Taylor, you get back here."

She stopped with her hand on the knob. "You know I *hate* when you use my middle name," she said, clenching her teeth.

"You leave this room, young lady, and I'll have security haul you right back."

"You wouldn't dare," she hissed in an outraged whisper as she turned back, but her father's jaw was clenched and his nostrils were flared. Morgan knew he would do as he said, so she tossed up her hands and paced again.

Taking a deep breath, her father sat down. "Stop walking back and forth and take a seat, Morgan. You're making me tired just watching you."

"Fine." With an air of dignity, she sat in the leather wing-back chair in front of her father's desk.

"Thank you. Now, let's talk this through until we come up with something that works for all of us."

"I can go along with that as long as we understand I'm leaving for Yellowstone next week." On that, she wouldn't bend.

Dean cleared his throat, and she spared him a look. "Morgan, as Chairman of the Trustees, I have full authority to pull the plug on this whole assignment. In fact, you'll have to convince me not to."

"Pull the plug for all I care." She leaned forward in her chair. "My friends are dead, not yours. I *will* finish this lynx project *and* find out what happened to the team while I'm at it."

"Morgan." Her father closed his eyes, pinching the bridge of his nose.

"No," she snapped with a determined shake of her head. "I won't hear any more. It's been two weeks, and they have nothing—not one damn lead. The police are clueless. We're affiliated with the federal government, for heaven's sake. Solving these murders should be top priority. Their funerals are this weekend, and the families have more questions than answers." She stood again, unable to sit still. "It's unacceptable."

"You're not a cop, sweetheart." Her dad's voice gentled as hers radiated with pain.

"You're right. I'm not. I'm a biologist who wants to do her job." *And a friend who desperately needs to know what happened.*

The men exchanged glances.

"Let me think, Morgan. I'll find a way to make this work."

She wanted to soften as her father had, but if she stared too long at the pleading look in his eyes, she might change her mind. She had to do this. "Fine, but I'm leaving Monday. Can I go now, or will you call security?"

His brow winged up, mirroring hers.

"Good night, then." Morgan walked to the door, closing it with a hard click behind her.

———◆———

"That girl is so goddamn stubborn," Stanley grumbled as

he scrubbed his hands over his face now that he and Dean were alone.

"I wonder where she gets it from." Dean smiled. "Morgan's beauty comes from her mother and her wretched temper from her dear old dad. You're two peas in a pod, Stan."

Stanley laughed.

Dean sipped his tea. "I'll pull the funding for the project. I was about to submit paperwork when you called me up here."

"I don't think it'll make a damn bit of difference. She'll go anyway. If the funds stay in place, she'll be busy tracking animals instead of getting herself into trouble searching for a killer." The very thought made the hair stand up on the back of his neck.

Dean set down his cup and walked to the window as lights blinked on around the city. "This isn't a good idea. The remaining members of her team have already been reassigned. I won't risk any more of our field scientists on this, and she can't go alone. Short of hiring a bodyguard, how will you make this work?"

Sitting up straighter, Stanley slammed his hand on the desk. "Why, Dean, you're a genius—a damn genius."

Dean turned with an incredulous laugh. "You can't be serious. A bodyguard? Where are you going to find someone willing to hike out into backcountry Montana and keep Morgan out of trouble? It's absurd."

"I happen to know a man out in LA who owns one of the best security firms in the country—hell, in the world. His father and I roomed together in college. I'll put in a call."

"Christ sakes, Stan. Wiring alarms for people and standing at some actor's gate aren't the same as what you're looking for."

"I'm still going to ask. If he can't help me, perhaps he'll put me in touch with someone who can."

"You do what you need to, but let's be clear on one point: The Bureau will not be paying for a bodyguard."

"I'm aware of that. Money is the least of my worries." Stan found the number for Ethan Cooke Security and lifted the phone.

"This should be interesting. I'll leave you to your call. I'm curious to see what you come up with."

↷ CHAPTER FOUR ↶

THE PHONE WOKE HIM. HE'D BEEN ON DUTY FOR FOR-
ty-eight hours straight and asleep for three. Hunter
lay on his stomach with his cheek squished against
his pillow as he felt around the side table for his cell phone
and knocked his alarm to the floor with a bang. His fingers
made contact with the plastic, and he grabbed hold, pressing "talk" with his eyes closed. "If you're calling me at this
hour, somebody better be dead."

"Hunter, it's Ethan."

Rolling to his back, he blinked, staring up at the patterns
the early morning sun left on his ceiling. "Yeah, I know who
this is. What do you *want*? I'm trying to sleep here."

"I've got the job of a lifetime for you, man."

"I'm pretty sure you said the same thing last week, and
I spent two days at a spa in northern California with four
rich-bitch ladies who thought they were important enough
to warrant protection. I still can't figure out why. One of the
women's daughters, who is barely legal by the way, came on
to me—several times. She pinched my ass and flashed me.
Thoughts of coming home and killing you got me through."

"I can't lie, Phillips—I would've paid to see that. Look on
the bright side; at least you weren't bored. Now, back to the
job of a lifetime."

Hunter stumbled out of bed in blue boxers adorned with

a grinning skunk that told someone to pull his finger. He made his way to the tiny efficiency kitchen, grabbed a gallon of orange juice from the refrigerator, and chugged while Ethan continued.

"Hear me out before you give me an answer."

He capped the juice and shoved the jug back on the top shelf. "Every time you start off your job-of-a-lifetime spiel with a disclaimer, I want to hang up and disconnect my phone."

"Stop being a cranky bastard and listen. The guy you'd be doing this for is a DC bigwig—an environmentalist or something. He's President of the Parks and Conservation Bureau. His family is big into politics."

He poured a huge bowl of cereal and dumped in milk. "I'm still waiting for the part where this is the opportunity of a lifetime."

"Stop interrupting me and I'll tell you. His daughter needs protection for a month. Let me speak off the record here for a minute—friend to friend—and say she's fucking hot, Phillips. I mean smokin'. I met her once a few years back at some party my parents threw. It was memorable." After a sigh of reverence that made Hunter smile, Ethan went on. "She's a biologist or whatnot like her dad. She's going out to Montana—backcountry—to trap animals. Something happened to her colleagues out there. I didn't get all the details, but basically Daddy wants to be sure she's safe while she's doing her thing."

Intrigued, he shoveled a bite of Wheaties into his mouth. This assignment would be a hell of a lot more interesting than standing outside a hair salon listening to women talk about who was screwing whom. After the past few weeks, he'd had all he could take of the spoiled Hollywood-type. Time away in the wilderness would be a nice change of pace.

"You haven't hung up on me. This is always a good sign."

"Just how hot is this daughter?" He took another bite.

"We're talking a solid ten, and I haven't even mentioned

cash yet. Stanley said money is no object."

"When would I need to head out? I want to make sure Sarah's all set before I take off."

"Morgan will be ready to leave next week. If you fly out to DC tomorrow or Friday, that would probably work best. Go visit Sarah today. I'll keep an eye on her while you're gone. We were planning to bring Kylee to the beach for ice cream tonight anyway."

"I know you will. I'll take the job. If I get there and find myself taking care of some hairy legged, bottle-thick glasses nerd for a month, you'll have to sleep with one eye open for the rest of your life."

"I guess I'll be sleeping soundly then. You won't be disappointed; I promise. I'll call you with the details after I talk to Stanley again."

"Sounds good."

———◆———

The sunny June afternoon was alive with the sounds of children playing. Hunter walked through the busy park, scanning the parents and kids, finally spotting the two blonds at the swing set as Sarah gave the baby swing another push.

Kylee laughed, kicking her chubby little legs back and forth, clapping. "More, Mama, more."

"You're high enough, Kylee."

"No, Mama, more." She clapped again.

Walking over, he grabbed the swing and pulled it up until his forehead rested against the angel-faced little girl's. He kissed her nose and let her go.

"Unke Hunte! Unke Hunte!" She held up her arms for him to take her out.

"You're getting closer, kid." He unfastened the safety clip, tugged up the bar on the seat, and pulled her from the blue plastic, settling her on his hip. "It's *Uncle Hunter*," he over enunciated, hugging her close.

Kylee put her fingers on his lips, and Hunter growled, trying to eat them, as was expected. Her deep belly laugh made him chuckle.

He smiled at Sarah and kissed her. "Hey, thanks for meeting me."

Kylee wiggled to get down.

He pushed her up over his head until little blond pigtails dangled and she stared down at him. "And where do you think you're going, ma'am?"

She grinned. "Sand."

"All right. Let's go." He set her on her feet in the sandbox.

Kylee plopped herself down with a pail and shovel.

"She's grown since last week."

Sarah smiled. "Kids do. It's part of the deal. Kylee, keep the sand in the sandbox."

Mischief and mutiny gleamed in Kylee's bright blue eyes, and Hunter grinned as little fingers curled around a sand-heaped shovel.

"Look at the way she's staring at us. She's trying to decide if she's going to listen or let it fly. What a piece of work."

"Don't encourage her. We're heading toward the terrible twos, and sometimes they really are terrible."

He frowned at the weary tone of Sarah's voice. "Are you okay? Are your parents helping you out?"

"I'm fine. She's just testing a lot these days. She's supposed to. She's a toddler."

"I wanted to let you know I'm going out of town for about a month. I'll be in the mountains and hard to reach. If Kylee's giving you a rough time, I can try to get out of my assignment."

"We'll be all right." Sarah took Hunter's hand and pressed his palm to her cheek. "You have a life of your own."

He glanced away, staring as Kylee shoveled sand into her bucket. "I promised him I'd take care of you two."

She nuzzled his hand still resting against her skin. "Yes

you did, and you do." Sarah sighed. "Hunter, we love you so much. You're such an important part of our lives, but you can't give up yours for us. Jake wouldn't want that, and neither do I. You put limits on yourself for us, and it has to stop."

"That's ridiculous."

"You were going to give up an assignment because Kylee's new favorite word is 'no.'" She gave him a hesitant smile. "I might make you angry by saying what I'm about to, but we probably should've discussed this a while ago."

He stared at her, already knowing he wasn't going to like whatever she had to say. "Well, go ahead."

Sarah pulled his sunglasses down the bridge of his nose. "You put limits on yourself for Kylee and me as punishment for what happened in Afghanistan."

"You're right," he said, snapping his glasses back in place and turning away. He didn't talk about Afghanistan. "You are going to piss me off. What a bunch of bullshit."

She placed her fingers under his chin, tugging gently until he faced her. "Just hear me out. You can be mad for a whole month before you have to forgive me again. What I said *is* the truth. When was the last time you had a relationship?"

"Is that what this is about? Sex? Don't worry, Sarah, I have sex when I want to."

"No, this is *not* about sex. I didn't ask you about your sex life. I asked when was the last time you had a relationship— you know, where actual emotions were involved? You've cut yourself off from any deep feelings."

Embers of resentment burned in his belly. Sarah sounded like the psychologist he'd been forced to see after he'd gotten back. "It'll take me two months to forgive you if you don't drop this. I have deep feelings. I love you and Kylee."

"I love you too, Hunter, but that's not what I mean. You're like my brother. I want you to be happy, and you're not. When will you stop punishing yourself for coming back?"

More than finished with the conversation, he started to stand.

Sarah placed her hand on his shoulder, stopping him. "You came back," she said again. "But six of your men didn't get the chance. They still aren't going to come home even if you try to pay for it every day. Do you think they would want that? Jake would want you to live, Hunter, really live. They all would. I've watched you for almost two years, and you pull back as soon as you start to get too close. Stop punishing yourself for something that was never your fault in the first place. There. That's it." She kissed his cheek and smiled. "Even if you don't forgive me for three months, I'll be okay because I've needed to say that for a long time."

He stared at her beautiful face, into her genuinely kind eyes, and his anger vanished. Sarah had the best of intentions. He brushed her lips with a quick kiss. "There's nothing to forgive, because you didn't say anything wrong."

"Good." She grabbed a package of crackers from Kylee's pink diaper bag. "Let's go feed some ducks."

An hour later, Hunter walked Kylee and Sarah to her car while Kylee slept on his shoulder. "I guess feeding the ducks did her in."

"It usually does."

"Ethan's going to check in with you while I'm gone, and my mom is two miles from your house. You have keys to my place. Don't hesitate to use them. You know where I keep extra money. I'll call you when I can."

Sarah glanced at him, grinning. "You sound like I did the first time I left Kylee with Hailey. We're going to be fine. I'm a big girl. Will you do me a favor while you're gone?"

They stopped by her navy blue sedan. "Name it."

"Think about our conversation and try to enjoy yourself." She unlocked the doors.

"Unke Hunte," Kylee said groggily when he fastened her in her car seat.

He brushed her nose with a kiss as her eyes drooped closed again. "I'll be back soon, baby girl." He shut Kylee's door, giving it a testing wiggle. "Are you sure you're going to be okay?"

"Yes." Sarah hugged him and eased away. "Go play in the woods. I'll see you next month." She got in the car, buckled her seatbelt, and rolled down her window as she backed up.

Leaning through the window, he gave her a final kiss. "Don't let her grow too much."

"She'll practically be a teenager by the time you get back. Bye. Have fun." Sarah drove off, tooting her horn.

Guilt consumed him as he waved.

❧ CHAPTER FIVE ❧

MORGAN STOOD BY THE MARBLE COUNTERTOP IN her parents' spacious kitchen, adding a spoonful of honey to her tea. The gentle breeze ruffled the sheer white curtains, bringing in the scent of roses from the gardens as she made her way to the table in the sunny breakfast nook. "Good morning," she said, smiling as she snagged a piece of her mother's whole grain toast—a habit begun twenty years ago.

"Morning, honey." Mom smiled and winked. "Did you enjoy your jog?"

"Absolutely. I need the runner's high these days. Hi, Dad."

He glanced up from his newspaper. "Hello, Peanut. How are you?"

"Not too bad. My schedule's jammed full today, but with a little planning, it's doable. I'm picking up supplies for the trip next week."

"Ah, I'm glad you brought that up." Dad picked up his steaming mug of coffee and took a sip as her mother slid him a glance.

Morgan narrowed her eyes, realizing something was up. "Oh yeah?"

"I thought I should tell you I hired someone to accompany you on your trip to Montana."

Morgan's light mood vanished along with her smile as she

sat in her chair. "You did what?"

He set his cup down. "I hired someone to go with you to Montana."

"And what does that mean, exactly? Who did you hire?"

"A bodyguard."

Her eyes widened as she laughed. "You've got to be kidding." She chuckled again, looking at her mother. "Mom, what is he talking about?"

The frown on her mother's face told Morgan they were in on this together. "I'll admit I agree with your father. Neither one of us is happy about your choice to continue with this assignment. You're taking too many risks."

"I'm going to track animals in backcountry like I've done for the last several years. I'm pretty sure that's what you two paid for when I went to college. Every job has risks, Mom."

"You know that's not what we're talking about. If you insist on going, we won't stop you. Our only condition is that you bring this man for protection."

Morgan took a deep breath, trying to find her patience. "I just don't see why this is necessary. I know my team was murdered. I can't think of much else, but I truly believe they surprised a poacher and the bastard killed them. With all the police combing the area, he has to be long gone." *But I'll find him somehow.*

Dad folded his paper. "I don't understand why you're making this into such an issue. You can't go into backcountry by yourself anyway. It's unsafe and against Bureau policy."

"So I'm supposed to depend on some guy whose bicep is bigger than his brain to help me track and monitor the animals? That definitely sounds like a recipe for success." She let out a frustrated sigh. "If Dean hadn't reassigned Jim and Dave so quickly, I could've taken them."

"I told him to," Dad said, tapping his fingers against the table—a sure sign of irritation. "I wanted the three of you back in the field as soon as you were ready. I thought work would help."

"But—"

"You said we would find a solution suitable for both of us. This is what I came up with. You're going and you'll be safe. That's the way it will be."

She recognized the finality in his voice and shrugged. Pushing him too hard wouldn't be a good idea if she wanted to keep the funding for the project in place. "Fine. You're right. But he better not screw anything up."

Her mother eyed her as she spread strawberry preserves on a piece of toast. "Nice attitude, darling."

Morgan recognized the scolding disapproval and blew out another breath.

"Morgan." Dad took her hand. "This man was a highly decorated Recon Marine. He's not some idiot off the street. Ethan says he's the best on his payroll, and my research confirms it. You'll be well protected, and he knows how to rough it. He was in Afghanistan for a year. Before that, he spent plenty of time in other volatile areas."

"Such as?"

"I can't say."

"Why not?"

"It's classified information."

"Oh." She stared at her mother's eyebrows drawn together in concern and the worry plaguing her father's eyes, regretting the whole situation. The last two people she ever wanted to cause distress were her mom and dad, but she had to go. She had to do this. She needed the answers to her friends' deaths. Their blood was on her hands. She could only blame herself for their murders. If she'd altered the groups and gone to Yellowstone herself, the end result might've been different, but she'd let Ian talk her out of it, and now she could only wish she'd changed the plans despite his objections. "I'm sorry. I don't want you guys to worry. Thank you for thinking of my safety. I'm sure this man will be handy to have around. What's his name, anyway?"

"Hunter Phillips," Dad said as he popped his multivitamin in his mouth, swallowing the capsule down with his daily glass of orange juice.

"All right then. I should get to my errands. When does this Hunter Phillips arrive in DC?"

"He'll be in town this afternoon." He glanced at his watch. "I'll meet him at the office before he heads over here."

"I'll be back to introduce myself later." Kissing her parents, she departed for the guesthouse she lived in and dressed for the day in cropped skinny jeans and a pink spaghetti-strap tank. She stood in front of the bathroom mirror, applying clear gloss to her full lips, and narrowed her eyes as she thought of the whole bodyguard situation. Hunter Phillips, huh? He was bound to be a pain in her ass. She would just have to make everything perfectly clear from the beginning: She had her own plans and agenda. Nothing mattered more than finding answers. As long as he didn't get in her way, things would be fine. Her father was paying him, so in essence she was his boss. Her new *bodyguard* was probably used to taking orders anyway.

Feeling better about the whole thing, she glanced in the mirror once more and pressed her slick lips together before leaving to take care of her errands.

———◆———

Hunter arrived at The Bureau right on time. He walked up to the homely older woman sitting behind a receptionist's desk as she spoke on the phone. He studied the tight bun coiled at the top of her head and her eyeglasses, straight out of the sixties, resting on the bridge of her nose. She reminded him of the stern librarian who had scared him witless as a young boy. Her workspace epitomized office efficiency. Needle-sharp pencils with The Bureau's insignia stood soldier straight in a glass holder. Papers were neatly stacked in color-coded files lined along the left edge of her blotter. The dark cherry wood had been polished within an inch of its life. She replaced the receiver and looked up, smiling warmly.

"You must be Mr. Phillips."

"Call me Hunter." He glanced at her nameplate and smiled. "Helen."

"It sure is kind of you to fly all the way out here to help our little Morgan."

"I'm happy I could offer my services."

"Morgan's a lucky young lady. You're a handsome one if you don't mind me saying so—remind me a lot of my Charlie, you do. He had a dimple in his chin and blue eyes too. We had forty wonderful years together before cancer took him."

His smile disappeared. "I'm sorry to hear that."

"I can't be sorry when we were blessed with forty years. Can I get you something to drink, Hunter?"

"No, thank you. I'll just see Mr. Taylor if he's available."

"You go have a seat. I'll let him know you're here." She sent him a saucy wink.

Charmed, he grinned and winked back, watching her blush as he sat down. He took in the posh surroundings of the office suite. This wasn't what he'd had in mind when he thought of an environmental agency. Plastic chairs and linoleum floors were more on par with what he'd envisioned, not plush carpet and leather furnishings.

"Hunter, Mr. Taylor is ready." Helen added a little extra sway in her hips as she walked him down the hall and opened a door, signaling for Hunter to follow. "Meet Mr. Hunter Phillips, Mr. Taylor."

Stanley Taylor exuded power as he stood and stepped from behind his desk in a charcoal-gray designer suit. Salt and pepper hair set off his serious, dark blue eyes. "Mr. Phillips, it's good to meet you. Come take a seat."

Hunter glanced around the classy office, taking in lush green plants set on dark wood, several plaques hanging on one wall, and a small marble-topped beverage station occupying the right corner of the room.

"It's nice to meet you too, sir." He sat in the leather wing-back chair in front of Stanley's desk and zeroed in on an eight-by-ten picture in a silver frame, staring at the smiling, dark-haired beauty with green eyes and a smooth olive complexion. If that was Morgan Taylor, Ethan would live after all.

"That's my Morgan, Mr. Phillips. I trust Ethan has filled you in on the situation."

He couldn't take his eyes off of the face in the frame. "Yes, although I wouldn't mind going over everything again. And please call me Hunter."

Stanley nodded. "Two weeks ago, three members of my daughter's wildlife research team were found shot. There are no witnesses and no leads. They were out in the middle of nowhere. It doesn't make sense. We aren't sure what the hell happened; all I know is three talented young people are dead."

"Do you believe her colleagues were targeted, that Morgan will be a target when we get to Montana?"

"Honestly, I can't be sure, but I don't think so. From what little the police have been able to gather, we can only assume they were in the wrong place at the wrong time. Whatever the case, I won't be taking chances with my daughter. That's why you're here. Ethan tells me you're the best, and I feel confident with his endorsement."

"With all due respect, sir, if you're this concerned about her safety, why don't you send her somewhere else?"

"Do you think I haven't *tried*? She'll go anyway. Morgan is damn stubborn when she sets her mind to something. She's determined she's going to do this. You try to stand in her way and she gets nasty."

"Aren't you the boss?"

This time Stanley let out a full-throated laugh. "Oh, Hunter Phillips, you're in for quite a surprise. No one is Morgan's boss but Morgan. She has a mind of her own—has since the day she was born. She's a love and as sweet as they make 'em, but once you cross her..." Stanley winced. "Well, you'd better protect your balls, son." He took a sip of his water. "I guess this is a good time for me to tell you I sprang all of this on her at breakfast this morning, and she isn't exactly happy you'll be joining her on the assignment. But she'll go along with it because she knows the line has been drawn in the sand. She just needs a few days to adjust. Morgan is fiercely independent—what you might call...spirited. Overall though, I think you'll get along quite nicely."

Hunter doubted it. "I'm sure it'll be memorable, Mr. Taylor."

"I imagine so. Why don't you go on over to the house, meet Morgan and Ilene, and get yourself settled in."

"Sounds like a good idea." He stood.

"Thank you again, Hunter."

"I'm glad I could offer my expertise, Mr. Taylor." He shook the man's hand.

"Call me Stanley. Oh, I almost forgot. We're having a fundraising event tonight—black tie. I hope you'll join us."

———◆———

"Great. Just fucking great." Hunter stabbed the button for the garage as he stepped into the elevator and stuffed his hands in his pockets, cursing fate. Was it too much to ask for an assignment that didn't involve a high-maintenance, self-important Hollywood-type? What happened to the business tycoons and diplomats who needed protection overseas, or a good high-stakes government function that required his security clearance and reconnaissance expertise?

Instead of enjoying a low-key duty with the added perks of backwoods hiking and camping, he'd signed up for thirty days of princess sitting at a time when his patience for pampered purebreds was at an all-time low.

Ethan would pay for this one. Technicalities kept his pal free and clear of a major ass kicking. Ethan hadn't lied, after all. Morgan was smokin'; her picture confirmed it. He just forgot to share the part about her being a spoiled bitch.

He should've figured that out before her father more or less corroborated his suspicions. Stanley's office screamed "filthy rich." She probably held her position at The Bureau because Daddy was CEO and she'd wanted it, not because she was qualified and had earned it. Serious wildlife biologists didn't look like that. He'd never actually met a wildlife biologist, but he doubted many had movie-star looks. Weren't they au natural? Didn't they have hairy armpits and wrinkles from the sun? That certainly wasn't Morgan Taylor. No, she was Grade A. He knew the type—saw it every day: There wasn't a hair out of place or an activity attempted that could break a nail.

Halfway through his conversation with Stanley, it became apparent he would be spending most of his days in a salon in Montana instead of LA. She would probably get bored with the whole animal-tracking thing after a day or two and be ready to go home early. He figured he'd be on a plane back to LA in less than two weeks. He could deal with her for two weeks. Spirited, was she? Well, he could be pretty damn spirited himself.

Cheered by his own thoughts, he smiled as he stepped from the elevator and walked through the parking garage. He hopped on the Harley he'd rented and drove toward the address Stanley had given him.

❧ CHAPTER SIX ☙

MORGAN DROVE HER JAM-PACKED CONVERTIBLE
down the long drive of her parents' estate, glancing
at lush grass spreading over the vast grounds and
green, leafy cherry trees long past their bloom. Smiling, she
passed a grouping of smaller trees she and her father had
planted when she'd been a little girl. It was one of her most
cherished memories—her father's large hands covering hers
while they gently tamped soil around young, tender roots.

She rounded a sharp bend and adjusted the visor closer to the windshield as the late afternoon sunshine poured
against the faded brick of her family's massive home and
reflected off acres of glass and pillared white columns. She
pulled up to the walkway leading to the guesthouse, careful to avoid the catering trucks parked by the kitchen of the
main house.

Florists bustled about, setting up lavish arrangements
on either side of the enormous, double oak front doors, and
cherry trees and childhood memories were quickly forgotten. Guests would be arriving in a little more than three
hours; she and her mother had so much to do yet. If she
was quick, she could drop off her supplies, grab a snack, and
head over to help in less than ten minutes.

Getting out, she popped the trunk with the button on
her key and walked to the back of the car, pausing when the

deep rumble in the distance interrupted her thoughts. She watched as the black and chrome motorcycle pulled up next to her, stopping inches from her feet. The engine deafened, making her want to plug her ears as she stared at the man sitting on the Harley, taking in every impressive inch. His arms were well muscled and tan, filling out the sleeves of his white t-shirt. He wore his Dodgers ball cap backwards, giving her a good look at high cheekbones and a deep dimple in his square jaw. Oakleys covered his eyes.

He turned the key, killing the engine, and dropped the kickstand. In one efficient and surprisingly graceful swing of his leg, he stood next to his bike in blue jeans, snug in all the right places, accentuating his mouthwatering build.

She stared at his broad shoulders and solid chest before pulling herself together. She recognized the red and black insignia printed on the breast of his shirt— Ethan Cooke Security—and was certain this could be none other than the man who would be tagging along with her for the next thirty days.

In an attempt to move beyond her irritation with the situation in general, she extended her hand in introduction, pulling back when he glanced in the trunk, smirking and shaking his head. Her thin eyebrow arched above her black Wayfarers and her friendly smile disappeared. *Just what is his problem?* She felt the low burn of her temper coming to life and finally broke the tense silence humming between them. "So, you must be the muscle my father hired."

"That's me." He shrugged. "You got a problem with it, talk to him."

Yup, he was going to be a pain in her ass—*great*. Deciding it was better to say nothing more, she turned and reached for the bags she'd temporarily forgotten about. Although her hands were full, several items remained in the trunk. She walked toward the house, glancing back, hoping Hunter would offer to help. He didn't move. "Could I get a hand?"

He backed up, palms out. "Let's get one thing straight,

sweetheart. I've been hired to protect you—life and limb. I'm not a servant."

Oh, that's it! She placed her bags on the driveway and quickly closed the distance between them, stopping toe-to-toe. The top of her head met the bottom of his chin, and she had no choice but to look up to make eye contact. "Listen, *sweetheart,*" she poked him in the chest with her index finger as she emphasized the word, "I don't know who the hell you think you are, but I won't put up with you talking to me like this."

He pushed his aviators onto his cap. "You gonna tell Daddy?"

His potent grin and shocking blues eyes left her blinking and her heart stuttering. In defense, the temper she'd tried to hold on to snapped. "You're an even bigger idiot than I first feared. I was hoping you might have manners. Customarily when you see someone with their hands full, it's polite to help them or at least offer."

"I'll try to keep those manner things in mind." He flicked her sunglasses down the bridge of her nose. "Perhaps over the next month you can teach me more. By the time we get back, I just might be civilized."

She narrowed her eyes to slits. "Oh, I seriously doubt it." Snapping her glasses back in place, she reached down for her bags and walked off without giving him another glance.

———◆———

"Holy shit," Hunter muttered, letting loose a slow breath as he stared after Morgan walking toward the small house adjacent to the enormous lagoon-style swimming pool. Her back end was as spectacular as her front. The picture in her father's office had done her little justice. She was even more striking in person, and she smelled great. Her perfume fit her perfectly: dark and sexy. The bears and insects would eat her alive if she wore that in backcountry.

A slow smile spread across his face. Perhaps a few bug bites would be good for her. It wouldn't hurt to knock Princess down a few pegs, and he felt honor-bound to do so— free of charge.

Morgan opened the door to her cottage-sized house. Seconds later, wood cracked against wood as she sent it slamming home. There was certainly plenty of attitude packed into that hot little body of hers.

His gaze followed her as she moved past a large picture window. Christ, what a stunner. Physically, she couldn't be any more perfect. He'd never seen eyes as big and boldly green as hers. They should have looked odd with her small nose and full lips, but they didn't. And he'd enjoyed a peek at her firm breasts and silk bra when she'd bent down to collect her bags after giving him the business. It was too damn bad he couldn't stand women like her. First impressions told him he'd hit his mark: She was privileged and useless.

Taking his eyes from her windows, he stepped back, scanning the enormous ramble of house, her high-end sports car pulled close to the posh guesthouse, and zeroed in on the dozen or so shopping bags remaining in the trunk.

He sniffed at her expensive perfume still lingering on the air, and with a shake of his head, started toward the mansion he would be staying in for the next few days, damning his luck. Morgan Taylor was a first-class bitch, and he was stuck with her for the foreseeable future.

❦ Chapter Seven ❧

I
T WAS PAST NINE WHEN HUNTER JOINED THE FUND-
raising event, wearing the black suit he'd been smart
enough to pack. At least two hundred people wandered
the grounds of the Taylor estate. He'd expected formal and
boring, but the twelve-piece band tearing it up under the
tent hinted that there might be a little life to this party.

The evening was warm, the sky clear and twinkling with
stars. Spacious grounds spread as far as the eye could see.
The trees closest to the house sparkled with white lights, and
the scent of summer flowers surrounded him as he made
his way to the outside bar set up next to one of the many
gardens. Grabbing a beer, he scanned the crowd, spotting
several of the nation's most influential leaders. Ethan wasn't
kidding—Stanley Taylor was a big fucking deal. He nodded
to a man discreetly tailing the Senator of Indiana—poor
sucker was on duty. Happy he wasn't, he turned toward the
guests beyond, looking for the boss-man. He would finish
his beer, find Stanley, and make his excuses.

The bottle of Corona was halfway to his mouth when
he saw her in the dim lights of the tent. The short, black
backless dress she wore gave him an eyeful of gloriously
toned arms and legs. The thin string tied at the nape of her
neck kept the silky fabric from falling in a heap at her feet.
She brushed a long lock of shiny brown hair curled loose-

ly around her shoulders behind her ear, and the diamond bracelet at her wrist winked as she laughed at something the handsome, ebony-skinned man standing next to her said. Hunter gripped the bottle tighter as the smoky sound carried on the air, washing over him.

An older couple joined Morgan and the man at her side. She exchanged air kisses and smiles. He knew the moment she spotted him: Her smile vanished. He tipped his bottle in salute and took a deep drink as she excused herself and made her way over to him.

"So, you decided to join us."

His pithy remark withered on his tongue when her face lit with warmth as she grinned and waved to a woman across the lawn. Damn, she was beautiful. He took another pull from the bottle.

"I'm going to have to introduce you around. I'm not telling people you're my bodyguard." Morgan scowled as she said the word. "I'll say you're an associate of mine."

He shrugged. "You're the boss."

"That's right, and—"

"There you are, Hunter." Ilene walked up to his side and kissed his cheek. "We weren't sure if you would make it." Ilene Taylor was just as lovely as Morgan in her black off-the-shoulder dress. She was also a hell of a lot friendlier than her daughter.

He grinned at her. "I got tied up with a couple of things. I wouldn't have missed your event, Mrs. Taylor." He glanced from Ilene to Morgan, studying mother and daughter. Morgan favored her mom. They shared the same delicate build, golden coloring, striking eyes, and small nose that turned up ever so slightly at the tip.

"I want you to call me Ilene, Hunter." She hooked her arm through his, smiling. "I'm sorry I left you by yourself this afternoon. I've been a terrible hostess."

"Don't worry about it. You've had your hands full. Everything looks great."

"Thank you. Morgan and I had to work quickly to get this ready." She gestured to the people surrounding them. "Is your room comfortable?"

"It's perfect." He was curious about the event in question and the really bad timing. Her co-workers had been slaughtered just weeks before, and they were already throwing parties. Unbelievable. With an internal shrug, he glanced into Morgan's cool, measured stare. Some people had ice water for blood.

"Oh." Ilene interrupted his thoughts with a gentle hand on his. "I thought I should tell you, I talked to Helen, Stanley's secretary, earlier today. She's quite taken with you."

Morgan's eyes widened in what could only be surprise.

"What? Not all women detest me on the spot," he said to her.

Ilene frowned, tsking in Morgan's direction. "Has my daughter been nasty to you, Hunter? I'm sure she's only surprised by Helen's reaction because Helen doesn't like many people."

"Her nickname at the office is 'Dragon Lady,'" Morgan said. "I can't imagine how, but you've charmed the beast."

"*Morgan*," Ilene gasped, closing her eyes. "Go take Hunter around and introduce him. Dance with him. Make him feel welcome. You two will be spending a lot of time together."

"Mom, I know how to be a good hostess."

His brow winged up, and Morgan frowned.

"Go have fun."

He extended his arm to Morgan.

She stared a moment, then locked hers through his.

He watched her exchange a glance with her mother as they walked off into the crowd.

After being introduced to the throngs, he was left alone as Morgan excused herself to speak to her parents. Desperate for quiet, he wandered toward an empty corner of the tent where a large, draped table held dozens of framed pictures. He bent down for a closer study when he realized Morgan was in several of the shots. She didn't look like the sophisticated woman he'd spent the last two hours with. In many of the photographs, she posed with five other people. He recognized the man she'd been standing with earlier in several of the photos. Apparently he was an identical twin.

Numerous shots showed Morgan and the men or a pretty blond woman in various stages of tagging wild animals. The pictures captured the group of six working in all four seasons, wearing shorts and t-shirts in some photos, parkas and snow pants in others. The only consistent thread in each picture was that the elegant Morgan Taylor from Washington, DC ceased to exist.

In most of the photographs, she wore a red bandana wrapped around her hair. In every shot, she was grubby or even filthy and appeared blissfully happy. The dirt and grime didn't take away from her beauty; it somehow accentuated it.

Hunter's eyes widened when he spotted one snapshot in particular. Morgan and a well-muscled man had their hands in the mouth of a tranquilized lion. Her long, graceful fingers held a caliper to a massive tooth while her partner wrote data in a notebook. Hunter frowned. The woman in these pictures definitely knew what she was doing.

After several seconds, he moved to the last photograph. The group of six stood next to an empty cage, a forest of trees around them. Someone had written *Back Where I Belong* on a makeshift sign taped to the metal pen. Morgan smiled triumphantly, and Hunter stared, captivated, hypnotized by her eyes. He shook himself free of his trance and glanced away, watching the guests gathered in upper-crust herds, talking, laughing, and sipping champagne, before he turned back to the table.

He avoided Morgan's frozen smile, concentrating on the five other faces in the same shot. Three of those people were dead. The blonde woman he knew for sure, but he wasn't certain about the men. Had the man he'd seen Morgan with that evening lost his twin? What about the well-built guy with the rakish grin who'd helped Morgan with the lion? Or the thin man with the thick glasses? He focused on the groups' arms linked around each other's shoulders in one long chain. Morgan's team had been close—connected. The obvious bond pulled at him.

"Excuse me."

He glanced up at Morgan on stage as she spoke into a microphone.

"May I have everyone's attention, please?" She waited for the crowd to quiet. "On behalf of my family, I would like to thank you all for joining us this evening. Tonight we gather in memory of three of the best people I've ever had the pleasure to know."

Murmurs spread through the group.

"Shelly Simmons, Ian Ledderbeck, and Thomas Smithson will forever be remembered as great scientists, dedicated advocates, conservationists, and most importantly, amazing friends and human beings. It is with..." She paused as her voice thickened, took a deep breath, and continued. "It is with a heavy heart, I introduce to you our first annual fundraising event for a scholarship that will be set up in their names. With your generosity, we'll be able to keep their dreams alive by helping aspiring wildlife biologists make a difference in the lives of the animals they worked so hard to protect. Thank you, again, for joining us."

The band kicked into high gear with something fast and fun. Everyone clapped as Morgan stepped from the stage. Those wanting to offer their sympathies surrounded her, suffocating her with hugs and handshakes. Her eyes met his across the room, wide and desperate.

He cut through the crowd, putting his arm around her waist as he whisked her from the mob, leading her from the tent down the long paved paths of the massive gardens. They walked until the light grew dim and the music and conversation faded.

Morgan stopped abruptly, looking up at him. "I guess you're pretty good with a quick exit."

He took a step back. "That's how I make the big bucks."

She gave him a small smile. "Thank you for getting me out of there."

"No problem." He preferred the temper he'd seen in her eyes earlier to the misery clouding them now. Thinking fast, he stepped forward again. "You still owe me a dance."

Long, heavy notes from a saxophone echoed on the air.

"Oh, that's okay. You don't—"

"I'm pretty sure your mother told you to make me feel welcome."

Morgan eyed him as she let loose a long, weary sigh. "You're right. I think I do." She held up her hand for him to take in a more formal dance, but as they came together, he settled his hands on the exposed small of her back. She hesitated and laced her fingers at the back of his neck, holding his gaze as they moved in a slow circle.

Testing himself and her, he caressed his thumbs along her soft skin, feeling her quick shiver of response. "I saw the picture of you and your team," he said, ignoring the tug low in his belly. "You did some amazing work together."

"Yes, we did. I still can't believe they're gone. I just don't understand it. How could someone end three people's lives like that?"

He knew she wasn't asking him, that she didn't expect an answer.

"They must've been so scared." Looking down, she shook her head. "I can't think about it. I can't bear to." She looked up as her eyes shimmered with pain.

Who was this woman he held in his arms? She wasn't whom he'd initially judged her to be. There was more to Morgan Taylor than wealth and a stunning face. Her vulnerability moved him. He trailed his hand up her spine, to the center of her back, surprising himself when he pulled her closer, wanting to comfort her.

She rested her head on his chest, and her soft hair brushed his chin as the scent of her shampoo and perfume surrounded him, intoxicating.

His heart beat faster and sweat beaded on his forehead as unease bloomed in his stomach. What was she doing to him? Abruptly, he pulled back and reached out, catching her as she fell forward. "Sorry. I'm sorry." He had to get out of here. "Let me walk you to the tent. I'm calling it a night."

Her brow furrowed as she searched his face. "I'm okay. I could use another minute. Go on ahead."

"I'll take you." He put his hand on the small of her back and pushed her forward, eager to drop her off and get to his room. "We're pretty far from the house."

"Hunter, I'm fine. I'm in my own backyard, for heaven's sake."

As his panic increased, his patience grew thin. "It isn't safe to be out here by yourself. It's dark. Let's go." He snagged her by the elbow and started walking.

"What is wrong with you?" She yanked back, trying to break loose. "You were acting like a human being a minute ago, now you're being a jerk again." She tried to stop, but he kept her moving forward. "Let go of my arm."

He didn't say anything as he guided her along. Moments later, they reached the tent, and a couple stopped them.

"Why, Morgan, are you going to introduce us to your gentleman here?"

He forced a smile for the older man and woman. "If you'll excuse me for just one moment." Not waiting for a response, he turned his back and walked toward the house, leaving Morgan staring after him.

—◆—

Hunter turned on the light and locked the door as he entered his room. He hurried to the bed and sat on the creamy white comforter, ripping off the tie that felt as if it strangled him and the jacket that was suddenly too tight. Closing his eyes, he took deep breaths and unballed his fists, consciously trying to relax them on his thighs. Muffled conversation and laughter from the party below drifted through his windows as he counted to two, inhaling through his nose, then to four, exhaling through his mouth. The gallop of his heart steadied and the sick fear subsided as he collapsed back on the bed. What the hell?

He hadn't experienced an episode in months. After his return from Afghanistan, panic, anxiety, and wrenching nightmares plagued him almost daily. With time, his symptoms had faded, only sneaking up on occasion. The military shrink had called it post-traumatic stress disorder. Hunter called it bullshit. He remembered the quack telling him that until he was ready to deal with the guilt and pain of his losses and he could willingly explore strong emotional attachments with others, he might suffer occasional bouts of anxiety. The asshole didn't know what he was talking about. What did a dance with Morgan Taylor have to do with crap talk like that?

—◊—

Long after the last guest left, Morgan sat by the pool, wide awake and comfortable in cutoffs and her ratty gray alma mater sweatshirt. She dangled her feet in the heated water, moving her legs in restless circles, creating waves and small whirlpools as cricket song surrounded her. Her parents' home was dark but for the three upstairs windows of Hunter's guestroom. She could see him walking back and forth in gym shorts and a t-shirt as he talked on his cell phone, gesturing with his hand.

Hunter had occupied her mind from the moment he'd pulled up on his bike. No matter how she'd tried, she thought of little else. She had watched for him from the crowds at the fundraiser, waiting. After two hours, she'd figured he wouldn't come and was shocked by her disappointment.

When she'd glanced over and saw him staring at her in his sexy suit, her heart had pounded as their eyes locked. She had never seen anyone as perfectly handsome as Hunter; although, handsome was too tame a word for his in-your-face good looks. And his kindness surprised her. Her first impression had been perfect features, amazing muscles, and an ego to go with them, but when he pulled her against him, looking at her with understanding in his eyes, she thought she might've made a mistake. Shockwaves had coursed through her body when his fingers brushed and caressed her skin. Then he pulled away as if she'd grown fangs, and he'd gotten all pushy-shovey, bossing her around in his irritating tone. And just like that, the ass she'd met in the driveway had been back.

She pulled her feet from the water and stood, drying off her legs. She stopped abruptly when she felt Hunter's gaze on her and glanced up to his window. Despite the distance, their eyes locked, and a slow grin spread across his lips, making her pulse bump up a notch. Unsettled by her reaction, she turned her back on him and walked to her house.

❧ CHAPTER EIGHT ❧

THE FLIGHT ATTENDANT WALKED DOWN THE AISLE carrying a trash bag bulging with cups and napkins. She stopped short when Hunter held up his empty water bottle. Their fingers brushed as the plastic exchanged hands, and the pretty blond gave him a wide smile, showing off her straight, white teeth. Her gaze flicked over Morgan as she stepped away and moved along, looking back once, smiling again. Hunter sent her one of his best grins. Why the hell not?

"Ladies and gentlemen," the pilot said, "our descent into Bozeman will be delayed momentarily due to a medical emergency on another flight. We'll be circling for a short time until we get the all clear for landing. Sit back and relax. We'll have you on the ground shortly."

Hunter closed his book, recognizing the mechanical whirr of the wing flaps extending, and gently shook his shoulder, which Morgan was sleeping against. "Hey." He bent close to her ear, breathing in the tropical scent of her shampoo. "It's time to get up. We're almost there."

Murmuring something inaudible, she snuggled closer, nestling herself against the crook of his shoulder. As she wrapped her hand around his bicep, her hair brushed his jawbone, and her breathing deepened, steadying out again.

He cleared his throat and moved his arm once more.

When she didn't respond, he sighed and let her be.

Morgan had lost her battle with exhaustion shortly after they'd changed planes in Chicago. Hunter had watched
her head bob to her chest several times before she'd finally
pushed her seat back the miserly half-inch it allowed and
gave in to sleep. By the time pretzels and drinks were served,
he'd had a shoulder-full of Morgan. She'd been dead to the
world ever since.

When they met at Reagan International for their nine
a.m. departure, she'd looked like hell. Attending three funerals in one weekend had taken its toll. The light purple
circles under her dull green eyes had been the only color on
her face.

"Ladies and gentlemen, we've been cleared to land."

The plane dipped slightly, and the landing gear descended
from its belly as the lights of Bozeman were visible through
the droplets of rain scattering across the window. Hunter
shook his arm, moving his shoulder up and down. "Morgan,
we're going to land. Wake up."

She blinked several times and bolted upright in her seat,
staring at him with wide, sleepy eyes, the creases from his
shirt imprinted on her rosy cheek. "Sorry," she said as she ran
a hand through her hair.

He shrugged. "You don't look quite as bad as you did this
morning."

She narrowed her eyes. "I bet you say that to all the girls."

"No. Just you."

"Aren't I the lucky one?" She hissed out a breath as she
smoothed her hair again.

The plane swayed from left to right, jolting as the wheels
made contact with the runway, and the whoosh of the aircraft's quick deceleration filled the cabin. Morgan gathered
her belongings from under the seat as the jet taxied to the
gate.

He pulled down his shirtsleeve that had ridden up while
Morgan rested upon it and frowned as his fingers made

contact with the dark, wet circle in the center of the fabric. "Christ," he muttered, wiping his hand on his pants. "You drooled all over me."

She glanced at his shoulder, and a smug smile played across her lips. "Don't let it go to your head. I assure you it wasn't because you're irresistible." She gave his thigh a quick pat.

Before he could respond, the plane rolled to a stop, and his seat was jostled from behind as passengers moved into action. The flight attendants thanked everyone for choosing them as their carrier while Morgan stood and stepped into the aisle, opening the top latch. She grabbed her overhead baggage and made her way toward the front without looking at him again.

Loaded down with luggage, they walked through the sliding doors of the airport into the patchy fog and misting rain. Hunter held a rental contract and keys in his hand. "We're looking for lot C-twelve. The lady said the car should be down a row and to the right." He walked off, leaving Morgan to struggle with her bags as he scanned the cars, stopping when his gaze landed on the black Buick Regal lit up by the street lamp. "Here we are." The brake lights blinked twice when he hit the button to unlock the doors and pop the trunk. He threw his pack and carry-on in and turned to see Morgan limping toward him, weighed down by the suitcase she dragged at her side.

"I told you not to bring all of this." He strolled over, hefting up her bag.

"I wouldn't have if you'd brought some of the stuff yourself."

He took the rest of her belongings and crammed them in, then slammed the trunk closed. "I'll drive. We need to make a quick stop."

"Fine. Whatever. I just want to go to bed." She settled in and rested her head against the seat.

"Why don't you grab another nap? It's going to be a good half hour or so before we check in."

Her gaze whipped to his as she gaped. "But we're ten miles from our exit."

He took a left out of the parking lot. "I said I have to make a stop."

She muttered an oath and something about how the hotel would have food and toothbrushes.

They merged on the interstate, and he punched a number into his cell phone. "Cooke, it's Phillips."

"I take it you're in Montana."

"We just landed. Is everything all set?"

"Yeah. A man named Frank is waiting for you. He'll hook you up with what you'll need."

"Good. I'm on my way now." He passed a car and moved back to the right-hand lane.

"Let me know if you have any problems."

"Will do." He closed the phone and glanced at Morgan dozing off again.

◆

The car came to a stop and Morgan opened her eyes, frowning as she realized they sat in front of a small warehouse instead of the drug store or fast food chain she'd expected. "Where are we? What are we doing here?"

"Lock the doors. I'll be back in a couple of minutes." Hunter got out and knocked on the heavy metal door of the grimy building. A hulking man with a long silver beard let him in.

What was he up to? She got out of the vehicle, intending to follow him, but when she tried twisting the doorknob, she realized it was locked. "Damn." She walked through the shadows surrounding the building toward a small, lighted window covered with dirt and cobwebs and glanced over her shoulder, uneasy in the creepy silence of the dark. Standing on her tiptoes, she peered inside, watching while Hunter spoke to the man with the beard. The guy laid a pistol on the counter and Hunter picked it up, aiming at something, then nodding as he put the weapon into a leather holster under his shirt. *He isn't really going to bring a gun...*

Hunter shook the man's hand and headed toward the front of the building.

She hurried from the window as the door opened, meeting Hunter as he stepped outside. "What are you doing?" She ripped the paper sack he carried from his hand and pulled it open, staring at two boxes of bullets. "Are you out of your mind?"

He yanked the bag back. "Get in the car."

"I absolutely will not until you tell me what you're thinking. We're going to a national park tomorrow. It's illegal to discharge a firearm."

"Don't worry about it." He walked back to the vehicle. "Get in so we can get out of here."

She stormed over to his side, slamming the door he'd just opened. "You're not bringing a gun onto federal property. You could—"

"Listen to me," Hunter interrupted as he grabbed her by the arms.

She gasped, frowning. "Get your hands off me."

"In a minute."

"No." She struggled. "Now."

He tightened his grip. "This isn't your show anymore, got it? I was hired to protect you, so that's what I'm going to do. I won't tell you how to do your job. Don't tell me how to do mine."

She fought harder. "Let me *go*, you bastard."

He pulled her closer until they stood nose to nose. "You don't seem to understand, Morgan. You aren't the boss. You're on my watch now, which means you do what I want when I say. That's how I keep you safe."

"You can go to hell. You're here with *me*. I tell *you* how things will be." She jerked her knee up to prove her point, but his reflexes were fast.

Hunter yanked her forward, killing her momentum. In a flash, he turned them around, pinning her against himself and the car. "That wasn't a good idea," he said between clenched teeth.

Her breasts rose and fell against his chest as her breath rushed in and out. Her heart pounded, partly in fear but mostly because of...something else. She knew he was angry, but her instincts told her he wouldn't harm her.

He moved his face closer until the warmth of his breath tickled her lips. His gaze darted to her mouth and he hesitated, stepping back, letting her go. "Get in the car."

She walked around to her side and slammed her door, glaring at him. "You have some nerve."

He lifted his eyebrow in the shadows and she steamed out a breath, staring out her window as he started the car and navigated his way through the industrial park.

Damn him, she thought. What was he thinking bringing a gun into Yellowstone? What if he accidentally shot an animal, or even another person? And he'd *grabbed* her. Who did he think he was? In charge of her? Do what he said when he said? The hell with that. This was her assignment. He was just along for the ride.

She glanced at his profile—hard-set and tense but stunning nevertheless. She folded her hands, her knuckles whitening as she remembered the way his electric blue eyes had locked with hers while she stood pressed against his hard, muscled body. When his lips had been a whisper from hers and his gaze flicked down to her mouth, she'd thought he would kiss her—and she'd wanted him to. Surprised by her own admission, her frown returned. She was going to have to think about that.

They checked in to the upscale hotel and walked to their rooms in silence. Hunter waited while Morgan swiped her keycard and stepped into her room. She flicked on the light, turned to look at him one last time, and with smug satisfaction, slammed the door in his face. With any luck, she'd broken his nose. She sent the deadbolt home just as someone knocked. Blowing out a breath, she turned back the lock and opened the door, staring at Hunter.

"You forgot to ask who I was." He leaned against the doorframe with his hands in his pockets.

"What do you want?"

"Since I'm officially on duty and we'll be in separate rooms tonight, I wanted to do a quick safety check. You failed the first part."

With a frustrated huff, she shut the door again and walked to the king size bed, placing her carry-on and laptop case beside her as she sat on the mattress. Closing her eyes, she sighed and moved her tense shoulders in slow, smooth circles. Coils of strain began to release before she heard the rapping sound against her door once more and ignored it.

The knock came again, and her eyes snapped open. She wasn't going to answer. Determined that Hunter wouldn't get the better of her, she walked to the window with a view of the pool, closed the curtains, and flicked on the television. The rapid, steady bang of knuckle against wood continued. Damn it, he was *insufferable*. Swearing, she rushed forward and yanked on the knob. "What *is* it?"

"Yikes. Failed again. You still didn't ask who I was, but I just wanted to say goodnight. You forgot to say goodnight."

Morgan stared into eyes, which danced with humor, and glared. "*Goodnight*, Hunter." She shut the door and peered through the peephole, waiting for him to knock again. Instead, she saw him grinning as he turned and walked to his room. Morgan blinked, realizing she was grinning too.

⍋ CHAPTER NINE ⍋

"**D**AMN IT, MORGAN. ARE YOU AIMING FOR THE POT-holes?" Hunter asked, clutching the grab-handle above his window.

"Well, where do you suggest I drive to avoid them?" She glanced over, frowning, and gave her attention back to the road. "It's either the dirt road and potholes or the forest and trees. I'll let you decide."

The tall pines and Rockies in the distance created a stunning picture, but the bone-rattling bumps and threat of whiplash made the view nearly impossible to enjoy. "Try for a little more finesse. Jesus." He lurched forward again and swore as the front tires bounced through a lake-sized hole. The last mile and a half had been full of them. Maintenance on the back roads of Yellowstone clearly wasn't a high priority.

"If you think you can do better, you drive next time. Oh, good. There's the turnoff for the ranger station."

"Thank *God*." He'd learned two things as they drove from Bozeman to the northeast entrance of the park: Morgan couldn't drive for shit, and a person's life really did flash before their eyes prior to death. He'd seen moments of his flicker by when she cut off a tractor-trailer on Interstate Ninety. But the white-knuckled ride hadn't stopped there. He'd foolishly dozed off. When he awoke thirty minutes later, the orange needle on the speedometer had hovered at eighty-five while Morgan danced in her seat, belting out Pink's latest song along with the radio. Instead of telling her to slow down, he'd stared in utter fascination, cringing when she hit the rumble strip and had to yank the steering wheel to pull them back in their lane. After that, Hunter had checked his seatbelt—several times—and waited for their exit.

Morgan took the right turn into the small parking lot and pulled into a spot.

Hunter got out and looked to the sky, outstretching his arms. "I'm alive! I'm alive!"

A reluctant smile tugged at her mouth as she walked to the back of the car. "Very funny, Bodyguard Phillips."

"There's absolutely nothing funny about your driving, Morgan. Nothing." He joined her, pulling the large suitcase from the trunk.

"So I've been told. My team teased me often." She hoisted her pack and laptop case, grabbed her carry-on, and started toward the trail that would lead them to the remote ranger station.

"Didn't you forget something?" He looked down at the enormous suitcase at his feet.

She glanced at the piece of luggage, then at him, smiling. "Nope. Don't think so." She started through the trees, disappearing from his sight.

He was tempted to leave it but hoisted the suitcase and followed, breathing in fresh pine and crisp mountain air as they moved along the half-mile path.

"Whew. It's getting warm." Morgan stopped to pull off her sweatshirt, exposing a quick glimpse of smooth flesh before her pale green t-shirt settled against her blue jeans. "I think we're almost there."

"Well, that's super." He dropped the suitcase that had to weigh more than she did and flexed his cramping fingers. "When we leave this place, you'll be carrying your own damn luggage."

"Think of it this way: You're also carrying half of *your* luggage. Since you didn't trouble yourself to bring half of the items necessary for our backcountry outing, I brought them for you. Wasn't that nice of me?" Picking up her belongings, she flashed him a grin that wasn't entirely friendly and continued along.

"I brought everything I need."

"Yeah, if you're Crocodile Dundee. You can thank me later when you have a mattress pad under your sleeping bag."

"And who gets to carry all of this when we start hiking? It sure as hell isn't going to be me. I told you before, I'm not your servant."

She stopped in her tracks, whirling to face him. "Listen to me, you jerk. I don't have servants. I take care of myself. The only reason you're here is because I couldn't find a way around it. Believe me, I tried." She sent him a withering glare and turned her back on him, walking again.

Minutes later, the small path steepened and the tree line thinned, growing rockier with every step. They came to a clearing where a dark brown cabin sat nestled among a grouping of tall pine trees. "Not exactly the Hilton," he said, scanning their surroundings. The square, one-story building wasn't any larger than a small summer cottage. A large picture window trimmed in white occupied most of the left wall next to the front door. Smaller windows winked in the sunshine at the side of the house.

"This practically is the Hilton compared to what we'll find in the wilderness. I thought you knew how to rough it." Sneering, she shook her head. "Let's just remember you're my associate when we meet the rangers who live here."

"Whatever you want."

"Well, now there's a change."

"Don't get used to it." Christ, she was a spitfire.

Two men dressed in park service uniforms stepped out the front door, waving.

Hunter felt an itch between his shoulder blades as Morgan returned their greeting.

"Hello. I'm Morgan Taylor." She offered her hand to the attractive, baby-faced blond.

"Hi, Ms. Taylor. I'm Miles Jones. We're glad to have you with us."

The tall fifty-something standing next to Miles stepped forward, taking her hand next. "Robert Hammand, Ms. Taylor. Welcome."

"Thank you." Morgan flicked Hunter a glance when he didn't make a move to introduce himself. "This is my associate, Hunter Phillips."

Hunter shook Robert's outstretched hand, deciding on the spot he didn't like something he saw in the man's eyes. "Thanks for having us."

"We're happy to." Robert smiled.

"You two found the bodies of Morgan's colleagues?" He watched Robert and Miles closely, gauging their reactions as he ignored Morgan's sharp intake of breath.

Robert's smile disappeared. "Yes. I'm afraid we did—a real tragedy."

"Not to mention random, don't you think? You and Mr. Jones were the last to see them alive, right?"

The well-built twenty-something glanced at Robert.

"Please excuse my associate," Morgan said, wide-eyed and staring, her shock and warning for him to stop unmistakable.

"I'm just trying to get everything straight," he continued.

Robert held Hunter's gaze a moment longer. "Let's show you two to your room." He gave Morgan a friendly smile and turned, walking toward the station. "Your equipment arrived from The Bureau late last week, Ms. Taylor. We put the cases in storage." He pointed to the brown building set back from the cabin.

"Great. I'd like to do inventory at some point today."

"Sure. Just ask me or Miles. We'll open the shed for you."

Hunter followed Morgan and Robert into the tiny house.

The scent of stale coffee mingled with pine cleaner as they walked into the wood-paneled office that made up the majority of the station. A short hallway sectioned the galley kitchen, two bedrooms, and bathroom from the rangers' official work area.

"We'll put you and Mr. Phillips in here," Robert said to Morgan as he moved down the hall and stepped into the small bedroom.

There was barely enough space for two bodies to stand, let alone three, so Hunter peered in from the doorway at the two twin beds crammed together in the room. Someone was going to have to crawl over the first bed to get to the second. A small shelf had been nailed to the wall above the beds where a dented metal lamp took residence in its center. Apparently they would be sharing the closet. The amenities didn't include bureaus or chests of drawers. There simply wasn't room.

"Sorry about the accommodations, folks. This room is meant for one. Miles usually sleeps in here. We shoved this other bed in, but..." Robert shrugged. "It's going to be pretty close quarters. I wish we had something else to offer. If this is too awkward—"

"No. No, this is fine." Morgan touched Robert's arm. "We appreciate your hospitality."

"I'll leave you to settle in and give you fair warning: The shower doesn't always cooperate. Sometimes we have hot water, but it's never guaranteed."

"Thank you, Robert." Morgan smiled.

Hunter stepped in when Robert left.

Morgan closed the door and whirled. "What is your problem? Why were you so rude?"

"I wasn't." He dropped her suitcase on the scarred floor with a thud.

"Close enough. You didn't go out of your way to be friendly, and the first words out of your mouth were practically an interrogation. We're going to be living with these people for the better part of a month. That was completely unacceptable. I expect you to apologize."

"I wouldn't hold my breath on that one." He set his pack on the bed.

She closed her eyes and sighed as she pressed her fingers to her temple. "You're *impossible*. I'm going out to inventory my equipment. I'll put my stuff away after you've finished."

He stepped in front of her, blocking her path to the door. "I want you to wait for me."

"Forget it."

He grabbed her arm as she tried to walk by. "If you go to the shed, you stay put. Don't wander off."

She gave him a "fuck you" scoff as she skirted around him and stepped from the room.

"I mean it, Morgan," he said, as she walked down the hall and out the door without sparing him another glance.

Her dark scent lingered, and he clenched his jaw. If he'd ever met a bigger pain in his ass, they certainly weren't coming to mind. Her stunning looks were equally matched by her ugly attitude. If this kept up, she wouldn't have to worry about potential threats from others; he'd kill her himself.

———◆———

Morgan stepped outside, catching site of Miles as he headed toward the government-issued pickup. The cloudless blue sky cheered her instantly, and she fought to forget the irritating man she'd left behind. Feeling friendly again, she called out, "Excuse me, Miles. Could you unlock the shed? I would really like to get a look at my equipment before I use it this week."

"Sure, Ms. Taylor." His brown eyes warmed as he smiled.

"Please, call me Morgan."

"All right, Morgan. I'd be happy to open the shed." He unlocked the padlock and walked away.

"Miles?"

He stopped and turned.

"I want to apologize for Hunter's rudeness. He can be pretty impossible."

He smiled again, shrugging. "Don't worry about it." He walked to the truck, got in, and drove down the narrow access road.

She entered the shed, pulling on the string to the light as the door slammed shut in the breeze. Dust danced around the bulb, making her cough as she glanced around at rope, shovels, and other items the rangers would use to aid them in their job, spotting her equipment in the corner. Before unlocking the two metal cases The Bureau had shipped, she walked to the door, opened it, and found a rock to rest against the wood, allowing fresh air to blow into the small, mildewed space. Satisfied, she brushed her hands free of dirt and headed back to the cases, going through her checklist, noting that everything was where it should be.

Finished with the task at hand, she looked past the doorway to the tall pines in the distance as birds twittered among the trees. She took the camera from one case and the tranquilizer gun from the other as the thought of a walk tempted her. Taking pictures would be so relaxing. If she was lucky, she might get a few good shots of the local fauna. Hunter told her to stay close, but she wouldn't go far. Walking half a mile, maybe a mile down a trail wasn't a big deal, especially when she was taking precautions. She patted the gun tucked in the waist of her jeans. She would be back before he noticed, anyway.

She locked the case, turned to leave, and ran straight into Robert. "Oh. I'm so sorry. I didn't know you were there." She dropped her hand from her heart. "I was just heading out for a walk."

"No problem, Ms. Taylor. I apologize for scaring you."

"Not at all. Please, call me Morgan. Which path do you recommend? I'm looking for a little exercise."

"If you head down the southwest trail, you might spot a

deer or two. It's not particularly common this time of day, but you never know."

"I guess I'll mosey down that way. I'll be back soon." She took two steps and stopped. "Robert, I want to apologize for my associate. We got off on the wrong foot."

"Don't you worry yourself over that. Losing close friends is upsetting."

She was about to tell him they weren't Hunter's friends but stopped herself. "It is. I'm going to be on my way. See you soon."

—◆—

Twenty minutes later, Morgan sat in a clearing just off the path of the southwest trail with her jacket and tranquilizer gun at her side. She breathed in clean, crisp air and relaxed as a hawk circled overhead, letting out a high-pitched screech. The mighty Rockies, snowcapped and gray in the distance, took her breath away. She'd needed this, the tranquility and peace she hadn't been able to find in the weeks since her friends' deaths. She closed her eyes, clearing her mind of the guilt and worry, knowing it would all be back to haunt her before long.

Refreshed, Morgan opened her eyes, blinking against the sunshine, and caught sight of a mama mule deer and her two babies. Grinning, she watched, delighted as the mother grazed on the lush, green grasses while one of the calves suckled. Morgan laughed when the calf's sibling moved in for his turn, despite his sister's annoyed bleats and head butts.

Enjoying the show, she picked up her camera and focused on her shot, taking picture after picture. She stood and walked farther into the clearing, looking for a new angle. She never heard him come up behind her.

—◆—

Hunter tossed his luggage in the closet, not bothering to unpack. There wasn't any place to put his stuff anyway. He turned around and let out a deep sigh as he studied their sleeping arrangements again. The twin beds were so close they might as well have been a full-sized mattress. He and Morgan would more or less be sharing a bed for the next few weeks.

After he put the extra bullets for the Glock in the bottom of his pack, he headed out to see if Morgan finished her inventory. Maybe they could take a walk, relax, and try to clear the air. It was going to be a very long month if they couldn't find a way to get along. He stood in the doorway, zeroing in on the closed padlock on the shed door. Instantly uneasy, he stepped outside, scanning the dirt parking lot and trees close to the cabin. Where was Morgan? He walked around the corner of the house, expecting to see her, but she wasn't there. A small tingle of panic bloomed as he hurried to the other side. She wasn't there either. "Son of a bitch." He rounded to the front and spotted Robert. "Have you seen Morgan?"

"Yeah. She said she wanted a walk. She headed down the southwest trail about fifteen minutes ago."

"Goddamn it!" Hunter took off running, moving at a dead sprint, cursing her the entire way as he booked it down the uneven dirt path littered with sticks and rocks threatening to trip him with every hurried step. A half-mile turned into a mile and his worry compounded. He should've come across her by now. Where the hell was she? What if something had happened to her? He broke through the tree line and spotted her standing in the valley with a camera in hand, smiling. Relief swamped him before hot, ripe anger flooded his veins. He was going to teach her a lesson she wasn't about to forget.

Hunter never broke his stride as he caught her in a tackle and rolled with her, taking the brunt of the impact. The camera went flying, and the deer ran away. When the momentum of the roll stopped, Hunter lay on top of her. He stared into her huge green eyes as she blinked up at him. "What the hell is your *problem*? I told you not to go anywhere. So what do you do? You take off anyway."

"Get off of me," she said quietly, still dazed. "You're crushing me."

He didn't move. "What am I going to do with you? You don't listen to a goddamn thing I say. How can I do my job if you won't fucking *listen*?"

"So this is your solution—tackling and crushing me? I just went for a walk. I brought a weapon, and don't you *dare* talk to me like that!"

Hunter looked over at the gun and back again. If he wasn't seeing wavy shades of red, he might've laughed. "The tranquilizer gun? That's your weapon? Are you *serious*?"

"Perfectly." She shoved at his shoulder as she raised her chin, answering him in that haughty tone that drove him insane. "Now get *off*."

Completely out of patience, he grabbed her wrists with one hand and pushed them over her head. Firm breasts pressed against his chest, and he wanted her with a power so swift it took his breath away, making him even more furious. "Don't you get it, Morgan? You're completely defenseless right now. You didn't even hear me come up behind you. How can you protect yourself with a tranquilizer gun or anything else for that matter when you're so caught up in your pictures, you don't know someone's coming? What if I wasn't a nice guy? I could do—"

"You're not," she spat.

"You're right. I'm not. I think I'll show you what happens to a woman who goes out in the middle of nowhere by herself." He had to taste her.

She went perfectly still when his mouth brushed hers, testing, teasing. Her eyes burned into his as he nipped her full bottom lip, tracing lightly with his tongue. Her breath turned ragged and her eyes fluttered closed.

Helpless to do anything else, he crushed his mouth against hers and let go of her wrists still trapped above her head. Bracing himself on his elbows, he cupped her face in his hands, changing the angle of the kiss, deepening it, tasting her exotic flavor as his tongue tangled with hers.

A hum of surrender purred in her throat as her hands found their way into his hair. Her fingers stroked the nape of his neck, sending a shiver down his spine.

He was losing his shaky grip of control. As abruptly as he initiated the kiss, he ended it, lifting his head, staring into eyes that had gone dark with passion. His heart hammered against hers, and he pushed himself up, standing while Morgan lay on the ground, looking up at him. He turned away, staring hard at the trees in the distance. "If you ever take off on me again, I swear I'll handcuff you to my goddamn wrist. Get your stuff and let's go. Hopefully I've made my point very memorable and very clear."

"Bastard," she hissed as she got to her feet and stormed passed him, grabbing her tranquilizer gun, broken camera, and other belongings, and started up the trail.

His heart still pounded as she walked away. He scrubbed his unsteady hands over his face and let out a deep breath as her dark flavor lingered on his tongue. He'd meant to prove a point and got a hell of a lot more than he'd bargained for. Flickers of something long dead had come to life when he'd lost himself in her.

He hadn't realized he gave a damn until she wasn't where she was supposed to be. She made him *feel*. He didn't want to feel anything for Morgan Taylor. He didn't want the responsibility of being in charge of anyone's life he cared for ever again.

Hunter kept Morgan in sight as he started up the trail after her, but he gave them both their distance.

♥ CHAPTER TEN ♥

WITH THE PACE MORGAN KEPT ON THE HIKE BACK, she made it to the ranger station in record time. Both pickup trucks were gone from the parking lot. Good. She wasn't in the mood for polite conversation with her new housemates. She needed a few minutes to herself—desperately.

Morgan stepped onto the small porch and glanced over her shoulder. Hunter's long strides closed the distance quickly. She was tempted to shut the door and lock it, but he would just find a way inside. Instead of indulging in petty satisfaction, she walked to the bedroom for her shower gear. The tension that vanished while she sat in the clearing was back with a vengeance, squeezing at her aching shoulder blades.

He was such a *jerk*. She knew Hunter had it in him, but she'd never realized he could be cruel. Why did he have to go and kiss her like *that*? He'd taken her breath away, confusing her and hurting her all for a lesson, a game. Well, score one for Bodyguard Phillips. He'd won that round.

She said nothing as he followed her to the room. She gathered her tote and fresh clothes, turned to leave, and stopped short, almost running into him. He held her gaze as she tried to move around him, but he snagged her arm at the door. She waited for him to say something—anything—as his eyes searched hers in the humming silence. She yanked her arm, trying to pull free. "Let me go."

He looked at her a moment longer before he let her pass.

———◆———

The plumbing in the bathroom hummed and clacked moments before water hit the tiny shower stall. When Hunter was certain Morgan stood under the spray, he headed into the ranger's office and called LA. "Cooke, it's Phillips. What did you come up with?"

"You have a meeting with Darren. He flew into Montana a couple of days ago to see what he could dig up."

"That's what I wanted to hear. What time?" he asked as he leafed through paperwork, hoping to find a report on the deaths of Morgan's team.

"Four o'clock in Merkly. How's it going? She still giving you a hard time?"

"Nothing I can't handle." He opened a drawer, searching through files.

"I've gotta admit, I envy you, man. If I had the wilderness skills you do, I would've taken the assignment myself. I can think of worse ways to spend a month. Sharing a tent with centerfold material doesn't sound too bad to me. You're a lucky bastard, Phillips. One lucky bastard."

"I'll try to remember that the next time she aims for my balls." He closed the drawer, hanging up when Ethan laughed and glanced at his watch, calculating the drive time from the station to Merkly. He would have to ditch Morgan for a while. After his initial meet and greet with Robert and Miles, he was interested to see what the PI on Ethan's payroll found. He opened drawers on the second desk, searching, finding nothing.

Standing, he licked his lips, tasting Morgan, and his stomach fisted into knots as his mind wandered back to the way her curvy body felt pressed under his. He blew out a breath and picked up the phone, dialing Sarah's number, needing to hear her voice. Her easy friendship always settled him.

———◊———

Refreshed and steadier, Morgan opened the bathroom door dressed in comfy jeans and a gray scoop-neck t-shirt as thoughts of work crowded her mind. She moved down the hall, pausing when snatches of Hunter's one-sided conversation registered. He sounded different somehow—more relaxed and happy. Curious, she walked past the bedrooms, toward the office, stopping just shy of entering the room.

"Yeah, put her on. Hey, baby girl. How are you? You almost have it. You're so close. It's Uncle Hunter," he over enunciated. "Oh, did you play at the park? Ducks? Yes." Hunter made a quacking sound.

Morgan's eyes widened with surprise as she peeked around the corner and saw him grinning while he looked out the window. Sun blazed into his eyes, making the brilliant blue more shocking. He chuckled and her heart stuttered as she nibbled her lower lip.

"All right, baby girl. Give the phone to Mommy. Love you. Sarah, are you sure you two are okay? Ethan's checking on you? I'm trying. I'll talk to you soon. If you need anything..." He grinned again. "I know. I love you."

Who was this man who sounded so kind and gentle? Morgan suddenly and desperately envied the woman on the other end of the phone. His unexpected sweetness tugged at her, pulling until she felt herself softening, knowing nothing good could come from it. If she were smart, she would sprint in the opposite direction.

Hunter moved to the desk, hung up, and turned. His gaze met hers, and his smile disappeared.

Morgan watched the warmth vanish from his eyes, and her chin rose slightly, automatically, before she walked to the bedroom, trying to shrug off the unexpected hurt brought

on by his cool reaction. She had a job to do—reports to
write. Who cared what he thought anyway?

———◈———

An hour later, Hunter stood in the bedroom door, watching Morgan as she sat on the mattress closest to the wall with
her back against the paneled wood. Her laptop rested on her
crossed, outstretched legs as she stared down at the papers
next to her, typing rapidly, muttering to herself.

"Knock knock."

She glanced up, her eyes unfocused in her concentration.
"What?"

"We need to go out for a while."

"No, *we* don't." She returned her gaze to the laptop. "I
have stuff to do. If you need to leave, go ahead."

He stepped into the room. "Come on. I don't have time
for this."

She stopped typing. "I have reports to finish before we
can head into backcountry. I wasn't planning on hiking the
trails anymore today. Your 'memorable lesson' did the trick.
Nice work, champ. I'll be good and won't leave my room.
Promise."

"Damn it, Morgan. You are the most unbelievably stubborn person I've ever met." He scrubbed his hands over his
face. "I have somewhere to be, and you have to come. That's
how this works, remember? I can't protect you if I'm not
with you."

"I have an idea. You do what you need to, and I'll stay
here and do the same. We'll pretend you did your job. Hell,
I'll even sign off saying you were with me the entire time.
No one has to know. I'm safe, completely free of danger. I'm
in the ranger station for heaven's sake." She turned the page
in her notebook with a snap and got back to work. "See you
later." She took her hand off the keyboard long enough to
wave her dismissal.

He didn't move. "That's data for the animal you need to track, right?"

She let out a frustrated huff. "Yes, among other things. Now go away. I can't concentrate with you hovering over me."

Hunter ripped the papers off the bed. "If you want these back, you'll get your ass up and get ready to leave. I have an appointment in an hour and we're going to be there."

"Why are you doing this?" She crawled over the beds and stood. "Why won't you just leave me alone? You don't care about me or my safety. Just get in the damn car, go away, and don't come back."

"You're my job, Morgan, my responsibility. I get paid to keep you safe and to pretend to give a shit. If you don't like that, talk to your father. Unfortunately, we're stuck with each other for the next month, so deal with it."

Something moved through her eyes, and she glanced away. He closed his, blowing out a breath. "Okay, that was a little harsh. I—"

"No." She shook her head. "You're right. I apologize. I keep forgetting you're as stuck with me as I am with you. I'm giving you my word that from this point forward, I'll cooperate with you fully. It'll make things smoother all the way around. The sooner I track and tag these animals, the faster we can get out of here." She grabbed her purse and jacket and walked to the door. "Let's go. You're going to be late."

<hr />

They arrived in Merkly forty minutes later. The small, tidy town of ten thousand bustled with its own rendition of rush hour. Main Street was a hot bed of action as pickups stopped at traffic lights in front of refurbished brick buildings dating back to the early nineteen hundreds.

"I'm meeting my pal in there." Hunter pointed to the busy diner across the street as he spotted the PI sitting in a booth by the window, sipping coffee and talking to a waitress.

"Fine. I'll browse the bookstore right next door, or I can take a different table in the restaurant if you'd rather."

"No. Go ahead and get yourself a book, but don't go anywhere else."

Morgan got out and shut her door. "If I'm finished before your meeting's over, I'll come sit here." She gestured to a wrought iron bench shaded by a tree close to the vehicle.

He nodded. He'd be able to see her exit the bookstore and would have full view of her from the diner window. "I shouldn't be too long. Do you want me to grab you anything to eat?"

"No, thanks. I'm fine." Her voice lacked its normal enthusiasm and fire.

He walked her across the street.

Morgan opened the door to the pretty little shop and stepped inside. "I'll see you in a bit." Her eyes briefly met his as she turned away.

He watched her walk to a stack of books and browse the selection, sighing, realizing he'd hurt her. He hadn't meant to. He didn't know he could, but she'd pissed him off. She was very good at that. Letting out another deep breath, he walked next door and let himself into the diner.

ᙜ Chapter Eleven ᙝ

HUNTER SCRUTINIZED THE CRIME SCENE PHOTOS OF Morgan's team. "I just can't believe they don't have anything. How can that be?"

"I don't know what to tell you." Darren Norwell shrugged as he took a bite of his apple pie a la mode. "They were out in the middle of nowhere. There were no witnesses, no signs of struggle."

"It doesn't add up, though. The woman, Shelly—" Hunter tapped the picture showing Shelly's grisly wound and blank, staring eyes. "She turned on her GPS out of the blue. She knew she was in trouble, so why didn't she radio in to the rangers?"

"Like I said, I don't know, but from what I've been able to find out, it doesn't seem like the boys in blue are working all that hard to figure this case out."

Hunter flipped to the next picture. "And doesn't that seem off to you? These people were biologists working on a project for the federal government. You'd think this would be a top priority at the local level. Did you run the names of the rangers Ethan gave you?"

"Yeah. They came up clean. That Robert character has an armed forces background. He's decorated. Apparently he's an expert tracker and quite handy with a gun. The kid's from up north of here. He's a couple years removed from college and clean as a whistle."

Hunter glanced at Darren. "You know what they say about whistles? They're not that clean."

"Well, according to the law and anything else I could find, he's your average boy next door."

Hunter shook his head. "Something feels off. I don't know what it is yet, but I got a bad vibe. I want to take these pictures and the police reports with me—give them another once over. How did you get this stuff?"

Darren smiled, his beady gray eyes almost disappearing in the folds of his fleshy face. "Trade secrets, my friend, trade secrets."

Hunter opened his mouth to speak but closed it as he watched Morgan exit the bookstore, cross the street, and sit on the bench by the large shade tree. She peeled a banana, took a bite, and opened her book as a light breeze played with her silky brown hair. He couldn't take his eyes off of her.

"That your assignment?"

"Yeah."

"Jesus. *Look* at her."

Hunter narrowed his eyes at the blatant lust in his colleague's stare. "Should we get you another napkin to wipe the drool from your chin?"

Darren's gaze darted to Hunter's. "Well, well, well."

"What the hell's that supposed to mean?"

Darren smiled. "Not a thing." He took a last bite of pie and stood. "I should probably head out. Don't want to miss my flight. I'll see you back in LA, Phillips."

———◦———

Morgan glanced up as someone approached. She watched Hunter walk toward her with a file folder in hand, studying his smooth, confident strides, begrudgingly admitting that he was simply spectacular. A lock of his blond hair fell loose against his forehead, and he swiped it back. His black t-shirt fit over his muscled torso like a second skin. Her gaze wandered down, noting the small grass stain on the knee of his jeans from where he'd tackled her like a damn linebacker.

Surges of pleasure careened through her system as she thought of his firm mouth on hers and his bold tongue diving deep, tangling with hers. Blowing out a quiet breath, she stared down at her book, trying to rein in her revving hormones.

Hunter stopped in front of her. "I'm ready whenever you are."

"Let's go then." She dog-eared her page, hoping she appeared unaffected as she stood. "I have a lot of work to do."

They walked side by side to the car. Hunter frowned as he placed the folder on the trunk and bent down, examining one of the tires. "Looks like the air's getting a little low. We'll have to put some in when we stop for gas." He moved along to the next tire and pushed against the rubber with his thumbs.

"Let's make it fast. I want to get back to the station. I figure we can be in backcountry by the end of the week if I get all of my paperwork finished and submitted to The Bureau in the next day or two. The red tape of working between dual agencies is unbelievable." As she spoke, she picked up the folder and opened it. "I'm eager to—" She caught sight of the photograph of Shelly and dropped the folder as if it had scalded her. Pictures scattered on the pavement, and she stared in horror, stunned, unable to look away from the gruesome images of her dead friends.

Shelly's eyes were open and staring. A single drop of blood had run from her forehead into her hair. She couldn't tell if Ian's or Tom's eyes were opened or closed; the exit wounds at the top of their heads had left a mess. Some of the pictures were close-ups—others had all three bodies lined up, capturing the entire crime scene. Shelly had fallen straight back from the lethal blast of the bullet. Her head bent unnaturally, dangling over her pack. Her long, blond hair lay matted with blood and dirt in the pine needles on the ground.

Ian and Tom lay face down in dark red pools of their own dried blood and tissue. Their heads were turned just enough to see that there wasn't much left of the faces she once knew. The horrid images intermingled with the life and vitality she remembered on Ian's handsome face. His roguish grin flashed through her mind, and the sharp stab of pain slashed her heart.

The last picture broke her. Tom's bifocals, spattered with blood, lay next to a bright yellow evidence tag. The thick glass had been shattered in one lens while the other lay untouched. She could see Tom pushing the same pair of black-framed glasses up the bridge of his nose. How many times had she watched him do that, never thinking anything of it? Oh, *God*. Look what someone had done to her friends. Morgan tried to speak, but all she managed was a barely audible sound in her constricted throat.

"Sorry about that." Hunter stood after checking the second tire and turned at the quick blast of a car horn. He saluted Darren as he drove off in the busy flow of traffic. "You're eager to what?"

She knew Hunter had spoken, but couldn't find her words. She was helpless to do more than stare at the ground.

"Morgan, what..." He took a step forward. "Shit. Why did you get in my stuff?" He knelt down, quickly picking up the pictures.

"I—I thought..." Unable to hold back the churning nausea, she ran to the barrel by the bench, stumbling once on unsteady legs.

Hunter threw the folder in the back seat and walked to where she stood with the bottle of water she'd set down on the trunk.

Morgan gripped the sides of the trashcan, taking deep breaths while her stomach heaved.

"Here." Hunter held the water out to her. "Take a drink."

She continued to grip the trash barrel.

He brought the water to her lips. "Take a sip, Morgan. Get the taste out of your mouth."

She did as she was told, spitting the first mouthful into the trash and swallowing the second, easing her raw throat.

"Sit down before you fall. You're white as a sheet."

Morgan dropped to the bench, waiting for the sickness to pass, and stared at the cracks in the blacktop. "I thought those were the papers you took from me. I was going to look them over on our drive back."

He knelt down in front of her, taking her hand. "It's okay. I'm sorry you saw that. Do you feel like you're going to get sick again?"

She shook her head, never taking her eyes from the ground, too sick at heart to care that she'd just barfed in front of Hunter.

Hunter pulled her to her feet, putting an arm around her shoulders.

She gave in, sagging against him, taking the support he was willing to offer as he guided her to the car.

———◆———

Morgan clutched at her elbows, watching the pine trees rush by as Hunter turned into the parking lot. Somehow the forty-minute drive had gone by in an instant.

"We're here. Let's get you to the cabin."

She tore her gaze from the window, nodding as their eyes met.

"You still look a little shaky. Do you want me to carry you?"

She sent him a small smile, surprised he would offer. "No. I can walk, but thank you."

The short hike back to the station felt like a major climb. For a moment Morgan wished she'd given in and let Hunter carry her. Her legs trembled with every step as she fought a fog that tried to overtake her racing mind. Everything seemed to move in slow motion. The crisp air and stunning scenery she'd enjoyed only hours ago no longer held any charm.

When they made it to the small cabin, she walked directly to the bedroom, ignoring Miles and Robert's friendly greetings. She didn't have it in her to socialize. She listened to Hunter make excuses when both rangers stopped playing their card game and stood, concerned, commenting on her sickly, pale complexion.

Still shaken and sick to her stomach, she collapsed on the edge of the bed, covering her face with her hands. Her friends. Her poor friends. They didn't deserve to have died that way.

The door closed with a quiet click, and the mattress sagged as Hunter sat next to her. She smelled soap and the fresh air from their hike on his skin. "Why? Why would someone do that to them?" she asked, hearing the agony in her own voice.

"I don't know." His muscled arm came around her. "I really don't."

"They were so good." Her voice broke. "Such good people."

He pulled her closer until her head rested against his firm shoulder.

Morgan desperately wanted to hold on to him, to hang on to the strength he offered, so she stood with her back to him. She didn't want to need him as she had in her weak moment by the bench in the parking lot. She was a job. He'd made that very clear. He was paid to care, which meant he didn't care at all. It was important to remember that. "You know, I'm okay. I really am. I'm going to be all right." Her voice sounded hollow and weak, even to herself. "I'm going to bed."

The mattress squeaked as he stood and rested his hands on her rigid shoulders. "I'll give you a couple minutes to get ready, and I'll be back."

She closed her eyes. "No. You don't have to. I'm all right."

Maybe if she said the words enough, she might believe them. She didn't dare look at him; she would fall to pieces if she did. Breaking in front of him, showing him any type of weakness wasn't an option.

"I'm coming back. I'll do some work in here on my laptop. We can turn off the light, and you can get some rest."

She didn't have the strength to argue. "I need to get undressed." She walked to the bathroom, going through the motions of her nighttime routine, running on autopilot while she rubbed moisturizer on her face and brushed her teeth. She just wanted to go to bed and not think about what she'd seen anymore. How would she get those images out of her mind?

Every ounce of energy left her body on the way back to the bedroom. Her legs threatened to buckle with each step, so she hurried, changing into her green tank top and crawling onto her side of the bed. She sighed as her head nestled the pillow, and she covered herself with starchy sheets, curling into a protective ball, praying for the oblivion of sleep.

The bedroom door opened with a creak and closed. She continued to stare at the wood-paneled wall, pulling her knees tighter to her chest, listening to Hunter move around the room. As much as she hadn't wanted him to come back, she was glad he did. She found comfort in knowing he was close by. He didn't talk to her as he sat on his side of the bed, powering on his laptop. The screen cast a blue tint throughout the tiny room, and she drifted off to the sound of Hunter's fingers tapping against the keyboard.

———◆———

Late into the night, Morgan whimpered in her sleep, reliving the horror of the pictures she'd seen over and over. The photo of Shelly staring with blank, milky blue eyes and blood on her forehead monopolized her subconscious. The picture came to life, and somehow Morgan was there, standing over her, helpless to do anything.

Shelly continued to stare with her head bent back against her pack. Her hands reached out, trying to grab Morgan's legs as her mouth began to move. She screamed and begged Morgan to help her.

Morgan turned to run, but Ian and Tom lay in her way, bloody and missing most of their faces. Their hands made a grab for her ankles, and she jumped back, shrieking, surrounded by the dead.

She cried out and shot up in bed, covered in sweat, her breath sobbing in and out.

Hunter sat up next to her. "Hey, hey, hey—Morgan, it's okay." He pulled her close.

Terrified, defenseless, she let herself relax against his warm chest, listening to the steady beat of his heart.

"You're shaking." He tightened his grip, wrapping his arms around her. "It's all right. Just take some slow, deep breaths." He drew her away. "I'm going to get you a glass of water. I'll be back in a minute."

She wanted to cling to him, to tell him to wait. She wasn't ready to be alone, but she nodded anyway. As soon as Hunter left the room, she switched on the light, terrified of the dark.

He came back moments later, handing her a glass.

"Thank you." She swallowed a sip of cool water, relieving her dry throat as she took in the sight of Hunter's naked upper body. He was broad and chiseled. His black mesh shorts hung low on his hips, accentuating his six-pack. A large scar, circular and puckered, stood out on his well-muscled shoulder. And there was a tattoo of a cross on the side of his left bicep with a date under it. She wanted to ask him what it symbolized but stopped herself, putting the glass on the shelf above the bed instead. The blanket pooling at her waist fell away.

Hunter's eyes traveled the length of her legs before she adjusted the sheet back in place. Letting out a deep breath, he sat on the edge of the bed. "Are you feeling better?"

"Yeah, thanks. Thanks again for the water."

"You're welcome." He got under the sheet.

She moved farther over on her side and cleared her throat. "I'm going to work for a little while before I go back to sleep. I have to generate graphs on my laptop. I won't need the light, so I shouldn't disturb you." She wasn't ready to close her eyes again and see the images that might come. If she stayed awake, she could block them out with the demands of her job.

Hunter turned off the lamp.

She bit her lip, forcing herself not to cry out, and took a deep breath, scolding herself for being ridiculous as she sat up in the pitch black. "Um, I need a minute to get my computer."

The bedsprings creaked as Hunter pushed himself over to her mattress, his leg brushing hers, sending small shockwaves skittering along her skin as he got under her covers and tugged on her arm until she collapsed against the bed. "Come here." He pulled her toward him, tucking his arm around her waist.

"What are you doing?" She tried to push herself up, but he held her to him.

"I'm being your friend. We haven't tried that one yet. You need to sleep. You're pale and exhausted. Close your eyes and turn it off for a while."

She didn't speak, didn't move as she held herself rigid. It felt good, comforting and safe, to be pressed against his body. As the minutes ticked by, she relaxed and fell into a deep sleep.

❧ CHAPTER TWELVE ❧

HUNTER WOKE FLAT ON HIS BACK ENVELOPED IN Morgan's dark, sexy scent. He lifted his head from the pillow, staring at Morgan's cheek resting on his chest and her hand lightly fisted over his heart. The soft skin of her stomach pressed against his side where her tank top had ridden up during the night and her knee lay bent, crossing over his hip. He moved his hand, realizing it rested upon her naked lower back.

His current situation gave him a jolt. He hadn't woken with a woman in his arms in over two years. He'd had his fair share of sex since his return from Afghanistan. He just hadn't stuck around for the morning after. The complications were never worth it.

He studied Morgan's spectacular face and her bombshell body practically glued to his, well aware that she was the mother lode of the sticky complications he'd tried to avoid. For some reason he found himself admiring her more and disliking her less, which worried him. Morgan was tougher than she seemed; that counted for a hell of a lot in his book. She'd had quite a shock yesterday and handled herself far better than he'd expected.

She didn't become hysterical, faint, or scream, despite the graphic pictures of her team. They made him a little squeamish himself, and he'd seen the results of violent death more times than he could count. When she sat on the bed, sick with horror and grief, he'd wanted to make everything better, to give her what comfort he could, but she hadn't wanted him. The more she tried to push him away, the more he needed to be there for her.

While he held her close last night, he realized the need to find out what happened to her team had less to do with the protocols of keeping her safe and everything to do with giving her peace. In a week's time, feelings he'd tried to avoid were coming to life—feelings he didn't want. How the hell did that happen?

Flutters of anxiety started twisting in his stomach. Feeling trapped, he gently lifted Morgan's wrist, attempting to pull himself free of her, but he woke her instead.

She stretched out the arm he still held, bringing herself closer. With every movement, her shirt climbed higher, exposing more of her excellent body.

Need, bright and hot, burned in his belly, quickly replacing any traces of panic. He grit his teeth, fighting the urge to reverse their positions and take what he wanted.

Morgan opened her eyes, staring into his. Her full mouth creased in a slow smile and vanished as she quickly boosted herself up to sitting. As she pulled away, he caught a teasing flash of her amazing breasts and toned stomach before her tank top slid back into place. She yanked the covers up to her neck, looking like a sleepy sex goddess with her disheveled hair and flushed cheeks. "I, um, I didn't mean to...lie all over you," she finished lamely as the flush in her cheeks darkened and she glanced away.

"Don't worry about it." Desire roughened his voice as he sat up, wanting to put some distance between them, needing to get them back on an even keel. "You look like you were able to get a little sleep."

"I was. I didn't have any more dreams. Thank you for everything."

"You're welcome." He propelled himself to the front of the

beds and got up, rifling through his bag until he found a t-shirt to put on.

"Why did you have those pictures? Where did you get them?"

He turned, staring at her and blew out a breath. "I'm not going to tell you everything, but I will tell you I asked Ethan to look into your friends' situation. I need to know what I'm dealing with if I'm going to keep you safe."

"The police told my father they're pretty sure the team was killed by a poacher. They were in the wrong place at the wrong time."

"That's the official line, but no matter how I spin it, it doesn't fit. Something doesn't feel right. Now that I've seen the pictures, I know it's not."

"What do you mean?" Frowning, she crawled across the beds and stood in her skimpy tank top and pretty panties riding high, showing off her shapely legs. "What are you saying? Do you think they were intentionally targeted?"

God, she was killing him. She needed to get dressed. Clenching his jaw, he threw her the pair of jeans she wore yesterday.

Her eyes grew wide when she glanced down, and she quickly tugged on the denim.

"I'm not saying anything at this point, but think about it. Everything's off. Nothing makes sense. Three people are taken out by one poacher? Three healthy, athletic adults under the age of thirty are shot without a struggle? You saw the pictures and wounds. If they caught a poacher by surprise, they would've been shot at random, not execution style."

"I never really thought it all through, but you're right. Oh my God." She sank down to the mattress. "What happened out there? What did they walk into? What do we do?"

"We don't do anything—not yet." He crouched in front of her, staring into her eyes. "I never thought there was any real threat to you until I talked to my PI friend yesterday. Now I'm not sure. You have to stay close. I don't know what the hell is going on around here, but you have to cooperate and stay close."

She nodded. "I told you I would. I will."

"Let's get up and get on with our day. Don't say a word about this to anyone. No one—not even your father."

She frowned. "But—"

"No one, Morgan. Not yet."

She nodded again. "Okay."

———◈———

Morgan followed Hunter to the kitchen, ready for breakfast.

Robert read the paper, sipping his coffee while Miles ate his bowl of cereal at the small table. Both men glanced up when Morgan and Hunter walked in.

"Are you feeling better, Morgan?"

She smiled at Miles. "Yes, thank you. I must've been over-tired."

Robert set down his paper. "You've put in a lot of travel time over the past couple days. It's easy to get rundown. There's plenty of food for the two of you. The Bureau sent money for provisions. Help yourselves to whatever you find."

"That's very kind." Morgan opened the refrigerator, scanning the shelves, and pulled out eggs, ham, and cheese. "Hunter, do you want an omelet?"

"I wouldn't turn one down." He poured a cup of coffee and joined Miles and Robert at the table. "I'll take good food while I can get it—before we head out."

Robert set his paper down again. "Are you going out into backcountry?"

"In a couple more days. It really depends on when Morgan gets her paperwork finished."

Robert sipped his coffee. "Where do you plan to go?"

"I'm not sure. I'll let the boss answer that question." Hunter met Morgan's gaze as she poured beaten eggs into a pan.

"At this point, I'm essentially starting from scratch," she said as she chopped ham on a cutting board. "My team didn't get a chance to start their research. They never made it back to report their findings. I know they didn't tag an animal, because we never received a transmission signal. Shelly always kept a journal when we—" She stopped, looking up, her eyes locking on Hunter's as her heart stuttered in her chest. "Shelly always kept a journal when we were on assignment. She kept a log of what we did professionally, but it was a personal diary. She would've recorded their itinerary. There might be a clue as to what happened to them. Did the police find it? I need to call my dad and have him ask Shelly's family. Why didn't I think of this sooner?" She pulled the eggs off the burner. Omelets could wait. She ran to the bedroom and was back less than a minute later. "My cell phone doesn't work up here. I can't get a signal. Do you mind if I use the office phone, Robert? I'll reverse the charges."

"No, go ahead. Miles and I should get to work. We'll see you tonight."

———◆———

Hunter sat down to his omelet and whole-wheat toast as the pickup's engine faded in the distance. "Are you sure Shelly kept a journal with her?"

Morgan cut a piece of egg and looked at him. "Yes. I'm one hundred percent certain. She and I worked together for three years. She always brought her journal when we went on assignment. She would usually write at night after we settled in. She called it her 'me time.'"

"She took one *every* time you traveled?"

"Yes, Hunter. Every single time. Why are you questioning me on this?"

"Just curious." He shrugged, wanting to play things casual, but he had an idea of where the journal ended up. He sampled a bite of fluffy egg and melted cheese and thought he'd gone to heaven. "This is really good."

"Thanks. You think the person who killed them took it."

He stopped chewing and met her steely stare. "It crossed my mind."

"Why didn't you just come out and say that? I'm pretty intelligent. I can connect the dots." She stood. "If you expect me to cooperate with you, I expect you to do the same. They were my friends." She put her plate in the sink and walked off.

He took his last bite as she moved down the hall. He wasn't interested in cooperating—just in her safety. He'd watched his new roommates when Morgan first mentioned Shelly's journal. Robert had been about to take a sip of his coffee when he paused and set down his mug. Miles' eyes had darted to Robert's before he'd taken another bite of his cereal. Hunter's shoulder blades had itched the entire time. Those two men were connected with her friends' deaths; he just didn't know how yet. He would be keeping that to himself for a while.

✀ CHAPTER THIRTEEN ✀

BRIGHT AND EARLY FRIDAY MORNING, HUNTER AND Morgan stood at the kitchen table, preparing for a day hike. Morgan placed first-aid supplies in her pack, followed by a blue insulated bag that held their lunch. She picked up her list—again—to quadruple check that she had everything.

Hunter ran his tongue along his teeth, rocking back on his heels, trying hard to be patient. When Morgan muttered to herself, glancing back and forth from her daypack to the paper she held, he rolled his eyes, letting out an impatient breath. "Are you almost ready?"

"Yes. I just want to be sure I'm not leaving anything behind. I would hate to have to come back."

He stared at the computer-generated list and neat checks Morgan had placed in the boxes next to each item as she packed it. "I don't think we have to worry."

She frowned. "There's nothing wrong with being prepared. In fact—"

"You're right." He didn't want to fight with her. "Let's go find that animal."

"The lynx."

"Right." He glanced over his shoulder through the large picture window, more than ready to go. "So, what's the plan?"

She folded her list and placed the paper in her pack. "I'm

not entirely sure to be honest, but I'll have a better idea after today. The last lynx tracks were measured and photographed north of here almost three months ago. Lynx are nocturnal unless food is scarce, so I don't necessarily expect to see one, but I do want to go to the last documented area of activity. I think it'll be best to start there, since these animals are almost never seen."

Hunter pulled a light gray hoodie over his head. "I'm just along for the hike. You do what you have to."

"We're looking at four miles one way. We'll be gone for a good part of the day."

"Let's do it. I'm going stir crazy in this place." He'd spent the last two days stuck in the ranger station while Morgan completed her initial report for The Bureau. He'd checked in with Ethan several times, hoping for new information on her friends, but there wasn't any. He'd read a true crime novel cover to cover and played all the Solitaire, Free Cell, and Mahjong Tiles he could stand. He needed fresh air and physical activity and was looking forward to watching Morgan in professional mode. The pictures he'd seen of her with her team—covered in grime and wearing the red bandana in her hair—flashed through his mind. He wanted to see that side of her, the facets of her life that intrigued him and added substance to her privileged existence and stunning beauty. The confident, intelligent, career-focused woman Morgan appeared to be attracted the hell out of him.

She gave him a smile as she zipped her windbreaker and slipped the daypack on her back. "Let's go. I need to stop by the shed and grab my tracking equipment."

They stepped from the cabin into the cool morning air as he shouldered his own bag and cinched the shoulder straps along the way. "Why don't I carry your stuff?"

"I can handle it. I'm only bringing the absolute essentials today, so my pack is pretty light. I've packed the tranq gun and collar with my supplies just in case." She unlocked the shed and grabbed the small nylon bag from inside the door.

"Are you sure you don't want me to carry that?"

She shook her head. "Really, I'm good."

Hunter made a circling motion with his finger. "Turn around."

When she did, he took the equipment bag and unzipped her pack, placing it inside.

She turned, facing him, giving him a small smile. "Thanks."

He smiled back, enjoying the tenuous peace they'd come to find over the past couple of days. They'd gone almost forty-eight hours without a single argument—a miracle in his estimation. "No problem."

The steady twitter of birdsong played through the trees, growing louder as they moved closer to the trail leading north of the ranger station. Hunter took a deep breath, filling his lungs with crisp, clean air, appreciating the lack of smog that was a part of his everyday life in LA. The sun continued its rise over the majestic mountains, bathing snow-capped peaks in light, cloaking the valleys below in shadows, enhancing an already breathtaking view.

The first mile of the hike passed quickly with the steady pace they kept. Hunter's muscles warmed, and he was ready—eager—for a full day of exercise. His body, used to grueling workouts, craved to be taxed. Morgan led the way with him two steps behind. He was pleased that her petite body could move.

She pulled a small map from the side pocket of her cargo pants and traced her finger along the blue line, announcing they were at the halfway point.

He glanced at his watch. They were making excellent time.

Farther up the trail, the path twisted and turned. Massive tree roots and large rocks peppered the ground, forcing them to slow a bit as the terrain became more uneven. Hunter's breath began to puff with the effort of the climb. This was a perfect way to spend the day.

When the path evened out, Morgan fell into step beside him. "So, this must be better."

He met her gaze. "What?"

"Being outside." She made a sweeping motion with her arm. "Being in the fresh air. Moving around."

"I certainly don't hate it."

"You must've been miserably bored these last couple days. I feel kinda bad."

He shrugged. "There's a lot of boredom that goes along with my job. The movies make it look pretty exciting, but mostly it's planning and waiting around."

"Do you like it?"

He shrugged again. "It pays the bills."

"Care to expand on that?"

"Not really."

"You're quite the conversationalist. You must be boatloads of fun on a first date."

He smiled. "I don't get many complaints."

She rolled her eyes. "I'm sure you don't."

He chuckled as she grinned. "All right. You want to talk, let's talk. I'll ask the first question. Now that you've finished with the damn paperwork, can we finally head out into backcountry?"

"Ah, a professional exchange. Boring, Hunter. Very, very boring, but I guess we'll start there."

Morgan began to answer his question, but he soon stopped listening. The occasional rustle in the distance caught his attention. The sound was too persistent and patterned to be debris falling from trees or animals moving about. He knew they were being followed. The steep, rocky terrain on one side and sheer drop on the other made a quick retreat back to the station all but impossible. He had two choices: find cover and disable their tail, or keep going. If someone was keeping an eye on them, there was a reason. They were making someone nervous, and he planned to figure out why. He debated whether he should tell Morgan and stopped.

She halted beside him. "What are you doing?"

He took her hand and pulled her close, turning her slightly, shielding her body with his and a pine tree as he wrapped his arms around her in a hug.

She stiffened, standing rigid. "Seriously, Hunter. What are you doing?"

"Smile."

She frowned. "What?"

"Just do it."

She did.

"We're being followed."

Morgan's eyes widened, and the fear showed.

His arms tightened around her waist as she started to pull away. "Stay right here. Keep looking at me, right into my eyes and listen. I don't want him to know I'm on to him. We don't have many options at this point, so we'll keep moving. You'll look for your lynx, and I'll keep you safe. We'll both do our jobs."

"But—"

"No buts. We're going to continue hiking. You'll do exactly what I say. You'll walk slightly ahead of me. That's all you have to do at this point." He kissed her cheek as if they were two lovers on a pleasure hike. "Trust me, Morgan. Do what I say and we'll be fine."

She nodded.

"We need to turn to the right just a little. You'll reach under my sweatshirt and unsnap the holster on my gun. Keep smiling at me. Move your hands slowly and calmly, as if you put them on me all the time, like they belong there. I'm sure the fucker has his binoculars trained on us right now. We'll let him think he's about to enjoy a show."

He nuzzled Morgan's neck and turned her to the right as her hands casually moved down his body. Her fingers snuck beneath his hoodie, trembling against the t-shirt he wore underneath. He grazed her ear with his lips. Despite the situation, he couldn't help but feel the heat sizzle through his system when her breathing quickened. "You're doing fine. Did you find the snap?"

"Yes." She released the strap and slowly removed her hands from under his sweatshirt.

She still trembled as he captured her face in his hands and stared into the depths of her green eyes, pulling her closer as their breath mingled. His pulse pounded, and he no longer knew if it was due to the kick of adrenaline brought on by the danger they faced or the surge of desire she made him feel. "Take my hand for a minute while we walk. I want this to look natural. I'll give you a little squeeze when I want you to let go. Remember to stay ahead of me and don't look around—only straight ahead. Everything will be all right." He brushed his lips against hers, watching her frightened eyes grow bold and determined. She nodded, and he had no choice but to let her go.

They continued along the rocky terrain with hands clasped tightly. Hunter gave her fingers a gentle squeeze, feeling her hesitation before she let go. She stayed in front of him, and he adjusted his movements so his body blocked hers while he focused on the occasional crack of branches. They were still being followed.

———◆———

They made their way to the coordinates Morgan marked on her map by mid-morning. Two hours had passed since they left the cabin, but after Hunter's announcement, time seemed to stand still. Her initial reaction had been to run, but he'd held her close, calming her, hypnotizing her with his blue eyes and steady voice. Although someone followed them, she'd only thought of him as his callused hands cupped her cheeks and he assured her everything would be all right.

The reality of their situation had come rushing back when he drew her away, breaking eye contact. She hadn't felt safe after that. Letting go of him had been one of the hardest things she'd ever done. As the warmth of his palms left her skin, she'd realized how much she'd come to depend on him, how much she needed him.

He'd kept close as the terrain steepened to an almost forty-five-degree pitch, slowing their pace considerably, making her calf muscles scream, but they finally arrived at their destination. Huge boulders and tall pines occupied much of the area—a great hiding place for a lynx. Rigid and tense, Morgan turned to face Hunter with her map in hand.

"We're here. This should be the spot. What do I do now?" she asked.

"What you came here for. We have pretty good coverage with all of the rocks and trees. Just do what you normally would and let me take care of the rest. If our plans change, you'll be the first to know."

She studied him as she reached into her pack for her field book and notes. He didn't seem overly concerned. "I want to do a small search of the area and see if I can find any fresh prints or guard hairs. We'll expand our radius from here."

"What the hell's a guard hair?"

Her shoulders relaxed as she smiled. "It's the outer coat of a mammal's hair. The hairs help keep the animal dry. If I get a sample, we can send it out for confirmation that a lynx has been in the area. The tracks photographed are consistent." She showed him a picture of the footprint and pointed to the identical print in her field guide. "But we always want to be sure." Unable to help herself, she glanced behind her, knowing somewhere close someone watched, and her shoulders coiled tight again.

Hunter put his hand on her arm. "Hey."

She turned back, staring into his eyes.

"I've got this. We're safer here among these boulders and trees than we were on the trail. Trust that I know how to do my job, that I know how to keep you safe. I'm not going to let anything happen to you."

Believing him, trusting him fully, she placed her hand

over his, giving a gentle squeeze before she nodded and glanced back at her field guide.

———◆———

After an hour of crawling around on the forest floor, looking for fresh tracks and scanning branches for hairs without luck, Morgan sat on a rock with her bottle of water. Hunter settled on a fallen tree close by, blocking her body from any possible openings.

"It's actually pretty warm up here." She unzipped her jacket and took it off.

"It's July. It should be. Hell, it should be hot. If I were back in LA, I wouldn't be wearing a damn sweatshirt. I'd be in sandals and short sleeves."

"We're pretty elevated up here. It'll be cooler than the summer temperatures we're used to, but I'm not complaining. At least we're on the northeast side of the park. It's warmer and drier than other sections. We could actually get snow, but now that summer's in full bloom, we don't have to worry too much." Her eyes darted about as tension strained her voice despite their casual conversation. She pressed a hand to her growling stomach and bent forward, reaching into her pack. "I'm on edge, but I'm also starving. Are you ready for lunch?"

"Yeah, I could eat." On full alert, Hunter continued his scan of the trees in the distance. Fifty yards from where they sat, the quick flash of sun on glass caught his attention. He didn't want to alarm Morgan or make whoever followed them aware, so he made sure his eyes continued their scan— as if he were enjoying the beauty of the nature surrounding them. He gave Morgan a small smile when she handed him a sandwich thick with ham and cheese from the double-sealed container. He took a bite. "Mmm. Good."

"Enjoy it while it lasts. Cold cuts won't be on the menu when we head into backcountry. We'll both be sick of beans, rice, and pasta by the time we're done here." She flashed him a quick smile and took a bite of her sandwich. A twig cracked in the distance, and she stopped chewing. "Did you hear that?"

Hunter lost sight of their tail as another branch snapped, much closer this time—a little too close for Hunter's liking. He unholstered his gun and stood.

Morgan started to stand. "What—"

"Get on the ground by the rock and don't move," he said, putting his hand on her shoulder, keeping her down.

"But what—"

He didn't stick around for her question. Instead, he took off, sprinting in a zigzag pattern, hurdling rocks with his gun in hand, ready to fire. He caught quick glimpses of a man wearing army fatigues and a boonie hat, running at a fast clip. He knew their stalker was long gone, and the chase was pulling him too far away from Morgan. He wanted to pursue, to track the bastard down, but it wasn't an option. With little choice, he stopped, listening until the footsteps faded. Confident the man wouldn't be back, he ran to where he left Morgan, holstering his gun, slowing to a steady jog as he got closer.

Wide-eyed, Morgan stood. "My God."

He stopped in front of her. "I didn't tell you to get up. Never get up until I give you the all-clear."

"Okay, fine. Whatever. Why did you take off? Hasn't he been following us all day?"

"He got too close." He took off his hoodie and guzzled water.

"Do you think he's the killer? What if he was going to try to murder us? Maybe this is the game he played with Shelly and the guys. I bet it's some sicko who stalks his prey for fun before he shoots them."

"I didn't get that impression. He had several opportunities to shoot at us, but I don't think that was the goal. Someone is keeping tabs on us, but why? There's the real question. If

I'd thought we were in trouble, I would've taken care of the situation long before now."

Her eyes grew wide again. "What does that mean? You would've killed him? You say that like it's no big deal."

"No. It's a very big deal, but I'll do what I have to in order to protect you. I think we should consider hanging this whole thing up. We need to have a serious conversation about pulling the plug and heading back to DC."

She shook her head. "No."

He was surprised by the battle light burning in her eyes. He knew she'd been on edge for most of the day and figured she would be more than happy to follow his suggestion to go home.

"I'm not about to let some jerk scare me. I have a job to do here."

"That may be, but that was before someone decided to tag along on our hike."

"I can't go. I won't. If you want out, fine, but I'm staying."

He didn't miss the hint of desperation in her voice and wondered about it. "Then I guess we're staying together, but I'll give you fair warning. I don't like what's going on here. If I continue to not like it, I'm putting you on the first plane back to DC."

"That isn't the agreement you made with my father. You're being paid for the month. When the month is up, I'll put *myself* on a plane and go back to DC."

Her haughty tone irritated him. "If I call your father and tell him what went on here today, he'll come out and get you himself."

She took a step forward. "You go ahead and call whoever you want, but I'm not going anywhere. My father isn't in charge of my life—I am. As I said before, if you're out then get out, but don't you dare talk to me as if the two of you make my choices." She picked up her pack and headed back toward the ranger station.

———◆———

Morgan walked down the steep, slippery path riddled with dry pine needles. She slowed her pace as her anger faded, not wanting to get too far away from Hunter—not that he would allow that to happen. And truth be told, the arrangement suited her just fine. Followed...they had actually been followed. She shuddered at the idea of having her every move watched. If Hunter hadn't made her aware of the situation, she would have gone through her day oblivious and that terrified her.

But why? Hunter was right: That was the question. Why did a day hike to track an animal make someone nervous? How had the person known their plans? She looked deep into the surrounding trees, wondering if she was still being stalked.

Hunter picked up his pace, walking closer—no more than four or five steps behind—and she relaxed. She played back their latest argument and sighed. She didn't want him to leave her here to do this on her own. It shamed her to think she'd almost agreed with him. She'd almost let herself be talked into going back to DC without answers. Didn't her friends deserve them?

A smile ghosted her mouth as she remembered their last night together—the music, the laughter, the fun. Shelly, Ian, and Tom had been so carefree, so *alive*. Her smile vanished as pictures of their violent deaths circled through her mind, replacing the good memories of an evening that seemed so long ago.

Her fault. She would never forget that three people had died as a result of her poor planning. How many times had she damned herself for not changing the teams? Why did she let Ian talk her out of it? Physically, Shelly and Tom had been the weakest of the crew, and the terrain of Yellowstone was so much more difficult than Maine's. What if they'd had to run for their lives? Shelly and Tom had never been very fast, and Ian never would have left them behind. Had they fought and struggled only to lose in the end? Would physical strength have made the difference?

She would never know, but she could only blame herself for the tragic result. She'd followed along with rash decisions, fully aware that the crew who went to Yellowstone never should've been there in the first place. And now she could do nothing more than find their killer or killers. She owed them. Nothing was going to stop her—not fear, not her father, and definitely not Hunter. She would stay, even if it meant she stayed alone.

ᥨ CHAPTER FOURTEEN ᥩ

A COLD FRONT MOVED THROUGH THE MOUNTAINS during the last mile of their hike. Dark, heavy clouds and gusting winds promised a strong afternoon storm. Morgan opened the door to the station as thunder rumbled and the first fat drops of rain hit the ground. She closed herself and Hunter inside and moved to the window, peering out into the storm-darkened forest, wondering if she and Hunter were alone. Shuddering, she turned to meet Hunter's gaze.

He stared at her, clearly studying her. "Whoever followed us into the woods didn't follow us back." He walked to their bedroom, stopping abruptly at the door.

Morgan crept up behind him. "What are you—"

Hunter put his finger to his lips as he pushed her behind him. Rushing forward, he forced the door open with a powerful kick. Wood slammed against the paneled wall with a loud crack.

Morgan followed him into the cramped space. "What are you doing?

Frowning, he shut the door behind her, securing the lock as he glanced around the room. "Our door was open. I closed it before we left."

"Maybe you thought you did."

His eyes stopped scanning, locking on hers. "I know I

shut it."

If no one followed them back, why was he making this into such a big deal? "It was barely cracked. I'm sure the wind caught it or something."

"Yeah, or something." He took his suitcase from the closet and rifled through his clothing. "Boot up your computer and search the history. What's on there?"

"Why?"

"Just *do* it." He powered his on as well. "Look through your stuff. Is anything missing? Has anything been tampered with?"

She pressed the power button on her laptop, glimpsing over her shoulder at their stuff. Everything looked exactly as it had when they left this morning. "Is this another one of your 'memorable lessons?'" She glared at him. "I don't know why you're trying to scare me. I already told you I'm not going back to DC."

"I got your point loud and clear."

"Are you suggesting someone broke into the station?"

"No, I'm *telling* you someone went through our stuff while we were gone."

Frowning, Morgan scrutinized their space. Everything was in its place. "Give me a break," she said with less conviction as she studied the rigid set of Hunter's body and his humorless eyes. He certainly didn't appear to be joking.

"I'm not kidding."

"How can you tell? Nothing seems disturbed. I know someone followed us, but I think it's a bit of a stretch to think they came here first. They wouldn't have had enough time to do both."

He looked back at his computer. "Just trust me on this one."

Picking up her laptop, she hit a couple of keys, accessing her security settings as she remembered the kiss he'd planted on her after he'd tackled her to the ground in the name of teaching her a lesson. His methods of proving his points left her unwilling to believe him. "I think you're being para-noid. I think—" A flashing red box popped up on her screen, alerting her to a failed log-in attempt just as a loud blast of thunder shook the station, making her jump.

"Not so paranoid after all, huh?"

She swallowed the dredges of fear, ignoring his smug tone. "How—how did you know?"

"I get paid to know."

"No, really—how could you tell? I'm looking around and everything seems the same."

"I set up my things in a certain way so I can tell if any-one touches them. I always leave my stuff flush against the wall, creating a ninety-degree angle. The suitcase is now at eighty-five. The apple on my computer faced the other way when I powered it down before we left."

"Oh," she said lamely, staring at his carry-on. "We should tell Robert and Miles. They might want to check their stuff too."

"No. We aren't saying anything about any of this."

She opened her mouth to argue as someone knocked on the door.

Hunter stood. "Not a word," he said before he answered.

Miles smiled. "Hey. I wanted to make sure you two made it back. That's a pretty crazy storm out there."

She joined Hunter at the door, returning Miles' smile. "We did. It's certainly a loud one." Thunder clapped as she spoke, and she laughed, rolling her eyes to the ceiling when Mother Nature followed her cue.

Without warning, Hunter put his arm around her shoul-ders, pulling her closer to his side. She slid him a glance as he moved his fingers in long, slow strokes against her skin, sending shockwaves of need through her body.

Miles looked from Hunter to Morgan and cleared his throat. "Well, I'm glad you're back safely. I'm on supper duty tonight. We usually eat around six if that works for you."

Morgan pulled away from Hunter's hold, fighting to

steady herself. "It works just fine. Can I help out?"

"I'll never turn down an extra hand." Grinning, he sent her a friendly wink. "What do you say we get started in an hour?"

She smiled again. "Perfect."

Miles walked off, and Morgan closed the door with a snap. "What was that?"

Hunter wandered to the bed and sat down, staring at her as if he had no idea what she was talking about. "What was what?"

"You know." She gestured wildly with fluttering hands. "Why did you put your arm around me that way, as if you and I are...involved?"

He shrugged. "I didn't like the way he was looking at you."

"You didn't like the way he was *looking* at me?" She settled her hand on her hip as her temper started to heat. "And just how was he looking at me?"

Hunter picked up her laptop, busying himself with the information on the computer screen. "Like he wanted to take a bite out of you," he replied absently as he tapped at the keys, breaking through her security systems within seconds. "So what kind of information do you store on this thing anyway? I'm trying to figure out what someone would want to access."

She yanked the laptop from his hands, slamming the top closed, and tossed it on the bed. "Forget the damn computer. Miles was being perfectly polite, and once again, you were incredibly rude. What signal was he giving off, Bodyguard Phillips, that led you to believe I was somehow in need of your 'protection?'"

Hunter sneered as he shook his head. "He was mentally undressing you while you talked about the weather. Hell, Morgan, you were about to lose your panties before dinner even made its way into the conversation."

Outrage left her gaping. "You're *despicable* and crude, but that's beside the point. Who do you think you are? You don't get to make decisions about my personal life. If Miles is looking at me as if he 'wants to take a bite out of me,'" she emphasized with exaggerated air quotes, "that's his choice. If I want him to take a bite out of me, that's mine." She turned toward the door.

"Where are you going?"

"I can't be around you right now without wanting to hurt you. I'm going to help Miles with supper. We'll eat early. You've got a hell of a nerve." She left the room without a backward glance.

———◆———

Morgan and Miles' happy chatter drifted back to the bedroom while Hunter stared at the computer screen he'd opened again after she left. The rain drummed on the roof but failed to drown out Morgan's laughter. The smoke and velvet sound had his jaw clenching and his hands in fists at his sides. When he'd had all he could take, he strolled down the hall to the kitchen. During the half hour he'd spent alone, he'd had time to think about what she'd said, knew she was right, and didn't like it.

He stepped into the doorway and narrowed his eyes when Miles touched Morgan's hips as he slid behind her to get to the refrigerator. The kitchen was small, but not *that* small.

She glanced over her shoulder, smiling as Miles passed by. She turned her head, meeting Hunter's stare, and her smile vanished as she looked down, putting the freshly rolled meatballs in the hot olive oil.

Robert walked through the front door with water dripping off of his bright yellow slicker. "That's one hell of a storm out there. Miles, we'll have to check the roads for washout later."

"Great. That's just how I want to spend the evening. Morgan and I are making spaghetti and meatballs."

Robert's gaze passed over Hunter before he gave Morgan a smile. "Smells great. I look forward to it. We'll have a hearty meal before we head out into this bitch of a storm."

He winced. "Begging your pardon, Morgan."

"Don't worry about a thing," she assured, as she dried her clean hands on a towel and walked over to Hunter with plates and silverware, shoving them into his arms with more force than necessary. "Set the table for us, *honey*."

His brow drew together as she walked away and smiled at Miles again. Oh, they were going to talk about this later.

———◆———

Fifteen minutes later, they sat around the table with plates full of pasta and meatballs, garlic bread, and salad.

Robert took a big bite of a meatball and spaghetti dripping with sauce. "This is delicious, Morgan, absolutely delicious. Where did you learn to cook?"

Miles waved his hand. "Hey, I helped too."

"You don't cook like this."

Morgan chuckled as she looked from Robert to Miles. "You were a wonderful assistant. Actually, I learned from my mother. She's amazing in the kitchen. She started teaching me when I was a little girl."

Miles sipped his Sprite. "Maybe I could get a couple of lessons before you leave."

"Sure. I'd be happy to give you a lesson or two." She met Hunter's smoldering stare as he chewed his salad. Still miffed and unconcerned with his mood, she turned her attention back to Miles. "Just think of a few dishes you'd like to learn, and we'll find some time. It'll have to be in the next couple of days, though. We'll be heading into backcountry soon."

Robert wiped his mouth with his napkin. "This morning you weren't sure where you'd go. Did your hike give you any ideas?"

"The last documented tracks were found north of here. I imagine we'll continue in that direction. Perhaps we'll go northwest."

"Hmm, northwest. I would think you might want to try

south of the location."

She cut her meatball in half and rolled spaghetti on her fork. "You think so? I just figured that since the lynx typically comes down from Canada, north would be the most logical choice. Although we did look north today and I didn't see anything. I guess it couldn't hurt to go south of the tracks." She shrugged. "They're such an elusive species. I'm pretty much flying blind here."

"It'll certainly be a difficult animal to tag." Robert put down his fork. "This really was delicious. I hate leaving the mess behind."

"Don't worry about it. Hunter and I'll get it." She flicked him a glance as his brow shot up. He hadn't said a word during the entire meal. "Riding around in the pouring rain sounds like a miserable task."

"It is, but it has to be done. We'll be awhile. I can't imagine we'll be back before you're asleep." Robert brought his plate to the sink, with Miles following behind.

On their way out, Miles stopped in front of Morgan's chair, taking her hand and kissing her knuckles. "Thank you for an enjoyable evening. I'm eagerly anticipating my next cooking lesson."

She didn't dare look at Hunter as she gently pulled her hand free from his. "I had fun too. Goodnight. Be safe out there."

✂ CHAPTER FIFTEEN ✂

ORGAN STOOD GATHERING DIRTY DISHES FROM the table when the door closed behind Miles and Robert. In an attempt to drown out the tense, uncomfortable quiet, she turned on the countertop radio and fiddled with the dial until she found the one station that played Top 40 music instead of country. She hummed along with The Script as the sink filled with hot water and lemon-scented soap. Plunging her hands into the bubbles, she began to scrub.

Hunter grabbed a towel and took the dripping plates she handed him, drying them in stony silence.

She was shocked he'd stuck around to help but was even more surprised he had nothing to say about Miles kissing her hand. She'd expected some sort of pithy comment, but it seemed he would rather stand inches away from her and brood in his pissy mood. Apparently Hunter didn't like being put in his place.

When the kitchen was spotless, Morgan headed to the bedroom, congratulating herself on finally putting him there—until she thought of the way Miles had looked at her before he left. She gnawed on her bottom lip as guilt swamped her for leading him on. She wasn't attracted to him or interested in anything more than friendship, but it had been important to prove her point to Hunter. He didn't have a say in her personal life. She would cooperate for safety's sake, but she would be damned if he was going to start dictating her relationships. She didn't know how to handle things with Hunter—she never did—but she could make everything right with Miles by making sure he understood they were friends and give him a couple of cooking lessons.

With her conscience clear, she gathered her items for a quick shower. A relaxing night with a good book was just how she planned to end this long, tense day. She glanced at the small curtained window in their room, hating that having Hunter close by on this dark, rainy night was more comforting than annoying. She still had the willies when she thought about someone watching them.

Clean and refreshed, Morgan walked back to the bedroom, anticipating her warm bed and the new best seller she'd brought along. She looked forward to getting lost in a good novel and the problems of the characters for a while—and forgetting her own. Her pleasure dimmed when Hunter lay on his side of the bed, reading with the covers settled around his waist. He wasn't wearing a shirt again. She couldn't help but stare at his chiseled torso and wonder what it would be like to run her hands along all of that smooth, golden skin. She felt the tug low in her belly and let out a quiet sigh as she closed the bedroom door behind her.

Hunter glanced up from his book. "Squeaky clean, *honey*?" Scathing blue eyes traveled down her body and back up, locking with hers.

Suddenly self-conscious in her black tank top and tiny white boxer shorts, she pushed a strand of her wet hair behind her ear, nervously licking her lips as she glared, recognizing his mocking tone for what it was. Turning, she put her bathroom tote on the floor, hung her towel on the peg, and bent down for her book. She'd be damned if he would spoil her night. She turned, gasping when she slammed into his naked chest. "God, you scared me. Why are you always *doing* that?" Having had more than enough of Hunter for one evening, she tried to maneuver around him.

He wouldn't move.

"Excuse me. I'd like to get by."

He pulled the book from her hand, tossing it to the floor, and gripped her shoulders, walking her back to the wall.

"Let go of me," she said weakly as her heart pounded, but it wasn't fear that made it race.

"Not yet," he murmured, sliding his hands down her arms, sending sparks of desire along her skin. He pulled her bottom lip between his teeth, nibbling gently, as his gaze burned into hers. "I'm the only person around here who'll be taking a bite out of you, Morgan. You remember that." He captured her mouth, roughly, angrily.

She knew she should shove him away, but instead she wrapped her arms around the back of his neck, returning his potent kiss.

He trailed his fingers down her waist, stopping at her hips, sneaking his hands under her shirt on the way up. He found her breasts and sent shockwaves through her system as he teased and caressed.

Her breath caught in her throat and rushed out as she skimmed her palms over his muscled back, relishing his warm, firm skin pressing against hers. She cupped his butt over the black mesh of his shorts and pulled him closer, feeling her effect on him.

He tipped her head to the side, nipped at her earlobe, and wandered, skimming kisses along her neck and over her collarbone, making her whimper. "You smell good. You always smell so good. I want you," he shuddered out, picking her up.

She wrapped her legs around him, feathering kisses along his firm jaw, biting gently at the dimple in his chin as he carried her to the bed. She flicked her tongue along his earlobe, smiling when he hissed out a breath.

The mattress springs squeaked when they collapsed on the bed, with him landing on top of her. Hunter pulled her shirt up and off, groaning as he stared. "God. Look at you. You're perfect." The resentment in his strained voice registered, but her thoughts scattered when he traced his tongue around her nipple, taking her into his mouth.

Her hands went wild in his hair and she moaned, rocking her hips in invitation as she started to throb.

His mouth came back to hers as she opened her eyes, seeing his before he closed them again. There was no tenderness there, only anger.

She wanted him, but not like this. Putting her hands on his shoulders, she moved her chin up so her lips were out of reach. "Stop, Hunter. Stop. I want you to stop."

He stared at her, breathing hard. After a moment, he untangled himself from her and walked out of the room.

Suddenly cold, Morgan pulled her shirt back on and stared at the ceiling, trying to catch her own breath. She'd never wanted anyone the way she did Hunter. There'd been a moment where she almost let him keep going, but she couldn't bear the thought of him looking at her with such... derision while he moved inside her. She had deep, complicated feelings she knew he didn't return. It shamed her to know she'd almost settled for whatever he would have given her. Crawling to her side of the bed, she pulled up the covers, turned off the light, and stared into the darkness until she finally fell asleep.

Hunter walked to the bathroom and turned on the sink faucet, splashing frigid water on his cheeks. He pressed his face into a towel and hung it on the hook, taking a deep breath as he stared at his reflection in the mirror. What the hell was he *doing*? Had he really believed he was proving a point by kissing Morgan and putting his hands all over her sinful body? He leaned against the door, running his trembling fingers through his hair. Every time he looked at her, he *wanted* her. He didn't know how to stop.

He'd set out to show Morgan—and himself—that she wanted him just as much as he did her. He'd been angry and jealous when Miles had been all over her. He didn't do jealous—never had. Only she could make him feel such ugly emotions, and he didn't like it at all.

Hunter dropped his hands, resting them on the sides of the sink. He was on shaky ground. His feelings for her were growing stronger. They were more than he wanted. If he chose to be honest with himself, he could acknowledge they were more than he could handle.

He would be keeping his hands to himself for the rest of this assignment. It was never wise to mix business with pleasure, especially in this business. And he never had. His objectivity was compromised. He knew he should call Ethan and request a change of assignment, but he wanted to see this through—had to, he realized.

In a little more than two and a half weeks, he would be finished with Morgan Taylor. He wouldn't have to talk to her, look at her, or think of her again. He glanced in the mirror, staring into his own blue eyes, knowing that forgetting her wouldn't be so easy. Sighing, he turned, twisting on the shower. He stepped into the steam and stood under the hot spray as the miserly stream pelted his back, easing most of the tightly coiled tension. He closed his tired eyes and stretched his neck with slow, smooth rolls, thinking of the many shitty events that had piled up high and fast throughout the day. It wasn't a huge surprise that his temples were throbbing.

After a quick rinse, he shut off the water, toweled himself dry, and pulled on his boxers and shorts. He opened the tiny medicine cabinet hanging above the sink, shook two extra-strength Tylenol into his hand, and swallowed them before heading toward the bedroom, having no idea what in the hell he was going to say to Morgan—whatever it was would start with an apology. He couldn't deny he'd been way out of line.

He reached their door, and relief washed through him when the ugly lamp on the shelf above their beds had been turned off. He could see Morgan asleep from the light in the hallway—thank God. They both needed time to settle after what had passed between them. He would apologize in the morning.

Now that he didn't have to worry about bumbling his way through a dicey conversation, he wandered down the hall to the kitchen. His stomach growled as he opened the refrigerator door and studied the shelves, looking for something to eat. He glanced at the ceiling as steady sheets of rain began pounding on the roof and the wind gusted, battering against the windows, compounding the quiet emptiness of the cabin. This was the perfect opportunity to take a look around. Perhaps a quick shakedown of Miles and Robert's room wouldn't be such a bad idea. There was no guarantee he would get another chance.

He closed the fridge door and made his way to the front of the house, double-checking the locks for the third time. Confident the door and windows were secure, he walked to his room and grabbed a small flashlight from his pack, glancing at Morgan once more before heading to the next room.

He turned the cheap chrome knob, opening the door to darkness, breathing in the scent of Old Spice wafting through the small space. Stepping inside, he used the harsh light of the hallway to do an initial scan of the room, making mental notes of the way everything looked, determined to do a hell of a lot better job than the person who'd been through his and Morgan's stuff earlier in the afternoon. He wasn't exactly sure of what he was looking for, but he had little doubt he would know if and when he found it.

Starting in the closet, he slid his fingers up and down the shirts and pants hanging on the hangers, then passed the beam of his light over every wood-paneled inch of the rest of the small space. Finding nothing, he checked the beds, sneaking his hand under the pillows and on top, squishing the feathers down within and smoothing the cases out to remove his indented handprint.

Something rattled outside the bedroom window, and he froze in his tracks, his heartbeat quickening as he reached for his gun, muttering a curse. The Glock usually resting in the holster against his ribs was in the other room. He scanned the dark for some sort of weapon as a howling gust of wind sent something crashing against the side of the house. The rattling stopped and he remembered the birdfeeder hanging on a hook next to the window frame. Robert had filled it yesterday while he and Morgan chatted about the damn animal she was searching for.

He stood still, listening for the noise for several more seconds, confident the feeder had been the culprit. Then he left Robert's room to check on Morgan just to play it safe. She hadn't moved.

His pulse leveled as the adrenaline ebbed in his veins, and he went back, picking up where he left off by running his hands in between the mattresses. Coming up empty again, he peered under the beds and searched the one dresser in the larger room, moving from drawer to drawer. He lifted neatly folded boxers, felt jeans and shirts for anything that didn't seem like it belonged—still nothing. He moved the dresser out slightly, scanning the back with the flashlight, and stopped, coming to attention when the beam landed on a six-by-six-inch false panel cut into the scarred flooring. Interesting.

Hunter slid the dresser farther out and squeezed behind, crouching. He pressed on the edge of the panel, tugging on the corner jutting out slightly, and pulled the board free, then shined his flashlight into the opening. A small, pink book decorated with fancy white flowers had been taped to the inside.

"Bingo," he muttered as his shoulders tensed. This had to

be Shelly's journal. He removed the hardback book from the tape and replaced the panel, putting the furniture back. He scanned the room one last time, making certain everything appeared the same as it had when he entered, and brought the book back to his bedroom.

Easing onto his side of the bed, careful not to cause the bedsprings to squeak under his weight, he sat, beaming his flashlight on the pages while he flipped through the journal. There wasn't a lot to see. He skimmed several entries from the team's trip to Washington State, but they hadn't really had a chance to start much of anything in Yellowstone. With every page he turned, he got a slight whiff of fading perfume. He pulled the book close to his face and sniffed. The frilly, feminine scent reminded him of a warm spring day, and he felt a sudden tug of loss for a woman he'd never known. In life, Shelly must have smelled like this.

He didn't want to think about that. It made her real instead of just an image in a gruesome picture and a mystery to be solved. He didn't want to feel closer to her. He didn't want a reminder that the woman who'd lain sprawled over her pack with dull, staring eyes had been a human being full of life only weeks before. More than that, she'd been a good friend of Morgan's.

Hunter's gaze wandered to Morgan's stunning face relaxed in sleep, and he brushed his fingers over her soft hair. Catching himself, he fisted his hand and settled it at his side. This small piece of Shelly's humanity touched off a flood of tenderness for everything Morgan had been through over the last month. He wanted to make it better and take away her pain. He wanted to turn back time and somehow change it all. Shaken by the need to protect her—more than life and limb—he looked away, trying to block it out.

Focusing on the book again, he scanned the words. Nothing remarkable caught his eye. Frustrated, he blew out a breath, rubbing at his pounding head. They weren't going to find anything this way.

Continuing on, he glanced at more pages, reading the thoughts that had passed through Shelly's mind: She and the team hadn't found anything yet; where had all of these feelings for Ian come from; he wanted to be with her, but what about taking over as lead researcher in Los Angeles; did she love him? Yes, absolutely...

Hunter turned to the next page and sprang up. "Holy shit." He winced, glancing at Morgan, hoping he hadn't woken her up. She slept on, and he read Shelly's entry.

May 25, 2012

As I sit by the light of our campfire tonight and write, I still find myself in complete disbelief. It feels like today was a dream. We will certainly have a story to tell when we get back to DC.

Ian, Tom, and I traveled northwest for three days and found little to nothing that would aid us in our attempt to locate and tag our animal. Truth be told, our luck has been terrible so far. It's been colder than average and rainy with it. One of the tents leaks, and we haven't located any evidence that verifies a lynx lives in the area. I hope Morgan and the guys are having more luck in Maine than we are here. I'll ask Mr. Taylor for an update when we check in.

We stopped for lunch this afternoon and decided—unanimously—to make our way back to the station if we still had no findings to add to our data. Perhaps we need to start over and try a different area of the park. As we gave it our last shot and journeyed along the banks of the Slough River, we didn't find the lynx, but something far more disturbing. Large carcasses, which appeared to have been mule deer, were scattered about every few hundred yards in different states of decomposition.

After closer examination, we saw that they had been shot. It was unclear as to why. They weren't killed for meat and their heads were left behind, which ruled out shooting for trophy. I believe the poor animals were murdered just because someone carried a weapon and could. We tried radioing our location to the station, but we were too far out of range. The guys and I traveled well beyond the typical tourist destination. With few options, we noted the area on the map and planned to share our findings as soon as we could make radio contact again.

Just as we were about to turn and head back, a loud blast shook the area. Ian thought we should check it out, but Tom and I were hesitant. Ian reasoned that perhaps we would find a clue as to why the animals had been killed. We followed the river for another half-mile before we came to the large clearing and hid ourselves in the shelter of the trees. From there, we could see what was going on. After a thorough examination through our binoculars, we concluded a gold mining operation was taking place on federally protected land. Ian wanted to confront them, but Tom and I talked him out of it. The situation was too dangerous. We were outnumbered and unarmed.

We left as quickly as we could and hiked our asses off. A hike that should've taken two days ended up taking one—my aching feet can attest to this. If the station wasn't still a good day from here, we would've kept going and told the rangers in person, and I would be writing this entry in the comfort of a bed.

After several attempts, we finally made radio contact with the northeast ranger station. Tom started to tell the ranger what we'd discovered, but the man interrupted Tom and had him switch to another frequency. He asked us for our location and said we should stay put for the night. He plans to meet us here by midmorning, and we'll bring him back to the spot where we found the mining operation.

All of this is so crazy. It makes me wish for Morgan and the rest of the team. It's strange not having everyone together, and it's too quiet. I can't wait to get back to the station and make contact with The Bureau. Perhaps if we time things right, I can get a call through to Morgan's hotel. She will be shocked when I tell her what we've been up to. She'll be envious of our adventure; although, I'm looking forward to its ending.

I'm eager to be back in DC. During the nights when I'm cold and sometimes wet, I keep reminding myself I have my Farewell to Shelly Party to attend, and it immediately lifts my spirits. I mentally leaf through the few dresses I haven't packed away, but none of those will do. This one has to be special.

Perhaps Morgan and I will make a quick trip to the little boutique just down the road from her house. We'll walk in, she'll scan the selection, and within seconds I'll be making my way to the dressing room with the perfect outfit. I don't know how she does it, but she never fails. I want to look amazing. With Morgan and Ilene putting this little soiree together, it's guaranteed to be quite an event. It's going to be great.

The only sad part in all of this is I really am going to miss the team so much. I guess they'll have to come visit me out in LA—a lot.

I wonder what Morgan will think when I tell her Ian is coming with me. I guess my Goodbye to Shelly Party will actually be a Goodbye to Shelly and Ian Party. He wants to be with me. He wants us to make a go of it, and surprisingly enough, so do I. I don't know when all of this happened—it sort of just did. It almost seems too good to be true.

I left Morgan dangling with bits of a long story, which wasn't very fair, but we'll talk when I get home. This is all so new. I'm in love and I can't wait to tell her everything.

Well, until tomorrow. Here's to hoping for a dry night of sleep and a quick resolution to our most amazing discovery.

Hunter turned the page and found another entry. The handwriting no longer appeared pretty and looping. It looked as if it had been written in a rush.

Something's wrong. The ranger came with two police officers. It feels off. When they met up with us, every instinct

in my body shouted at me to run. I think the guys feel it too.
Ian and Tom are going to try something, but we're outnum-
bered—three guns to none.

After looking at our map, they told us we would hike
north-northwest to find a shortcut. They've been grilling us
with questions. I'm turning on my GPS so The Bureau can
track us. I want to go home. I'm so scared.

I think

He flipped through the rest of the pages. They were
blank. He held the book upside down, shaking it from side
to side, hoping the map they'd marked might be stuck to
another page. It wasn't. Mentally filing the information
away, he got up to put the journal back and pulled the panel
from the floor. Before he put it away, he felt around for more
loose boards, hoping the map would be there, but there was
nothing else. He secured the journal under the tape as the
bright beam of headlights cut across the room. Wet brakes
squeaked just outside the cabin. "Shit." He closed the panel
and moved the dresser into place, hustling back to the bedroom seconds before the front door opened.

Hunter stared into the dark long after the house was quiet
again, thinking about what he'd read. If the team had turned
around instead of following the noises they'd heard, they
would all be alive. Sighing, he ran his fingers through his
hair. So much for a month-long, vacation-like assignment.
His plans for a somewhat relaxed trek through backcountry
had been shot to hell in less than twelve hours. He and Morgan were living with at least one shady ranger. He had little
doubt Robert was in this up to his eyeballs, but what about
Miles? Did he know? And the cops. How many dirty cops
were involved with murder?

Since he couldn't convince Morgan to go back home, and
there was little he could do at this point to force her, they
might as well get to the bottom of all this. The answers lay
along the banks of the Slough River.

He and Morgan would have to move in that direction to-morrow. If they hiked hard, it would take them the better part of two days. He would keep the journal to himself for now. Once he confirmed what Shelly and the team had seen and got the exact coordinates, he would get Morgan the hell out of Yellowstone before the shit hit the fan—whether she liked it or not.

❧ CHAPTER SIXTEEN ❧

HUNTER WOKE INSTANTLY WHEN MORGAN'S LEG brushed his as she attempted to crawl over him. He trailed his gaze over her sexy body, remembering the way her soft skin felt pressed beneath his. Despite his promise to keep his hands to himself, he wanted to grab her and finish what they'd started last night.

Her foot left the mattress and touched the floor, making the bedsprings squeak. She winced and glanced over her shoulder, pausing in her crouched position as their gazes locked. Her chilly green eyes narrowed to slits, and the apology for his behavior last night withered on his tongue. Any tenderness he'd felt for her while he read through Shelly's journal dried up like a desert pool. Perhaps he wasn't sorry for his actions after all. His gruff, "We'll leave tomorrow," was the best he could do.

She stood, pulling on her jeans and a bold red sweatshirt, covering the black tank top he'd peeled off of her hours before. She opened the bedroom door without a backward glance and shut it with a hard snap behind her.

"That went well." Sighing, he scrubbed his hands over his face and got out of bed, opening the door. He wanted to be able to hear any conversations coming from the office or kitchen. He yawned, desperate for a cup of coffee, but ignored his craving, deciding Morgan could use some space, especially when he heard a cupboard close with a bang, the refrigerator door shut with a rattle, and her spoon and bowl clatter against the kitchen table. A shot of caffeine wasn't worth dealing with that; they'd seen enough of each other already. Resigned to start the day without his java buzz, he pulled his laptop from its case and got to work, getting lost in his latest project.

Throughout the afternoon, the motorized sounds of a vacuum sealer and the occasional clang of dishes made their way back to the bedroom. Preparations for the backcountry hike were in full swing. Morgan had made it clear she didn't want his help. When he offered to organize supplies, he was met with an icy, "I'm all set." He was eager to be on the move but knew they had to wait. Last night's torrential downpours put a wrench in his plans. Hiking backcountry through thick mud and over slippery rocks was an accident waiting to happen. Minor injuries could turn into major hassles when miles of wilderness separated a hiker from proper medical treatment.

He utilized the time Mother Nature had given him, spending much of the day sitting on his bed in front of his laptop, taking advantage of the security clearance he'd earned as a Force Recon. He hacked into government satellite imagery of the Slough River, comparing the images on the computer to the map he and Morgan would bring when they left early tomorrow, trying to pinpoint where Shelly, Ian, and Tom had found the mining operation.

The river went on for miles through Wyoming and Montana. He focused on the northern border of the park—well into the forest where few tourists traveled. Most of the waterway was exposed to open valley, except for small patches of trees scattered along the banks. He pressed the right button on his mouse, zeroing in on a segment of water that disappeared under a large section of thick vegetation. He was willing to bet they would find what they were looking for there. Tree cover would disguise the operation, keeping it from detection by satellite and flyovers. He and Morgan were in for quite a hike. A good five to ten miles of their trek appeared treacherous—jagged peaks and steep valleys.

As he searched, he covered his tracks, constantly erasing his computer's history. He still hadn't shared the information he'd discovered in Shelly's journal with anyone. He wanted to brief Ethan but knew he and Morgan were being watched. Robert and Miles were suspicious. He didn't exactly fit the bill of a wildlife biologist or any other type of associate Morgan would have through The Bureau. He couldn't be certain his calls weren't being monitored. If Miles and Robert had something to do with all of this, they weren't working alone.

As dusk fell, Miles walked through the front door of the station, greeting Morgan.

Hunter glanced toward the hallway, clenching his jaw, fighting the urge to wander out to the kitchen. Instead, he focused on the map at his side and continued to prepare.

Moments later, Morgan's smooth voice told Miles he was about to have his first cooking lesson. Amazing, spicy scents drifted through the air, along with Morgan's laughter as she and Miles discussed the southern route she planned for tomorrow.

Hunter grit his teeth, listening to their casual friendliness. If it bothered him that he rarely experienced the warm, sweet side of Morgan—the side she shared so willingly with everyone else—he chose to ignore it. Consciously, he relaxed his jaw and stared at his computer screen, willing the gnawing frustration away.

He still hadn't clued her in to their change of plans. If everyone believed they were heading south, they were less likely to be followed.

CHAPTER SEVENTEEN

THE SUN ROSE OVER THE ROCKIES, CASTING SHADOWS among the trees as Hunter and Morgan donned their heavy packs and headed south from the ranger station. Morgan gave Robert and Miles a final wave before they disappeared into the tree line and headed toward the southeast trail. Birdsong filled the brisk morning air along with the productive sound of twigs snapping as they walked their first mile over rocky terrain. Hunter kept his ears trained and his senses tuned for a tail. When he was sure they weren't being followed, he stopped.

Morgan slammed into his pack, letting out a whooshing breath as she stumbled backwards.

He turned, grabbing her hand, catching her before she fell.

"Geez, tell me when you're going to stop next time, will you? What's the matter? Did you forget something?"

"I want to turn around. I think we should head northwest."

"What? No way. We tried that already and it got us nowhere."

"I want to head northwest," he repeated.

She shook her head. "Absolutely not. This is *my* call, not yours."

"Well, I'm making it mine."

Her brow shot up as she stood hipshot, crossing her arms. "Why?"

Had he really thought she would go along with this without an explanation? "Let's just call it a hunch."

"Screw your *hunch*, Hunter. Why can't you just answer my questions? Why are you always so damn evasive?"

He shrugged. "It's just another one of my many charms."

She grumbled her frustration. "You're absolutely *impossible.*"

"You've mentioned that."

Her nostrils flared. "You're also on my turf. This is the part where you cooperate with *me.* I've kept my word. I've done what you've asked. Now you're supposed to do the same. Robert thinks I'll have more luck tracking the lynx if we head south."

"And Robert's an expert on the lynx?"

She scoffed. "He's a forest ranger. He knows a hell of a lot more about the fauna in this area than you do, that's for sure." She yanked off her pack and pulled off her jacket, stuffing it in the top of her bag.

"That may be, but I still think we should head back."

"Spotting the lynx in this park is very rare," she went on as if he'd never spoken. "Although we have recently documented tracks up north, I agree with Robert's reasoning. Their main food source is more abundant farther south this time of year." As she spoke in her haughty tone, she put her pack back on. "Last time I checked, a career in security didn't require a deep knowledge of wildlife behavior. How about we both play to our strengths: You use your muscles, and I'll use my brain. If I need you to lift something heavy, I'll let you know. I said we're going southwest, so that's what we're doing." She started walking off.

Out of patience, Hunter grit his teeth as he snagged her by the elbow, turning her around to face him.

She shrugged away from his hold. "Let go of me. Why do you always think you can put your hands on me?"

"You didn't seem to mind the other night."

Her eyes widened as she sucked in a sharp breath. "You're the most despicable human being I've ever met. Just two more weeks and I can be rid of you."

"Believe me, sweetheart, I've been thinking the same thing."

Sighing, she closed her eyes and rubbed at her temple. "Look, the sooner I get this job finished, the faster we can go our separate ways." She gave a decisive nod, as if that solved everything, and turned away to walk again.

"I think I have a lead on your friends."

She took three steps and paused, whipping around. "You do?" She reached out, clutching his arm as her eyes filled with hope. "What is it?"

"I'm not going to say at this point."

With another scoff, she dropped her hand to her side. "That's not a good enough answer."

"It's the only one I'm giving you. You'll have to trust me." He grabbed the map he'd studied from his pack. "We need to head northwest and follow the Slough River."

She took the map from his hand, tracing the route he'd planned with her finger. "That's a good day's hike from here—and that's being optimistic. What's so important about the river?"

He only flicked her a glance. He'd given her enough information for now.

"Give me something here, Hunter. I have a right to know about this lead."

"It's a strong lead. That's all you're going to get." He held her gaze for several seconds.

"Well, I guess I don't have much of a choice if I want to find out what happened to my friends."

That was exactly what he'd hoped for. "Guess not."

She stared at him long and hard before she checked her compass and led them off the trail in a northwest direction.

After hours of walking over steep, brutal terrain, they found a clearing next to a fast-flowing stream ten miles from the Slough. The flat patch of dirt fifteen yards from the water was the perfect spot for camp. The skyline was a picture of shocking oranges and pinks, fading into purple as the sun made its descent for the night. Morgan and Hunter sat in silence while the stove heated their evening meal.

He'd set up the tent and appeared completely relaxed as he rested against a rock with another true-crime novel in hand while she sat close by, exhausted and achy, her legs trembling with unaccustomed fatigue. She couldn't remember the last time she'd felt so drained. She was used to this type of work—the tax and challenge it placed on her body. She thrived on it, had always loved it, but not today. As the adrenaline of the hike wore off, she was tempted to crawl into her sleeping bag and rest until morning, but her stomach growled as the enticing gravy scent of beef stew grew stronger. If she wanted to regain her strength, she had to eat.

Crickets began their nightly chorus—such a lonely sound—and the heavy weight of grief suddenly swamped her. In that moment, she noticed the lack of laughter and absence of the five voices as familiar to her as her own. It hit her then that she would never have that back. Nothing would ever be the same. There would never again be card games by firelight or late-night chats under the stars with Shelly, Ian, and Tom. They were truly gone.

Tears welled, threatening to spill, but she blinked them back. Crying wouldn't help her friends, but finding answers would help their families. Sitting up straighter, she fought to shake off the looming depression. Hunter had a lead, and she was going to follow it.

She'd been quiet for some time. Hunter snuck a peek as Morgan stared off into the trees, looking as exhausted as she did sad and lost. The final two miles of the hike had been agony for her. He'd watched her energy vanish with each step she took, but she hadn't complained or asked to stop. She'd pushed herself until he knew she didn't have much left. He admired her for that.

Morgan tore her gaze from the trees and pulled off her boots, wincing and lunging forward as she pressed her toes back. "Ow, ow, ow. Cramp."

He set down his book. "You should drink more water."

"I'll get some in a minute," she said, massaging her foot frantically. "After all this, you better have really good information about my friends."

He said nothing as she stood, noting the misery in her voice she tried to disguise with half-hearted temper.

"I'm going to clean up while the stew finishes heating."

"I think that's a good idea," he snickered as he looked her up and down. Pissing her off always seemed to give her a little spark, and he was more than willing to do his part.

She frowned. "You don't exactly look fresh yourself, you know."

"If you fill the shower bag, save some water for me, will you?"

"We'll see."

He smiled when she turned away with a flash of temper heating her eyes. That was better. He picked up his book again, as she grabbed the portable shower bag, her soap, washcloth, and towel. His gaze wandered from the words on the page when she peeled off her t-shirt, standing in a gray tank. She stopped at the water's edge and wrapped the towel around her waist, pulling down her pants. The towel stopped at the top of her shapely thighs.

He gave up with the book altogether and watched her wade into a small, knee-deep pool separate from the rest of the stream. Droplets splashed up, leaving glistening trails down her legs, and she closed her eyes, tilting her head up to the sky.

After several moments, she dipped the shower bag into the water, struggling to hold it and keep her towel in place. She glanced over her shoulder, and their eyes met.

He couldn't hold back his grin. "Got yourself a little problem there. Don't get that towel wet. You won't have anything to dry off with."

Scowling, she turned back, bending slightly with her efforts. The towel loosened around her waist, and she grabbed the end, catching it just before it hit the water.

His grin turned into a roar of laughter.

"I'm glad you find this so funny." She walked closer to the bank and threw her towel down.

The laughter died in his throat as his eyes widened. Her bikini-cut panties showed off her tanned, glorious legs. When she pivoted to rescue the shower bag on the verge of sinking, he read *Too Hot* printed in big black letters on the ass of her pink underwear. He couldn't agree more. He wanted his hands all over her shapely, sculpted butt.

She turned again with her small biceps bulging from the weight of the bag. Their eyes locked as desire pounded through him in time with his rapid pulse. She stepped from the stream and bent over, tying a piece of sturdy rope around the handle of the makeshift shower, and walked off.

He cleared his throat. "Don't go too far. It'll be dark soon."

Moments later, Morgan swore.

He turned as she stood on tiptoes, her arms raised above her head, trying to get the rope over a sturdy branch. Her calf muscles bunched, and her tank top rode high, showing off her impressive backside.

He walked toward her, picking up the shower supplies she left behind, and came up behind her, grabbing the bag she struggled with. She fell back, and her body brushed against his front. The contact was shocking, like a bolt of lightning.

She stepped to the side, staring at him with the same heat

and surrender he saw in her eyes the night before, when she had wrapped herself around him as he carried her to the bed.

Clenching his jaw, he remembered his vow to keep his hands to himself. "Are you going to take this stuff so I can hang the damn thing up or are you just going to look at me?"

She blinked and stepped over to grab her things. "Sorry."

He knotted the rope and walked away. As he approached the campsite, steam from the bubbling stew caught his attention. He spun on his heel to tell her supper was ready, and the words died in his throat as she turned toward the shower, pulling her tank top over her head. She was the most spectacular thing he'd ever seen. His gaze wandered over her petite, athletic body, remembering the way she'd moaned when he touched her, the way her exotic scent made him want more.

She stood with her back to him, gasping as the first drops of spray hit her. The water cascaded down her hair and skin, turning pink underwear a darker shade and accentuating her taut body beneath.

He took a deep breath and turned away, looking forward to his turn under the spray. He desperately needed a cold shower.

◌ৎ Chapter Eighteen ৩◌

Sexual frustration burned hot through Hunter's blood as his need to touch Morgan, to be inside of her and pound and plunder away all of the *want* went from smoldering to flashpoint. He used his energy to create a fire pit, willing the visions away. The sweaty work of gathering heavy rocks to construct an ornate circle did little to erase the picture of cool water sluicing over her golden skin. In the end, Hunter sat in front of the fire, staring into the flames with his muscles wound tight, hoping the images torturing his mind would vanish. By the time Morgan approached from behind, he'd found a tenuous grip on his unrelenting need. He used the small ladle to scoop a bowl of simmering stew.

"You can't have a fire out here. This isn't a designated area."

He glanced up, clenching his jaw as she stood next to him wearing nothing but her towel and her dripping wet hair.

"They'll have to fine me. I'll put it out in the morning before we go." He spooned up a bite of carrots and beef.

"I forgot to grab clean clothes. It's getting cold." She took pajamas from her pack and stepped behind him. "No peeking."

It was tempting—too tempting. He knew how to be a gentleman when it suited him, and it did now. If he looked back and saw her, he'd take her. Desperate to think of something other than Morgan's hot body, he changed the subject. "The stew's good. You're really an amazing cook. I'll admit I'm surprised."

"Oh, yeah. Why's that?" She put her towel and other clothes over a fallen tree and sat down next to him wearing snug white long johns and a black fleece top. She scooped herself a healthy portion of stew.

He shrugged. "The image doesn't fit. I didn't think someone like your mother would know how to cook. I figured you had a cook."

Frowning, she put the spoon back in her bowl. "What's that supposed to mean, 'someone like my mother?'"

"I wasn't being insulting. She's a great lady."

"Yes, she is. My grandmother taught her, and she taught me. Just because you have financial advantages as an adult doesn't mean you had them as a child. She didn't. She was raised by a single mother who worked her butt off in a factory. It's my dad who comes from money."

"Your grandmother was a senator. I kind of figured that out." Hunter scraped the rest of the stew from his bowl. "Like I said, I wasn't trying to insult you or your mother. I was raised by a single mother myself."

She perked up. "You were?"

"Yup. She's a pediatric nurse back in LA."

"Have you always lived in Los Angeles?"

"Born and raised."

"Do you have brothers and sisters? I heard you talking to your niece the other day."

He thought of Jake and instantly shut down. "Neither. It's just me and my mom." He stood and walked to the tent.

"I feel like I said something I shouldn't have."

He turned, seeing the questions in her eyes. "Don't worry about it. I'm going to shower off real quick. Will you be okay if I leave you here by yourself for a few minutes?"

"Of course. You'll just be over there." She gestured toward

the darkened area by the trees. "I'll wash the dishes after I finish up. I might be down by the stream when you get back."

"All right. Stay close to camp and bring a flashlight." He strode off into the darkness.

———◆———

Morgan walked away from the light and comfort of the campfire, wondering what she'd said to upset Hunter. She played back through their conversation again, trying to figure it out. If he didn't have any siblings, how did he have a niece? She would've asked him about the little girl he clearly adored, but his eyes had changed. They'd grown so cool and distant in the firelight, and his voice had lost its inflection while he spoke. He'd actually shared something about himself, and she couldn't help but be sorry that the moment ended so quickly. She wanted to know the man who slept inches from her every night.

Shaking off the sense of loss, she scooped up water in her collapsible bucket and started toward camp as a wave of unease hit her and she stopped. Her eyes darted back and forth in the pitch black, and her pulse jumped. Someone was watching her. She grabbed the flashlight and shot the beam into the distance but saw nothing. Laughing nervously, she cursed her overactive imagination, but she couldn't shake the feeling.

Spinning slowly, she examined her surroundings as she snatched up the pail with hands that shook, dropping it again and spilling the water. "Damn it." Her voice trembled. She went back to the stream for more, even as her instincts told her not to. Her breathing quickened as she dipped the bucket into the current, suppressing the overwhelming need to run. She took a step back from the water's edge, heard the snap of a branch to the right of the stream, and pivoted with the flashlight, scrutinizing the dark.

She walked quickly as her chest constricted and her

breath sobbed in and out. Someone was definitely watching her, and they were close—very close. She whirled again and screamed.

———◆———

Hunter was freezing his ass off as he washed. The cool night air and frigid water were a bad combination. Goose-bumps covered every inch of him. Clenching his jaw, he fought against the racking shudders threatening to chatter his teeth. He couldn't wait to get back to LA. He wanted the hot summer sun. Turning on the shower nozzle again, he sucked in a sharp breath, cursing the ice-cold water as he rinsed the Campsuds he'd lathered in his hair. He turned off the nozzle, dried himself, and threw on his boxers and jeans. He was about to pull on his shirt when Morgan's bloodcur-dling scream echoed through the air.

With his heart in his throat, Hunter grabbed his gun and flashlight and sprinted forward in bare feet. He wanted to call her name and tell her he was coming, but he had to stay quiet until he knew what he was dealing with. He ran until he saw the beam of her flashlight and came to a dead stop. Of all the scenarios racing through his mind, he hadn't ex-pected this. Morgan gripped a big rock in her hand as a pair of green, glowing eyes stared at her in the light's reflection. He racked the slide on his Glock and held the gun over his head, firing into the air.

Morgan jumped, screaming again as the cougar ran off into the night.

Hunter walked to where she stood and yanked the flash-light from her hand, training the beam into the distance, making sure the animal had left. When he was certain it was gone, he shined the light to see her more clearly. She didn't look scared. Her eyes were glistening bright with excite-ment. He'd almost had a heart attack, and she was grinning from ear to ear. Christ, she was something. "That cougar was about to pounce on you. That doesn't seem to bother you."

"Thank you for not shooting him." She rested her hand on his arm. "I was scared breathless until I heard you coming. I could see that he was going to leap, but he didn't. This is *amazing*. Sightings of the cougar are fairly rare—not as rare as the lynx, but still." She spoke rapidly with her enthusiasm. "This is great. He was *so close*—just inches away. We must be in his territory or too close to his kill. From his size, I'd be willing to bet he's about two years old. Often times, a cougar his age will have just separated from his mother and be on a search for his own territory. Attacks are rare but more likely during that time."

Hunter's pulse steadied as he continued to stare. "Fascinating."

"Oh, I know."

He raised his eyebrow, realizing his sarcasm was completely lost on Morgan in her delight.

"I'll have to record this in my log and get some pictures of his tracks—measurements too," she continued with her hand still resting on his arm. It was damp and clammy, but he had to give her points for her guts. She started forward to pick up the pail she'd dropped and turned back. "Thank you." She sent him one of her knock 'em dead smiles.

He fought to keep his breath as he gave her a brisk nod. She was absolutely stunning.

She turned again. "Well, let's get things cleaned up and go to bed. Tomorrow's bound to be another long day."

"Yeah," was the best he could do as he watched her walk toward the stream for another bucket of water.

After Morgan took her pictures and recorded measurements with his assistance, they settled into their sleeping bags in the bright-orange two-person tent. Morgan's deep, steady breathing told him she slept. She seemed as accustomed to sleeping here in the great outdoors as she was her posh guesthouse in DC. He wondered what she would think if they found the mine tomorrow—how long it would take her to start piecing together her friends' murders. He had no doubt she would. She was too damn smart not to.

❧ Chapter Nineteen ❧

B Y LATE MORNING, HUNTER AND MORGAN MADE IT TO the banks of the Slough River. The sun blazed bright in the cloudless blue sky, baking the tall grass in the valley surrounding them. The mountain breeze, usually plentiful and refreshing, blew stingily, offering little relief from the stifling heat. Hunter swallowed the last of his water as they approached the blessed shade of several tall pines, one of the few groupings of cover along the river. "Let's stop here for a while and take a break. We can refill our bottles and look at the map again."

"When are you going to tell me more about this lead? I just can't figure out what the river has to do with the team's deaths. We're *miles* from where Shelly turned on her GPS and where Robert and Miles found their bodies." Taking off her pack, she sanitized her hands and reached in for the double-sealed package of trail mix. She popped a handful of raisins, peanuts, and chocolate pieces into her mouth as she sat next to Hunter on a small boulder while he scanned the map.

"I've already told you, I'm not saying anything until I confirm the information I've been given." If they were able to verify Shelly's journal entry today, he wouldn't have to say a thing, but that was still a big if. "The last thing I want to do is get your hopes up. There's a possibility this could turn out to be nothing." Without thinking, he snagged Morgan's wrist as she brought another handful of trail mix to her mouth and brought it to his own, dumping it in. His lips brushed the soft skin of her palm, and she stiffened. He instantly realized his mistake as their gazes met and he saw the flicker of desire in her eyes.

She pulled free of his grip, darting her tongue across her lips in a nervous gesture he recognized from the night things got out of hand—the night they'd almost become lovers.

"What was that?" she asked, clearing her throat.

"I haven't sanitized yet, and I'm hungry." He chewed his mouthful of food, trying to play it light, even though she was driving him crazy.

She grabbed the sanitizer from her pack and set the small container in his palm. "You sanitize and eat. I'll take care of getting us some water."

He let out a long, slow breath as Morgan took his empty bottle to the edge of the river, filled it, and did the same with her own. As she checked for cracks in the filters and capped the bottles, he admonished himself for touching her. The violent need snapping through his system proved he would have to keep his hands to himself, even in the most casual of ways.

She walked back to the shade and shelter of the trees, stuffed the bottles into the mesh side pockets of the packs, and wiped her dripping hands on the hips of her pants.

He ate another handful of dried fruit and nuts, staring out into the vast green of the valley beyond. He estimated they were about two miles—three at the most—from where he thought her friends had discovered the mine. He wanted to proceed cautiously, uncertain of the mine's security measures. Had they beefed it up after Shelly's team made the discovery, or was everything status quo, thinking they'd taken care of the problem by killing three people? Either way, it was worth taking precautions before approaching any farther. Hunter looked at Morgan, studying her bright yellow top and black zip-off cargo pants as she bent over and tidied the front compartment of her pack.

"Do you have anything you could put on that might blend in with our surroundings?"

She frowned, glancing down at her clothes. "Yeah, I guess. Why?"

He shrugged. "I just think we should try to blend a bit."

Her frown deepened. "You think we should try to blend a bit?"

"Yeah."

"That's all you're going to say?"

"Pretty much."

She stared at him, crossing her arms, her brow now raised in a stubborn line.

He blinked, staying silent, unwilling to bend. He meant what he said when he told her he didn't want to get her hopes up. The river was miles long. It was more than possible they weren't even in the right spot.

Huffing out a breath, she rolled her eyes. "Fine. I have a brown or a dark green top."

"Go dark green. Change your pants too. Do the khaki you wore the other day."

She dug the clothes from her pack, muttering something about idiots and secrets as she neatly replaced the items she'd disturbed.

He looked at the map again, catching her movements in his peripheral vision as she lifted her shirt over her head, exposing her skimpy powder blue bra and beautiful breasts spilling slightly from their cups. He dropped all pretense of looking at the paper in front of him as his eyes wandered from her sinful underwear to her firm, smooth torso. He fisted his hands, itching to touch her.

She reached for her shirt, pausing when she glanced his way. "Do you mind?" she asked, her voice going husky.

His eyes stayed locked on hers as she nibbled her bottom lip and swiped at a lock of hair that came loose from her ponytail. He stood, wrestling with his need to keep his distance and his want for her. Images of water raining over her amazing, panty-clad body flashed through his mind, and lust won out. His tight tether of control unraveled, and he suddenly didn't give a damn that this wasn't the time or the place. He let the map fall to the ground and closed the distance between them.

Short, shallow breaths escaped her mouth, feathering his lips, driving him half-mad.

He flicked the clasp of her bra, releasing her breasts into his eager palms.

She gasped as he reveled in the feel of her, tracing her sensitive skin.

"You asked me if I minded—"

"I don't. I don't mind," she shuddered out, clutching his cheeks in her hands, pulling his lips to hers, kissing him first this time as she raked her fingers through his hair. Her tongue dove deep, sliding against his, eager and teasing.

Groaning, he backed her against the tree, meeting her demand for demand. He kissed her jaw and explored the soft skin of her neck, skimming her rapid pulse point on his way to her breasts.

Her breathing quickened to whimpering pants as she laced her fingers around the back of his neck, forcing him closer, inviting him to take more.

He nipped and nibbled, savoring her exotic flavor and sexy moans.

She tugged on his shirt, pulling it over his head as their eyes met in a searing-hot moment. She smiled, sending her small, confident hands trailing down his arms as she pressed open-mouthed kisses across his chest.

He closed his eyes, clenching his jaw, his stomach muscles quivering as her clever fingers danced toward the button on his pants. He yearned to feel her hand wrapped around him, but he wanted to touch her more. Pushing them heat to heat, he trapped her hands, preventing her from making the first move.

When her palms lay flat against his lower stomach, he made quick work of her snap and zipper, teasing and tracing just above the silk of her low panty line while their tongues danced and her hips rocked, begging him to make her come alive. He hooked his thumbs in her belt loops and tugged.

"Yes," she whispered, digging her nails into his shoulders as her pants cleared her hips. He made certain her pretty blue panties followed the same path while he traced her collarbone with his tongue.

Purring, she closed her eyes and let her head fall back.

Her throaty sounds were making him crazy. He had to have her right now. He eased back enough to let her deal with his pants, ready to fulfill them both, when the drone of a plane's engine finally registered. Pulling back, he broke their embrace and glanced up as a single engine plane flew overhead.

He noted the time on his watch—a long-ingrained habit—and looked at her. Her cheeks were flushed and her lips swollen from his kisses. The moment passing between them vanished as he watched her eyes follow the small, white aircraft through the sky.

"That was really low," she said, covering her breasts with her arm.

He picked up his shirt and yanked it over his head, grunting instead of responding as he struggled to get his hormones under control.

She swallowed and looked at him, then turned away, quickly fixing her underwear and pulling on the clothes he'd suggested. "I, uh, I didn't realize tourist planes came this far north. I've never been in one that flies so close to the trees. I thought they focused on the southern part of the park where visitors can see the waterfalls and buffalo population."

"Yeah, I don't know." But he did. He knew they were close now. There was no way in hell that was a tourist plane. That was a security flyover. This had to be a hell of a mine to require flyovers and the murder of three federal employees. Luck had been on their side when they'd stopped under the tall pines instead of the wide, open space of the valley surrounding them. There would be very little cover for the next two or three miles until they hit the heavy forest again.

Morgan changed her socks, damp with sweat to prevent blisters, while Hunter picked up the map and scanned it again, focusing on the area he wanted to check out. Satisfied with his route, he folded the paper and placed it in his pack as the sound of the airplane came back, flying so low instinct had them both ducking. "Shit. That was too close." He stood from his crouched position and looked at his watch. "Eight minutes," he muttered.

"Why are they flying like that?"

"I'm not sure."

"But you have an idea. I can tell by your voice."

"They're lower than I like. I don't know if they saw us. Hurry and get your boots on. I want to make it to the next tree line before they come back." He jammed her clothes in her pack while she tied her laces. Then he hefted her pack for her as she got to her feet. "Can you run with this?"

"I want you to tell me—" she stopped, shaking her head. "Never mind. Of course I can run with my pack." She took it from him and settled it on her shoulders.

"Good. If I'm right, this plane should circle by every eight minutes. I've only timed them once, so hopefully that's it. The next tree line is about two hundred fifty, maybe three hundred yards away. Can you make it?"

"Yes, I can make it. Let's go."

They ran hard to the next section of cover. The heat and the weight of their packs left them winded.

Hunter glanced at his watch again. "We should have about two and a half minutes before they come back. I want to get as far away from the first clearing as possible and up into the dense woods."

"Tell me what's going on."

Ignoring her, he brushed his forearm across his sweaty forehead. He didn't plan to say anything until he was certain they were safe. He wanted Morgan focused on running and doing what she was told. "The next break is much shorter—about one hundred yards. The one after that is going to be a bitch, though. It's about three-quarters of a mile. I think after we get to the next, we should wait a while and make sure we're fresh. We can't afford—" A huge blast cut him off, vibrating in his feet.

For a flash, he was back in Afghanistan and Jake's voice echoed in his mind. *"I'm hit, Hunt. I'm hit!"* Jake's blood dripped from his hands as he looked down at his dying friend. Then he sat in the dust and dirt with excruciating heat radiating through his shoulder where a bullet pierced his flesh. Then, somehow, he was in the chopper, staring at the white sheets flapping in the wind, covering six dead soldiers—his men.

Wide-eyed, Morgan grabbed his hand. "What was that? What the hell was that?"

Unable to answer, he turned away, trying to fight off a full-blown panic attack. Closing his eyes, he took long, slow breaths. He wasn't in Afghanistan, he reminded himself. He was in Montana.

"Are you okay?"

He said nothing as sweat dribbled down his forehead, and he concentrated on taking air in through his nose and blowing it out through his mouth.

Morgan reached for his white-knuckled fist at his side, holding it, caressing his skin. "Hunter, what's wrong? Are you all right?"

He was tempted to pull her into a hug and hold on to the comfort she was offering as the gory images shook him to his core. The fear and pain was as fresh and raw as it had been the day he was ambushed. He opened his eyes, looking into the compassion and concern in hers, and yanked free of her gentle hold. "I'm fine. Just leave me alone for two fucking seconds."

Her eyes widened with surprise and she stepped back. "Fine." She walked over to her pack and sat down, staring out into the endless, open land as the plane flew overhead, and she flinched.

Still shaken but in control, he studied her, sighing. He'd been harsh, but he couldn't make himself apologize.

She glanced up, making eye contact, and looked away.

He slid his hand through his damp hair, absorbing the stab of guilt as she made him feel like a piece of shit with one wounded look. Her sad eyes were all the more potent, because she tried to disguise her hurt feelings with a subtle shrug of disinterest.

She sipped her water and continued staring out into the vastness surrounding them. "We should probably go after the next flyover," she said dully. "I can run all of it."

He shook his head. "No. We're going back. We've seen and heard enough to confirm that something sketchy's going on up here. We'll head for the ranger station tomorrow, go to the airport, and call your father." When the plane flew over the last time, Hunter spotted a man sitting in the passenger seat with an M-4. This wasn't worth it anymore. This was the big time, and they were getting the hell out while they still could.

Morgan put on her pack and stood. "Like hell we will. Something sketchy *is* going on, and I want to know what. It's clear my friends died for whatever it is. I don't know the hows and whys behind it, but I will. I'm not leaving until I do."

It was on the tip of his tongue to tell her, but she would be safer if she knew as little as possible until they were back in DC. They'd gotten close enough for him to give her father and The Bureau an accurate-enough location to find and bust up the mining operation.

They stood in tense silence, eyeing each other as the plane flew overhead again. As the sound of the engine faded in the distance, Morgan turned, taking off in a sprint.

"Goddammit, Morgan!" Hunter grabbed his pack and ran after her, but she was fast. Her powerful, petite body could move. She made it to the next grouping of pines in just over a minute with Hunter close at her heel.

He slowed a bit under the trees, gearing up to give her a verbal ass kicking as anger boiled through him. What the hell was she thinking? What right did she have to put them both in danger? Sure, they'd made it easily enough, but they were moving in the wrong direction. He wanted her out of here. Morgan didn't belong out here, just miles from danger. He wanted her back in DC, living her pretty, safe, privileged life.

Before he could react, she ducked and dodged the trees and kept going, breaking cover and running into the wide-open valley. Fear slid greasily in his belly as he broke into a dead sprint, trying to catch her and bring her back before it was too late. They would never make it to the next shelter before the plane circled by again. "Morgan!" He gained on her quickly, making a grab for her.

She looked back and dodged.

He swore. They were too far from the last shelter. There was no choice but to keep going.

With an eighth of a mile left to go, Morgan's pace began to slow. The plane's engine droned in the distance, coming closer with every step. Hunter calculated they had less than a minute before they were dead meat. He grabbed her arm, pulling and helping her along. They met the shelter of the mighty pines with barely a moment to spare as the plane passed over the initial tree line they'd run from, over the second, third, and finally the one they were under now. The breeze from the plane rustled the treetops overhead.

He paced back and forth with his hands laced behind his head, sucking in huge gulps of air. "As soon...as I catch...my breath...I'm going...to kick...your ass."

She flicked him a glance as she threw her pack to the dirt

and rested her hands on her thighs while her breath heaved in and out. Moments later, she took her water from the mesh pocket of her bag and gulped.

He walked over, ripping the bottle from her hand, and threw it. The bright blue plastic cracked against a tree, spewing liquid everywhere.

"Oh, well that was brilliant. Now we're down a water bottle. You're lucky that wasn't one of our filters."

"You'll want to shut up right about now," he said through clenched teeth, looming over her.

"Stop talking to me like that! What gives you the right? Who do you think you are?" She put all her weight into giving him a good shove, but he didn't move.

"Knock it off." He grabbed her arms, ignoring her struggle to free herself. "What the hell were you thinking? Do you know how close you came to getting us killed? Did you not notice the fucking machine gun the guy had trained out his window?"

She stopped moving. "I—I didn't see the gun. Honestly, I never thought—"

"Well, start thinking, damn it." He gave her a small shake. "Wake the hell up and use that brain you're so fond of. You almost got us killed." He let her go.

"I went for it because you would've stopped me." She pivoted away. "We're close. I can feel it. I don't know what we're close to, but I'm about to. Can't you understand that I have to know what happened to my team?" She whipped back around. "I owe them. I owe their families. I can't get those pictures out of my mind. When I close my eyes, it's all I see. I want to know what was worth their lives." She sat on the ground and leaned against a fallen pine, then wrapped her hands around her knees and pressed her face against them. Another explosion shook the ground, making her jump, and she hugged herself tighter.

The blast was louder, but Hunter was prepared this time. He stared down at Morgan, muttering a curse. She looked so small and defeated. Another wave of guilt wormed its way through his conscience. He'd yelled at her for putting them in danger, but he hadn't shared the details of why he'd brought her here. That wasn't exactly fair. Taking a deep breath, he sat next to her, his leg brushing hers as he got comfortable and rested against the rough bark of the tree. "I know you're looking for answers." His voice gentled as he spoke. "But it's time to go back. This isn't safe. We're in way over our heads here."

Her head whipped up as she looked at him. "I can't. I won't," she said with a hint of desperation. "I thought you were supposed to be some big bad Marine. I thought you were supposed to be a trained killing machine. It sounds to me like you're just a washed-up bully. You don't mind manhandling and bossing me around, but when things get tough, you're ready to give up and go home. My dad told me you were in Afghanistan for a year, that you knew how to rough it. I think that's bull. You were probably—"

He clamped a hand over her mouth when he heard footsteps. She struggled until he knew she heard them too. "Get down on your stomach and tuck yourself against the tree. Don't move," he whispered as he lay next to her and took the pistol from its holster, aiming toward the sound. He spotted the water bottle he'd thrown as the footsteps moved closer. There wasn't time to crawl forward and get it.

A man in army fatigues walked toward them carrying a machine gun. He scanned the area, turned to leave, and stopped.

Hunter moved his finger, resting it on the trigger, as his heart pounded, but his hand stayed steady, ready to land his kill shot if the man glanced their way.

The guard reached into his shirt pocket and pulled out a cigarette. He put the cigarette between his lips and grabbed a lighter from his pants pocket. Smoke tinged the air as he blew out his first exhale and continued on his way.

For several seconds, Hunter and Morgan lay silent as the

plane flew overhead and another explosive detonated in the distance. Hunter studied the thick cover of trees beyond, the open valley to the left, right, and behind them. They were trapped. There was no way Morgan would be able to make the run back to the trees they left behind before nightfall, and they couldn't risk being discovered. Their only option was finding a way into the deep forest patrolled by the guard. Holstering his gun, he sat up.

"What are we going to do?" Morgan whispered.

"I don't know yet. I'm going to have to go check things out. I don't know the layout of the security perimeter. I need to know how many guards I'm dealing with. I have to find us a way around them so we can get the hell out of here. You have to stay here."

"No. I want to come with you." She gripped his arm as her eyes pleaded with him. "I'll be quiet."

He shook his head, trying to ignore the fear in her eyes. "You have to stay put and stay down. It's too risky to bring you. It's broad daylight. I don't know what kind of cover I'll have."

"What if they find you and shoot you? What should I do? How will I be able to find you and help?"

His eyebrow shot up. "They aren't going to shoot me. I've been in a hell of a lot messier situations than this." He grabbed the cracked water bottle, handing it to her. "Stay right here. I'll be back as soon as I can. Remember what happened to your friends." He hated that he made her flinch and remember the grisly images that had given her nightmares, but he needed to be sure she would do what he said. If he had to fire his gun, they were both dead.

After covering their packs with a pair of pants, pine needles and sticks, he left silently.

———◆———

Panic washed through Morgan in a violent flood as she

watched Hunter disappear among the trees. Her stomach clenched while she fought the urge to get up and run after him. Only the fear of not being able to find him kept her still.

A quick flash of gleaming white brushed the treetops when the plane flew overhead again. Her mind raced as she tried to stay calm, but her imagination ran double-time, thinking of the terrible things that could happen to Hunter. In need of a distraction, inspiration struck as the sound of the engine faded. The plane would fly over again in eight minutes. Eight minutes was four hundred eighty seconds. She would count the seconds until Hunter came back. Thrilled with the idea of having something to do, no matter how trivial, she began.

"Nine hundred thirteen," she whispered, smiling when footsteps finally rustled the pine needles and broke twigs close by. She turned her head, and her relief quickly turned to dread. The man wearing army fatigues walked toward her, scanning the area. "Shit, shit, shit." Her eyes widened as she pressed her lips firmly together. Was she saying that out loud? Did he hear her? She glanced around for a stick or a rock but didn't dare move toward any possible weapon she saw.

He walked closer, and she swallowed, staring at the threads attaching the soles of his boots to black leather, listening to the fabric of his pants rubbing together with his hurried movements. If he kept up his pace, he would step on her—if he didn't shoot her first.

Closing her eyes, she held her breath, waiting for the bullet that was surely only seconds away, and opened them again when the commotion began.

The crack of a large branch breaking in the distance stopped the man in his tracks—just feet from where she lay. Seconds later, irritated birds squawked, flying off in a massive flock, the racket insane.

The guard put his finger on the machine gun's trigger and

rushed toward the noisy disorder.

The drumbeat of Morgan's heart throbbed in her skull as she trembled. *Come on. Pull yourself together. You're made of tougher stuff than this.* She closed her eyes again and took a deep breath, trying to believe what she told herself, trying to stay calm. Becoming hysterical wasn't going to help the situation. She opened her eyes and turned her head, gasping.

Hunter sat next to her.

"Oh. Oh, my God, Hunter." She rushed up and crawled onto his lap, gripping him hard in a hug. "He almost found me. He almost found me," she shuddered.

He tugged on her hips so she sat more truly against him and wrapped his arms around her as she twined her legs around his waist.

She tightened her arms, burrowing closer, trying to control her shaking.

"It's okay," he soothed as he nestled her head on his chest and pulled the tie from her hair, running his hand through it. "I'm right here. I'm not going to let anything happen to you."

His heart beat strong and steady, calming her as did his arms holding her. She took another deep breath and loosened her grip, staring into his eyes. "Did you find us a way out?"

He continued running his fingers through her hair, occasionally picking out stray pine needles. "Yeah. It shouldn't be too bad. We'll get a little closer than I'd like, but we should be able to make camp where we did last night."

She nodded.

"Let's have something to eat, wait for the guard to come back by again, and leave after he does."

"I'm not very hungry."

"You have to eat to keep up your strength. We'll have to haul ass through the little compound they have going on here. I want you resting until we leave."

Feeling steadier, Morgan scooted off of Hunter's lap and grabbed his pack, taking out the makings for an energizing lunch. She heaped crackers with Goober peanut butter and jelly, handing several off to Hunter and eating plenty herself.

Hunter poured pouches of Gatorade into their water. "Of all the days for it to be hotter than a bitch in heat, it had to be this one."

"Weren't you telling me just a couple of days ago about how you couldn't wait to get back to your California weather?"

"I also mentioned sandals. I forgot the shorts, though— and the cold beer. Mmm, ice-cold beer. See, now I'm getting homesick."

She smiled. "Get us out of this mess, and I'll buy you a round myself. How *are* we going to get out of here? What's the plan?"

"For you to eat more food and relax." Hunter downed Gatorade.

"I'm good. That scared me, but I'm fine now." A thought struck her. "You said this was a compound. They must traffic drugs through here. It makes sense. The team must've found it." She paused, staring unfocused into the distance. "My friends died for drugs. I thought knowing what happened would help somehow, but it doesn't. It makes everything worse."

Hunter opened his mouth and shut it just as quickly, shaking his head.

"What? What were you going to say?"

"Nothing." He glanced at his watch. "I think we have about fifteen minutes before the guard comes back. I've been able to time him twice, so it's a rough guess, but it's all we've got. We can't afford to sit here again. That was a close call."

"You're telling me. You made that racket so he wouldn't find me, didn't you?"

He shrugged. "I created a little diversion, that's all."

"But he could've seen you."

"I was careful, and he was all but on top of you." He shrugged again. "Let's get back to Operation Get the Hell Out of Here. We'll move out right after the guard takes off. It should take us about half an hour to get to the front of the compound. We'll have to book it from there. I don't know where the plane flies and what they can see. We're going back a different way. I can't be sure of our cover." He looked down at the map, tracing a line with his finger while he spoke, sitting against the tree, calm and steady despite the danger they were in.

It gave Morgan a start to realize he'd saved her life by risking his—again. She hadn't really appreciated the meaning or sacrifices that came along with his profession until now. She thought of how quickly he'd reacted when the guard passed them initially, pulling and readying his gun before she'd had a chance to blink. His eyes had turned cold and deadly while his finger flirted with the trigger. He'd been prepared to shoot and kill because she put them in danger. She cringed, thinking of the despicable things she'd said to him not even an hour ago. The man sitting next to her certainly wasn't a coward. He was good and honorable, and she'd been way out of line. "I want to apologize for the things I said to you earlier."

"Don't worry about it." He brushed her off as he continued his study of the map and chewed a bite of his protein bar.

"No. I was wrong and unkind." She put her hand on his arm.

He glanced up.

"I didn't mean a word I said. I'm very sorry."

He stared at her for several seconds, and she fought the urge to nibble her lip.

"It's okay. We're both under a lot of pressure right now."

She shook her head. "That's no excuse. There's no excuse for the way I behaved. I—"

"Morgan, I accept your apology." He gave her hand a gentle squeeze and focused on his map. "Eat up. We're running out of time."

ෆ CHAPTER TWENTY ෨

HUNTER PILED PINE NEEDLES IN THE CENTER OF HIS map and walked back to where Morgan sat, stuffing the leftover contents of their hasty lunch into his pack.

She glanced up, frowning when he stopped in front of her. "What are you doing with that?"

"Covering our tracks. I don't want to take any chances." He twisted his wrist and peeked at his watch. Time was running out. "We need to hurry."

She stood, shouldering her pack and grabbing his.

"Why don't you wait over by those trees while I finish this up?" He dropped clumps of dried needles, scattering them with his hand, careful not to leave any footprints behind. When he dumped the remainder on the ground and folded the map, he stepped back, examining the area with a critical eye. Satisfied the spot appeared untouched, he brushed his hands off, grimacing when sap clung in patches. His index and middle fingers stuck together as if they had been glued. "Well, shit." He spread his palm wide, pulling them apart.

Morgan snorted out a laugh and glanced down when his narrowed gaze met hers.

"Can I get some sanitizer?"

Biting the inside of her cheek, she dug into the mesh pocket of the pack and handed him the small bottle. "Sticky, huh?" She cleared her throat in an attempt to disguise another laugh. "I hate when that happens."

"I can really feel the empathy." He grinned as humor danced in her eyes.

She aimed her killer smile his way as he squirted a large glob of liquid into his hands and rubbed them together. The alcohol in the sanitizer took care of most of the sticky mess. He handed the bottle back.

"Better?" she asked.

"It'll do. Come on. We need to find a hiding spot." He grabbed his pack and placed it on his back, watching the traces of fun vanish from Morgan's face. He was sorry for it.

They walked farther into the thick of trees, waiting. Minutes later, the armed guard stopped by the fallen log they had rested against. Thank God they'd chosen to move on. Things would have turned sour fast if they hadn't.

The man scanned the area and went back the way he'd come, his footsteps eventually fading.

Hunter nudged Morgan's side, nodding, and they rose from their crouched positions, stepping from their hiding place, following behind at a safe distance. A thin dirt path cut through the forest of massive pines—just wide enough for them to walk side by side if Hunter angled his body close to Morgan's. "Be careful where you step," he whispered, rubbing at his cheek when wisps of her hair tickled his skin. "Try not to break branches with your pack or step on any large twigs. Let's not give him any reason to circle back and check things out. We have a pretty good distance between us, but I don't want to take chances."

She nodded.

"The guardhouse won't be far once we get closer to the river," he continued. "We'll have to be extra careful through that area. I want to get as close to the house as we can. We'll wait at a spot I saw on my pass through. After this bastard heads back out, we'll keep moving. If things go wrong, I want to deal with one machine gun at a time."

Her eyebrows winged up. "There's a comforting thought."

"Just do what I tell you and we won't have a problem."

One mile turned into two, and the dense forest thinned. A cool breeze blew off the wide river's edge as the hum of several engines echoed through the air.

"What in the world is that?" Morgan asked, her eyes briefly meeting his before wandering back to the water. "It sounds like a construction zone."

Instead of answering, he pushed her farther into the tree line as cover became sparse. Filthy, dark brown water rushed past the large gaps among the trees.

Morgan's frown returned. "Ugh, look at all of that sediment. I should really try to get a sample."

The steady warning beeps of a heavy-duty truck joined the chorus of noisy water rushing by, and Morgan moved closer to the river.

Hunter pulled her back as excavators and backhoes dug deep into the earth, piling their loads into a dump truck. Another dump truck backed up, off-loading its pile into an enormous machine vibrating the dirt down a long slide, rinsing what was left with water at the bottom. Farther in the distance, a man worked by the water's edge, blasting sand from the riverbed with a large, high-powered hose.

"What's going *on* here? Look at what those bastards are doing. They're completely destroying the land. This is protected property. Why would they..." She stopped, turning to look at him.

He'd watched the range of emotions flicker over her face—the furrowed brows of puzzlement, the clenched jaw of fury, the wide eyes of disbelief. He knew the moment she figured it out.

"Not drugs, Hunter. Gold. They're mining gold."

"Yeah. That's what it looks like to me." He gave her arm a tug. "We have to keep moving. If anyone sees us, we're going to have a big problem."

"I can't believe this. This is insane. I—"

"You need to be quiet. We're getting closer to the building." He pulled her along as she continued staring in the direction of the destruction along the river.

"They cut down so many trees. And look—they've been blasting into the rocks. That must be the awful noise we heard earlier. How has this not been discovered?"

"We'll talk about it later. You need to be quiet now."

"Shelly, Ian, and Tom must've seen this," she continued, despite his warnings. "The guards must've found them and shot them. That has to be it. It makes sense."

"Hey. Look at me." He stopped, gripping her by the shoulders.

She met his gaze, but her eyes kept wandering to the river.

"Really look at me, Morgan, and listen." He gave her a small shake, aware that he didn't have her full attention.

She took a deep breath. "I'm sorry. I'm listening."

"I'm sorry about your friends. I truly am, but if you want to get out of this alive, you have to do what I say."

She nodded.

"We have to keep walking if we're going to pull this off. We can't let the guard get too far ahead of us. We're close now. When we make it to our cover, we'll wait for this guard to head back out on his rounds. When we know he's well on his way, I'm going to leave you and deal with the other one. Are you following me?"

"Yes."

"Good. You'll give me six minutes to get to where I need to be." He gave her arms an urgent squeeze. "Six minutes, Morgan. Not five-and-a-half, not six minutes and fifteen seconds—exactly six minutes. When we hit the six-minute mark, you'll carefully and steadily head southeast from the left corner of the building. Got that?"

"Got it."

He nodded, certain that she did. "Let's synchronize our watches." He adjusted his to match hers. "Okay. The vegetation is sparse for the first fifty yards. You'll have to be quick.

After that, you'll hit a thick tree line. When you get to what you estimate to be one hundred yards from the building, run. Fucking sprint. I want you to be careful, though. I don't want you to fall and hurt yourself. Just run until you can't anymore. You also need to be sure you stay where the trees are thick. We can't afford to have the plane spot you if it flies in that direction."

"What about you? How will I find you?"

"Just follow your compass in a straight, southeasterly direction, and I'll find you."

"What if you don't?" Her voice tightened with hints of panic. "What if they kill you?"

"They didn't get me last time, did they?" They walked on until he pulled her behind an area abundant with bushy pine trees, and they crouched down, hiding when they came to the edge of the newly constructed building. The structure was the size of a small pool house with large windows on each side and a stovepipe poking through the roof. It was the same dark brown as the ranger station, blending well with the surroundings.

"All right," he whispered, "we'll wait here." He scanned the small clearing, looking for potential problems with his plan. Two guards, the one he and Morgan had followed and the one on lookout at the building, stood close to the door, laughing, dragging deep on their cigarettes. Hunter glanced down at his watch and a movement in the distance caught his eye. "Shit."

"What?" She grabbed his wrist. "What is it?"

"There's a third guard. He wasn't here before."

"What are we going to do?"

He studied her wide, weary eyes and mouth pressed firm in a tense line. Morgan was unraveling. This wasn't the time for her to break. As soon as they were safe she could fall apart. He was losing control of the situation, and that wasn't an option. "We're going to do just what we talked about," he reminded her, his voice cooling several degrees. "You go on six minutes and run southeast. Your spoiled, rich-bitch princess roots are shining through, Morgan. Pull yourself together. If you can't do it for yourself, do it for Daddy. I'm sure it'll be worth a new diamond necklace when he hears about your troubles."

She recoiled as if he'd slapped her and glared. "Wow. Don't hold back, Hunter. Tell me how you really feel."

Satisfied that he'd seriously pissed her off, he knew she would do what she needed to. "Just do your part so you don't get us killed." He glanced at his watch as the guard crushed his cigarette on the forest floor and walked away from the guardhouse.

"I wouldn't worry about them," she whispered, gesturing to the men with a haughty toss of her chin. "I just might kill you myself, you bastard."

He bit the inside of his cheek, stifling a grin. Morgan was definitely back.

They both stood perfectly still as the guard passed within feet of them. Hunter watched him follow the narrow path until he faded among the trees. He looked at Morgan one last time. "Six minutes and then southeast from the building." He waited for his second hand to land on the twelve and took off without another word.

———◆———

Morgan noted the exact second Hunter left her side. She looked up from her watch just as he vanished among the trees. With her eyes and ears trained, she waited for a movement—any movement—but she didn't see or hear him again. It was as if he'd melted into the forest. How did he *do* that? Sheer terror and paranoia had her eyes darting back to the minute hand on her watch. What if she messed up the timing? She shook her head. She wouldn't. She couldn't.

Two and a half minutes ticked by. It felt like two and a half years. Her legs tingled and ached as they began to fall asleep in her crouched position. The pack added extra weight to her frame, compounding the discomfort.

The guard lit another cigarette close to where she waited, puffing several times. A cloud of smoke wafted in her direction, and she struggled not to choke, breathing a sigh of relief and fresh air when he walked toward the other man standing in the building's doorway.

Mopping sweat from her forehead, she chewed her bottom lip, checking and rechecking her watch as her six minutes came closer to an end and the guards still stood feet away. On the four-minute mark, a distant pop rang through the trees, and her heart stopped. Oh God. Hunter. Had another guard found him? Had he been shot? She shook her head, stifling the sob rising in her throat. No, it couldn't be. He said he would find her, so he would.

The two men standing by the house glanced at each other and swore as one of them picked up a two-way radio. "Single gunshot heard north of the guardhouse. Possible security breach. Carlson and I'll check it out."

The man named Carlson dropped his cigarette, and he and the other guard took off running in a northerly direction toward the sound.

Morgan had a minute before she was supposed to start running herself. She scanned the tree-lined area as the men disappeared. Her gaze trailed back to the orange-tipped cigarette smoldering on a small patch of dirt surrounded by dried pine needles. One good gust of wind and she'd be dealing with bigger problems than two men with machine guns.

She glanced back at her watch as the second hand ticked down her final fifteen seconds, ten seconds, five. Gripping her compass, she looked at her watch, realizing she was four seconds behind. Swearing, she checked the area to be sure she was still alone. With the coast clear and her heart pounding, she broke cover, tamping out the cigarette, then quickly walked to the back of the guard house, pausing when she approached the left corner of the building. She pointed her compass, found north, and ran southeast from that direction.

She reached the thick tree line, looking behind her, ever fearful of discovery, and took off at a sprint. Dodging branches and hurdling fallen limbs, she continually checked her compass as she ran among the trees until her legs, weak from exhaustion, threatened to give out.

Something rustled in the distance, and her head shot up as terror poured through her veins. A bird flew from a tangle of branches and soared toward the sky. The quick flash of dread caused a much-needed adrenaline rush, and she used it to keep going.

When would Hunter catch up? She wanted to stop and wait for him, but the fear of someone else finding her first kept her moving. She stumbled but caught herself, preventing a fall as the energy burst that reenergized her vanished as quickly as it had kicked in. She tripped again and fell hard to the ground. Gasping for breath, she struggled to lift herself to her hands and knees. Nausea churned in her stomach, and she vomited from the exertion and heat.

When her breathing steadied, she grabbed a tree trunk and hoisted her weak and trembling body from the ground, took off her pack, and dug in. Water and food were a must. She wouldn't be able to go much farther without refueling. The thought of eating made her shudder, but she uncapped her drink, determined to battle back against the weakness and nausea. She was playing the game of survival, and she was going to win.

She sipped at the Gatorade Hunter had prepared earlier. The sweetness of the drink made her heave. Taking another sip, she held the liquid in her cheeks until she knew she could swallow and keep it down. After several successful sips, she peeled a badly bruised banana and nibbled on the few good spots. Bringing the fruit to her mouth for another bite, she noticed the smear of blood on her right hand. A small gash ran along the heel of her palm, soiled with dirt from the forest floor. She knew it needed to be cleaned. A small cut could turn into an infected nightmare in backcountry.

She pulled out the bottle of hand sanitizer and squirted it on her injury. "Damn, that stings." She blew on the cut, shaking her hand. "Damn, damn, damn." Blowing once more, she covered the wound with a Band-Aid.

As her stomach steadied, Morgan finished what she could of the banana and took bigger sips of Gatorade. Next she grabbed dried fruit and nuts from her bag and ate while she walked. As her energy started to return, she walked faster until she was moving at a steady jog.

Ⓒʒ CHAPTER TWENTY-ONE ⒷⲞ

HUNTER PLAYED A RISKY GAME BY FIRING HIS GUN. The northern area of the compound, where the river zipped in and out of the trees, was a mystery. On high alert, he tuned his senses to his surroundings, always looking and listening for an unexpected guard. The coast was clear for now, but he knew that would change soon enough. Holstering his weapon, he climbed a tall pine, thankful he'd ditched his pack a mile back. The branches toward the bottom were few and far between, but he made it well above eye level with little trouble.

He nestled himself into a grouping of rough, thick limbs and glanced at his watch. Exactly six minutes had passed since he'd left Morgan. He needed to believe she'd stuck with the plan. If she hadn't... He couldn't think of that.

It wasn't long before the men from the guardhouse moved in his direction. He clung to the branches holding him, praying they wouldn't break as the guards walked past him—never glancing up while one of them spoke into the two-way radio. "We don't see anything. We'll continue looking around before we head back. It was probably just a poacher or some shit like that farther north of here."

A man on the other end of the radio ten-foured them.

The team of two disappeared among the trees, and Hunter checked his watch again, anxious to be on his way, waiting for the guards to circle back from their search. Finally they returned, stopping and standing directly beneath him. "The area's clear. We're on our way."

When the twigs and branches littering the forest floor no longer snapped, Hunter quickly and carefully made his way down the giant tree, following behind the guards, giving them plenty of space. Eventually he found his pack and pulled out his anti-reflective binoculars as he moved closer to the guardhouse. Stopping, he zeroed in on the bushy patch of pines where he'd left Morgan, breathing a sigh of relief that she wasn't there. "She did it," he muttered.

He put his binoculars back and swallowed several gulps of Gatorade as he made his way in a southeasterly direction. It only took him minutes to pick up Morgan's trail. He spent time erasing a good half-mile of her tracks before he slid his feet along the ground, making exaggerated footprints through pine needles and dirt, creating a false path leading in the opposite direction.

Satisfied with his work, he backtracked and picked up her trail again, running a steady pace until he came to the spot where she'd clearly fallen. Hand and knee prints disturbed the scattering of pine needles among the dirt and tree roots. Nearby a lone banana peel lay in the dirt. He picked it up and threw it far into the distance. There was no need to leave further clues.

He ran three more miles before he finally spotted her. She jogged along slowly, lethargically through the uneven terrain. He stepped on a branch and her head whipped up as she stopped.

Her fists bunched and relaxed, bunched and relaxed as she looked around from left to right.

He walked out of the trees, watching her blink back tears suddenly filling her eyes.

She started toward him with her arms extended, as if she was going to hug him, but she stopped, smiling instead. "You found me."

"I told you I would."

She nodded, blinking again as she glanced away, taking several unsteady breaths. "You were gone for such a long time. I thought they shot you. I thought you weren't coming back. I almost turned around half a dozen times."

He brushed back a strand of hair that had escaped her ponytail and tucked it behind her ear. "I'm glad you didn't." Trying to keep the mood light, he gave her a gentle elbow bump to her side. "You did a good job. You're in one piece." Although she looked like she was ready to drop. Her green shirt clung to her, soaked with sweat, and her flushed face dripped from forehead to chin with fat drops of perspiration.

She cleared her throat. "Yeah, I'm fine. I'm ready for a dip in a ten-foot pool, but I guess a shower with stream water will have to do." She took a long drink of her Gatorade and turned to walk again.

He fell into step beside her. "Why don't we sit down for a few minutes?"

She shook her head. "No. I want a shower."

"We're a good two miles away from the stream. I want to rest." He could've kept going for miles, but he was worried about her. Her cheeks were so red, and her hair soaking wet.

"Then go for it. I'm going to keep on. I know where we are now. Catch up when you're ready." She looked at him. "I'm—I'm glad you made it back safely." She cleared her throat again and walked away.

They hiked the last two miles in silence.

——◆——

Morgan saw the knee-deep pool she'd waded in last night and the ash pile they'd tamped out as they left earlier in the morning. It seemed like days since they'd been here, not hours. She dropped her pack with a thud by the edge of the quick moving stream, took off her boots, and walked into the chilly water with her socks and khaki pants on. Tipping her head skyward, she moaned as the cool liquid moved against her legs.

Hunter wandered over with the shower bag he'd dug from her pack. "Feels pretty good, huh?"

"It's heaven." She watched him fill the bag and tie it to the tree where they'd showered before.

He stripped off his filthy shirt, took off his grubby pants, and turned on the nozzle full blast. The steady stream of water rained over him, and his boxers clung like a second skin.

Desire tugged low in her belly as she stared at him, remembering the weight of his magnificent body pressing hers into the mattress at the ranger station, and the way he'd touched her as they leaned against the tree in the valley not that long ago. She studied every muscled inch of him when he closed his eyes and let all five gallons of water drain onto his back without picking up the bottle of Campsuds.

Shaking her head, she snapped out of her sex-hazed trance and put her effort into maintaining her balance while she stripped down to her panties and green t-shirt in the stream. Despite where her thoughts drifted, she felt her body temperature returning to normal even as her pulse still pounded. She had no plans to leave the blissful coolness of the water anytime soon. Her pants landed on the bank with a wet plop as Hunter walked back to the river.

He waded in, filling the bag for the second time. "I'll give you fair warning: I'm taking it all off for a good rinse." He gestured to his underwear. "If you don't want your sensibilities shocked, I wouldn't look over by the tree for the next few minutes."

She raised an eyebrow, giving him no hint as to where her mind had wandered just moments before. "I'll try to control myself."

He smiled, sending a tidal-wave-sized splash her way.

She gasped as chilly water soaked her shirt, then laughed and splashed him back.

He cast another wave in her direction.

Unwilling to be outdone, she gave as good as she got. Before long, they both dripped from head to toe, breath heaving, and called a truce.

While Hunter tied the shower bag to the branch again, Morgan got out of the water and dug through her pack, finding the ultra-long-range radio she brought with them. She tuned into the frequency she knew the northeast ranger station used and tried to radio in. "Robert, Miles, are you there? Can you read me?"

There was only static.

"Northeast station, do you read? This is Morgan Taylor checking in."

When no one responded, she shrugged, turning it off. She put it back in her bag and returned to the deliciously cool water, unaware that the radio had been fitted with a beacon that activated when the radio powered on.

———◆———

"I can't begin to tell you how good it feels to be clean," Hunter said. "It's your turn if you want one."

She glanced over and lost her breath as he stood grinning, wrapped from waist to calf in a navy blue towel. Droplets glistened on his powerful body, trailing down his muscular build. He was perfectly beautiful, and she desperately in love. Stunned, shaken, she stared down into the pool of clear water. Hadn't she just looked at him? She hadn't felt anything then but a heavy dose of lust and longing, yet something had changed in a flash of a moment, and she knew she would never be the same. She sat back against a large, slippery rock, shaking her head, trying to deny the overwhelming feelings rushing through her. "Yeah, I'll take a turn. Just give me a minute," she answered dully.

"Are you okay?"

She looked up at Hunter standing before her, studying her. She stepped from the water, needing space and time to think. "Yes, of course. I'm just ready for a shower and a real meal."

He put his finger under her chin, inching her face up until their gazes met. "You need to rest."

She pushed his hand away. "I'm fine. In fact, I think we should keep going after I shower and we eat."

"Not happening. You're done for today."

She stared into his concerned eyes, confused. When he was kind and looked at her like he gave a damn, she wished for something that could never be. Her voice chilled in defense. "What do you care? The rich-bitch princess wants to keep moving."

He winced. "Morgan—"

She shook her head, walking backward toward the shower. "I'm sure if I tell Daddy I was brave and kept going—even though I broke a nail—I'll get a matching bracelet for that new diamond necklace. I'll be stripping down to nothing, so if you don't want your sensibilities shocked, you might want to turn around." Steadier, she turned without giving him another glance.

☙ CHAPTER TWENTY-TWO ❧

WHILE MORGAN SHOWERED, HUNTER SET UP CAMP. After staking the two-person tent to the hard-packed ground, he crawled inside and unrolled the navy blue sleeping bags, setting them on their mattress pads. He placed the small LED lantern at the head of the beds as his mind wandered back through the events of the day. With a weary sigh, he sat on his haunches, rubbing the tight knots of tension torturing the back of his neck. Christ, it had been a long one. There'd been too many close calls. He thought of the guard practically stepping on Morgan and the flyover that missed discovering them by seconds. No one could argue he wasn't earning his pay.

He was ready to finish this job. He hoped to wrap it up in the next seventy-two hours. It was time to get the hell out of Yellowstone. If they could make it to Bozeman without encountering any more complications, he could check this assignment off as another success. Morgan would return to DC in one piece—with the answers she'd come looking for—and he would be able to give Stanley the coordinates to bust up the mine. But first they had to walk the several miles back to the cabin and actually avoid another catastrophe. He was starting to wonder if that was possible. Morgan seemed to attract trouble like a magnet attracted metal. Wherever she went, disaster wasn't far behind.

Despite the chaos they encountered throughout the afternoon, he couldn't help but smile. Hell if he knew why that amused him. She was a piece of work. Their conversation moments ago played through his mind, and his smile spread into a grin. She'd certainly told him where to go with her frosty words and fiery eyes. Morgan could hold her own, of that he had no doubt. For such a tiny thing, she had one hell of a bite. It was easy to forget Morgan had a soft, sweet side and that she could be just as vulnerable as the next person. She didn't show her weaknesses often, which made them all the more powerful when she did—like earlier today when the guard almost found her.

His smile vanished, and he clenched his jaw, thinking of the way she'd looked at him—pale and terrified. He'd almost come undone when she crawled onto his lap, wrapping herself around him like a vine. Her heart had pounded against his while she trembled. As the scent of her soft hair surrounded him and her body pressed to his—molding perfectly as if she was made for him—tenderness engulfed him. He would have done anything to make everything okay, to make her feel safe again.

He unclenched his bunched fists, letting out another weary breath. It was definitely time to go. Seventy-two more hours, he promised himself, and then he could put this all behind him and get back to his life in LA.

With everything settled and little else to do, he backed out of the tent and started a fire for an early supper. He hoped the busy work of preparing a meal would distract him from his unwanted thoughts.

———◦———

By the time Morgan wandered to their small camp, towel clad and her hair dripping, chili was heating on the cook stove. Hunter sat comfortable and more relaxed in his convertible shorts, reading the novel he brought along. He flicked her a glance, sincerely wishing he hadn't as a hot ball of lust settled uncomfortably in his belly. He knew just what was under her towel and wanted his hands all over her soft skin.

"I told you I wanted to keep moving," she said. "It can't be more than four o'clock. We can put in several more hours before we call it a night."

Out of self-preservation, he stared at the words in his book instead of her. "I'm ready to stop. We've had a long day."

"I want to radio our location in to Miles and Robert tomorrow morning, when we get farther down in elevation. We have to tell them what we saw."

Hunter's eyes locked on hers as a shiver ran down his spine. If only she knew how closely her thoughts mirrored her doomed team's actions. He wanted to tell her about Shelly's journal and give her the rest of the answers she sought, but he couldn't risk it. She already knew too much. Eventually they would make it back to the ranger station. He was going to try his damndest to get them out of there without bumping in to Robert or Miles, but there were no guarantees he could pull that off. Morgan's grief was too raw, her loss too recent to disguise knowing who may have played a part in her friends' murders. If Robert and Miles had any idea she could put one or both of them away for life, she wouldn't live long. He wasn't taking that chance. "I think we should skip the radio and head back to the station. We'll book a flight home and tell your father everything when we get to DC."

She frowned. "That doesn't make sense. We'll radio in tomorrow. I tried while you showered, but I only got static."

"You did what?" He shot up, grabbing her arm. "Shit, Morgan, why did you do that?"

She yanked free of his grip. "Why wouldn't I? We found an illegal mining operation on federally protected land. They're rangers. That's exactly what I'm supposed to do."

"You should've told me."

"I just did, so what's the problem?"

"I don't have one. You shouldn't be using the radio, that's all." He thought quickly, covering his deceptions with more lies. "The guards at the mine have one. They might be able to pick up our frequency."

Her eyes filled with fear as she swallowed. "I didn't think of that. All I got was static. I don't think anyone heard anything."

"I'm sure everything's fine. Just tell me before you do something like that."

"Fine." She walked away, unzipped the tent, and crawled in.

Minutes later, dinner simmered in the pot.

"Chili's ready," Hunter called over his shoulder.

No response.

He hadn't heard a peep from Morgan since she'd disappeared. Curious, he got up and wandered over to the tent, peering through the black-mesh top he'd left open for ventilation. He stared at her as she lay asleep on her side with her towel still snug and knotted at her breasts. His first thought was to wake her, but he decided against it. She needed to rest more than she needed to eat.

He turned to leave but stopped when the gouge on the heel of her hand caught his attention. He winced, sucking in a breath through his teeth as he bent closer to examine the deep, purple bruising surrounding the ugly-looking gash. "Ouch. That looks nasty," he muttered. He would have to help her clean it when she woke up.

∽ CHAPTER TWENTY-THREE ∾

MORGAN OPENED HER EYES TO THE STARS WINKING in the sky. Cricket song echoed in the night as the stream rushed over rocks, creating a musical tinkle. She could just make out Hunter's profile from the light of the half moon as his chest rose and fell with each strong, steady breath. She sat up, and the towel she wrapped around herself hours ago came loose. Tucking the cotton tight again, she pulled back the sleeping bag Hunter must have covered her with and winced as the movement caused her injured hand to throb.

Ignoring the pain, she moved her hand along the bottom of the tent, trying to find the small flashlight she knew they kept between their beds. Her fingertips made contact with the cool metal handle, and she grabbed hold, putting it under her sleeping bag, hoping to have enough light to see but not wake Hunter. She blinked, squinting from the dim glow as she examined her palm. Her wound had been bandaged with gauze and medical tape. Clearly, Hunter had cleaned it too. When she moved her fingers, the gash stung like fire. How had she slept through *that*?

She kept the flashlight on while she pushed forward, grabbing the tank top folded at the foot of her makeshift bed. The zipper slid down with her movements, and she jumped when Hunter sprang up, reaching for his gun.

"Sorry. Sorry," she said, sending him an apologetic smile. "I didn't mean to wake you. I was trying to get dressed." Sighing, he scrubbed his hands over his face. "It's all right," he said, his voice rough with sleep. She pushed forward and lost her balance, catching herself with her sore hand. "Ouch!"

"Let me see that," he muttered, snagging her by the wrist as he grabbed the flashlight, his knuckles brushing her leg. She inched away from the quick contact, suppressing a shiver. "What are you doing?"

"Checking this out." He put the handle between his lips and shined the light on the gauze as he spread her palm flat with both of his hands.

"Hey." She frowned, trying to tug free from his grip as pain radiated through her palm. "Be nice."

He held her still, continuing his examination. "That's a nasty little cut you've got. It doesn't look red or swollen around the bandage, so I don't think we have to worry about infection. We just have to keep it clean."

Her eyebrow winged up. "I'm pretty sure it's never been cleaner. Did you leave any antiseptic in the bottle or just dump it all on tonight? It stings like *crazy*."

He grinned. "I only used what I needed. There's plenty left for tomorrow."

She rolled her eyes, smiling as she pulled her hand away. "Great."

He turned on the LED lantern and shut off the flashlight. "Here. Why don't you get dressed? It's cold out."

They both reached, grabbing for her shirt, and her head connected with his chin.

"Ow!" He jerked back, rubbing at his jaw as he swore. "I know you have a hard head, but Christ."

She laughed. "Oh stop. It's not that bad."

He continued massaging the sore spot, scowling. "It is from where I'm sitting."

She picked up the flashlight lying on his sleeping bag and

shined the beam in his face.

He squinted, blocking the glare with his hand. "What are you doing—besides blinding me?"

"I'm just making sure I don't need to perform emergency surgery." She leaned forward. "A bump to the chin can be a life-threatening injury."

He reached for the flashlight she kept moving out of his reach. When he finally grabbed it, he gave her a playful shove, grinning. "Smart ass."

She fell back laughing, looking up at him.

His eyes traveled down the length of her towel-clad body, and his smile disappeared.

Her laughter quieted as she sensed the sudden change in his mood. She sat up for her shirt, paralyzed by his gaze, her heart stuttering as she recognized hot, needy desire and wanted him.

He grabbed the front of her towel, pulling her to him. Their breath mingled as she swallowed, clutching his arms, waiting.

He captured her mouth, cupping her cheeks, instantly taking the kiss deep.

She moaned her surrender, getting to her knees and wrapping her arms around his neck, eager to feel her body pressed against his.

He only gave her moments to savor before he drew her away, looking into her eyes as he tugged at her towel, sending it to the floor. She quivered as his big hand lazily caressed her skin—from the valley of her breasts, stopping just above her center.

"I want you, Morgan." He hooked his arm around her waist, settling her on his lap.

She felt him, through his shorts, hard and ready, as she wrapped her legs around his waist, knowing tonight she would finally be his. She smiled, her lips a whisper from his. "Then take me."

He groaned as he took her mouth in a ravenous kiss, getting to his knees and laying her on the sleeping bag.

She sighed as he feathered kisses along her neck and sensitive collarbone, moving and nibbling the side of her breast, making her whimper as his teasing touches set off a firestorm of need.

He traced his fingertips over her nipples, and she sucked in a breath, arching. Hunter's blue eyes, darker in the moonlight, stared into hers as she settled her hands over the tops of his, pressing his callused palms to her breast. "Touch me, Hunter. Touch me."

"I'm taking my time." He moved her hands and continued with his caresses. "I'm going to make you as crazy as you've been making me."

Goose bumps covered her skin, and she shuddered, anticipating his promise.

He skimmed his knuckles up and down the sides of her waist and showered her with hot, moist kisses, stopping at her belly button.

She trembled as sensations built deep in her core, desperate for release. "Please, Hunter."

He walked his fingers down her hips, his mouth following, grazing her with his teeth, making her moan. He ran his tongue along her firm inner thighs, stopping short of fulfilling her.

She gasped, feeling his warm breath against her and his lips brushing over her skin, teasing. More. She needed more. Just a little more pressure would send her flying. Her fingers went wild in his hair as her hips rocked back and forth, urging him to finish her. Her eyes snapped open, looking into his as he made his way up her body, leaving her frenzied and unfulfilled. "Hunter. Please, Hunter."

He smiled smugly and took her mouth again.

She kissed him back, wild with need, running her palms over his smooth, sculpted back, and found her way into his shorts, moving over his muscled butt.

He groaned, closing his eyes, resting his forehead against

hers as her fingers skimmed his hips and wrapped around him.

She pleasured him, moving her hands up and down, listening to his shuddering breaths, feeling him clutch at her hair, enjoying his surrender. "Be inside me," she begged, pulling his shorts down his legs, eager for the heat, craving the ultimate connection. "I can't take it anymore."

He settled more truly between her legs, and she felt him hard against her, just inches from where she wanted him. She moved her hips, desperate to take him inside. The orgasm needing release built until she could hardly bear it.

"Not yet." One by one, he took her breasts into his mouth, licking, savoring.

Her hands fisted at her sides as her breath came in ragged gasps.

He moved farther down, spreading her legs wider, his eyes locking with hers, as he touched her with the tip of his tongue. The slight flick of moist pressure sent her into ecstasy.

She threw her head back, crying out, as the power of the orgasm ripped through her system. She built again, shattering as his tongue stroked and his fingers moved in and out. She came again, mindlessly calling his name.

He trailed his lips along her skin, lazily making his way back up her body, lacing his fingers with hers as he pulled her hands over her head, kissing her deeply. "Look at me, Morgan."

Her eyelids fluttered open.

He entered her slowly, hissing out a breath.

"Yes," she gasped, wrapping her legs around him as she closed her eyes, whimpering helplessly when he started pumping, his lazy rhythm pure pleasure.

"Look at me," he repeated against her mouth. "I'm going to watch you go over this time."

She cried out, her eyes going wide, her fingers tensing on his, when she pulsed around him.

He pulled his hands from hers, brushing them through her hair as he stared into her eyes, letting out several deep, ragged breaths. His stomach muscles contracted, and he groaned long and deep as his mouth covered hers, and he filled her.

———◆———

They were still until their gasps for air turned into steady breathing. Hunter lay inside of her as her legs stayed locked around his waist. She combed her fingers through his hair while the weight of his head rested against her shoulder. She'd never experienced anything so intense. Good sex, even great sex, wasn't new to her, but this was a whole different level of amazing. Hunter had moves that were killer, but it was more than that. Perhaps the experience had been so powerful because love had never entered the picture before. She'd teetered a time or two, but never like this. This was so strong, so vital, so...all-consuming.

When did it happen? The first time he drove up on his Harley? When he kissed her cross-eyed in the clearing by the southwest trail? It had been there—somewhere—hovering among the harsh words and nasty looks that passed so easily between them. She'd pushed it away, shoving at the troublesome emotions, always denying she could be in love, but it always circled back. When she thought she'd lost him to a bullet hours ago, it snuck back again, knocking her flat.

He raised his head, looking down. "You okay?"

She smiled. "I almost had a heart attack, but yeah, I'm fine."

He grinned. "You're spectacular." He brushed his lips against hers as he started to move.

She tightened her legs. "Where you going?"

"I'm moving so I don't crush you." He turned over and lay on his back in the sleeping bag, grabbing the thick fabric and covering himself.

She inched her way toward him, resting her head on his shoulder as she cuddled closer.

His hand hesitated before he settled it against her waist.

She smiled, pretending she hadn't seen him pause.

He smiled back, but something was different.

She studied him when he closed his eyes, running her hand down his arm and back up, playing with the puckered bumps on his shoulder. "How'd you get the scars?"

He opened his eyes. "On-the-job injury."

Her fingers wandered to his firm bicep, tracing his tattoo. "What does it mean?"

He stiffened and picked up her hand, moving it to his chest. "Nothing. It's just a tattoo."

She continued her examination of the ornate cross. "It's really a work of art. It has a date. What event in your life did you deem important enough to permanently ink into your arm?"

"I feel like we're playing twenty questions here." He pulled away, sitting up. "It's just a damn tattoo. It's no big deal."

She stared at him, noting the weariness in his guarded eyes. "Right. I'm going to get a drink and snack." She moved to her bed, yanking on her tank top and panties, then un-zipping the tent. "I missed dinner." She grabbed the lantern.

He snagged her by the wrist. "Morgan, wait."

"Really can't. Gotta pee." She didn't bother making eye contact as she pulled away and crawled from the tent. She walked to the packs Hunter tied high in a tree and tugged on the rope until hers came down. She selected a pack of chicken-flavored Ramen noodles, her fleece, thermal pants, and socks from the bag. The temperature had dropped con-siderably.

She swung the lantern around, making certain she was alone. She didn't want any more run-ins with wild animals— although she was certain she could take them on right about now. What the hell was Hunter's problem? They'd just shared the intimacy of mind-blowing sex, but he couldn't tell her about his stupid tattoo? Well, screw him. She put kindling on the sleepy campfire embers until they crackled back to life and heated water for her overdue dinner. Circling her arms around her knees, she stared into the flames. So much had happened over the past twelve hours, all of it leaving her miserable. She'd solved the mystery behind Shelly, Ian, and Tom's deaths, but the waste of it all left her sad and angry. She'd discovered love, the big L-O-V-E, but it would never work out. That ripped at her heart. She sat for a long time, until the campfire died again, and then she cleaned up. When she was finished, she dimmed the lantern and unzipped the tent. Her eyes met Hunter's as she crawled in. "I figured you would've fallen asleep." She turned and zipped the tent closed behind her.

He crossed his arms behind his head. "I was waiting for you to come back."

She tossed him a glance as she settled herself into her sleeping bag. "There wasn't any need." Lying down, she reached forward to turn off the light.

He took her hand, holding her gaze.

She waited for him to say something—anything—to voluntarily share a piece of himself with her, but he didn't. Hurt, she pulled away, switching off the lantern, and turned her body away, staring into the darkness.

———◆———

Several miles away, Robert stood alone in the dark office of the northeast ranger station. Miles had left the day before to spend the long weekend at his parents' home. Using his shoulder to press the phone to his ear, he fiddled with a paperclip, nervously twisting it out of shape as he spoke on the phone. "She tried to make contact this afternoon. The radio was only on for a minute, but it was long enough for me to figure out they aren't where they said they would be."

"Well, where the hell are they?"

He cringed. "The beacon placed them ten miles southeast of the Slough. I don't know where they went from there. It was late afternoon when she tried to check in. I imagine they probably hiked on. I'll send the guards out to take care of it. They shouldn't be too hard to find."

"No. Leave this to me. You've already fucked it up enough. You should've followed them. I'm going to regret offing her, but him, I'm going to make it real painful before I put a bullet in his brain." Wild laughter bounced through the receiver, leaving a trail of sweat down Robert's spine.

"What do you want me to do?"

"Wait for my orders. We'll take care of them soon, Robert, very soon. I'll get back to you when I figure out how I want to handle this."

The big boss hung up, and Robert stared into the dark shadows of the forest until he no longer heard his boss's mad laughter ringing in his ears.

⋖ CHAPTER TWENTY-FOUR ⋗

GRITTY-EYED AND IRRITABLE, MORGAN DECIDED IT was time to get up. It's not like she'd slept anyway. She shoved her cover back and sat up, glancing at Hunter. She glared, taking in the cozy sight of him sprawled across his mattress pad, lying facedown on his stomach with his cheek pressed against the pillow he'd made with his arm and sleeping bag. She spent the night tossing and turning while *he* slept soundly, completely unaffected by what had passed between them. The awkward after-sex snuggle certainly hadn't left him miserable and confused. How could it? His breathing had steadied out and deepened only moments after she'd turned off the lantern.

He hadn't bothered to clue her in as to why he'd gone from hot to cold in the blink of an eye. One minute he'd been the kind of lover every woman dreams of—passionate, attentive, *thorough*—the next he'd all but shoved her out of his sleeping bag and thrown up the *No Trespassing* sign. He'd made it clear that there wouldn't be any encroaching into the mind and heart of Hunter Phillips. Sex would be fine, but everything else was off the table.

Letting out a frustrated sigh, she pulled on her boots and unzipped the tent, stepping into the early light of dawn. She breathed in the crisp air as the sun rose over the trees, casting shades of purple along the horizon as far as she could see. Even in her exhausted, pissy mood, she couldn't deny the beauty of the morning. Gathering kindling, she placed the small pieces of tinder in the rock-ringed fire pit, returning the flames to life. Wood crackled and spit as she walked to the stream, filtering water for breakfast and filling their bottles for the day.

Cold to the bone and covered in goose bumps, she sat by the fire, absorbing the welcome heat radiating from the licks of flame. She stirred walnuts and raisins into her big bowl of instant oatmeal as rustling movements in the tent caught her attention. She paused, her fingers tightening on her spoon, as the distinct sound of the tent's zipper opening filled the still air.

Hunter crawled through the open flap and stood, pulling a green fleece over his head.

She looked him up and down while flashes of the night played through her mind, remembering what those hands, that mouth, his body could do to hers, what he could make her feel, and looked away. Despite her confused emotions, she glanced back, and their eyes met before he walked into the woods. And just like that, she realized there was nothing between them. There were no inklings of affection after a night shared in passion, just a brick wall of indifference. Staring after him, she subconsciously moved closer to the fire, seeking more warmth as she gripped her bowl until her fingers ached. It wasn't only the cool dawn air and icy mountain water that left her cold.

She ate quickly, wanting to get on with the day. The sooner they alerted the proper authorities about the mine, the faster she could get back to her lynx project. With the mystery of her team's death solved, she would be able to give her friends' families the whys behind it all. She hoped they would find some peace—even if she couldn't. Hunter would go home. Dave and Jim would come help her finish what the rest of the team couldn't. That was the way it should be. It was all for the best. Sorrow threatened to consume her as she took her last bite of oats and raisins, trying to believe the lies she told herself.

Hunter walked back through the woods, and Morgan's heart stuttered. She watched him—confident strides, breathtakingly gorgeous, wondering how someone she'd known for such a short time had become *everything*. Tomorrow, perhaps the day after, he would be gone, and that would be that. She damned him, knowing he would walk away and never look back, and she would always love him. Hunter was "the one," there was no doubt in her mind, but after last night, there was little hope he felt the same way. She shook off the despair sitting heavy on her heart and stood to wash her dish as Hunter came to join her by the campfire.

He cleared his throat. "You're up early."

She barely suppressed a scoff at his attempt to clear the air with small talk, wondering if he would bring up the weather next. Apparently he wanted to play things casual. She could do casual. "Yeah, I want to get going. We have a long day ahead." Burying her disappointment, she walked off with hot water in her small pail.

Hunter ate his breakfast, watching Morgan pack the campsite like a dervish on a mission. Her body was tense, her movements fast and jerky. He chalked it up to an awkward morning-after and hurt feelings about the tattoo. He didn't like to talk about it—never had. It was a tribute to his fallen brothers and nobody else's business.

Morgan came out of the tent dressed in hiking pants, with her fleece zipped over a dark brown shirt. She took the sleeping bags and air pads she'd rolled from the tent and began to break those down too.

"Where's the fire? If you wait five damn minutes, I'll help you. I haven't even finished my first cup of crappy coffee."

"I'm fine. I don't need help." She fastened the sleeping

bag sacks to their packs and attached the tent to his. "When you're finished with your crappy cup of coffee, you can get dressed and we'll leave. I'll even wash your dishes."

He looked at her injured hand. "We need to change your bandage."

"I'll take care of it after I wash your dishes."

"I can wash my own dishes. It's still dawn for Christ's sake. Sit down and chill out. You're rushing me, and it's pissing me off."

"I'm being productive. If you don't like it, too bad."

Swearing, he grabbed his clothes and walked off with his dishes.

By the time he finished dressing and cleaning up, everything was packed. Morgan sat on a ratty towel next to the campfire, pulling the tape from her wound. She blew on her cut, muttering curses, and he arched his brow, listening to the expletives rolling off her tongue. He had no idea she could be so imaginative. Stifling a grin, he put the clean dishes in his pack and wandered over to the fire. "Hey, Gutter Mouth, I said I would help you with that."

She flicked him a glance as she hugged her hand closer to her body. "I'm fine. I've got it. It's just a little cut."

Ignoring her, he sat down, gathering antiseptic, antibiotic cream, gauze, and tape from the first aid kit, then squirted sanitizer on his hands and rubbed them together.

"I said I've got it. I don't need any help here." She made a grab for the bottle of peroxide in his lap.

He slapped his hand over hers and held on, looking her in the eye. "I'm going to help you. We have to make sure your wound stays clean."

"I don't need your help," she said, spacing each word between her clenched teeth.

With his patience growing thin, he moved his face closer to hers. "I don't care. Now knock it *off*." He tugged on her wrist, and she lost her balance, falling against him. He hissed out a breath as he examined the swollen, red gouge.

Christ, that had to hurt. The deep purple bruise alone would be painful, not to mention the wound that looked like it might need a couple of stitches. "This thing's infected. Look how red it is. You're not stupid. You know what can happen out here if this isn't taken care of properly."

"I'm perfectly aware and more than capable of seeing to it on my own. I didn't say anything, because I knew you were going to freak out." Frowning, she tried to pull free. "You've proven my point."

He tightened his hold. "I'm not freaking out, but I am going to clean this wound. The sooner I finish, the faster we can get out of here."

Her cool gaze held his until she let out a deep breath. "Fine. Let's get it over with."

He took a long Q-tip and dipped it into the antiseptic.

Morgan looked away, flinching as he gently rubbed the swab over and around the gash. "Damn it, that hurts!"

"I'm sorry." He blew on the wound as he cleaned it. "I know it stings. I'm almost finished." He put the Q-tip down and blew on the cut again, frowning as he turned her palm from side to side. When he was satisfied the gash was as clean as he could make it, he rubbed antibiotic cream on a large piece of gauze and placed the sheet of cotton on the wound site, wrapping the heel of her hand before securing it with medical tape. "You'll have to keep your hand dry today." He let her go. "I'll change the dressing again when we stop for lunch. I think we can control the infection if we stay on top of it."

They both began to repack the first aid kit, and their hands brushed. Morgan paused, then started replacing items with hurried movements. "I can do this. Thanks for your help. Why don't you make sure you're ready, and we'll go."

He frowned as he stared at the top of her head. What was her deal? She'd hardly looked at him since he'd gotten up. "It sounds like you're dismissing me, like I'm your servant.

We've already established I don't take orders from you."

"Fine," she said on an exasperated huff, shoving the case toward him. "You put the stuff away. You can carry the bag in your pack." She got to her feet and grabbed the ratty towel, cramming it in her pack before she shouldered it and turned to leave.

He stood, catching the back of her bag as she walked by. "What's your problem this morning?"

"I don't have a problem. I just want to get out of here."

"I didn't think the bitter morning-after bitch routine was your style."

She stopped in her tracks and whirled, slapping him—hard.

He gripped her wrist as he ran his tongue around the inside of his stinging cheek, staring into her glowing green eyes.

"How *dare* you, you son of a bitch. You've got a hell of a nerve critiquing my after-sex style. I foolishly expected a small amount of affection from my partner afterward. But why mess up a good, cheap fuck with conversation and emotion when you can roll off of someone and go to sleep."

His hand tightened on her skin. "I didn't fuck you. There was nothing cheap about last night."

"Really? You could've fooled me." She yanked her arm free of his hold and started into the trees. "That's the interesting thing about sex, Hunter. There are so many different ways to interpret it."

"Wait a minute." He threw on his pack and doused the flame with his water bottle, hurrying after her. "Morgan—"

"Just stay away from me," she said as she kept walking, picking her way down the rocky terrain. "When we get to the station I'll call my father, and you can be on your merry way." Her voice wavered as she dashed her hand over her cheek.

He wanted to hurry after her and stop her, but what was the point? She was right. He kept hurting her, and he didn't know how to stop. He never stuck around for the after-sex snuggle—at least he hadn't over the past couple of years. The women he slept with knew that. There was always easy affection and fun with no strings attached. When Morgan lay against him afterward, he'd felt strings like a noose around his neck. The whole experience had been different with her. She'd been so responsive, so giving. When she'd cried out for him, lost in her ecstasy, it made him want to give her more. When he'd moved inside her, staring into her eyes, she'd looked at him as if he were all that mattered. It made him not only want her but *need* her. He didn't want to need her. He didn't want to need anyone. And yet, he did.

He'd never met anyone quite like Morgan. She intrigued as often as she irritated him. She wasn't just beautiful; she was also funny, intelligent, and a hell of a lot more than the rich bitch he'd accused her of being. Her bold, independent streak kept him on his toes, and hell if he didn't like it. He wanted to hold her close more than strangle her these days, and that just couldn't be.

It was probably best she thought what she did, even though last night meant more to him than he wanted to admit. It was time to move on. He'd get her home and they'd go their separate ways. He blew out a long breath, worrying when the thought didn't make him as happy as it once did.

∝ CHAPTER TWENTY-FIVE ∽

THEY WALKED FOR HOURS AT A GOOD CLIP THROUGH dense forest and wide-open valleys. The snow-capped Rockies that had left Morgan awe-struck days before lost most of their appeal as her focus shifted from nature's beauty to getting the hell out of Yellowstone and away from Hunter. She kept her distance as they walked, talking only when necessary, as their latest go-round played through her mind. Fuming, she put more effort into each step. He was really something. What a *jerk*. What had she been *thinking*?

"Hey, we should stop and take a break," he called. "We need to check the map and change your bandage. A little lunch wouldn't hurt either."

She wanted to ignore him and keep walking, but she shrugged instead, unwilling to let him see that his earlier comments still bothered her. "Fine. Let's stop over by those boulders. It looks nice and shady."

He nodded. "We'll do the bandage first, then take care of the rest."

"Okay." She sat on a large rock shaded by several tall pines and closed her eyes, letting out a long sigh. Her weary body sagged as she rested her back against the boulder. She'd been so distracted by her dark thoughts, she hadn't realized how tired she was. She opened her eyes again, watching Hunter take a long drink of his water before he pulled the first aid kit from his pack. He sanitized his hands and moved closer, until she could smell the Campsuds in his hair.

He unwrapped her bandage, pulling the piece of gauze from her wound. "Wow, okay. Now we're getting somewhere. This already looks a little better. A lot of the deep redness is gone. I don't see any signs of pus or drainage. I think this will be as good as new in a couple of days."

She lost the thread of their conversation as she studied him kneeling before her—the day's growth of dark blond beard accentuating the bold blue of his eyes. She itched to slide her fingers over the rough stubble and touch the deep dimple in the center of his chin. She yearned for him to look at her the way he had last night. Having him so close while he brushed his hands gently over hers made her want to pull him closer, and she cursed herself a thousand times for being a fool. "Um, you seem to know what you're talking about," she said, trying to carry on the conversation.

He glanced up, meeting her gaze. "Yeah. They give Force Recon pretty advanced medical training." He looked down again, swabbing the wound with antiseptic. "Sometimes it's not enough though."

She frowned. *What did he mean?* She was about to ask but decided not to. He wouldn't answer her anyway.

After he secured a new bandage, they ate lunch and studied the map.

"It looks like we're about fifteen miles from the station. We'll be back by nightfall, easy."

She swallowed a bite of apple. "Good. Then all of this will be over."

"Should be close."

Because it was easier to be civil, Morgan kept her tone light. "I want a real meal and a hot shower. Steak and potatoes with grilled veggies." She groaned. "That sounds like heaven. I can hardly wait. When we get back, we'll tell Robert and Miles about the mine and—"

"No."

Poised to bite into her apple again, she stopped. "What do you mean? Of course we will. They have to take care of this situation immediately."

"That's not how we're going to handle this. We're going to grab our stuff, get in the car, and go to the airport. We'll call your father when we get in the air."

"Why would we do that? The rangers are right here." She held his gaze, waiting for an explanation.

"Can we do things the way I want without all the damn questions? Just once, could we try it that way?"

"Yes, that's right. You don't like questions." She stood and put on her pack. "If this is how you want to handle things, fine, but you don't have to fly back to DC with me. I can call my father and take care of everything from here on out. This is a federal issue. You did your part; now I get to do mine."

"I'm coming with you. My job isn't over until my principal is out of danger. I'll officially consider you out of harms way when we've contacted your father and you're back in DC."

Her stomach sank. "Your principal?"

He shook his head. "Sorry. Security jargon. You know, my client?"

His client. "Yeah, I got it." There was no heat in her words, just the acceptance of what was. He couldn't have hurt her more if he'd slapped her. She turned and started walking off.

"That came out wrong." He hurried ahead, blocking her way. "You know I didn't mean anything by that."

"No, Hunter, I don't know much of anything when it comes to you." She tried to maneuver around him.

He stepped to the right as she did, pressing a halting hand to her shoulder. "Wait." He jammed his free hand through his hair. "Listen to me. I didn't mean to hurt... Have—have dinner with me when we get back to DC."

She wanted to say yes and almost did, but what would be the point? They would eat, he would leave, and she would never see him again. It was time to put an end to this here and now. "As your *client*, I think we've probably mixed more

than enough business with pleasure, don't you?" She skirted around him and walked off. "Let's get going," she called over her shoulder. "I want a shower before we board a plane."

Hunter stuffed the folded map in the side pocket of his pack and glanced at his watch. He and Morgan were making good time; they were no more than two miles from the ranger station. They would definitely be back before nightfall. He stared up at the vivid pinks painting the horizon as the sun began its descent toward the Rockies. The silhouette of massive mountains against the shock of color made a spectacular picture. He took it all in, thrilled that this would be his last night in Montana. There wasn't much he would miss about this place, but the sunsets never disappointed.

He caught glimpses of the valley through the trees as they kept to the woods. The wide, open space beyond was a welcome sight after hours in the dense forest. Spending time in the woods had never bothered him before. He'd spent months in the wilderness during his military training, but everything was different now. He needed to get home and put his life back on an even keel. Since he'd laid eyes on Morgan, nothing had been the same. He was afraid it never would be. He tried to shrug off his troublesome thoughts, but there was no use. It would be a long time before he was able to shake Morgan Taylor from his mind.

Moments later, he recognized the massive boulder he and Morgan had passed as they left the trail days before. They were close now—about a half-mile, if that. They skirted the perimeter of the enormous rock and stepped onto the walking path overgrown with ankle-high grass. He stayed two steps behind Morgan, watching her firm calves bunch in time with her gait, which had slowed considerably over the last hour. Their breaks throughout the day had been quick and few and far between. The lack of rest and her heavy pack were taking their toll. He fell into step beside her, attempting to start an easy conversation he knew she would rather do without. "I sure wish we could stick around for those steaks you were talking about. We'll stop for something good when we get closer to Bozeman."

She spared him a glance and kept walking.

"We might not be able to get a flight out tonight. In fact, we more than likely won't," he continued, trying to break through the icy shield she'd thrown up hours ago. It bugged the hell out of him that they were back exactly where they'd started from, that she wasn't going to let him in. "Maybe they'll have a room at that place we stayed in by the airport."

"Make it *rooms* and that'll be fine."

"Sorry—you're stuck with me for the next day or two. If we stay over, we'll be sharing. You can put up with me for one more night."

"You seem pretty sure of that."

"Look, I've obviously handled things poorly—" A sudden wave of unease washed through him, skittering along his shoulder blades. He stopped in his tracks. Nothing good ever happened when he felt the dreaded sensations. "Morgan, stop."

She did, and stepped closer to him. "What is it?"

He placed his body in front of hers, taking his gun from the holster as he searched the thick vegetation. "We have to move. We're too open right now."

"Open to what? To who?"

"I don't know. Get behind those rocks until I do." He pointed to a large grouping of boulders just beyond the tree line and grabbed her hand, running. They crouched behind their cover, and Hunter dug through his pack for his binoculars.

Morgan grabbed hers too. "What are you looking for? If you tell me, I can help." She put the binoculars up to her eyes. "Someone's coming. I think it's...yes, look. It's Robert."

Robert walked down the path in his service uniform,

stopping where Morgan and Hunter had moments before. He looked at the ground, his eyes trailing to the pile of rocks. He turned toward the forest behind him, making a waving motion.

"Hunter, what is he doing?"

He didn't answer as he watched Robert pull a pistol from his belt. Two police officers emerged through the trees.

"Shit. They're on to us. We made tracks in the grass." He dropped his binoculars long enough to slide the rack on his gun, waiting. "Stay down."

A bullet pinged off the rocks in front of them. Morgan threw her hands over her mouth, stifling a scream.

Hunter shoved his knee against her shoulder, pushing her closer to the ground as he dropped the binoculars he held one-handed and fired. The bullet hit one of the officers in the kneecap, and the man fell to the ground, screaming.

Two more bullets flew their way in rapid succession, ricocheting off the rocks. Tiny pebbles bounced backward, nicking Hunter in the cheek, stinging on impact. Blood dribbled, and he swiped at it with his shoulder.

The uninjured cop ran from the cover of one tree to a large pine just feet away.

Hunter zeroed in on his target and fired, hitting the officer in the right ankle. He fired again, severing the man's Achilles heel on the opposite foot as he fell to the ground. Two down, but he couldn't find Robert. Where was the bastard? He bent forward to pick up the binoculars he'd dropped and caught a movement out of the corner of his eye just as Morgan screamed.

Robert lunged around the side of the rocks, aiming his gun.

Instinct kicked in and Hunter jumped into a high spin kick, knocking the pistol away. "Get the gun, Morgan!"

She sprinted ahead to the weapon and turned, aiming at Robert with trembling hands as he lunged toward Hunter again. Her finger moved to the trigger just as Hunter used

Robert's momentum to throw him over his shoulder to the ground.

In the blink of an eye, Hunter knelt down, striking Robert with an elbow to the chest, and jammed the heel of his hand into his face, rendering him unconscious.

Morgan's breath shuddered in and out. "Did you—did you kill him?"

He glanced up at Morgan still holding the pistol. "Put down the gun before you shoot me."

She stared at the weapon as if she had no idea how it got in her hand and dropped it to her side. "You didn't answer me. Is he dead?"

"No, but he'll be out for a while." He stood, taking the pistol she held.

"You're—you're bleeding."

"Just a little." He swiped at his cheek with his shoulder again.

Standing on her tiptoes, she took a closer look as her cool, clammy fingers brushed the skin of his face. "We'll have to clean these cuts." Her thumb traced his cheekbone, making two small circles. "You'll have some bruising." Her gentle fingers soothed as he met her gaze. They didn't have time for this.

"We'll take care of it later." He dug through Morgan's pack and cut a piece of the rope from the shower bag, tying Robert's hands behind his back. "Let's get out of here. Stay behind the rocks until I tell you."

She nodded.

Hunter peered over the boulders at the police officers, who were both writhing and moaning in pain. He stood, breaking cover, and aimed both guns in their direction. "Listen to me, you bastards. I didn't shoot to kill, but I will if I so much as see you move. Let's go, Morgan."

She stood and shouldered her pack.

Hunter walked backwards, shielding her body, holding both weapons trained on the officers, keeping his aim until they'd vanished from his sight. He holstered his gun, secured the safety on Robert's, and shoved the muzzle in the back waist of his pants. "Run. Hurry. We need to get to the station before Robert comes to." He held Morgan's hand as they ran as fast as they could. He pulled her along as her energy flagged, knowing they had very little time. "Screw our stuff. Let's get to the car."

"What about the keys?"

"I'll hotwire the damn thing. We have to get to the airport."

They made it to the parking lot minutes later. The tires on the car had been slashed. "Fuck. Let's go to the station." Hunter yanked Morgan back toward the trail. "We'll take one of the pickups." But when they got to the cabin, it was clear they wouldn't be taking one of the trucks either. The rims of the wheels rested stubbornly against the dirt of the small driveway. "Okay, I guess we'll hike." He looked at Morgan. "Grab food and get more first-aid supplies from the bathroom. You know what to do. I'll call this in to The Bureau. Hurry."

Miles walked from the woods as they took the first step to the door.

Morgan gasped, stumbling back. "Oh, God, Miles, you scared me."

"Geez, sorry. I just got off duty. You guys are back early. We weren't expecting you for a day or two yet."

"We made good time," Hunter said as he walked over to Miles with a smile on his face and his hand extended.

Miles reached out to return the gesture. "It's good to have you—"

Hunter grabbed hold of Miles' arm and pivoted, elbowing Miles hard in the solar plexus. He followed up the first blow with an elbow to the chin, sending Miles to the ground in an unconscious heap.

"Why did you do that?" Morgan stepped back, staring at Hunter in disbelief. "Why did you hurt him? He could've helped us."

"Because I don't know if he's working with them. Get the stuff, Morgan. Hurry up."

She opened the door, and Hunter dragged Miles inside, leaving him on the office floor. She hesitated next to Miles' limp body, nibbling her lips as she looked up.

Hunter held her gaze, watching the internal struggle playing out in her eyes. "Having second thoughts about whose side you're on? This would be a bad time to decide you don't trust me anymore." After everything they'd been through, the idea that she might not burned deep.

"Of course I trust you, Hunter." Her gaze held steady. "How could I not?"

He nodded. "We're running out of time."

They started down the hall, stopping short when the police scanner in the office belched, "Two officers down by the northeast ranger station. Yellowstone. Be advised and on the lookout for..." Descriptions matching Morgan and Hunter blared through the speaker.

"Move, Morgan. Move. We have to go." He hurried to Robert's bedroom, grabbing what he needed as Morgan ran to the bathroom. He stepped out, stopping short of slamming into her as she emerged from the bathroom, loaded down with supplies.

"I didn't get the food. I need a couple more minutes."

"That's all we've got. This place will be surrounded in fifteen minutes or less. I'm guessing less. The fact that we're out in the middle of nowhere is working on our side."

She dashed to the kitchen, opening and slamming cupboards, appearing moments later with boxes of pasta and canned goods. She shoved them into his pack and headed back for more.

Hunter placed a call to California.

"Hello?" Sarah's friendly voice answered on the second ring.

"Sarah, it's Hunter. Don't talk, just listen."

"Okay."

"You need to take Kylee to your parents'. Don't go back to your house until I call and say it's okay."

"Hunter, I have a full schedule of photo shoots tomorrow, and my parents are out of town."

"Cancel your appointments. Go to Ethan's."

"I can't just—"

"*Do it*." He took a deep breath. "Please, Sarah. I've gotten myself into a hell of a mess and may've put you and Kylee in danger. I called you on phones that might be tapped. Don't go to my house. Pack a quick bag. Have Ethan go back for the rest. Tell him I'll call as soon as I can. I really have to go. Promise you'll do it. I'm sure I'm overreacting, but I need to know you're safe."

"Okay, I promise. I love you, Hunter. Be careful."

"I will. I love you too." He hung up.

Morgan yanked dirty items from their bags and stuffed their packs with fresh clothes as Hunter placed the next call.

"Parks and Conservation Bureau. This is Dean Jenkins."

"This is Hunter Phillips. I need to talk to Stanley Taylor immediately. It's an emergency."

"I'm sorry—he's in a meeting."

"Interrupt him."

"I'm afraid I can't do that."

"Listen to me, *Dean*. I don't know who the hell you are, but—"

Morgan ripped the phone from his hand, tilting it so Hunter could hear. "Dean, it's Morgan."

"Hello, Morgan. Is everything all right?"

"Actually, it's not. You're going to have to take a message. It's life or death."

"What are you talking about?"

"Just listen," she snapped. "We found an illegal gold mining operation in the park on the northeast side of Montana—on the Slough River. I can't get you exact coordinates, but the authorities won't have any problems finding it. I think that's why the team was killed. The guards must've gotten to them. We need to be picked up from the park. It's—"

Hunter took the phone back. "Listen carefully, Dean. We need to be picked up in Tower Junction, Wyoming, in three days."

"What kind of mess are you in? What if you don't make it in that time frame?"

"We will. Just have someone there."

"How will we find you?"

"I'll find you."

"Wouldn't it just be easier to go to the airport?"

"You'd think, but I don't know who the hell I can trust anymore. There's at least one dirty ranger and two cops involved with the operation. I don't know how far up the chain this thing goes. An APB has been issued on Morgan and me. If you or Stanley could call and explain the situation to the authorities, it would take some of the heat off of us here. We'll stay in the wilderness until we find The Bureau agent. Three days, Dean. We've gotta go." Hunter hung up.

———◆———

Moments later, Stanley returned to his office. "Dean, what are you doing here?"

"I stopped by to see if you'd like to join me for dinner."

"Great idea. Ilene has a commitment tonight. A night out with an old pal sounds good."

Dean smiled. "Perfect. I'll drive. You just missed Morgan's call."

"You answered my phone?" He looked at Dean as he gathered items from his desk and transferred them to his briefcase.

"I'm sorry if I overstepped my bounds, but I knew it was your personal line. I thought I would take a message for you."

"No, that's fine. What did she say?"

"Oh, nothing much—just that she and the bodyguard

aren't having a whole lot of luck with the lynx. She's going back out into the wilderness first thing tomorrow morning."

"Ah, well, that's a hard animal to track down." He snapped the case closed and stepped from behind his desk.

"Yes, it is. Let's go get ourselves a bite to eat." Dean waited next to Stanley while he locked his office for the evening. "Oh, by the way, Stan, I have to go out of town for a couple of days. Connie's brother is having some trouble. We're going to give him a hand. I'll be leaving first thing in the morning."

❧ CHAPTER TWENTY-SIX ❧

HUNTER AND MORGAN SECURED THEIR PACKS AND took off into the night. The distant wail of sirens echoed off the surrounding mountains, following them deep into the forest. Thick, ominous clouds moved across the sky, covering what should have been a half moon. Wisps of fog snaked among the trees, hovering just above the ground. Minutes after they left the station, a chilly drizzle began to fall. Without the light of the moon, Hunter had little choice but to shine the beam of his flashlight along the path he created. "I know it's hard to see, but we have to hurry. They'll have canine units searching for us before long. I want to stay in the vegetation, but we can move faster if we get to the edge of the clearing."

In the true country black of night, Morgan held tightly to the back of his pack, following behind. "Dean would've interrupted my dad's meeting immediately. He should be calling the authorities by now—if he hasn't already."

"It'll take time to get word down to the local level. I don't know about you, but I don't want a German Shepherd snacking on my arm while we wait, so we'll keep moving for now." He felt Morgan stumble, and reached behind, grabbing her before she went over. "Are you okay?"

"Yeah. I can't see where I'm stepping, and I'm a little tired, but I'm fine."

If she was actually admitting it, she was way past a little tired. "I know you are. As soon as I think we're in a good place, we can stop. I imagine we have a small window of time before they call out the helicopters. They'll try to find us on foot first. If that doesn't work, they'll call in the big guns."

"Why haven't they already? That's what they do on those cop shows."

"Procedures are a little different in rural areas. The dogs have a better chance of picking up our scent versus a helicopter spotting us. We're like a needle in a haystack. We should stop and get into our thermals and raingear or we'll freeze our asses off and have even bigger problems to deal with."

"I was just thinking the same thing."

Hunter guided Morgan deeper into the trees, where they quickly dug into their packs for thermal underwear, rain pants, and the Gor-Tex shells for their jackets. Changed and as warm and waterproof as they were going to get, they continued on.

Mile after mile, they walked as quickly as the miserable conditions would allow. The light drizzle turned into a steady rain, creating muddy, slippery surfaces. The open space and easy maneuverability of the valley terrain vanished as they climbed. Sharp rocks, thick tree cover, and dangerously deep drops promised to break bones—or worse.

By ten, their pace had slowed to a crawl. The police had yet to find them, but it was still too risky to attempt headlamps. They continued to work by the tiny beam of Hunter's small flashlight.

"Are we far enough away to stop for a few minutes?" Morgan's teeth chattered as she shivered. "I need to change my socks and layer up some more. I'm getting cold."

"Yeah, I think we should be able—" He paused, listening to the thump of chopper blades in the distance. "What the hell? They're still looking for us?" He grabbed Morgan's hand, and they moved deeper into the cover of tall pines. He turned off the flashlight, and they braced themselves as close to the trees as possible, waiting for the helicopter's bright, bold searchlight to pass by.

"We've been out here for a couple of hours, at least. My dad should've taken care of this by now."

It was hard to miss the weariness in her voice. "Yeah, he should have," he said as he gave her hand a gentle squeeze. Something wasn't right. He needed to get to a phone and call Ethan. "All we can do is keep going. There's probably been a little snag."

Morgan changed her socks as rain began to fall in unrelenting sheets and the wind gusted with a violent howl. She looked up, blinking rapidly. "You know, I'm beginning to think things aren't going to go well for us tonight."

Rain whipped against his face like cold needles. Despite the hellish conditions, he couldn't help but smile. "I don't know where you'd get an impression like that. You're such a pessimist."

She smiled back.

"Things are actually looking up. They'll have to land the helicopter. They don't fly well in this weather. We'll take the rain. Let's keep moving."

The blinding rain and strong winds continued into the night. The battle with the unrelenting elements and brutal terrain was beginning to wear on him. If he was tired, Morgan had to be toast. "We'll stop for a little while," he yelled into a gust of wind.

Morgan shook her head and looked behind her. "I want to keep going."

"We have to rest, or we won't be able to move tomorrow when we really need to. This rain isn't going to last forever. If the search hasn't been called off, the weather has seriously slowed them down. We're safe for now."

She nodded. "Okay, you're right."

"What do you say we make ourselves a shelter and get out of this rain for a while?"

"That sounds good—really, really good. Can we set up the

tent?"

He shook his head. "It'll take too long to break down if we have to move quickly. We can leave the tarps behind, but we don't want to be without the tent." He took a folded tarp from his pack, and Morgan helped him tie the ropes attached to the vinyl around four large tree trunks. They pitched it at an angle, allowing the water runoff to flow into the rocks and trees instead of puddle on the ground tarp they laid down. Hunter gathered pine branches, placing them around the sides of their makeshift shelter.

With the tarps settled in place, they stripped out of their dripping Gor-Tex and sat in mostly dry hiking pants and fleece tops. Morgan turned the LED lantern on low and started making sandwiches, piling rye bread with cold cuts she'd taken from the refrigerator. Hunter turned the small camp stove on to heat water for packaged chicken noodle soup.

"Here." Morgan handed him his sandwich.

"Thanks." He groaned over his first bite of ham and cheese. "Now this is a sandwich."

"It should be." She smiled before taking a ravenous bite of her own. "You've got about a half-pound of meat and cheese between your bread. I wanted to use it all tonight before it spoils." She added a packet of broth to the boiling water and stirred. "It's great to be dry again, even if it's just for a little while." She handed him a cup brimming with steaming broth and noodles.

He blew on the soup, cautiously sipping the salty liquid, certain he'd gone to heaven. "Who knew powdered broth and dehydrated noodles could taste so good. Make sure you have some too. You need the warmth and energy."

"Don't worry. I'll eat. I'm starved."

When he finished his meal, he unsnapped the mattress pad and sleeping bag from his pack and took them from their waterproof covers, laying them on the tarp, careful to avoid any water splashing in on the vinyl. "Go ahead and get in when you're ready."

"What about you?"

"Oh, I'm sleeping too. We're sharing tonight. There's not much of a choice. This tarp isn't big enough for two sleeping bags and a spot for our clothes to dry out. We'll keep each other warmer this way, anyway."

She didn't hesitate as he thought she might. She crawled toward the makeshift bed as he set the alarm on his watch—just enough time to rest—then they would have to keep moving.

He took off his hiking pants, fleece, boots and socks and laid them out on the tarp to dry.

Morgan stripped down to her thermal pants and long-sleeve shirt, eagerly sliding into the sleeping bag, sighing when her head rested on the small bump of a pillow the mattress pad provided.

He checked the safety on his pistol, keeping the gun close by, and squeezed in awkwardly behind her as she leaned forward, letting him in. He pulled the cover over them, and she zipped them into very close quarters, lying back against him.

"It's so cold out here tonight. I can't get warm."

He settled his arm around her waist, snuggling her into the warmth of his body, resting her bandaged hand against his forearm. "We'll fix your dressing when we wake up. I'm giving us three hours."

"I haven't slept in nearly twenty-four. I'm so tired, but I don't think I'm going to be able to fall asleep."

"Try to relax. As much as it sucks, the rain is working to our advantage. We created a decent distance." He watched the pounding rain pour from the bottom pitch of the tarp like a fast-flowing waterfall, thinking about what Morgan had just said. She hadn't slept in twenty-four hours—since they'd had sex. It bothered him to think she'd been that upset with the way things ended between them. She had lain inches from him—sleepless—while he'd slept on. When she returned to the tent after eating her late dinner, he remembered the way her eyes had pleaded with him to give her something—some small piece of himself. He recalled the hurt as she'd looked away and dimmed the lantern to darkness. He'd shrugged it off—his habit. He didn't deal with messy emotions—they weren't for him. Uncomfortable with his cowardice, he brushed it all aside as Morgan shifted again. "Why aren't you asleep yet?" he asked quietly next to her ear.

"I can't settle. Talk to me, Hunter, about anything. I don't want to think anymore."

"Okay." He tried to think of something soothing, but there weren't many relaxing things going on. Instead, he said the first thing that entered his mind. "I'm curious to know how Robert and those two cops will explain their injuries. They'll have to come up with one hell of a story."

"I still can't believe this is really happening. Robert knew about the mine."

"It certainly looks that way."

"How did he know we found it?"

"I still haven't figured that one out yet."

"Those were some pretty impressive moves you had. I didn't know you knew karate. That was karate, right?"

"It was a mix of disciplines. Now go to sleep."

"Did you learn in the Marines?"

He didn't want to talk about his time in the military, but her voice was thick and sleepy. If he kept up the conversation, she would eventually go out. He caressed his thumb along her hand, waiting for sheer exhaustion to take her over. "I've studied martial arts since middle school, but we definitely used it in the Marines."

"What level are you?"

"We don't call them levels. They're belts. I'm a third-degree black belt. Close your eyes, Morgan. Relax."

"I'm trying."

He moved his thumb across the soft skin of her hand, listening to the rain pounding against the tarp as the minutes ticked by, relaxing when she finally slept.

"Thank you for everything," she said.

"Morgan—"

"I know. I need to sleep and so do you, but I want to say thank you first. Your lead about the mine was right. Now my friends' families will finally know what happened. It's not much, but it's something. I don't know how Ethan found out, but I'm grateful. And you've saved my life more times than I can count. So, thanks." She lifted his hand to her lips, kissing his knuckles, and settled his arm back around her waist.

He ignored the flash of guilt as he let her believe Ethan had given him the information. It was still safer this way. "You're welcome. Now stop talking and go to sleep." He wrapped his arm around her again, listening, until her breathing finally grew deep. He moved in closer, nestling his cheek against her neck, and fell asleep too.

———◆———

Her eyes had only been closed for seconds when Hunter's watch started its monotonous beep—or so it seemed. Morgan groaned. "Let's go back to sleep. Another hour or two won't hurt."

Hunter awkwardly stretched as much as their current arrangement would allow. "I wish I could say yes, but we have to get up and get moving. We'll try to stop later." He pulled the sleeping bag's zipper down and dragged the cover back. "Hey, the rain stopped."

The frigid air hit her like a shocking slap. "Yikes, it's cold out here." With a shudder, she yanked the cover back in place. "What time is it anyway?"

He pulled off the cover and sat up. "Three."

She groaned again, reluctantly crawling from their warm bed. "You're a cruel man."

They dressed quickly and took the time to heat water for strong coffee and hot cereal. Hunter changed her bandage by the low light of the lantern. The bright, angry red surrounding the wound had faded to a dull pink. "This looks better. We caught the infection just in time."

"Does this mean you'll stop swabbing that damn antiseptic all over it?"

"I think you already know the answer."

She smiled. "It never hurts to ask."

A slow grin spread across his lips while he put the first aid supplies away.

"What are you doing?" She put a halting hand on his shoulder. "It's your turn."

"Huh?"

"We're going to take care of your cheek. We should've cleaned it hours ago."

He brushed his fingers over his cuts. "Nah, it's fine."

"Let's not risk it. Those are some deep nicks." She pulled the sanitizer and antiseptic free from the pouch and cleaned her hands before dipping a Q-tip into the bottle. "Scooch over a bit. I can't reach."

He stayed put, eyeing her.

"Afraid it'll hurt? Don't be a baby, Bodyguard Phillips. If I can take it, you sure can."

"Those sound like fighting words." He moved closer, knee to knee.

Pushing her face close to his, breathing him in, she stared into the vivid blue of his eyes. "I can take you," she said, her voice thickening with reluctant desire.

His gaze wandered to her mouth. "Are you sure? I know karate."

The warmth of his breath feathered across her lips. If she moved her chin just an inch... What was she *doing*? This wasn't going to happen. She remembered the swab in her hand and jabbed it forward, making Hunter wince. "Yeah, but I have hydrogen peroxide."

His fingers curled around her wrist, nudging her away. "Shit, that stings."

With his curse, the shaky moment passed. Good. "Stop. Let me do this." She removed her arm from his grasp, concentrating on her work as she swabbed the Q-tip over and around the scratches on his cheekbone.

Hissing out a breath, Hunter pulled away. "Damn, Morgan."

"I'm sorry." She pulled him close again. "I'm almost finished." Blowing on his raw skin, she traced the last of his scrapes. "There. All set."

"Thanks...I think."

"You're welcome." She put the supplies away and shoved the small kit in her pack as her knees brushed Hunter's. The contact was too much. She pushed back, giving herself some space, and poured herself more coffee she didn't want, sipping the bitter brew, shuddering. "Ugh, this stuff's awful."

Hunter topped off his own cup. "Yeah, but it's all we've got."

"Then it'll do."

Certain they were back on solid ground, she relaxed and moved closer to Hunter's side as he pulled out the map.

"We should plan on cutting across this mountain here. I would like to stay close to the road and follow the river into Tower Junction, but I don't think it's a good idea. It's too obvious. We won't have as many water sources this way, but there're enough to get us by." He pointed to smaller rivers and streams along the route they would take.

"It looks like we'll be fine."

"We'll have to push pretty hard today to put some distance between ourselves and whoever the hell is after us. I don't know if your father straightened everything out with the authorities, and it'll be a while yet before we know what kind of resources we have working against us." He took another sip of his coffee. "The mine must be producing pretty damn well if they were willing to murder three people and buy a couple of cops. In my opinion, they won't stop until they find us. They seem to have the money to use any means necessary. We're the loose ends that can fuck everything up. Even if your father straightened stuff out and the mine has been busted up, it's going to take time before all of the players are taken down." He glanced up from the map, staring into her eyes. "People will be looking for us. We're literally running for our lives. I need to find a phone and contact Ethan."

"I understand the gravity of our situation, Hunter. I'm ready to do whatever we have to to get home."

"Let's get to it then."

They drank the rest of their coffee, packed up, and resumed their trek.

———◆———

Stanley woke with a start at three-thirty a.m. The phone on his bedside table rang twice before he finally answered. "Yes, hello."

"Stanley, it's Ethan Cooke. What the hell's going on?"

He sat up, alerted by the tension in Ethan's voice. "What do you mean?"

"Hunter called a mutual friend of ours several hours ago, saying he'd gotten himself into a hell of a situation and that he would call me when he could. I haven't heard from him. I've been trying his cell phone, but it goes to voicemail. Has Morgan contacted you?"

Stanley shook his head. "I'm confused. She called earlier today. Everything was fine."

"She didn't say anything to you about what Hunter was talking about?"

"No. I didn't actually talk to her. She spoke to one of my colleagues. I was in a meeting when the call came in." He put his hand on Ilene's shoulder as she stirred.

"Well, I can tell you this, Stanley: Things aren't fine.

They're far from it. I did a little hacking into the Montana PD computer system. They've issued an APB on Morgan and Hunter. Hunter shot two cops and roughed up a couple of rangers. If he did, there was a damn good reason. I would suggest you put in a call and find out what the hell is going on."

He ran a hand through his tousled hair. "All right. I'll call you back as soon as I know something. I'll call Dean first and find out just what he and Morgan talked about."

"Good. I'll—"

"He's taking care of her, right?" Stanley interrupted. "Hunter's going to keep my little girl safe?"

"I'd bet my life on it. I'm not sure what's going on, but I know he won't let anything happen to her."

"Okay. I'll get back to you." He hung up, looking into Ilene's worried eyes.

"What's the matter, Stanley? Is Morgan all right?"

"She's fine, honey. There's been a small complication. I need to make some phone calls. I'll be able to tell you more after." Walking from the bedroom, hoping he appeared calm for Ilene, he picked up his pace when he made it to the hallway, running for the office with fear resting heavy in his heart. He flipped on the light and dialed Dean's home number. The phone rang several times.

"Hello?" his wife answered sleepily.

"Connie, it's Stanley. I'm sorry to call at this hour, but I need to talk to Dean. It's very important."

Connie cleared her throat. "Stan, Dean left for the airport hours ago. He said he had to take a last-minute meeting for you tomorrow."

His eyes hardened as dread curled in his stomach. "Good heavens, Constance. You're exactly right," he said with a calm he didn't feel. "I'm so sorry to have disturbed you. I did send him for that meeting. I'm half asleep." He booted up his computer while he listened to Connie's groggy chuckle.

"You had me worried for a minute. Go on back to bed.

We'll talk to you soon."

"I'll do that. Bye now."

"Bye, Stan."

When the dial tone buzzed in his ear, he punched in the number for the Montana State Police.

CHAPTER TWENTY-SEVEN

MORGAN AND HUNTER TOOK ADVANTAGE OF THE early morning dark, moving as quickly as the treacherous landscape would allow. Rocky terrain, still wet and slippery from the night of rain, made the journey down the mountain excruciatingly slow. With little choice, they risked the use of headlamps. The probability of being discovered in the wee hours of the morning was less likely than the promise of major injuries on the dicey descent.

After hours of nonstop hiking, they reached the valley at the mountain's base and removed their headgear as the sun crept over the massive ranges in the east. They ran at a steady jog, making their way to the base of the new mountain they would climb throughout the day. Tower Junction, Wyoming, lay on the other side. They started the trek up, heading deep into the cover of the trees, knowing it was only a matter of time before the helicopter circled again.

"Do you need to rest?" Hunter asked, while he adjusted his pack with a quick shrug of his shoulders.

"No, I'm good. We're safer if we're moving now—before it gets any brighter." She took a deep breath. "It's going to be hot and muggy again. I can feel it in the air."

"Ah, the perfect conditions for hiking a large, steep mountain. I can't think of anything else I'd rather be doing today."

She grinned. "I can think of a million. The first on the list would be a shower. I keep fantasizing about warm water, real soap, and good shampoo and conditioner. It's the simple things that make me happy."

He winged up his eyebrow as he glanced at her. Did she really believe that? Even with her hair pulled back in a messy knot and her hiking clothes wrinkled and dirty, she didn't look simple. She was a bundle of contradictions and complications. Morgan exuded wealth and class with every breath she took. It was marrow deep. She was a purebred used to the finer things—had never known anything less. "I wouldn't have believed that when we first met."

She frowned. "What do you mean by—"

The distant drone of a low-flying aircraft bounced off the rocks. "Shit, they're at it already." He looked around, gauging its direction. "They didn't give us much time."

She glanced up, shading her eyes. "No, they certainly didn't."

"We'll have to stay close to the tree cover today, which will get tricky the higher we climb. This mountain is pretty damn barren toward the top." They ducked under a small grouping of pines as the plane flew over, and Hunter looked at his watch. "I'd like to stay put and time the flyovers, but I don't think we should risk it. If we make it to that tree line up ahead and use the vegetation to our advantage, we should be good for now. It'll be slower, and we may have to change our route as we get closer to the peak, but there isn't a whole hell of a lot else we can do." He shrugged. "Depending on how aggressive they are with their search, we might have to consider traveling at night until we get through the desolate section farther up."

"Maybe we should plan on it."

He thought of headlamps and deadly drop-offs. "Let's see how things go for a while before we decide."

By mid-afternoon, they had exchanged their thermal gear for short sleeves. Morgan hadn't missed her mark: It was hotter than hell and muggy with it. The lack of tree cover along the way intensified the already miserable conditions, creating logistical nightmares and leaving few places to rest and hide. At each stop they checked the map, measuring distances closely to ensure they would make it to a hiding place before the next flyover. Like clockwork, they scrambled for cover, standing under a small grouping of pine trees as the security plane's engine droned closer, making its circle.

"They're unbelievable, absolutely unrelenting," Morgan said.

Hunter wiped at his damp forehead with the bottom of his shirt. "Yeah, but at least the police helicopter stopped joining in on all the fun."

She smiled, rolling her eyes. "You would think we'd discovered a huge national secret, not a small-time gold mine." She sat on the rocky ground, the landscape of the last several miles. "I need to rest for a minute."

He sat next to her. "I don't think the mine's all that small."

"I imagine you're right." She uncapped her water and drank. "This is just so unbelievable. I'm still having a hard time wrapping my mind around it." Her knuckles whitened against the bright green plastic of the bottle. "I—I can't stop thinking about Shelly, Ian, and Tom. I can't make everything add up. They were really smart, every one of them. They were cautious, especially Shelly. I just feel like we're missing a piece—something important." Her gaze met his. "I keep coming back to what you said about the three of them not putting up a fight. The guards walked them a long way from the mine before they shot them. Their bodies were found *miles* from the river. I just can't believe they didn't try..." She capped her bottle as her voice grew thick with emotion, and she pressed her lips together in a firm line, shaking her head.

He stared into her pretty green eyes clouding with hurt, and he hated it. She looked so wounded and *vulnerable*. He brushed his fingers down her arm. "I wish I could give you the answers." And because he could, because he knew everything yet said nothing, he looked away from her haunted expression, reminding himself he was making the right decision.

"Ian was so strong," she said, interrupting his thoughts. "He wouldn't have given up without a fight, and I'm pretty sure he was in love with Shelly. He would've fought for her— for Tom too. We were a family. They would've fought for each other." Her lips quivered as she blinked back tears.

Christ, he felt like an asshole. "It's a horrible tragedy. Maybe when all of this is over things will make more sense."

She shook her head. "None of this will ever make sense."

He gave her hand a squeeze. "Things might be clearer at least."

"I hope so. I'm still shocked that Robert knew about the mine. He seemed so kind."

He drank his water—a good excuse not to reply. He didn't want to talk about this anymore. "We need to get moving."

She stood. "I'm ready to go if you are."

"I think we can reach the base of this beast by nightfall if we keep up our pace."

Thunder rumbled in the distance. Morgan stopped, watching the blackened thunderheads plow forward from the west as they cleared the latest peak. "We're walking right into a storm."

"Looks like a doozy," Hunter agreed, scanning the area. "Let's find some sort of shelter before we get dumped on."

"Where?"

"I don't know," he said, shaking his head, glancing toward the ominous clouds. "I have to admit I could do without the rain, but any trail we might've left behind will be wiped away. The damn plane will have to land too."

The lack of sleep was taking its toll as she searched for something optimistic to add. "It will also cool things down, and we can *rest*." She batted her eyelashes as she emphasized the last word.

He grinned as lightning flashed, followed by a deafening clap of thunder. "Let's pick it up a little. With the terrain so rocky through here, we might be able to find an overhang. We definitely need to find something."

The wind picked up as the boiling black clouds rolled closer. Morgan pulled her hair free of the elastic, smiling as her long locks danced wildly around her face. "This feels awesome!"

Thunder rumbled again, and the sky opened up, instantly soaking them. She stared into the torrents pouring down and held out her hands as refreshing droplets puddled in her palms. She grinned. "This isn't exactly the shower I had in mind, but I'll take it. At least it's warm, unlike last night."

"Break out the champagne." Hunter grabbed her in his arms and began to move in a complicated jig.

"What are you *doing*?"

"Dancing in the rain. Tell me you've heard of it."

Delighted, her smile brightened as she attempted to follow along. Completely missing the rhythm, she fell against his chest, laughing.

He hugged her tight and kissed the top of her head as he eased back, grinning. His blond hair lay plastered against his forehead as fat drops of rain coursed down his face, spiking his lashes and clinging to the dark stubble of his beard. His bold, blue eyes held her captive until he glanced down at himself. "What are you staring at? Doesn't the drowned rat look work for me?"

She studied his shirt plastered to his torso and the shorts sticking to his well-muscled thighs and glanced down at her own sopping clothes, snorting out a laugh. "It's certainly a statement."

He chuckled. "You wear it better than I do. Let's keep moving." He took her hand, pulling her along. "Come on."

What had just happened? Who was the stranger who appeared and vanished just as quickly? She'd seen glimpses of Hunter's softer side, but his moment of spontaneity shocked her. As his long strides ate up terrain and he scanned the area ahead, all remnants of fun vanished. It was almost as if she'd imagined the whole thing. Several slippery steps later, they approached an incline leading to a rock face. "Look." She pointed into the distance. "There's an opening."

"Great. Let's go for it. The lightning's getting pretty close."

They ran for the dark gap in the rocks and found that it gave way to a large cave. Hunter turned on the lantern. "We should probably make sure we aren't sharing with anything bigger than we are."

"Good thought. It's so roomy in here." Her words echoed, and she laughed. "You'd have to stand on your tiptoes to touch the ceiling. I'm glad it isn't too deep though. That would be creepy." She looked around at the discarded water bottles and wrappers littering the cave. "I see we aren't the first to discover this spot. It's certainly big enough to set up our tent." She gave him a pleading look as water dripped from her clothes to the cave floor.

"I think we can make that happen. No one will be wandering around in this mess."

Deafening thunder echoed off the walls as she took the lantern from Hunter and walked the perimeter of the cave, eager to investigate their home for the evening. "Yes! Some wonderful soul left wood in here from their campfire. I'm going to put our bucket in the rain, heat up water, and spoil myself with a warm bath—so to speak."

Enthused by the idea, she dug through her pack until she found the collapsible pail and stuck it out of the mouth of the cave straight into the downpour. "Let's get this campfire up and running. We'll get a little crazy tonight and heat up some pasta too. I'll open a package of that creamy cheese sauce. We'll eat it over shells. I never thought I'd be so excited about macaroni and cheese." She grinned at Hunter as she laid the wood in the stone circle other campers had used before them and struck a match, holding it to the dry pieces of timber. With little effort, flames began to dance, bringing orange-tinted light to the rock walls.

Hunter pulled off his pack and riffled through it. "I'm going out to find more wood. I'd like to keep the fire going through the night. I saw a couple of downed trees by an underhang not far from here. The wood might be dry. I'm pretty sure I'll be able to see the cave from there."

"Okay, whatever you want. Just don't get struck by lightning. You'll ruin our crazy night of cave fun."

He grinned. "I wouldn't want to go and do that. I shouldn't be too long." He pulled his survival knife and miniature ax from a small pouch and dropped them into his waterproof sleeping bag sack.

She checked her bucket, pleased to see it filling quickly. "All joking aside, be careful. This is a really nasty storm."

"I'll be fine. Stay here," he said as he left.

"You don't have to tell me twice," she called as she bustled around the cave, thrilled with the idea of being warm and dry for an entire evening. She had the tent upright in minutes with the sleeping bags unfolded on top of their mats inside.

With that job finished, she poured half the bucket of water into the cooking pot and shoved the pail back into the rain, spotting Hunter hacking away at a downed tree by the smaller cave opening. The underhang was keeping him dry, but just barely. His Under Armour t-shirt lay plastered against his muscled back while his biceps bunched with the effort of each whack to the tree. Morgan pressed her hand to her heart as it beat hard in her chest. God, did she love him.

Shaking her head, she turned away. It would never work. Sorrow threatened to ruin a night she was determined enjoy. Sighing, she pushed away her depressing thoughts and brought the bucket in with her, adding cool rainwater to the steaming pot. Ready to savor her "bath," she took off her clothes and washed. "You're living the high life now, Morgan

Taylor." She chuckled as she shaved her underarms and legs with dirty water.

Clean and refreshed, she placed the bucket outside to re- fill for Hunter and focused on the stove as water bubbled in the cook pot. She grabbed the baggie of pasta and pack- age of creamy yellow cheese as thunder boomed, echoing through the cave. When Hunter returned, she would add their dinner to the water and have the meal ready in no time. She stood, rubbing at her arms, chilled despite her fleece and long johns. Hunter would be frozen for sure; the tem- perature had dropped considerably. She rinsed the pot she'd used for her bath and prepared water for him, then grabbed clothes from his pack, laying them on his sleeping bag. She reached in for his towel, frowning when her hand brushed a small hardback book.

She grabbed hold of its spine for a quick peek at Hunter's latest novel and stared in shock at the white calla lilies dec- orating Shelly's journal. She opened the cover, breathing in Shelly's perfume wafting from the pages, and pain gripped her heart. She closed her eyes, taking another deep breath, desperately missing that wildflower scent. Opening her eyes again, she stared down at the pretty, looping handwriting on the first page. She treasured Shelly's secret thoughts and words, knowing this was all she had left of her best friend. She read about the new feelings simmering between Shelly and Ian, remembering that they never got the chance to talk about the big kiss. A tear ran down her cheek, and she shook her head with the injustice of it all.

They'd been in love. Somehow that made everything worse. Shelly and Ian never had the chance to see where it could lead. Would they have married? Shelly had always wanted children. As the possibilities of what could have been hit her, a new wave of mourning flooded her with wrenching grief. "Oh God," she whispered.

Her thoughts circled back to Shelly's pretty blond hair and Ian's roguish grin, to the whole team laughing and dancing the night away before everything changed. Then she remembered the pictures: Tom's cracked, blood-spattered glasses; Shelly's empty eyes; Ian's black hair matted with blood and tissue. She pressed her fingers to her forehead, willing the images away. She couldn't stand them, not when she could still smell the cheerful, springtime scent of Shelly's perfume.

Forcing herself through the rest, she made her way to where the words ended on May 25. Her hands shook as she read the short passage over and over again. It wasn't the guards. Shelly never mentioned seeing any guards. It had been Robert and the two cops. Robert killed her friends, and Hunter knew. He'd known all along and never said a thing.

☙ CHAPTER TWENTY-EIGHT ❧

HUNTER WALKED INTO THE CAVE, LEAVING PUDDLES with every step he took as water coursed down his sopping-wet body. "Now that's a storm. I haven't seen weather like this in a long time. It's starting to hail." He put the bag of wood next to the dry log pile and crouched by the fire, warming his hands. "I'm freezing. I think I'll have some coffee. Do you want a cup?"

Morgan didn't answer.

He glanced over his shoulder. "Hello? Earth to Morgan."

She kneeled with her back to him, not moving or speaking.

The smile touching his lips disappeared, and he frowned, standing when he saw his pack lying open at her knees. Stepping forward, his stomach sank as Morgan clutched the pink book in her hands. *Shit.* He shoved his bag out of the way, crouching in front of her. Tense seconds passed while he watched her, searching for something to say as she stared at Shelly's journal, white-knuckling the book, sitting still as stone. One lame excuse after another flew through his mind as panic clutched his belly. He wanted to reach out and brush his thumb along her skin, but he knew he wouldn't be welcome.

"You knew all along."

He strained to hear her quiet voice over the pounding

rain.

"All this time you knew and you never told me."

It felt like hours before her eyes met his—grief-shattered and swimming with tears. He clenched his jaw as she undid him with a look. He would've preferred another slap over the devastation he saw on her face, knowing he'd caused it. Guilt threatened to choke him, so he battled back with anger, ripping the journal from her hands. "Why were you in my pack? You shouldn't go through other people's stuff. Nosy people find things they shouldn't."

Morgan stared at him as if he'd torn out her heart. "That's it? That's all you have to say? You've been lying to me for who knows how long, and that's *it*?"

Jesus, he couldn't stand the disgust and betrayal he saw radiating in her voice and eyes, so he got to his feet and paced. "I didn't lie to you. I just didn't tell you."

She stood. "What's the difference?"

"There's a huge difference. I didn't tell you because you wouldn't have been safe if I did."

A humorless laugh escaped her trembling lips as her gaze zeroed in on the holstered gun resting against his ribs. Shaking her head, she rubbed her fingers along her temple. "When did you find it?"

He stopped pacing and met her stare, jamming a hand through his hair. She knew everything, but he resisted with the rest. He would lose her after she had it all, and the realization terrified him.

Rushing across the cave, she shoved at his chest. "When, dammit?"

He grabbed her arms. "The night they left to check for washout."

"Days ago, then. You've known for days." She struggled against him. "You knew what we would find when we went north to the river, what we were walking into. You knew Robert killed them, what my team's last moments were." Her voice broke on a sob. "And you didn't tell me." She fought harder, and he pinned her against him.

"Morgan—"

"How could you? How could you do this to me?" Her hands bunched into fists against his chest as he hugged her to him.

"I had to," he said, desperate to make her understand. "I have to keep you safe. If I'd told you, you would've been in more danger than you already are. There's no way you would've been able to look at Robert and not give everything away."

"Just stop! I don't want to hear anymore. Let me go." She struggled. "Let me *go!*"

Reluctantly, he released his grip.

She turned away, walking toward the mouth of the cave.

"Don't run, Morgan. I'll only come after you."

She went to the tent instead and crawled inside.

He stood, listening to her ragged breaths echoing off the rocks as she fought her tears. "Damn it." He yanked off his sopping shirt and threw it against the cave wall. It landed on the floor with a soggy plop. He took off his hiking boots, pulled off his pants, and went to his pack, taking out dry clothes. Warmer and dry, he crawled into the tent as Morgan lay on her side, trembling and rocking herself. Her hands covered her face while her breath heaved in and out. He lay next to her, pulling her close, and she stiffened, trying to pull away.

"Leave me alone."

"If I could, I would." But he couldn't. Somewhere along the way things had changed and gotten complicated. He couldn't leave her. He didn't want to. "You can hate me in a minute. Just hold on to me for now and let it go."

Seconds later, her sobs echoed off the walls of the cave as tears streamed down her cheeks and her body shook with the power of her grief.

Hunter turned her toward him, looking down at her devastated face, stroking her hair as he cradled her close to his chest. "I'm sorry, Morgan. I'm so sorry. I didn't mean to hurt you. I wanted to keep you safe."

She moved closer against him, putting her arm around his waist, clinging.

He rubbed her back until her helpless weeping turned to shaky breaths. Easing away, he dabbed the tears from her face with his shirt. Her eyes, red and swollen, stared into his as he ran his thumb over her cheek and kissed her forehead. "I'm sorry. I really am."

She dropped her gaze, and minutes passed before she spoke. "I—I know you did what you thought was best, and I can't change that. Shelly, Ian, and Tom are dead because of the choices I made. I can't change that either." She sat up and scooted toward the opening of the tent.

"Whoa, wait a minute." He snagged her hand before she got any farther.

She shook her head. "Not right now. I need to be busy. I'm going to take care of dinner and get to bed."

He let her go and sat up. "If that's what you want." Needing to touch her, he slid a strand of her hair behind her ear. "We can talk while you keep busy."

"I don't want to talk." She picked at a thread along the hem of her pants, glancing at him before she looked down again. "There's hot water in one of the pots for you to clean up with."

He noticed the sleeve of his thermal top peeking out from under the tangle at the foot of his sleeping bag. Reaching forward, he grabbed hold of the shirt and pulled the matching bottoms free. Realization struck and he closed his eyes, blowing out a deep breath. She hadn't been snooping when she found the journal. She'd been doing something nice for him. Goddamn. Could he be any more of a dick? "Morgan... thanks."

"Yeah, no problem," she responded, her voice flat as she crawled from the tent.

Muttering a curse, he followed. The worst of the storm

had passed, but the rain still poured as they emerged. Morgan walked to the fire, tore open the package of shells, and dumped them into the boiling water.

He grabbed the other pot and brought it over by their packs, taking off his shirt. He dipped his washcloth into the warm water and wrung it out, washing his arms. "I know you're pretty upset with me right now." And he couldn't stand it. The way she'd cried, knowing he'd caused her pain, ripped him apart.

She shook her head as she stirred the pasta. "Let's forget the whole thing."

"I can't."

She glanced at him with her eyes still damp. "I'm not angry with you, Hunter. I'd really rather drop it."

"Okay. Fine." Guilt ate at him as he dried off his upper body and set down the towel. "No, let's not drop it. You can't look over here with those big, sad eyes and tell me to forget it. I might be able to let it go if you were pissed, but you're not."

"All right. I'm upset but I'm not angry. I was at first, but what's the point?" She walked to her pack for bowls, the compact strainer, and silverware sets. Standing, she faced him. "And you're right. I wouldn't have been able to hide that I knew about Robert, but we left Robert behind two days ago." She fidgeted with the silverware as she continued. "I've been desperate for answers, and you've had them. You keep talking about trust. You want me to trust you—and I do—but it hurts to know you don't trust me. You don't seem to think much of me at all."

"That's not true." He held her by the shoulders, squeezing gently. "We're a team. I'm depending on you as much as you're depending on me."

She nodded and started to turn away.

"I mean that."

She nodded again.

He tightened his grip. "I don't have the right to ask, but

I'm going to anyway. Why do you feel responsible for your team's deaths?"

"Because I am."

He arched his eyebrow. "Dig a little deeper," he said, thinking of the crime scene photos and police reports he'd read, trying to find the connection between the murders and her statement. As far as he could tell, there wasn't one.

"I knew the teams were mismatched, and I didn't change them." Her eyes filled with tears. "It was my responsibility to do so, but I didn't. Now they're dead and—"

"Wait a minute," he interrupted, brushing her hair behind her ear. "I don't see how that makes any of this your fault." He ran his hands down her arms, lacing his fingers with hers.

In a moment of surrender, she rested her forehead against his chest. "You're being nice to me. It makes this so much harder to get through without crying again."

He winced. "Am I that big of an asshole?"

She glanced up, meeting his gaze. "You certainly can be."

"I'll have to work on that."

She gave him a watery laugh, nestling against him.

He leaned forward, kissing her hair. Morgan rarely caved to her weaknesses. Seeing her so undone flooded him with a need to be everything he hadn't been. He brushed his lips against her temple, speaking softly next to her ear. "I know I haven't made things easy, but lean on me tonight. Let me help you. Tell me the rest."

Taking a shaky breath, she drew back, looking into his eyes, and nodded. "Okay." She clutched at his fingers as she took a deep breath. "Shelly and Tom were amazingly intelligent. Shelly had a photographic memory, and Tom was a genius. They were very much the brains behind our team."

"You aren't exactly a chump yourself."

A fleeting smile touched her lips. "Shelly and Tom were a whole 'nother level of smart. Physically, however, they were the two weakest members of our group, and I knew that.

They should've been placed on separate teams with either Ian and Jim or me and Dave."

"Why? A good brain can get you out of a lot of bad situations."

"Yes, but so can brawn. If the teams had been more evenly matched, they would all be alive. In my heart of hearts, I believe that." A tear spilled down her cheek. "From the beginning I knew it was wrong, and I didn't do a damn thing to fix it. Something felt...off from the get-go, and I ignored it. Why did I let Ian talk me out of changing the groups?" She tugged her hand free, bunching it into an impotent fist. "Ian and Jim could've taken those guys, and I know Dave and I sure as hell would've tried." Closing her eyes, she took another deep breath. "She was so afraid, Hunter. I'm sure they all were, and I can't stand it. I can't stand knowing that."

He pulled her into a hug, and she held on as if her life depended on it. He recognized the burden she carried, the crushing weight of guilt that consumed and ate away at the soul until nothing remained but self-hate and regret. He didn't want that for her. "So you made them get on a plane and come to Yellowstone after they voiced their concerns and told you how uncomfortable they were with the arrangements?"

Morgan dashed at her tears as she shook her head. "Well, no, of course not. But—"

"None of this was your fault." He brushed the next tear away with his thumb as he cupped her cheeks in his hands. "I want you to hear me. Not one single part of what happened to your friends is a result of your actions. Don't take that on. Greed killed your team, not you."

"But—"

"I'm not finished. All of you could've come out here together. Nothing would've prevented the outcome. The only difference would be six dead bodies instead of three." He muttered a curse when she flinched. "What I'm trying to say is the people in on this mine aren't fucking around. If they know you've seen too much, consider yourself a dead man. There are no mercy rules out here."

She opened her mouth to speak as the water in the pot behind them boiled over. Starchy foam bubbled and hissed as it hit the flames. "Shoot." She broke free of his embrace and hurried over to their dinner. "I forgot about our shells and cheese. The pasta's going to be mush." She took the pot to the edge of the cave and poured the rest of the boiling water to the ground, came back, and added the cheese. Moments later, she handed him a bowl heaped with overcooked shells.

"Thanks." He sat across from her.

"They aren't going to be as good as they should be."

He blew on a spoonful of creamy cheese and soggy pasta and took a bite. "Tastes fine to me."

She pushed the food around in her bowl. "Do you think they'll find us if we stay here tonight?"

Apparently their conversation was finished. He would let it go for now. "No. We have a good enough lead. We should be fine. The rain helped us out again today. Any trail we left behind is virtually gone, and I haven't heard the damn air traffic for a while." He paused for another bite. "Tomorrow's going to be hell, though. The rocks will be slippery and the forest a mess, but we're on schedule even with our early stop. We'll probably be in Tower Junction by mid-afternoon."

"Good. I'm ready to be finished with this nightmare. I still haven't tracked a lynx. We'll have to call this trip a professional flop. When we get out of here, I think I'll try Maine again. Yellowstone and I need a break."

"So you're trying to tell me this isn't a typical assignment? Being chased and shot at, it's not all in a day's work?" He smiled.

"Maybe for you, but I prefer something a little less adventuresome." She scooped up a bite of pasta. "Are most of your assignments like this?"

He snorted out a laugh. "Hell, no. On my last assignment,

I spent two days avoiding my client's oversexed teenage daughter. She kept pinching my ass. I haven't been shot at since Afghanistan, and I can guarantee they weren't shooting at us with a Glock." As soon as he said it, his smile disappeared, and he stared down at his dinner. Where the hell had that come from? He'd never spoken of Afghanistan outside of the psychiatrist's office, and even then he'd only said what he'd had to say to get through the twelve mandated sessions.

"Your scar," Morgan said softly, "your on-the-job injury. You were shot while you were over there."

He looked at her, not answering. He wasn't going there. He wasn't bringing it all back, not even for her.

She hesitated and placed her hand over his. "It was—it was bad."

It wasn't a question; it didn't have to be. His eyes remained locked on hers. He saw the compassion and the comfort she offered, but he couldn't take it. Because it was Morgan, because she was different, he gave her what he could. "Yeah. It was bad—as bad as it gets." His stomach clenched as his pulse raced. He felt himself shutting down—a well-honed defense mechanism constructed to block out the images that could come out of nowhere and crush him. He broke contact and stood. "I'm going to finish cleaning up."

She nodded. "I'll wash the dishes."

○ઝ CHAPTER TWENTY-NINE ৪০

ORGAN WOKE IN THE DARK TO THE SOUND OF Hunter's erratic breathing. She reached above her head, groping for the lantern, and turned it on low, staring at his face and chest sheened with sweat in the dim light. She yanked back her covers, freeing herself from her sleeping bag, and placed her hand against his brow, fearful of fever, but he didn't feel overly warm.

Hunter mumbled something in his sleep, and she relaxed. He wasn't ill; he was dreaming. His body jerked as she felt the rapid hammer of his heart slam against his chest, and she brushed her fingers through his hair, wanting to rouse him from whatever hell his subconscious had dumped him into. "Hunter. Hunter, wake up. You're having a nightmare."

His hands fisted as he thrashed.

"Come on, Hunter." She rubbed his shoulder, swallowing a trickle of fear when she couldn't bring him around. "Hunter—"

"Jake! No, Jake!" He bolted upright, glancing around wildly while his breath heaved in and out. His wide eyes met hers, and he fell back against his sleeping bag, covering his face with his hands.

"It's okay," she said quietly, reaching out to soothe him. But she pulled back, wanting to give him his space.

"I'm all right," he said through his hands.

Was he trying to convince her or himself? "Can I get you anything? Water maybe?"

"No. I just need a minute."

"Okay." She put the water bottle by the lantern on his side, just in case he changed his mind, and got into her sleeping bag, turning over, trying to give him as much privacy as their situation allowed.

He sat up, and she turned back, needing to see for herself that he was okay. He swung his legs from the bed and crawled forward, unzipping the tent. His gaze met hers. "Stop looking at me like that. I said I'm fine, all right?"

She nodded.

Sighing, he closed his eyes. "I just need some air," he said more gently.

She nodded again, laying her head back against the small bubble formed by the mattress pad.

He let loose another long breath. "Sometimes I have nightmares about Afghanistan."

As much as she wanted to, she refrained from asking him questions.

He sat back on his sleeping bag. "They usually happen if I think about it too much."

"I asked you about it earlier. Did that trigger the dreams?"

He rubbed his fingers along his forehead. "I don't know. Maybe."

Horrified by the idea of causing his nightmares, she sat up. "I'm sorry. I didn't know it would upset you. I won't ask again." Taking his hand, she squeezed. "Why don't you go get some fresh air? Maybe you'll be able to rest after you clear your mind."

He reversed his palm so their fingers laced. "It's not your fault. They just sneak up from time to time."

Surprised by his gesture, she glanced down at their intertwining fingers and his large hand all but swallowing hers. She didn't know what to do for the suddenly vulnerable man sitting next to her. "Are you sure I can't get you something?

Sometimes a cup of tea helps me."

"No, thanks. I'm good." He rubbed his thumb over her knuckles, staring at her.

She gnawed her bottom lip as their gazes held. What did he want? She couldn't figure him out. Her first instinct was to hold and comfort, but he would only push her away.

He moved closer, until their knees bumped.

Her heart trembled as he brushed his thumb over her cheek and pressed his lips to hers, gently, tenderly. Need burned bright in his eyes as he moved in again.

She gripped his forearms, pulling him to her, deepening the kiss.

"I want to forget," he whispered.

Ready to give him whatever he would take, she nodded, skimming her lips along the bottom of his jaw and down his neck, tasting salt and Hunter.

He laid her down, bringing her mouth back to his as his callused hands slid down her arms.

She shivered from his touch, staring into his eyes, steeped in quiet passion as he cupped her breasts through the barrier of her clothing. She whimpered, already burning for him, wanting him to make her come alive.

As if he'd read her mind, Hunter lifted her, pulling off her shirt, and laid her back again. He trailed opened-mouth kisses down her neck and along the sides of her breasts.

She sighed, reveling in the tenderness passing between them, and bowed her back, offering him more to explore, wanting his mouth everywhere. She glided her palms down his waist and up to lay flat against his firm chest and strong heartbeat.

He journeyed down, leaving a lazy path of kisses, and tugged at her long johns until only her panties remained. He brushed his lips and hands along her legs, stopping at the skimpy V of black silk as he traced the lacy edges with his fingertips, dipping under fabric but never touching, never fulfilling.

Ready, throbbing, she gasped and moaned. "Hunter, I need... I need to—"

He silenced her with a kiss.

She grew hungry, eager for release, and dragged his hand to her center, pressing him against her, groaning in frustration when he pulled back to caress her breasts instead, only adding another layer to the flames. Frenzied, she tugged his mouth to hers, and her tongue dove deep, tangling with his. Lost in his taste, in the feel of his lips, in the thrill of his hard body pressing hers against the sleeping bag, she cried out, clutching at his shoulders when his fingers finally snuck beneath the lace and played her over the first violent peak.

He stroked and plundered, making her legs tremble, and she built again, erupting. Hunter swallowed moan after moan.

Wanting more, craving to feel him inside of her, she pulled off his shorts with unsteady hands.

He positioned himself over her and entered her slowly. Twin groans filled the tent.

He tortured them both with gentle thrusts, until her breath came in shuddering gasps. Tugs of ecstasy built deep in her belly, spreading, until they were too huge, too overwhelming. "Oh, God. Hunter." She tipped her head back, gripping his shoulders.

"Stay with me, Morgan."

Did she have a choice? She was with him. She was *his*. Throaty whimpers escaped her as she looked into his eyes. Unable to hold back any longer, the orgasm took her, stronger than before. Lost, undone, she clutched his ass, urging him on as he pumped faster and faster.

His breath shuddered out, growing harsh. Bracing himself on one arm, he used his other to scoop her hips high. With one last deep thrust, he emptied himself into her. He collapsed on top of her, his hot breath puffing against her neck, and rolled to his back, bringing her with him. "I'm always afraid I'm crushing you. You're so small."

"I'm small, but I'm not a wimp." She kissed him, smiling as her heart rate steadied. "I like when you're on top of me." She snagged his bottom lip between her teeth, tugging gently. "I like it better when you're in me."

He raised his eyebrow as his hand tightened against her lower back. "Keep talking like that and we'll get to it in just a second."

She traced his ear with her tongue and reached down, stroking him. "Promise?"

He groaned and rolled her to her back, plunging in again. "I never break a promise, Morgan."

She grinned. "Thank God."

Later, they lay together in his sleeping bag. Morgan stroked her hand along Hunter's arm, absently tracing his ornate cross tattoo. He glanced at her, and she stopped abruptly. "Sorry. Bad habit." She moved her hand to his chest, letting it rest there.

"I got the tattoo when I came back from Afghanistan."

"You don't have to tell me about it. It's okay."

He moved his fingers in lazy circles along her hip. "You want to know about the date."

"I don't want you to feel like you have to share. I know it's painful. I didn't the other night, but I do now."

"September 23, 2010, was the worst day of my life," he went on as if she hadn't spoken. "I don't think anything will ever be as bad." He steamed out a long breath and swallowed as the gentle drum of rain filled the cave.

She snuggled closer, letting him know he had her full attention.

"My men and I were heading out on a classified mission. We were off to bag Al-Qaeda's number three. Word came down through the chain that he was about to get away—again—so we went for it. We had four weeks left on our tour. We were going out in glory." He shook his head. "*God*, if I could go back and change it..." He scrubbed his hand over his face. "It was my job to plan the route. We had several options, but I chose the fastest, which was also the most dangerous. We couldn't let the fucker vanish into the mountains again." Bitterness spewed with his every word. "It was a bad call, but it was the one I made and will live with every day for the rest of my life. There were a thousand and one ways I could've done things differently, but I didn't." His voice grew strained as he stopped tracing lazy circles against her skin. "We were ambushed. Six of my men died and the bastard disappeared anyway."

"That's awful."

His restless hand relaxed and bunched on her hip as he blew out a long breath. "One of the men killed was my best friend, Jake. We were friends for so long, I can't remember not having him in my life." He paused again, swallowing hard. "I tried to save him. God, did I try, but his injuries were more than I could handle on the side of the road in the middle of fucking nowhere, so I sat there and watched him bleed to death."

"I'm so sorry, Hunter." She hugged him, trying to offer him comfort for something so much bigger than herself. She held him tight, attempting to imagine the horror he had lived through. Sitting up on her elbow, she stared down at him, brushing her hand through his hair as she remembered the tenderness that passed between them. He'd surprised her when he started sharing a part of his life with her. The pleasure of him finally opening up was quickly overshadowed by the tragedy he'd experienced. His story only made her love him more. It took courage to walk away from something like that and keep going, keep living.

He closed his eyes, and her finger roamed to the dimple in his chin. She wanted to hug this moment to her. There wouldn't be many more—when her body lay naked and warm, pressed against his. She slid his hair back from his forehead and pressed a kiss to his lips, wanting to savor one more minute before she turned off the lantern and let him sleep.

He opened his eyes, looking into hers.

She moved her hand to his cheek. "I thought you were resting."

"Not yet." He grabbed her wrist and kissed her palm. "Lay back down with me."

"I will, but first I want you to know you aren't to blame. What happened in Afghanistan wasn't your fault." As the words left her mouth, she saw the shutters come down over his eyes and felt the wall he put up between them so easily.

"Jake's daughter is growing up without a father, and his wife is a single mother. I am responsible for that. When you're in charge of a squad, it's your responsibility to get each and every soldier home to their families. I didn't."

She frowned. "That's not fair. You—"

"What's not fair is Jake watching his daughter come into the world and never getting a chance to hold her. What's not fair is Kylee will never know Jake. Sarah will never feel her husband's arms around her again."

"I thought you told me earlier that what happened to my team wasn't my fault. How is this any different?"

"It's completely different. My men didn't have a choice. They had to follow my orders, and I messed up. I don't want to talk about this anymore. Let it go."

Tears welled in her eyes as she looked away, nodding, wanting to understand.

He reached over and turned out the lantern. As he settled himself in his bed, his body no longer touched hers.

Hurt and desperately sad for him, she started toward her own sleeping bag, understanding that what they'd shared during the last hour was over.

He hooked an arm around her waist. "Where are you going?"

"I—I just figured you wanted your space."

"When I want space, I'll let you know." He pulled her back against his side.

She stared into the dark, resting her head on his shoulder, surprised yet again as he settled his arm around her waist and his free hand covered hers against his heart. Their fingers laced and she drifted off to sleep, content in Hunter's arms.

⚛ CHAPTER THIRTY ⚛

BY MID-AFTERNOON THE NEXT DAY, MORGAN AND Hunter made it to Tower Junction, Wyoming, a small tourist stop-off within Yellowstone's boundaries. Hiding deep among the trees on the outskirts of town, Hunter scrutinized the sea of visitors strolling about. He had no idea who pursued them, but the tingle along his spine and lead ball weighing heavy in his stomach told him that among the groups of happy, chattering families, people watched, eager to take him and Morgan out. They were a day early, and he had no way of contacting The Bureau or the agent who was supposed to get them the hell out of there. He needed to call Ethan, but he didn't dare use his or Morgan's cell phones.

He peered through his binoculars, keeping his eye on the small twelve-room motel, general store, and scenic center across the street from where he and Morgan hid. The three buildings were the area's main attractions. If someone waited—and he was sure they did—they wouldn't be far.

Morgan read a book while she lay on her mattress pad, resting her head on his lap. "The worst part of this whole thing is that there are perfectly comfortable motel rooms right across the way, and we're lying on the ground in a pile of trees being blinded by the sun."

He looked down at her, grinning. "One of us is lying down. The other is actually working. If you were sitting up, the sun wouldn't be in your eyes. It isn't bothering me."

Rolling her eyes, she mimicked him in a snarky tone.

He drilled his finger into her side, making her squirm and laugh.

"Okay, I'm sorry," she said, grabbing his hand, attempting to hold him off.

"That's better." Chuckling, he peered through his binoculars again as a silver Buick Lacrosse pulled into the motel parking lot. He came to attention when a man emerged from the car in an outfit too upscale for a day of fun at Yellowstone. The tall, fifty-something with black hair going gray at the temples wore Armani slacks and a polo shirt with thousand-dollar leather shoes.

"Unless you have something specific for me to do—"

"Hold up, hold up," he interrupted. "I think we might have something here."

The man looked around smiling as a navy blue Escalade pulled into the parking spot next to his. A man dressed similarly in black slacks and a white button-down nodded as he stepped from his vehicle. The men shook hands, talked, and turned toward the mountains. The stranger with the Buick gestured to something as he spoke. Hunter followed his hand as he pointed toward a wooded area far off in the distance.

"Can I see? I want to see." Morgan grabbed for the binoculars.

"Stop." Hunter moved, evading her hand. "I'm trying to watch a couple of guys who certainly don't fit the part of tourist."

"Maybe one of them is the agent from The Bureau." She tried for the binoculars again. "Just let me look for a second." She pushed herself up.

He handed them over, and she peeked through the lenses. "Who am I looking at?"

"Straight ahead. Twelve o'clock. The guys that look like they missed the turn for the country club."

A grin spread across her lips. "Pretty accurate description." Still watching, she shook her head. "I don't recognize—wait." Sitting up taller, she pushed forward through the trees. "The man standing closest to the silver car seems familiar. If he would turn just a little bit." As if on cue, he did. "It's Dean."

He yanked the binoculars back, peering through them again. "Who's Dean?"

"You know, Dean Jenkins, the guy we talked to on the phone the other night. What in the world is he doing here?"

Hunter didn't like it. It didn't sit right. He watched the men get back into their vehicles, reverse from their parking spots, and drive off through the chaos of visitors.

"I guess my dad sent him to pick us up. I honestly thought he would've come himself."

"Dean just left."

"What?" She yanked the binoculars back. "How can he just leave?"

"We're not supposed to be here until tomorrow." He needed to get to a phone and talk to Ethan—now.

"Oh, well, that makes sense."

Hunter put the binoculars in his pack. "We have to get out of here and find a phone."

"How are we going to do that and stay hidden?"

"I'm not sure yet, but sitting here isn't solving the problem."

He waited for Morgan to roll up her cushion. They put on their packs and walked away from the crowds, deeper into the trees beyond. A mile into the hike, they came upon a campground. Hunter spotted an older couple sitting outside their mid-sized RV, playing a round of Cribbage. A cell phone lay next to the woman's elbow on the card table. Hunter walked toward them. "Play along."

"What are you going to do?"

"Get us that cell phone." He picked up a dingy metal o-ring that had fallen from someone's camping gear long ago. "Put this on your ring finger."

She frowned. "Why?"

"Just do it," he said through his teeth, smiling as they moved closer to the elderly couple. He watched for a re-action, wondering if the police had shown up with flyers warning guests about the "dangerous criminals." When the couple only smiled, he began the show, glancing at Morgan's hand, making sure she put the ring in place. He slung his arm around her, bringing her toward him. "Good afternoon, folks."

The couple set their cards down. "Good afternoon to you, young man," the woman with the mop of curly gray hair said.

"Beautiful day to be camping," Hunter commented while he casually scanned their surroundings, looking at the other RVs parked close by.

"Sure is." The man with more wrinkles than hair and a hawk-like nose gave Morgan a friendly wink.

Hunter nudged her.

Morgan cleared her throat and flashed her knock 'em dead smile.

The elderly gentleman sat up straighter.

"We sure are sorry to bother you, but my fiancé and I broke down about a half-mile back."

Morgan's eyes widened as she slid Hunter a glance.

"Oh, now that's a shame. Is there anything we can do to help?"

Hunter added more charm to his smile. "Actually, if I could use your cell phone to call my brother that would be great. I was so nervous trying to plan the perfect romantic getaway, I forgot mine." He shook his head. "I was a wreck the whole drive here, trying to think of just the right way to propose. I was worrying myself sick—would she say yes? What would I do if she said no..." He shrugged, shaking his head again with a smile. "Thank goodness she put me out of my misery and said yes." He hugged Morgan tighter against him.

The older woman's eyes softened. "Now, Earl, isn't that just the sweetest thing you ever did hear?"

"Sure is, Ida, sure is. Of course you can use our phone, son."

The woman's gaze wandered to Morgan's hand. "Can I see your ring, honey?"

Morgan looked at Hunter.

"Go ahead, sweetie. Show them your ring." Hunter gave her a small shove forward.

Morgan hesitated and held out her hand.

The woman's eyes dimmed as she stared at the tarnished piece of metal.

"Pretty awful, huh?" Hunter grinned. "I forgot the ring too. Can you believe it? I planned the trip to propose, and I forgot the ring. I found that on the road near the campsite we stayed at. I hoped it would be good enough until we got home. It's the feelings behind the symbol that count, right?" He gave Morgan a quick but intimate kiss.

The older woman smiled as her eyes misted. "That's right, honey." She directed her attention to Morgan. "I see you were smart enough to say yes, even though you have a hunk of ugly metal around your finger."

Morgan smiled at Ida and looked at Hunter. "I sure was. It wouldn't have mattered if he hadn't had anything to give me. This made the moment all the more romantic." She glanced down at the dull metal, then at Hunter again. "When you find someone amazing, you grab them up before they get away." She kissed him.

He felt a jolt that shook him to his core and grabbed her arm in reflex, dropping it as he stared in Morgan's warm, smiling eyes, remembering Jake saying the same thing moments before he married Sarah. *If you're smart, when you find someone amazing, you'll grab her up before she gets away. That's my advice to you, man.*

"Aren't you a smart little thing?" Ida spoke again. "He's a handsome one, honey. Good for you." She winked.

Morgan struggled with a smile for the older woman as she glanced back at Hunter. Questions replaced the warmth in her eyes.

"Here's the phone, young man. You call your brother." Ida dropped the phone in Hunter's hand. "Your fiancé and I are going to go in and have a nice glass of iced tea."

"Oh, I really shouldn't. I don't want to put you out."

"It's no trouble, dear. You look like you could use something cool to drink, and we don't get a lot of company around here."

Ida held out her wrinkly hand, and Morgan took it.

While Ida and Morgan drank iced tea, Hunter continued the show for Earl. "I can't tell you how much I appreciate this."

"Not a problem, son. Go ahead and call your brother. Get your beautiful bride-to-be out of here."

Hunter gave Earl a nod and smile as he walked away while Morgan's words still buzzed through his mind. He clenched his jaw as he thought of the deep, intimate look she'd given him. It was as if she'd actually meant what she said to Ida. As quickly as he thought it, he dismissed the whole thing. He was being stupid. She'd gotten caught up in her role, trying to sell it to the older couple. But that didn't make him feel any better. It only troubled him more that a large part of him agreed with everything she and Jake had said. Morgan was amazing, and in a matter of days, she would slip away from him.

The Cribbage board fell to the ground with a hard smack, jarring Hunter from his thoughts. He stepped forward as Earl bent slowly to pick it up. Hunter winced as every bone in the old man's body popped and cracked with the effort.

"I've got it, son. Don't you worry. Go ahead and make your call."

"Only if you're sure, Mr... I never caught your last name."

"Bester." Earl grabbed hold of the board and stood as slowly as he'd bent forward. "Not quite as fast as I used to be."

"Looks like you're doing just fine." Hunter put his nagging thoughts away. They were pointless, and he had a job to do. He punched in Ethan's number and got him on the second ring. "Ethan, it's Phillip." He didn't want to use his real name in front of Mr. Bester.

"Where the hell are you? I've been going crazy trying to track you down."

The reception was shoddy at best. "Speak up. We have a bad connection. We had a little breakdown in Tower Junction, Wyoming." He casually walked farther away from Earl.

"Obviously you can't talk, so I will. You sure know how to get yourself into a hell of a mess, Phillips."

"Brother, you're telling me."

"Stanley Taylor is at Reagan International right now. He's due to take off in an hour. He's going ape shit trying to find you and Morgan."

"Good. When is he supposed to arrive?"

"I'm not sure of an exact time, but he's landing in Bozeman later tonight."

Hunter walked toward the rear wheels of the RV, lowering his voice. "Why the hell did he send Dean if he's coming himself?"

"Dean's there? You saw him?"

"Yes. At a crap motel here in Tower Junction. He was talking to some guy. He left with him thirty minutes ago. Did he tell Stanley about the mine?"

"What mine? What are you talking about?"

"Son of a bitch. You don't know?" Running his hand through his hair, he blew out a long breath. "Morgan and I found an illegal mine in the northern part of the park, on the Slough River. Morgan's team found it too. That's why they're dead."

"*What?*"

"I did a little digging around at the station and happened upon one of the team member's journal. Ranger Robert is dirty. I'm not sure about the kid, but I know Robert and those two bastard cops I took out killed Morgan's team."

"Holy shit, man. This is insane. Stanley's been having a hell of a time clearing your name. The boys in blue have been saying you went nuts and just started shooting. Somehow they've made you, Phillips. They know everything about you. They—they brought up your past, man, your issues after Jake—

"Goddammit." The slow burn of rage started deep in his stomach. "That's fucking bullshit."

"Of course it is."

The absolute and unquestionable faith he heard in Ethan's voice was a balm over raw wounds. He unclenched his fist, trying to concentrate on his job—getting him and Morgan the fuck out of Wyoming. "Are Morgan and I clear?"

"You have been since yesterday. Stanley pulled several strings at the Washington level to get the APB called off the two of you. You aren't going to like it, but he threw your military career, not to mention your gold star, in the faces of the local boys around—"

"How the hell does he know about that?" Hunter closed his eyes, sighing. He'd been awarded medals and commendations—a slew of them—but as far as he was concerned, he hadn't earned a damn one of them. Half of his group had gone home in caskets because of the decisions he'd made. He could hardly take credit for valor, and he sure as hell wasn't anyone's hero. His so-called triumphs were a slap in the face to six families who went through each day without their loved ones. His "box of achievements" lay buried at the bottom of his closet.

"His mother was a senator for fifteen years, and he's an incredibly wealthy and powerful man in his own right. I imagine he can find out whatever the hell he wants."

Hunter grunted his agreement.

"Anyway, back to what I was saying. I think the cops' stories weren't quite ringing true to at least someone in the department, especially since Robert went missing shortly after he was checked over for injuries."

"Bastard."

"If it makes you feel any better, you broke two of his ribs."

"Well, I guess that's something."

"They haven't been able to track him down, so watch your back."

"Noted. I'm going to try to get Morgan and me into the crap motel I saw Dean parked in front of for the night. I think it's our safest option at this point. It'll be easier to keep her safe inside four walls versus the great outdoors." He glanced over his shoulder, making certain no one was listening. Mr. Bester sat in his lawn chair, pinching deadheads from pansies in a small flowerpot. "If Robert's roaming free, he's close by. I'm sure he's figured out I have the journal by now. He'll want it back. When the dominoes start to fall, that's what's going to put him away for killing Morgan's team." He scanned the surrounding trees as he spoke. "You're going to want to get ahold of Stanley and fill him in on all of this. Have him call the state boys here in Wyoming and Montana. Have him tell more than one big guy. It's hard to say who's on the up and up right about now."

"I was planning on taking care of that after we finish."

"He'll want to be careful when he gets here. These ass-holes aren't fucking around. He'll be in as much danger as Morgan and I are once he breaks this open. You might want to suggest security—for Ilene too."

"I'll call in a favor and get a team in place within the hour."

"Good. I want Stanley to stay in Bozeman tonight. He'll be more easily protected there. He won't be in until late, and I want to do this in the daylight. I know he wants to see Morgan, but I don't want him coming to our motel tonight. If anyone knocks on our door in the next twenty-four hours, I'll be shooting first and asking questions later." His hand instinctively went to his weapon under his shirt before he dropped it to his side.

Mr. Bester stood, glancing his way.

Hunter knew he needed to hurry. His conversation with Ethan was taking longer than a call home for help should. He smiled and rolled his eyes, pointing to the phone as if Ethan kept him. He held up his finger, signaling for one more minute and spoke, giving Ethan the code that he wasn't able to speak freely. "The reception's no good."

"Well, make it good, Phillips. I have to catch Stanley before he leaves."

Ida stood behind the screen door and asked Earl to join her and their lovely guest for a plate of cookies.

When the door closed behind Earl, Hunter continued. "The reception just cleared. I want Stanley to meet us tomorrow at one thirty, right here at the motel. I want a four-car detail—make them SUVs. Stanley is to be placed in the second vehicle, where Morgan and I will meet him. I don't want him getting out. We'll exit the park west from Tower Junction and go north, which will take us directly to Bozeman."

Ethan's fingers tapped against computer keys in the background. "I'm pulling up the map. It looks like you'll be leaving on Grand Loop Road where you'll hit Eighty-Nine. I'll have the team come in from the northeast so they don't have to turn around. It'll be a direct exit. I'll scan the maps for vulnerable areas tonight and make sure the team you'll be working with is aware of them just in case I can't talk to you again until all of this is over."

"Fine. Sounds good. Once we get to Bozeman, we'll board the Taylors' plane. I'll stay with Stanley and Morgan in DC until we know Robert and Dean are apprehended. They have the most to lose right now. I think the threat to the Taylor family will cease when they're taken care of." Hunter peeked into the RV, frowning as Morgan sat at the miniature table, sipping tea with her hosts. Her hair was damp, and she'd changed her clothes.

"If Robert and Dean are caught before our scheduled departure tomorrow, I still want the detail to pick us up. We'll proceed exactly the same way, but I'll leave for LA after I put Morgan and Stanley on their plane."

The rapid tap of fingers against keys echoed in his ear again. He knew Ethan was as itchy to end their conversation as he was.

"Okay, Phillips. I'll get everything taken care of on this end. Stanley will meet you and Morgan at one thirty with a four-car detail, two guards per vehicle entering from the northwest. You'll exit the park via the north entrance and head to Bozeman from there."

"Sounds about right to me. I have to go."

"I'll talk to you soon."

CHAPTER THIRTY-ONE

HUNTER AND MORGAN WALKED AWAY FROM THE Besters, smiling and waving while the older couple did the same from the door of their RV. "Thank you again, Mr. and Mrs. Bester. We appreciate everything," Morgan said.

"Not a problem, dear, not a problem. You enjoy that food before it gets cold." Ida gestured to the Wal-Mart bag dangling from Morgan's arm, heavy with Tupperware containing chicken and dumplings. "You just send the bowl back to the address I gave you. Maybe you can send me a wedding picture too."

"We can definitely do that." With a last wave, Morgan turned away, and her smile disappeared. She hated lying to Ida and Earl. The deception was all the more upsetting because she wanted the lies to be the truth. The act was supposed to have ended after Hunter's phone call, but when he knocked on the screen door of the RV and attempted to hand Earl a twenty for the trouble, Mrs. Bester had scolded him for "such nonsense" and insisted he come in for a glass of iced tea and cookies.

With little choice, he'd joined Morgan around the tiny table, taking her hand and running his thumb over her knuckles, bumping the ugly piece of metal on her finger while the Besters made conversation. Morgan had let herself pretend, just for a minute, that the farce was real.

The charade ended when they stepped from the small camper. Now she felt depressed and empty, but this was their reality. Everything would be over soon. Before long, she and Hunter would go their separate ways.

"You take care of your fiancé, Phillip," Mrs. Bester called out.

Hunter put his arm around Morgan and turned, grinning, giving Mrs. Bester a thumbs-up.

Mrs. Bester's tinkle of laughter followed them into the trees. Hunter's smile vanished as he scanned the path they walked. It would only be a matter of time before Robert made his move. Tall pines scattered the forest, allowing large patches of deep blue sky through the skimpy canopy. The lack of cover finally worked to their advantage. Robert wouldn't be able to surprise them now. Satisfied that they were safe for the moment, Hunter relaxed fractionally and glanced at Morgan. She looked miserable. "What's wrong?"

She stared down at the path. "Nothing."

Bullshit. But he kept his thoughts to himself, knowing she would spill it sooner or later.

She huffed out a breath. "I didn't like lying to the Besters. They were so kind to us. They gave us a meal and drinks and let us borrow their phone. We lied to them."

"We needed the phone, and I couldn't be sure they would let us use it. I went with sappy love crap to be on the safe side. No one can resist a love story."

"We could've just asked."

"Yeah, we could have, but they might've said no. If two hikers came up to you out of the blue and said, 'Hey, can we use your phone,' would you let them?"

"It would depend on the circumstances."

"Exactly." He gave her a gentle bump to her side with his

elbow. "I just upped our odds of getting the right answer."

"I guess, but I still didn't like it." Her eyes stayed on the path in front of them.

"It was that or steal, and I didn't want to do that. They're old and traveling. It all worked out in the end, right? I spoke to Ethan, and the Besters still have their phone."

She made a sound of agreement in her throat.

He hated seeing her so unhappy. "I have a surprise for you."

She glanced up. "Oh yeah?" Intrigue sharpened her eyes, replacing the sadness.

"We're going to see if we can get a room in that little hole-in-the-wall motel."

She beamed, her green eyes brightening. "Really?"

He couldn't help but grin back. "Really."

She grabbed him in a hug, giving him a quick, enthusiastic kiss. "This is the best day ever—a shower at the Besters, a real meal, *and* a bed." She did a cute little boogie.

He chuckled and pulled her against him, pressing his lips to hers. He eased back, staring into her eyes.

She smiled.

Caught up in her beauty and the confusing mix of longing and fear she made him feel, he closed the distance, kissing her long and sweet. His tongue slid against hers as she rose on her tiptoes, wrapping her arms around his neck. He settled his hands on her small waist and hooked his thumbs through her belt loops. Where did this *need* come from? He thought back to what she had said by the Besters' RV, realizing he didn't know how he was going to let her go when this was over. Resting his forehead against hers, he sighed. "We need to keep moving."

"Can we stop by the general store and see if they have ice cream? If they have double-chocolate chunk, this day has the potential to go down in the "best day ever" history books."

Morgan looked at him with such hope in her eyes, he

would have walked through a landmine to get her the damn ice cream. "Yeah, we can see if they have chocolate chunk ice cream."

"You're turning into such a softie, Hunter." She poked him in the stomach as they started walking again.

They went to the well-stocked general store and found a pint of chocolate chunk ice cream. While Morgan paid, Hunter blocked her body and kept his eyes on the plated glass door, scanning the tourists walking by, waiting for someone to make their move. When nothing happened, they walked the dozen steps across the parking lot to the Tower Motel lobby.

Hunter pulled open the door, letting Morgan in before him as they stepped into a haze of cigarette smoke choking the air. Twangy country music belched from the ancient radio on a lopsided shelf that had been new decades before he'd been born.

Morgan wrinkled her nose as their eyes met and smiled as she shrugged, giving him the go-ahead to proceed.

He plucked two fifties from his wallet and placed them on the scarred, wooden countertop next to one of the several overflowing ashtrays. The heavyset woman with shocking orange hair didn't bother to look up from her book.

Morgan cleared her throat. "Um, excuse me—"

"Gerdie, do you have a room?" Hunter asked, cutting Morgan off as he read the attendant's nametag. Nice wouldn't get them anywhere with this woman.

Gerdie tore her eyes from the trashy novel with a half-dressed man on the cover, snapping her gum. "One left."

"We'll take it. Two nights."

Gerdie's black, painted-on eyebrow rose high as she looked Morgan up and down, naked envy shining bright. With a sneer, she gave them their total. "Sixty-five bucks."

Hunter slid the money forward. "I know customer service is your top priority around here, but we don't want you knocking on our door with fresh towels and chocolates for the pillows in the morning."

The attendant glared as she made change.

"We don't want to be disturbed." He grabbed Morgan's ass.

Gerdie's overshadowed eyes widened.

"We'll be very, *very* busy." He took the keys from Gerdie's limp hand, barely holding back a grin as they made their way out the door.

Morgan glanced over her shoulder. "You're looking awfully pleased with yourself. What was that for?"

"I thought I'd knock Gerdie down a peg. She was rude."

Morgan snorted out a laugh. "Did you see the look on her face when you grabbed me? I thought her eyes were going to pop out of her head."

He chuckled. "Yeah, it was pretty fun—on both counts."

She rolled her eyes. "I can only imagine. But seriously, why did you do that?"

"My method may've been crude, but I don't want anyone knocking on our door for the next twenty-four hours. I made that clear to Ethan, and I put it into terms Gerdie would understand. If someone knocks, I'll know we didn't invite them." He watched some of the lightness leave Morgan's eyes. "Hey, relax. It'll be a hell of a lot easier for me to keep you safe in a small room versus outside. We've done pretty well so far, right?"

She nodded.

He slid the key in the lock and opened the door. After a visual sweep, he had Morgan come in. "I know it's overkill, but let me check it out." He gave the room a quick search, checking behind the shower curtain and under the beds. Finally, he nodded his okay.

She set down her pack.

He walked back to the door, securing the bolt and snapping the curtains closed as he stood to the side of the glass, out of a potential bullet's path. Peering through the small slit he left in the grimy fabric, he scanned the visitors meandering about in the fading daylight. The skittering along his spine warned him danger still loomed close. He scrutinized the tourists, looking for the one that didn't belong, but he didn't see anyone in particular that stood out. His gut told him whoever wanted them dead was too smart for such a rookie mistake. With nothing else to do but wait for morning, he closed the curtain and turned to face Morgan.

☙ CHAPTER THIRTY-TWO ❧

MORGAN GLANCED AROUND AT THE THREADBARE carpet, the over-washed purple bedspread, and the tacky green lamp on the bedside table and almost wept with joy. "*Look* at this place. It's like a palace. I haven't been this excited about a room since the team and I were in Washington. We slept three to a bed and the bathroom was filthy, but we didn't care after spending a month in the rain."

Hunter looked around with less enthusiasm. "From a security standpoint, I can't complain too much. The bathroom wall blocks the bed from the window, and the deadbolt seems secure." He shrugged.

She pulled the cabinet doors open on the green monstrosity of a TV stand, and Hunter's eyes brightened considerably.

"Well, now we're on to something." He wandered over, touching the small television. "Nice. It's fairly new, and supposedly we have cable. If they have Sports Center, I'll second your palace comment. Now, where's the guide?" He pulled open drawers, stopping next to the phone. "I should call Ethan." He picked up the receiver and unscrewed the bottom piece, then replaced it before punching in the number.

Seconds later, Morgan heard him give Ethan the phone number for the room.

He hung up and looked at her. "Since I'm the only one

covered in dirt around here, I'm going to grab a quick shower. I still can't figure out how you wormed your way into the Besters'."

She smiled. "Women stick together. While we were sipping iced tea, I just happened to mention that it had been days since I'd had a real shower. She insisted I use theirs. It went blissfully well from there. Hurry with yours. I can smell the food, and my ice cream's going to be liquid at this point."

"I'll be quick. Just don't open the door—not for anyone or anything." He disappeared into the bathroom.

"Thanks, Dad, for the refresher on basic safety tips."

He stuck his hand through the doorway, giving her the finger.

She laughed.

The shower spray sputtered and finally hissed to life as her stomach growled. She took their bowls and utensils from her pack and grabbed a change of clothes, pulling on her black tank top and white boxers. Finally comfortable, she turned on the TV and slid off the piece of metal she'd carried around on her finger all afternoon. She placed it on the side table, staring at it, wishing it could be what it never would be.

Minutes later, Hunter emerged from the bathroom wearing his black mesh shorts and smelling like motel soap. He put his gun on the table closest to his side of the bed and walked to the Tupperware. "Let's eat. I'm starving." He scooped two big bowls of chicken and dumplings and handed them off, joining Morgan on the bed, resting on the pillows pushed against the wall. Sports Center ran through its highlights for the day. "Hey, Sports Center. Thanks."

"You're welcome." She took a bite of chicken in rich, gravy-like broth and closed her eyes, moaning. "Oh, Mrs. Bester, you're the best."

He winged his eyebrow in the air as he looked at her. "You're shattering my ego here. I don't think you get that excited for me." He took a bite. "Oh my *God*, Mrs. Bester. You *are* the best."

They looked at each other and grinned.

"I really do feel bad that we won't have a picture to send along with the Tupperware," she said.

Hunter handed her his bowl and crawled to the edge of the bed, rifling through his pack, pulling out his cell phone. "What are you doing? We can't use that."

"I know. Put the bowls down on the side table and sit close."

Confused, she set down the bowls and glanced over as he readied the phone. "Oh, a picture. Nice." She pushed herself closer his side and waited for him to tell her to smile.

"Smile and thank Mrs. Bester for the best chicken and dumplings ever." He followed up his statement with an obnoxious sex moan.

She stared at him, wide-eyed, and laughed.

He grinned and pressed the button, freezing the moment.

"Nice, but I don't think that's going to work." He scrutinized the picture, then held up the phone again. "Okay. Serious one now." He put his free arm around her, hugging her close as she rested her head on his shoulder and placed her hand on his chest. He laid his cheek against her hair, and they smiled as he pressed the button again. They examined the results. "That's the one we'll send with the Tupperware. I'll e-mail it to you when we're back in civilization."

"Sounds good." She moved to grab their food as he caught her arm.

"Wait. One more." He held up the phone and pressed his lips to hers.

She responded to the warmth of his mouth and closed her eyes as the phone clicked.

He drew away and shut the phone, throwing it toward his pack without glancing at the picture they made. "Now, back to those dumplings."

Shaken by the moment, she turned for the bowls. Hunter was a completely different person when he was relaxed. He was funny and sweet. He kept showing her small pieces of himself, making her fall deeper and deeper in love.

"Hey. Earth to Morgan." He gently tugged on her hair, winking. "I'm hungry over here."

"Oh, yeah. Sorry." Shaking her head, she handed him his bowl and sat back against her pillow, taking another bite of the stew she no longer wanted. "So, what did Ethan say when you talked to him?"

"That your father will be here to pick us up tomorrow."

She frowned. "I thought Dean was here for that."

He stared into her eyes.

She sighed, fully understanding his silence. "He's part of all of this too?" She shook her head. "There has to be a mistake. He's one of my dad's closest friends. I grew up with his kids. We go to their house every year for New Year's Eve."

"I don't think it's a mistake. He never told your father about the mine."

"Maybe he forgot. Maybe he..." She stopped when Hunter's eyebrows winged up, knowing she sounded ridiculous. "He tried to convince me to stay in DC, and he threatened to pull the funding for the project."

"I'm sorry, Morgan." He brushed his hand down her hair.

"There's more. Robert took off after our little showdown. They haven't been able to find him. I think he's the biggest threat to you. He has the most to lose if you survive."

She stared at the ugly purple bedspread, struggling to take it all in. "When will my dad come for us?"

"We'll meet him at one thirty. He'll arrive in a four-car detail. We'll head to the airport from here."

"Why can't he come tonight?" As she asked, looking into Hunter's eyes, she was glad he wouldn't come until tomorrow. Everything would be different when they got back to DC.

"It's too dangerous. He's going to blow this whole operation wide open. He's in just as much danger as you are, and he won't be landing until late. It's better for him to stay in

Bozeman. I want to be able see our surroundings when we head out."

"No." Fear rushed through her, and she stood. "I don't want him having any part in this. He should stay home with my mother."

"He's already on his way."

"Then who's with my mother?" she demanded as her worry compounded.

"Whoa, Morgan." Hunter stood. "Everything's all right." He pulled her close, settling his hands on her shoulders. "Ethan's taking care of this. When I talked to him, he was setting up a detail for your parents."

"But Ethan's in LA."

"He knows people all over the place. Ethan Cooke Security is known worldwide." He slid his fingers along her skin. "Your parents are going to be just fine. Ethan's setting up our detail for tomorrow. Let him do his job, your father too. It'll all be over soon. I bet the police are out making arrests as we speak."

"You're right—I know you are, but they're my parents. I don't know what I would do if something happened to them."

"Try not to worry. They've been placed under excellent protection, that I can promise you."

"All right. I need a minute." She walked to the bathroom and turned on the faucet, splashing cool water on her face, trying to remember that Hunter never broke a promise.

———◆———

The phone rang, and the water shut off in the sink. Hunter met Morgan's gaze as she walked out of the bathroom holding a hand towel. He picked up the receiver, placing it up to his ear, waiting.

"It's Ethan. You there, Phillips?"

"Yeah, I'm here. "

"Stanley called. You can relax. They're breaking up the

mine as we speak. They're running a raid on some ranch north of where you are. They've apprehended Dean and Robert."

"Good." He sighed his relief. "That's good."

"We'll keep the security detail intact for tomorrow, just to play it safe."

"Four cars to Bozeman," he agreed.

"Your crew landed with Stanley ten minutes ago. I was lucky to get the best of the best to head up the team on short notice—used to be Secret Service."

"What's his name?"

"Baker."

"Baker. Got it. I still want Stanley to stay put. It's safest until we get them on a plane. You can book my flight for LA—late afternoon works."

"Your ticket will be waiting. We'll grab a beer when you get back."

"Sounds good. I'll see you tomorrow." He hung up and walked over to Morgan. "That was Ethan. It's over. Finished. Your father called everything in. It's happening fast. The police just ran a raid at a ranch north of the mine. They found Dean and Robert. You and your dad will be on a plane back to DC tomorrow afternoon. You'll be able to put all of this behind you." He kissed her forehead and hugged her, staring at the dingy wall for several seconds as his words sank in. This was it. Tonight was it. He looked at Morgan, knowing she was thinking the same thing.

A sense of urgency fell over him as he held her gaze and captured her mouth. He walked her backwards, lifting her tank top over her head, and pulled her boxers down as she bumped into the bed. His breath rushed in and out in steamy torrents, mingling with hers as she stood in her flossy white panties. He flicked his wrist, sending the scrap of silk to the floor, and pulled her legs out from under her.

She landed with a bounce and a gasp, and his tongue was in her heat before she exhaled. She let out a long, loud cry, coming instantly. He used his fingers and his mouth, making her legs tremble as she called out to him mindlessly. He crawled forward, lying on top of her, and they rolled, reversing positions.

Morgan straddled him—all flash, all fire—kissing him as her hands went wild on his body, touching, exploring. She moved her lips to his neck, his chest, leaving opened-mouth kisses down his stomach. Her soft breasts rubbed against his skin with every frenzied movement, making him groan and crave more. She grasped him in her hand, playing him as she stared into his eyes. Her mouth replaced her busy hand, and he threw his head back, his breath tearing from his lungs as he fisted his hands in her hair.

"Morgan," he hissed out as she sent him to the edge, driving him crazy with her skillful tongue.

She journeyed up, capturing his lips as she straddled him, taking him into her silky depths. She gasped as he let loose a rumble in his throat, and she rode him hard and fast, the scent of her hair surrounding him as her soft brown locks cascaded around his face.

The bold green of her eyes captivated him. He was lost in her rhythm, her beauty. He dug his fingers into her hips as his breath came in ragged snatches.

She grasped his hands and laced their fingers, pulling them above his head—like he'd done to her the first time they were together.

With their faces close and their eyes locked, she moaned, arching her back and tensing, tightening around him. She cried out, coming, smiling her triumph.

"Morgan. Morgan," he choked out, panting as he jerked his hips, filling her.

She collapsed to his chest, and their hearts beat together.

He wrapped his arms around her, staring at the ceiling. It had never been like this. He'd had stellar sex before, but this was several notches into indescribable.

Moments later, Morgan sat up on her elbows, looking

down. She kissed him. "How was that? Better than Mrs. Bester's dumplings?"

He smiled. "What dumplings?"

"Right answer." She kissed him again. "I was starting to feel jealous of dough and gravy. I need a serious drink of water." She climbed off of him. "Want one?"

"Sure." Grinning, he watched her firm, sexy body disappear around the corner.

She turned on the faucet and filled two cups, then walked back, one already half empty by the time she reached the bed. "Here you go."

"Thanks."

Her cheeks were still rosy as she pulled back the covers and crawled in on her side. "It feels so *good* to be in a bed."

He handed her his cup and slid under the blankets, looking at her. "Are you tired?"

"Not really. Maybe there's a movie on." She picked up the remote and started flipping through the channels.

He playfully pounced on top of her, pulling the remote from her hand.

She laughed. "What are you doing?"

"I think it's important for you to know that I'm a very competitive person. I feel like I was outdone a few minutes ago. It's vital that I always come out on top." He kissed her. "Let me rephrase that and say it's only vital that I come out on top competitively."

She grinned, pressing her finger into the cleft of his chin. "I see."

What started in fun ended with Morgan lying under him, trembling and gasping for air. "You win. You're the reigning champion of amazing sex moves."

Hunter smiled. "Just remember that."

She lay pressed against him until they slept. They woke throughout the night, coming together over and over. The pearly light of dawn crept through the corner of the drawn drapes before fatigue took them under.

☙ CHAPTER THIRTY-THREE ❧

MORGAN ROLLED OVER WHEN HUNTER SWORE.
"Morgan, get up. We slept in."
Yawning, she rubbed her eyes. "What time is it?"
"Eleven-thirty."
"*What?*" She shot up in the bed. "I've never slept this late. Ever."

Hunter, sleepy-eyed and smiling, skimmed his fingers down her arm. "If you don't go to bed until sunrise, you sleep in. That's how it works."

"Ah, I see. Well, it sounds like you've had a lot of practice staying up till dawn." She tried playing things light as she pulled the covers back, but his cocky comment reminded her she was nothing special in the eyes of Hunter Phillips. There had been women before her, and there would be plenty after. She stood and winced, her well-used muscles protesting.

"Hey, wait a minute." He snagged her by the wrist and pulled her back down. "I didn't mean anything by that."

Let it go, Morgan. Just get in the shower and let it go.
"Yeah, I know." She briefly met his gaze, then stared down at the wrinkled sheets.

"Hey." He skimmed his thumb along her jaw and lifted her chin until their eyes met. "I've been up until dawn a few times before, but it's never been like this. It's never meant anything. I—I care about you, Morgan. You mean some-thing to me. You mean a lot."

And that was the problem. She loved and he cared. Her stomach clenched with the pain. "I know." Because she knew he gave her all he could, she nodded and pressed her hand to his cheek, giving him a quick kiss. "This surprised both of us. I don't think either of us planned on being here."

"I certainly didn't." He caught her hand as it fell from his face and kissed her fingers before he let her go.

His tender gestures confused her as much as they hurt. Unable to take any more, she stood again. "I need to clean up. We're running out of time." Their eyes met as her words hit home. She walked to the bathroom and turned on the shower. Within moments, steam plumed above the curtain and she stepped in, sighing as warm water sluiced over her hair and down her body. Not wasting any time, she dumped the sample bottle of two-in-one shampoo and conditioner on her head and lathered it through her hair, her muscles aching with every movement after hours of endless loving.

She'd never spent a night like that—so wrapped up in an-other. When he'd pulled her under him time and again, she'd given him everything she had. She'd savored every brush of his body, every joining of lips, committing them to memory, fearful that each touch might be the last. She washed the suds from her hair, wondering how it was possible for Hunt-er to feel so little when they brought each other such *heat*.

Physically, they were perfectly matched. Each time they'd been together, she'd been right there with him—thrust for thrust, beat for beat. Sexually, she had the power to bring him to his knees, and he was the only man who'd ever sent her over the edge with little more than a simmering look. No, sex definitely wasn't their problem. It was emotion that set them so far apart. She loved in a way she never would again, and he *cared*.

In a matter of hours, Hunter would head back to Los An-geles and carry on as if nothing had happened. Perhaps he would give her a call and pass the time with an e-mail or two, but she knew before long even that would fade into nothing. Teetering on the cliff of despair, she focused on the present and unwrapped a small cake of soap, rubbing the bar over her skin. Tiny bubbles coursed down her body, and she turned into the spray, washing the suds away.

Hunter pulled the shower curtain open.

She jumped, her hand flying to her heart. "Damn it, Hunter."

Without apology, he stepped in behind her and wrapped his arms around her waist. His lips, slick from the water, moved along her neck to her ear. "One more time," he murmured. "I need to be with you one more time."

Her heart raced as his muscled chest pressed against her back. Because this truly would be their last time, she gave in to her need—and his. She turned her head, and he captured her mouth.

Hunter took the soap and rubbed it over her stomach, tracing patterns against her skin. Her lips never left his as his hands journeyed up, finding her breasts, teasing her nipples to sensitive, slippery points.

Sighing, she closed her eyes, enjoying the pulsing tug growing stronger. Stretching, she locked her arms around his neck, playing with his hair.

"Fast or slow?" he asked as he skimmed his fingers over her, moving in slow, steady circles.

Her legs trembled, threatening to buckle as she moved her hips to the rhythm he set.

He nibbled her ear, each steady breath coming faster. "Fast or slow, Morgan?"

She rested her head against his chest. "I can't think." She grabbed hold of any thought she could, never wanting the moment to end. "Slow. Go slow."

He worked her, pressing and circling with torturous movements.

The tug and ache built, and she clutched her arms tighter

around the back of his neck. "I'm going... I'm going to... Oh, my God."

He entered her, thrusting hard and deep as the orgasm shattered her. He moved, unhurried, as water pelted her stomach, and he played with her breasts, sending her to a frenzied level she'd never experienced. He broke contact and turned her, pushing himself deep again before she had a chance to gasp. Hoisting her up, he pressed her back to the wall.

She wrapped her legs tight and kneaded his shoulders as her whimpering moans built to long, loud cries. Shutting her eyes, she trembled, resting her limp head against the wall, certain she'd die from the overload of pleasure.

He tightened his grip on her ass as his breath heaved. "Go over, Morgan. Go over." With a violent pump, he took her mouth, swallowing her screams as she orgasmed with such intensity, she poured around him. He grunted, stiffening as she did, pressing her solidly to the wall with each powerful thrust.

Spent and shuddering, she held on, laying her head on his shoulder as their gasps mingled and the cooling water splashed against them. She clung to him and he to her as she lifted her head and stared into his eyes. She took his mouth, kissing him a silent goodbye. Tongues met as the tender moment stretched out. She shivered, and Hunter turned off the faucet with a snap.

He brushed his lips over hers once more, then her forehead. "They'll be here soon. It's time to get ready."

With little choice, she nodded. "Okay."

He set her down and held her hand, lingering, before he left her in the bathroom.

———◆———

Comfortable in his blue jeans and a white t-shirt, Hunter checked his watch. Forty-five minutes till show time. His brow rose as Morgan stepped from the bathroom dressed identically in jeans and a white short-sleeved v-neck. Her damp hair dripped on her shoulders, leaving wet patches, and he remembered the way she'd gone wild in his arms just minutes ago—that hot body of hers bucking against him as she came, calling his name. How long would it be before she forgot? How long would she wait until she let someone else touch her the way she'd let him? He fisted his hands at his side. There wasn't time for this now. He had two hours on the flight home and the rest of his life to torture himself with thoughts of Morgan and her lovers. Their gazes met, and he gestured to his clothes and hers.

She smiled, but her eyes were sad. "Maybe I should change."

"I wouldn't bother. You look good. I look better, so we'll just leave it alone."

She chuckled as she walked to the bed. "That's one of the things I like best about you, Hunter: Your modesty."

He grinned, relieved when the sadness vanished from her eyes, and he glanced at his watch again. "We have about forty minutes. We need to get things separated and organized." He picked up Morgan's pack and dumped the contents in the center of the mattress, then did the same with his own.

"What are you doing?"

"This'll go faster if we do it this way. We don't have time for one of your tidy checklists. I have some of your stuff; you have some of mine. So let's sort it out." He tossed her things to one side of the bed and his to the other.

"Well, this is certainly one way of doing it." She followed his lead, and the massive heap quickly became two.

Hunter picked up a small box of tampons. "Um, I can't remember. Do these belong to you or me?"

She glanced up and snorted. "I'm pretty sure those are mine."

"Yeah, I guess you're right." Grinning, he tossed the package into her mountain of supplies and grabbed the long-range radio next, casting it among her things. Snatching up the first aid kit next, his gaze returned to the radio.

Morgan had attempted to contact the ranger station the night before Robert found them. By some "strange fluke," Robert and his two bastard cop friends just happened to roam the trail he and Morgan would most likely take on their trek from the Slough River. The coincidence was even more amazing since he and Morgan weren't due back for several days. Leaning across the bed, he snagged the radio and sat down, popping off the back. "Son of a bitch." Among the soldering boards, wires, and batteries lay a tiny red rectangular box with an antenna on its top.

Frowning, Morgan sat next to him. "What is it?"

He detached the wire, pulling the beacon from the radio. "This is how that asshole knew we'd found the mine. When you tried radioing in that night, this little beacon sent out our location."

"What?" Her gaze met his. "But it was only on for a few seconds."

He examined the small tracking piece. "That's all it would've taken."

She swallowed, shaking her head. "No. The beacon would've stopped transmitting when I turned it off."

"As soon as you turned on the radio, the signal was activated, telling him where we were, which wasn't anywhere near where we said we would be."

"You're right." She stood, turning away. "I can't believe this. The last four days have been my fault. If I hadn't turned on the radio, they never would've found out." She paced back and forth to the end of the bed, moving in quick, jerky movements. "I'm such an idiot. I put you and my parents in danger, maybe even your friend and her little girl."

"Stop," he said, getting to his feet and standing in her path, unable to stand the anguish in her voice.

"No. It's the truth. I'm so *sick* inside. Robert almost shot you. My parents are surrounded by security guards." Tears filled her eyes as she turned away again.

"Stop," he said again, easing her around. "If you want to take the blame, you'll have to share it. If I would have told you everything straight up, you wouldn't've tried to radio in. We both made decisions we thought best at the time. We can't change that. It's over now. It doesn't matter anymore. Let's pack up." He checked his watch. "We have fifteen minutes."

Morgan stared, battling back tears.

"I said it's not your fault."

"I heard you."

"Do more than hear me. Listen. It's not your fault." He took her hand and squeezed. "We need to pack."

She nodded and went back to sorting.

Ten minutes later, Hunter zipped his pack and rested it against the wall by the door. With five minutes to departure, he gave a final check of the area through the curtain and stepped to the door.

"Wait."

He turned.

"Um, all of this will be over soon, so I want to thank you for everything." She nibbled her lip, swiping strands of her hair behind her ear. "I know it's not enough, not nearly enough, but I really need to say it."

He wanted to reach out and pull her against him, but it was time to take a step back. "It's not necessary but you're welcome. If you're trying to say goodbye, let's wait. I'm going to the airport with you. We'll say our goodbyes then." He wasn't looking forward to it, but he would worry about that later. Right now he had a job to finish.

"Right. I'll take a last look around and make sure we didn't forget anything."

"Sure." He opened the door a crack, peering out. Tourists swarmed the sidewalks yards away. He couldn't do much until his team got there. Closing the door again, he relocked it. Risks were minimal to Morgan at this point, but he would feel better when he watched her plane depart. "We have about two minutes. Be ready."

"I am. Just let me double-check the bathroom." She disappeared around the corner as he scanned the bedroom. The o-ring on the side table caught his attention. He moved to grab it and hesitated.

Morgan popped back into the room. "Ready?"

"Yeah." He picked up the tarnished piece of metal and shoved it in his pocket. "Yeah, I'm ready. Let's finish this." Shouldering his pack, he looked out the window for the second time. "As soon as we see the detail, I'll step out and make sure everything's secure. When I tell you to, I want you to move forward. I'll be at your side at all times until we get to the vehicle door. Once you're in, stay down. Okay, here they come."

Four dark green Lincoln Navigators pulled up in front of the room. Hunter opened the door wide enough to throw a hand signal to the men on his team. The back door of the second Navigator opened immediately from the inside. "Let's go," he told Morgan, bringing her out against his side, shielding her as he closed the motel door behind them and whisked her into the SUV while speaking to Baker. He moved her so she lay on the floor, covering her from the seat until they got up to speed.

As the team drove away, the phone in the motel room began to ring.

CHAPTER THIRTY-FOUR

HUNTER GLANCED OUT THE WINDOW AS PINE TREES flashed by at breakneck speeds. He sat up, speaking to Baker as they moved west on Grand Loop Road. "Anything interesting on the drive here?"

Baker glanced in the rearview mirror. "Not so far."

"Good. Let's hope it stays that way." He looked down at Morgan staring up at him. "You can get in your seat." He held out his hand, helping her off the floor.

"I was wondering how long I was going to have to stay down there." She buckled in as Stanley popped up from the last row. "Daddy!" Morgan threw herself halfway over the seat, embracing him in a fierce hug. "I'm so happy to see you." She kissed his cheek.

Stanley eased her away, looking her over. "Are you okay?"

She nodded, smiling. "I'm fine. I'm good. Hunter took good care of me."

Hunter smiled, feeling awkward when he met Stanley's gaze. Not even an hour ago, he'd had his daughter naked and pinned against the wall of the shower.

Stanley gave him a firm nod. "Hunter, my boy, I can't thank you enough for keeping my girl safe. I've been worried sick, but I see she's in one piece." He and Morgan grinned identical grins as Stanley hugged her close again.

Morgan turned her attention to Hunter, extending her

smile to him.

His reply to Stanley withered on his tongue as his stomach clenched in reflex. God, she was stunning—absolutely breathtaking. Without thinking, he skimmed his thumb along her cheek, needing to feel her soft skin.

Morgan leaned into his touch, her pretty eyes staring into his.

Stanley's cell phone rang, jolting Hunter out of his trance, and he dropped his hand, catching the look passing between Stanley and his daughter.

Stanley's frown disappeared when Morgan gave her dad a quick shake of her head, and Hunter turned in his seat, scanning the trees again. What in the hell was he *doing*? Had he lost his *mind*? The two of them weren't alone anymore.

Stanley pressed "talk" on the third ring. "Hello? Hello? Nothing but static. I haven't had a signal since Bozeman. The service here is terrible." He pushed 'end.'

"We're in the middle of nowhere, Dad. You'll be up and running in no time."

The phone rang again. "Hello? Hello?" Stanley cursed, ending the call.

"Dad, why don't you just turn that off for now?"

"Maybe I can receive a text. There's nothing more frustrating than knowing someone's trying to get a hold of you," he said, fiddling with his phone. "Nothing. I can't get a damn thing."

Rolling her eyes, Morgan pulled the phone from Stanley's hand. "I know you can't live without it, but why don't I hold this for you?" She pressed another button, powering down the phone, and tossed it in her pack. "So, how's Mom?"

Hunter bit his cheek, holding back a grin as Stanley stared at the pack, blinking and sputtering his protest.

Morgan took Stanley's hand. "Dad, how's Mom?"

Stanley's gaze left the bag, meeting hers. "She's fine, but she's been worried about you. Ethan contacted a security firm in DC. They sent people right over. As soon as I can get a damn *signal*, we'll call her and let her know we're all fine."

"I can't wait to talk to her."

Hunter checked his watch as the SUV merged on Route Eighty-Nine. "Any more news on the mine, Stanley?"

"I spoke with the police just before we left Bozeman. The authorities found the mining operation late last night. From what I understand, they encountered a pretty heavy gunfight. One of the guards was shot and killed. The others were interrogated until they gave up names. Those names led to others—Dean's included."

Morgan's gaze darted to her father's. "Poor Connie. She must be heartbroken. And Michael and Jesse..."

Stanley shook his head. "We'll do all we can for them. I know Michael will want to see you. He'll need you now."

She nodded. "It's the first stop I'll make when we get back."

Hunter stared at Morgan, wondering who the hell Michael was. Just how close were they? Would she look at Michael the way she looked at him? Did Michael touch her the way he did? He choked down the bitter taste of jealousy, pulling himself back, attempting to focus on his job as he realized Stanley was speaking to him.

"...quite a number of people involved with the operation. A big-time ranch, Jone's Ranch, farther north of the mine, was raided. Dean was drinking a beer and playing cards with the owner when it all happened. They found Robert hiding in one of the bunk houses, nursing his broken ribs with an icepack."

"The bastard deserved more than that," Hunter said.

"Oh, I imagine he'll get it—along with the others. At this point, they're certain they have the key players. The head of the investigation feels confident that Morgan and I are safe. An officer will meet us at the airport to collect the journal Ethan said you have. After that, we can go home and put this behind us for the most part. I'm sure there will be follow-up questions and paperwork for the both of you."

"I still don't understand how Dean got caught up in all of

this," Morgan said.

"I'm not sure, honey. From what I've gathered, he and Robert go way back. It takes a lot of people and a lot of money to keep something like this quiet. Early estimates report the mine has produced several million."

"The mine cost more than it made. Three lives are worth more than that." Morgan's miserable eyes met Hunter's before she turned toward the window.

He wanted to reach out to her but kept his hand at his side.

Stanley squeezed Morgan's shoulder. "Yes, they certainly are."

Morgan rested her hand on her father's. This was better. As much as Hunter wanted to be the one to comfort her, they had less than an hour until they had to say their goodbyes.

"Phillips," the stonily serious Baker said as he glanced in the rearview mirror again, "we're fifteen minutes out. Everything's clear."

"Thanks." Hunter looked from the rearview mirror to Stanley and Morgan. "It should be smooth sailing from this point forward. What time is your plane set to take off?"

"I told the pilot we would be ready by four."

"Good." He met Morgan's gaze once more before she turned to stare out the window.

———◈———

The door marked *Private Plane Departures* slid open to reveal a large waiting area, and they stepped inside. Dark wood complemented several rustic paintings of Montana's epic landscapes. Morgan walked to a grouping of brown leather chairs and put her pack down while her father strolled over to the customer service counter. She stared through enormous panes of glass as private planes waited for their turn to take off.

A Cessna gained speed on the runway, lifting its nose to

the sky. She took a deep breath, steeling herself for goodbye. Turning from the window, she met Hunter's gaze, and her pulse beat faster as he walked toward her. He was so outrageously sexy in his jeans and t-shirt. Did he know women looked twice as they passed him by? She took another long, slow breath as the dread of losing him curled tight in her stomach and her heart began to break. She smiled, unwilling to let him see how much his leaving hurt her. "Hey."

"Hey." He brushed a strand of her hair behind her ear, a habit she'd come to expect.

Dad walked over, joining them. "Good news: They can get us in the air within the half hour. The mechanic needs to do our maintenance check, then we can board." He looked at Morgan, then at Hunter and back, clearing his throat. "I'm going to get myself a cup of coffee. I'll be back soon."

"I'll be waiting right here." Morgan kissed his cheek before he walked away.

Hunter grabbed her hand. "Come see me in LA."

She blinked her surprise as she stared into his blue eyes and hope began to bloom. "What?"

"Come visit me in LA after you get stuff figured out with work. You could stay for a long weekend or something. I'll take you out on a real date."

Laughing, she hugged him and closed her eyes when his arms tightened around her. Was this really happening? Her heart stuttered in her chest as she kissed him. "All right. It'll probably be a couple of weeks before I can manage, but—"

"Excuse me, Hunter Phillips?" A man dressed in khakis and a collared shirt approached.

Hunter turned to face him, breaking their embrace. "Yeah?"

"I'm Lieutenant Ryan Myers with the Montana State Police." He flashed his badge and put it away. "I've come to collect an item from you."

"Can I see your badge again?"

The officer stared at Hunter as he dug in his back pocket

and handed over his badge for Hunter's inspection.

Hunter met his gaze, nodding. "Let me get it." He walked to his pack, digging deep, pulling the pink journal with the pretty white flowers free. He placed it in the officer's hand.

Morgan couldn't take her eyes off the small book holding her friend's thoughts, dreams, and the horrors of her last moments alive. She wanted to yank the book back from the stranger, knowing that when he brought it to the police station, Shelly's thoughts would never be private again.

"Thank you, Mr. Phillips. Miss." The tall, serious man nodded and placed the book in a bag then walked off.

Hunter put his arm around Morgan, pulling her close and kissed her head. "Are you okay?"

She pressed herself against him, holding tight to the comfort he offered. "Yeah. It's hard letting him walk away with that. On one hand I feel like I'm betraying Shelly, but on the other I guess I'm glad he has it. Now they can put those bastards away for what they did."

—◆—

Officer Myers walked to his unmarked police car parked in slot A-3 of the parking garage. He opened the door, sat down, and put the pink book on the passenger's seat. He was about to close the door when the cold barrel of a silencer rested against the back of his head. It was the last thing he felt before a bullet pierced his brain.

—◆—

The gunman smiled at the mess he made of the good officer. He was just like those asshole tree huggers who didn't know how to stay away from places they didn't belong. He hurried to the other side of the vehicle and grabbed the bag with the journal in it, wiping away the spatters of blood and tissue on the seat.

With the book secured in the inside pocket of his jacket, he walked toward the airport, ready to finish the job. The bitch and her stud had ruined everything. Now they were going to pay.

❦ CHAPTER THIRTY-FIVE ❧

HUNTER SAT ON ONE OF THE FIRM LEATHER CHAIRS, waiting for Morgan to emerge from the restroom. In the next grouping of seats, Stanley leafed through a golf magazine, sipping his coffee with Baker at his side. Hunter glanced up as Morgan exited the bathroom and excused herself when she bumped into a frazzled woman with two cranky toddlers. Her eyes met his across the hallway, and she smiled slowly, fully. God, she was beautiful.

She made her way through the chaos of a family of ten and took the seat next to his. "Well, that was an obstacle course."

"It looked like one." He played with a strand of her soft hair, twisting it around his finger as she leaned against his shoulder. He'd surprised himself when he asked her to come to California. The invitation had been out of his mouth before he'd thought it through, but when he'd looked into her big, green eyes, he hadn't been ready to say goodbye. What they had between them wasn't anywhere near finished. He kept waiting to regret his impulsive decision, but he didn't. In fact, he felt good, even happy. Maybe he would fly out and see her a week or two after she got back from visiting him. They could get together a couple times a month. If she spent enough time in LA, she might think about applying for the job Shelly had planned to take.

"Baker's a pretty serious guy."

Morgan's comment interrupted his thoughts. "Huh?"

"Baker." She smiled, gesturing to her father and the big black tank of a man staring straight ahead. "He's pretty no-nonsense."

Hunter snickered. "Apparently. I've never worked with him before. At least you won't have to worry about him talking too much on the flight home."

She grinned. "There is that."

A cell phone rang in the distance, and Hunter remembered he hadn't turned his on. "I should grab my phone and check in with Ethan."

"That's probably a good idea. I'm surprised my father hasn't asked me for his—shocked, actually."

Hunter chuckled. "He definitely loves his technology."

"What time does your plane take off?"

"Four-thirty." He powered on his phone, and it beeped as the red message light flashed. "Shit. Thirty-two missed calls and twenty messages."

"Aren't you Mr. Popular?"

"Yeah, lucky me." He dialed Ethan's number and waited.

"Cooke, it's Phillips."

"Where the hell have you been?"

"Hold on. I can't hear you." He stood and walked to the window, watching a plane lift off the ground as he leaned against the glass. "The signal's awful here. Can you hear me now?" he joked.

"Did you get my messages? I thought I would've heard from you right away. I tried calling the motel room, Stanley's phone, Baker's, hell, even Morgan's."

Hunter's smile disappeared as he picked up on the urgency in Ethan's voice. "What are you talking about?"

"I got a call from the Montana State police about two hours ago. It was Miles Jones. All of it."

He stood straight. "Wait, what?"

"His father was the rancher involved with the mining operation. It wasn't Robert who pulled the trigger on Morgan's friends. The cops confessed they were with Miles when he killed Morgan's colleagues. He hasn't been apprehended. You and the Taylors are still targets."

"Damn it." He jammed a hand through his hair. "Why didn't the cop tell us when he came to collect the journal?"

"I don't know. Maybe he assumed you already knew."

He blew out a breath as his mind raced, and he reformulated his plans. "I'll see if I can get Stanley and Morgan on the plane now. We'll head back to—" He glanced over from the window, and fear froze his heart as Miles walked down the long-windowed terminal and broke into an all-out run, pulling a pistol from his jacket. Hunter dropped his phone and ran toward Morgan. "Get down!"

———◆———

Morgan was walking toward her father, flipping through her missed calls when Hunter yelled. Suddenly everything started happening in slow motion. Baker leaped out of his seat, flying forward, taking her father to the floor. He covered him as three quick pops echoed in the terminal and spatters of blood flew from a blooming red hole in Baker's thigh.

Morgan whirled, staring at Miles, crazy-eyed and smiling as he ran toward her, aiming a gun in her direction. Three more blasts shattered the glass directly behind her. Before the instinct to duck registered, Hunter barreled ahead, pummeling her to the floor. The weight of his body crushed her, and she gasped, losing her breath.

Hunter clutched her to his chest, hooking his legs around hers, and rolled them toward cover as linoleum flooring ricocheted around them when Miles fired again. With his gun in hand, Hunter extended his arm, and it jerked twice as two rapid explosions sounded close to her ear.

Miles' eyes widened, his body jolting when the bullets

pierced his chest. The pistol fell from his hand, and he stumbled, collapsing backwards.

Morgan stared at the soles of Miles' boots as her heartbeat hammered in her ears. With effort, she broke through the dim fog of shock, and the world around her came back to life. People screamed and cried as they huddled together. Airport security ran to the terminal, shouting.

Pale and shaking, Hunter dropped his gun with a clatter. He pulled himself into a sitting position, dragging her with him. As soon as her head rested upon his firm chest, he drew her away. "Are you all right, Morgan? Are you okay?" He yanked her back against him, crushing her in a hug before she had a chance to respond. His trembling hand brushed through her hair as his arm constricted around her back, making it hard for her to breathe.

"Hunter, you're going to break my ribs."

"You're okay." He continued to stroke her as if he didn't hear her. "You're all right."

"Yes, I'm fine. I'm just fine."

Her father barked orders, demanding a paramedic as he crawled out from under a groaning Baker. He looked over, meeting her gaze. "Morgan, are you all right?"

She nodded while Hunter continued holding her plastered to his body. "I'm fine, Daddy. Are you okay?"

Pale himself, he gave her a wink. "Not a scratch on me, thanks to Baker." He turned back, assisting his bodyguard.

Seconds later, a team of paramedics burst through the sliding door, rushing to the wounded man.

Miles hadn't hit her. Hunter's heart rate settled as it sunk in. He'd made it in time. She was safe. He eased Morgan back to help her to her feet, extending his hand to take hers when he noticed the bright red streaks covering his arm from his elbow to his wrist. Staring, his mind drifted, switching gears before he could control his thoughts. The wails and shouts within the airport flickered in and out as echoes of machine gun fire and chopper blades whirled, creating a confusing carousel of past and present. He sweated, consumed by heat and dust as Jake lay before him, bleeding out. Too much blood, too much... *I'm not going to make it, man. Take care of them...*

Morgan frowned. "What are you doing?" She grabbed his arm, gasping. "You're bleeding. You're bleeding, Hunter."

What did she say? Jake was dying. No. Jake was dead. His heart pounded and his chest constricted as he wheezed in each breath while his stomach churned until he was certain he would vomit.

Morgan's hands flew over his body, cool against his molten skin. "Where's it coming from?"

The sliding door across the room opened, bringing in more police, and he clutched hold of reality, struggling to bring himself back. He was in Montana, and Morgan needed him. Morgan. He looked away from the officers hovering over Miles and focused on her. Sweat beaded along her pale forehead as her brow creased. "Damn it, why are you just staring at me? Where's the blood coming from, Hunter?"

Back in the moment, he zeroed in on her shirt, wet at the shoulder. Horrified, he ripped the sleeve clean from the seam, wavering again. The wretched smell of burning flesh and vehicles intermingled with the tropical scent of Morgan's shampoo. Smoke spewed from Jake's truck, and Morgan's green eyes grew saucer wide as she stared at the bright red drops dribbling down her arm. "You're shot, Morgan." His own words startled him out of shock, and he moved forward in a rush, laying her on her back and raising her arm high above her heart as he pressed the t-shirt sleeve to her wound. "I need paramedics over here! She's been shot!"

Stanley ran over, taking Morgan's hand as a second team on standby swarmed in.

"I'm okay, Dad. It stings but I'm all right. I thought I hurt myself when I fell on the floor. I didn't realize I was bleeding. I thought it was Hunter."

A paramedic donning bright blue gloves dabbed at the wound on her lower shoulder.

Morgan examined her injury. "It doesn't look like a bullet hole, not like the one on Baker's leg." Her gaze wandered in Hunter's direction. "Are you all right?"

He flicked her a glance and zeroed in on her delicately muscled arm.

"You're going to be fine, ma'am." The paramedic blotted at her skin, wiping at the remaining blood as he smiled reassuringly. "You were grazed. We can treat you here. You'll want to see your physician when you get to your destination."

"No. She's going to the hospital," Stanley demanded. "Get us to the hospital."

"Dad, I don't need a hospital." She frowned. "Now that it's all cleaned up, it isn't any bigger than my thumbnail."

The paramedic covered her wound with a large piece of gauze and medical tape.

"Hunter, tell him I don't need to go to the hospital."

He met her gaze again, the stubborn line between her brows apparent. "Go to the hospital. Get yourself checked out."

She huffed. "This is ridiculous."

The crew working on Baker wheeled him away through the sliding doors.

"Poor Baker needs to go to the hospital. *I* certainly don't," she said as they all watched him being pushed into the back of the ambulance.

Hunter fisted his hand covered in Morgan's blood. He'd fucked up again, and the walls were closing in around him, the void of self-loathing threatening to swallow him whole. Twinges of anxiety clutched in his belly and tightened his chest as two years vanished before him. Fear for what could've been and the loss of Jake choked him, hurtling him back to the aftermath of Afghanistan. "Go for me." He wanted her away from him.

"All right. I'll go. Will you come with me?" Her fingers brushed his arm, her eyes pleading.

He clenched his jaw, staring at the white of her bandage, so bright against her golden skin—a cruel reminder of his failure. He hadn't done his job. He hadn't kept her safe. He wanted some space. It was all he could do not to walk away right then and there. "I can't. I have to go to the police station and give my statement."

"Okay. We'll see you after, then."

"Yeah." He didn't miss the way she cautiously removed her hand from his arm.

They wheeled her away on the stretcher, and she rolled her eyes at one of the paramedics, apologizing for the unnecessary trip to the hospital.

He turned to leave, but she caught his eye, questioning him with a glance, holding him prisoner until she disappeared into the back of the ambulance.

CHAPTER THIRTY-SIX

HUNTER DIDN'T MEET THEM AT THE HOSPITAL AS she'd hoped he would. Morgan spent two hours in the ER, waiting for the doctor to swab ointment on her wound, tape a new bandage in place, and tell her she was just fine. She walked out of the hospital and into the cab her father had called for them. "The police station, please," she said to the driver as they settled into the backseat and she looked at her dad. "I told you I didn't need to go to the ER. We just wasted two hours we could've spent somewhere else."

She wanted to see Hunter and feel his arms around her. After this rollercoaster ride of a day, she needed him—and he needed her. He'd acted strange, distant, but now that things were different between them, he could tell her what was bothering him. They would deal with it together. She wanted to put this nightmare behind her—behind both of them—and move forward. A smile ghosted her lips, and her pulse beat faster. He'd asked her to come to LA. She'd been so preoccupied with saying goodbye, she hadn't let herself believe in possibilities, but here they were before her. Hunter opened the door to hope, and she was running through it.

"The next time you get grazed by a bullet, I'll let you call the shots; although, there better not be a next time," Dad warned.

She settled against his side. "I can promise you I will never get shot again, no matter how minor."

His arm came around her shoulders as he smiled and kissed her forehead.

"Did you check on Baker while we waited *forever*?"

"Yes. He'll be fine after a little R and R. They were rolling him out of surgery when I called for the cab. His wife is flying in tonight. They'll go home the day after next."

"That's good. I'm glad he's okay." She stared out the window, watching the buildings pass by, and turned her attention to her dad again. "These past few days have been insane. It doesn't seem real. I can't believe Miles was behind everything. He seemed like such a nice person. I gave him cooking lessons, for heaven's sake." She shook her head. "He killed my friends, then he let me teach him how to cook." Her eyes wandered back to the passing buildings, still trying to absorb the gravity of the situation. "Hunter didn't like him. He was right about him."

"Hunter's a smart man."

She smiled. "Yes, he is." Her light mood fell away. "I wish this could've ended differently. I wish they were still here."

"It's terrible, Peanut, just terrible." Her father snuggled her closer. "I spoke to the police again while you were in with the doctor. Word about the operation itself is coming out. Early speculation is Miles' father kept him out of the seedier side of the business until he found out about it. They're saying he was always eager to please his old man and more or less took over—full throttle." He let loose a long sigh. "Unfortunately, he'll be spending eternity in the ground while his father rots in prison. And all for gold."

Morgan snagged his hand. "I'll never understand."

He gave her fingers a gentle squeeze. "It's hard to grasp. They certainly used Miles' profession to their advantage. He and Robert kept patrol of the area by the mine. That's why it stayed undetected for so long. It's just unfortunate the team got mixed up in the whole situation." He kissed her hair. "I'll be forever grateful you get to come home with me."

They pulled up in front of the police station and paid the cabbie. Her father opened the door to the noisy squad room, and Morgan walked in. She stopped short of bumping into Hunter as he made his way out. Smiling, she touched his shoulder. "Hey, there you are."

He didn't return her smile as he glanced from her to her father and back. "How's the arm?"

"Absolutely fine." Her brow furrowed slightly as she puzzled over the distance radiating from him. "It's pretty much a scratch. Are you finished here?"

"Yeah. I'm actually on my way out. I have to get to the airport."

Her smile vanished as she blinked her confusion. What was going on? "You're leaving right now? As in leaving for LA?"

Hunter didn't meet her gaze. "Ethan booked me a new flight that leaves in an hour. If I go now, I can just make it."

Her dad stepped forward, holding out his hand. "If you're on your way, Hunter, I would like to thank you for everything. Ethan was absolutely correct: You were just the right man for my daughter. I don't know how to repay you for getting her back to me."

Hunter shook her father's hand as he stared at her. "Morgan did a fine job of taking care of herself. You've got a pretty tough daughter."

"Well, son, thank you again. I'm going to talk to whoever's in charge of this damn mess." He walked off, leaving them alone.

Hunter glanced at his watch. "I really need to get to the airport."

He spoke as if they were little more than strangers, as if they hadn't shared anything special, and her heart shattered. "All right. I'll walk out with you."

"No, you should stay here. It's getting dark."

"I'll walk you out." She spun away and pushed through

the doors, stepping out into the warm evening. Clouds, brilliantly pink from the setting sun, decorated the sky. She stared into the beauty, unable to look at him, unable to say goodbye.

He stood on the step next to her while people brushed passed, going in and out of the building as the taxi pulled up to the corner. "That must be my cab." He signaled for the cabbie to wait. "The desk at the airport's holding your stuff until you go back tonight. The items you left at the ranger station are there too."

She faced him, studying his eyes. The sweet, funny man she'd shared so much with no longer existed. The cold, distant stranger standing before her wasn't the man who'd made love to her until dawn. He wasn't the person who'd laughed with her and held her tight. With a slow, deep breath, she asked him the question she could already answer herself. "Is this it, Hunter?"

"Job's up. It's time to go our separate ways."

She turned her back to him as her eyes filled, and she blinked ruthlessly, hoping her voice wouldn't betray her as well. "There aren't going to be any long weekends in LA, are there?"

"No."

Steeling herself, she swallowed the sobs that threatened and turned, facing his ruthless stare.

"We got caught up in something that'll never work. I'm fixing it for both of us. A clean break is better. Let's not drag this out with a weekend here and a weekend there. I don't know what I was thinking. You live in DC; I live in LA." His gaze moved to the bandage on her arm before he met her gaze.

She wanted to scream and rage, to tell him she loved him, that she would never want anyone but him, but she didn't. There was no point. He didn't want her. He didn't love her. She cleared her throat. "If this is the way you want it."

"This is the way I want it."

Sick at heart and to her stomach, she nodded, holding out her hand. She claimed a small victory when it didn't tremble. "It was a pleasure doing business with you." He grabbed her, pulling her closer. "Don't make it cheap." "Aren't you?" Yanking herself free from his grip, she looked into his blue eyes one last time and walked back into the station.

———◇———

Hunter stared at the door long after it closed and took a step toward the station just as the cabbie honked. Instead of going back inside, he walked down the sidewalk, hesitating before he got in the car. He was doing the right thing, he assured himself as he fisted his hand on the seat and Morgan's eyes flashed through his mind. Shaking his head, he willed the image away, desperate to forget.

Minutes later, the cabbie pulled up to the curb by *Departing Flights.* Hunter paid him off and ran for his plane. He made it seconds before the flight attendant shut the door. The jet taxied and took off, leaving the lights of Bozeman fading in the east. He looked down one last time, knowing Morgan was still there. Ending things and walking away was for the best, he reminded himself again.

While he answered questions at the police station, the terrifying moments at the airport replayed through his memory over and over. He'd almost been too late. One more second and—he couldn't think of it. He closed his eyes, bringing back the image of his hand covered with blood. Morgan's blood. If he thought too hard, he saw the crimson drops dripping down her arm and could hardly stand it. He glanced at the specks of her dried blood on his shirtsleeve, then back out the window into the darkness. He'd failed again, almost losing her the way he'd lost Jake.

He'd been so caught up in his feelings, in his *need* for Morgan, he'd lost his concentration. Plain and simple, he hadn't done his job. If he would've worried more about checking in with Ethan and less about planning foolish cross-country visits, the whole nightmare would have been avoided.

He clenched his jaw as their last moments circled through his mind. He'd seen the tears in her eyes and her struggle to keep them from falling. He'd wanted to pull her close one last time, to smell her hair and feel her body against his, to wrap his arms around her, but if he had, he wouldn't have let her go. Saying goodbye had been the hardest thing he'd ever done. He couldn't stand leaving her behind, but he couldn't deal with staying either, so he did what was best for both of them.

Despair left him weary. He rested his head against the seat and closed his eyes, seeing Morgan's beautiful green eyes and bright smile. He sat up as if fighting his way through a nightmare and stared into the black, wondering if she would always haunt him.

☙ CHAPTER THIRTY-SEVEN ❧

HER FATHER EASED THE LEXUS TO A STOP IN FRONT of their massive home. Despite the late hour, lights blazed in every room. "It looks like your mother waited up for us, Peanut."

Morgan mustered up a smile. "Sure does. I can't wait to see her." The police interviews and long flight home had drained her. She'd replayed every detail of her three weeks in Montana for the officers. With each word, she remembered a look she'd shared with Hunter or a conversation or a touch, and her heart broke a little more. While she sat alone, curled in a leather seat on her parents' jet, she'd stared into the night, replaying her last moments with him. What went wrong? What had she done to make him change his mind? What brought that cold, remote look into his eyes? How was she going to make it through the rest of her life knowing she would never see him again?

"Ready, honey?"

Her father jarred her from her thoughts. "What?"

"I said are you ready?"

"Oh. Yes." She unbuckled herself. "Let's go see Mom." Despite the warmth of the night, she shivered. Would she ever be warm again? She climbed the dozen steps with her father by her side and reached for the knob as his hand rested on her shoulder.

"Are you okay?"

She steeled herself against the tenderness in his voice and his three simple words. Was she okay? No. She was anything but. Gathering the last of her emotional reserves, she darted him a glance, just barely meeting his gaze, and nodded as she swallowed against the tight ball of emotion in her throat. "I'm fine." God, she needed to get out of here and get back to her own house. A quick hug for her mom and she would go. She stepped through the door, into the light of the grand entryway, and her mother shot up from an antique chair.

"Oh, thank God."

Morgan walked into her outstretched arms, breathing in the familiar scent of Chanel, relishing the comfort of her mother's soft hair against her cheek. Unable to hold back any longer, a sob escaped her lips.

"It's okay, sweetie," Mom cooed close to her ear, ushering her upstairs, leaving her father sputtering behind them.

Morgan lay on the pretty canopied bed, the one she'd slept in every night until she left for college, and cried as she never had before. The weight of helpless grief had grown too heavy, finally needing its release.

Her mother lay beside her, brushing her fingers through her hair and soothed her with gentle words, reminding Morgan her friends were in a better place.

Morgan realized her mom thought she cried over her ordeal in Yellowstone and let her. It wasn't important for anyone to know that Hunter Phillips had shattered her heart.

Long after her mom left her alone, Morgan lay against the pale pink comforter, empty, devastated. A tear trailed down her cheek, and she swiped it away, vowing that it was the last tear he would ever get. There would be no more crying over Hunter.

Although it was well past eight, Morgan sat at her desk filling out paperwork. The halls were quiet and the other offices dark. Most of the staff, except for the cleaning crew, had long since left for the evening, but she wasn't ready to go yet. When she stayed busy, she didn't have time to think. The small print on the documents in front of her blurred, and she rubbed her tired eyes, knowing it was time to stop. She'd let herself into the office at dawn. After fifteen hours of meetings and paperwork, her mind was finally sluggish and her body exhausted.

Closing her eyes, she rested her head against the back of her chair and massaged her throbbing temples. Hunter's grinning face flashed through her thoughts, sneaking past her wall of defense, bringing a fresh wave of pain. With a defeated sigh, she gathered a stack of files to lose herself in should sleep elude her—as it often did—and placed them in her briefcase. With her purse on her shoulder and her briefcase in hand, she locked up.

Instead of going to her empty house, she hopped on the elevator and rode two floors to her father's suite. The chrome door slid open, and a smile of relief ghosted her mouth as light blazed through his door. Morgan walked down the hall and stood in his doorway, watching him sign documents stacked in a tidy pile left by the ever-efficient Helen. She knocked, smiling when he looked up.

He frowned, concern shining bright in his eyes, before his features softened with understanding.

She wanted to run to him, to snuggle against him and weep like she had as a child. There'd been a time when a gentle tug on her pigtails and a kiss on the forehead made everything better, but that wouldn't solve anything now. And she would break the promise she'd made herself the night she returned from Montana.

Her father smiled, studying her face. "Hi, Peanut. You're still here."

"I had some work to finish up."

He continued to stare, nodding, as she circled around the desk to kiss his cheek. The bold red and black insignia of Ethan Cooke Security caught her eye. The itemized invoice covered two full pages. The grand total typed in the box at the bottom was insane. Hunter had saved her life and broken her heart for the bargain price of forty-eight thousand dollars and change. "I see the bill finally arrived." She picked up the papers.

Dad snatched them back. "Yes. The check will go out in the morning. Have a seat, Morgan. You look like you'll fall on your face any minute."

She sat in the leather chair in front of the desk, her lack of sleep making her feel as if she were floating. Fighting it, dismissing the weakness, she eyed the invoice, then looked at her father. "I want to pay for everything myself."

"Absolutely not. That isn't necessary."

"Please. It's important to me." After this she would owe Hunter nothing—all debts would be paid. In less than a month, he'd taken everything from her that mattered, but knowing she could do this for herself was an opportunity to start taking some of it back.

"Morgan, hiring Hunter was my decision. It's my bill—and a big one at that."

"I'll use my trust fund."

"Your grandfather didn't set it up—"

"Please don't fight me on this," she pleaded with a hint of desperation tingeing her words.

He blew out a long breath. "All right. If it's that important to you." He handed her the bill.

"Thank you." She tucked the papers in her purse.

"Have you given any more thought to the vacation I suggested? You haven't been yourself lately."

"I'm fine. I don't need a vacation. There's too much to do. I've been up to my eyeballs in paperwork since we've been back." She didn't need to rest. All she needed was her work. If she'd paid more attention to her job while in Yellowstone, she wouldn't be where she was now.

"Exactly. Three weeks of nothing but paperwork is enough to make anyone go crazy, especially someone who spends most of their time in the field."

"Things will change soon enough. I'm heading to LA next week to take Shelly's position for the month, and I have the field assignment in Maine. We're going to find that damn lynx if it's the last thing I do."

"Will you call Hunter while you're in California?"

Morgan looked down, escaping her father's questioning gaze. "No. I don't know why I would. We had a business relationship. It's over. I'll send off the check, and that will be the end of that." Or so she hoped.

⸺◦⸺

Late that night, as she sat in her silky pajamas by the soft lamplight, she tore up another sheet of paper and threw it in the wastebasket. Why couldn't she find the words? She went through draft after draft of the note she wanted to send with Hunter's portion of the bill, but they were all wrong. This was her last chance to say goodbye. She desperately needed closure. Perhaps that was why she had nothing to say—how could she say goodbye when all she wanted to shout was I love you?

Drowning in despair, she rested her weary head against her folded arms. She missed him desperately. The last three weeks had been hell without him. She'd thrown herself into her work with a vengeance, attacking reams of paperwork and rolls of red tape so she could complete the lynx project. Finishing the assignment had become paramount. It would give her the opportunity to close two painful chapters in her life. With the accomplishment, she could let the memory of her team members rest, and it would be one less reminder of a time focused so fully on Hunter.

The hard work she'd put in to get the green light from

the hesitant new Board of Trustees had been a gift of solace, leaving her little time to think—until late at night, when sleep wouldn't come, just as it wouldn't now. Thoughts snuck up in the darkness, thoughts that consumed and tore at her heart. They always circled back to remind her that Hunter had been able to walk away so easily.

Memories filled the nights while she lay in bed staring at the red glow of her clock—his smile, the sound of his voice, the feel of his touch. Each morning the pearly light of dawn would come, bringing another day of work and sweet relief from the heavy weight of heartbreak. Because there was nothing she could do to change what was, she did everything in her power to forget. What choice did she have but to go on? She filled her work schedule to overflowing, committing herself to project after project for the next six months.

In the end, she stuck only the check in an envelope, addressed it, and set it with the stack of mail she would send out tomorrow. The envelope lay on top of the package containing the Tupperware bowl. There was no happy picture to send along with the container that once held chicken and dumplings, only a short evasive note of thanks for the Besters.

❧ CHAPTER THIRTY-EIGHT ❧

HUNTER PULLED THE MAIL FROM THE BOX OUTSIDE his door and flipped through the envelopes, stopping when The Bureau's official insignia caught his eye. Stepping inside his tiny kitchen, he ripped open the envelope, and pain twisted in his heart as he zeroed in on Morgan's pretty signature sprawled along the bottom right-hand corner of the whopping check. God, he *missed* her. A day hadn't passed where he didn't think of her or need her. He'd picked up the phone several times over the last few weeks, only to slam it back down. He'd bought a plane ticket to DC and canceled it. Night after night he woke sweaty from nightmares where Morgan's blood covered his hands.

And that was the problem. He couldn't do it. He couldn't live through losing someone again. If it had taken him even one more second to get to her, he would've lost her. That thought tortured him every single day. Morgan was gone now, but on his terms. It was all for the best. She would move on and make a life she deserved.

He sat in a chair, sinking further into misery as he thought of her finding someone else, of some other man looking into her eyes as they darkened with passion, of her making promises for a lifetime that wouldn't be with him, of her body growing round and more beautiful with a child that wouldn't be his.

He ripped her check into tiny shreds, throwing the pieces in the trash, and picked up the ugly o-ring he hadn't been able to toss away.

———◇———

"My Mr. Ruff. My mama. My Unke Hunte," Kylee exclaimed enthusiastically from the back of Sarah's sedan.

Sarah turned in the passenger seat, watching her daughter grin and bounce about while holding her stuffed dog, Mr. Ruff. In a matter of hours, she and Kylee would be in Florida, spending seven days and six nights at the happiest place on earth. Hopefully Disney lived up to its advertising. She was counting on it. But first they had to survive the long plane ride without annoying two hundred other passengers. She glanced back at her energetic daughter, worried. With any luck, Kylee would tire herself out on the drive to the airport and sleep for at least some of the flight.

It would've been so much easier to drive the hour to Anaheim and spend a couple of days at Disneyland, but Jake had always wanted to go to Epcot. This was for Jake as much as for Kylee. Remembering that, she dug down deep for her sense of adventure. Everything would be fine.

Sarah directed her attention toward Hunter, tuning out the noisy chatter coming from the back. "Thanks for dropping us off. Ethan was going to give me a hand, but he had to take that last-minute assignment."

"I'm happy to help. I'll miss you two this week."

"I'll have you and Ethan over for dinner when we get—"

Mr. Ruff sailed through the air over the passenger's seat, landing on Sarah's strappy sandals. "My Mr. Ruff fly on plane," Kylee said, clapping.

"Kylee's excited," Sarah said to Hunter as she handed Mr. Ruff back. "I'm not sure if you can tell."

Hunter maneuvered the car through heavy Los Angeles traffic, giving her a small smile. "I got that impression. She's also very possessive these days. What's up with all the 'my' stuff?"

"Just another fascinating phase of toddlerhood. Oh shoot, I forgot—"

"My shoot, my shoot," Kylee interrupted.

Hunter grinned into the rearview mirror, chuckling while Kylee sang.

"Hey, there's that smile," Sarah said. "I haven't seen it in a while."

Hunter glanced at her and returned his attention to the road. "What are you talking about?"

"I haven't seen many smiles from you since you got back from Montana. Your eyes have been sad."

"Leave it alone, Sarah."

She knew that warning tone well and let the budding conversation go until she could find another opportunity to bring it up. "Consider it left alone." *For now.* She'd waited two months for answers; another week wouldn't hurt. "Can I use your phone? Mine is packed in the carry-on in the trunk. I forgot to tell my mother not to overwater the plant in my bathroom. She'll drown the poor thing if I don't give her a specific amount and timetable."

"Yeah, go ahead." He dug in his pocket and handed it over.

She flipped open the phone and gaped. "Do you call NASA with this thing or regular people? Look at all of these buttons." She pressed one at random, and a picture of an absolutely gorgeous woman laughing into Hunter's grinning face popped up on the screen. *Well, well, well, what's this?* She pushed the button again. Hunter and the dark-haired beauty snuggled together, smiling happily. She studied the background. A motel. The drab walls and ugly bedding did little to detract from the stunning picture they made. She pushed the button once more, staring at Hunter's mouth pressed to the woman's, and tears filled Sarah's eyes. She'd waited so long for this—to see the look in Hunter's eyes that said he was happy and that he'd found some peace. After his return from Afghanistan, she'd worried she might never see it again. But here it was.

"Are you going to make your call or stare at the phone?"

She met his gaze.

Hunter frowned. "What's wrong?"

"Who's this woman in these pictures?"

He ripped the phone from her hand and glanced down, flinching. He snapped the phone shut and tossed it in the center console, staring ahead at the road.

She knew she should back down but pushed anyway. "Who is she, Hunter?"

"No one. She's no one."

His voice roughened, pain echoing in his answer, and Sarah aimed below the belt. Desperate times called for desperate measures. "I—I thought we were friends." She faced the window, smiling when he huffed out a breath and muttered a curse—she figured that would do it.

"Her name is Morgan Taylor. She was my assignment while I was out in Montana."

"Those pictures look like she was more than that. Are you in love with her? I already know the answer. Do you?"

"I don't want to talk about this." He took the exit for LAX.

"I do, Hunter. I want to talk about this." The temper she rarely let loose boiled over. "I'm taking my daughter to Disney World by myself for her second birthday because her father and I always dreamed we would."

"I'm so sorry—"

"Stop that, damn it!" She ignored Kylee repeating her swear in another song. "I want you to stop that," she said, trying to find her calm. "What happened to Jake wasn't your fault. It isn't any more your fault that you came home than it is Jake's that he didn't. I miss him every day. Every day I want him to walk through my door, to kiss me, to hug our daughter, to just be here. I can't have that, Hunter, but you can. Have you looked at those pictures recently?"

He didn't answer.

"Well, have you?"

"No."

"You need to. Have you seen the way she looks into your eyes? Do you see the way you look into hers? She's here. She's *alive*, and if I know you—and I do—you've pushed her away. You're denying yourself what I wish I could have back. I'm angry with you for that." She blew out a breath and laid her hand on his shoulder. "Love is a gift, Hunter. She loves you. Go get her."

He parked the car and stared ahead. "I can't."

"*Why?*"

He looked at her with lost, miserable eyes. "Because I can't do it. I can't lose someone who means that much again. When her blood was on my hands... It brought everything back."

In all the years they'd been friends, she could only remember one other time his voice had wavered with such anguish. Poor Hunter. She unfastened her seatbelt and hugged him. He gripped her against him as if his life depended on it, and she kissed his cheek. "I'll back off for now, but this conversation isn't over." She turned in her seat, staring at her daughter, who'd gone quiet. "Are you ready to go to Disney World?"

"My 'sney World! My 'sney World!"

Hunter got out of the car and took Kylee from her car seat. He settled her on his hip. "Let's get you to your plane then."

"My Unke Hunte," Kylee said as she rubbed her hands up and down his cheeks.

He kissed her little nose and placed her in her stroller, then grabbed the large suitcase from the trunk.

Sarah took the carry-on bulging with books and other entertainment for Kylee and pulled the car seat from the back. "I think we're ready."

Hunter raised his eyebrows. "I certainly hope so."

With the luggage checked, Hunter held Kylee tight, dragging the stroller she refused to sit in as they wandered through the chaos of Los Angeles International Airport. After weaving their way through masses of people, Hunter and Sarah stood at the back of the ridiculously long security line. Finally stationary, Kylee squirmed, trying to get down. "Not yet, ma'am. It's too crowded." He put the stroller on top of the cart Sarah had grabbed, wanting a better grip on the tiny, blond escape artist in his arms.

Kylee pressed her hands against his chest, pushing and fussing. "No. Down."

In an attempt to keep a tantrum at bay, he bounced her about, making her giggle while he spoke to Sarah. "I'll pick you up next week, as close to your gate as I can get. I have the flight information at home."

"Sounds good. I'm serious about the meal at my house. You and Ethan plan a night that works for you. As long as I don't have any photo shoots scheduled, I'll make you dinner."

"I can't imagine either of us turning that one down." He scanned the countless people putting their bags in gray tubs for the x-ray machines, and his eyes stopped dead on the farthest line to the right in disbelief. There she was.

Morgan bent down in her snug blue jeans, taking off her black sandals, and put them in a bucket. Her purse and laptop case went in next. She took off her casual black business jacket and put it in with the rest. She looked amazing, breathtaking in her white spaghetti-strap top with her hair piled on her head in a messy knot.

"What are you looking at?" Sarah followed the direction of Hunter's stunned gaze.

He could only stare as his heart pounded and his gut clenched with need.

Sarah smiled, grabbing his arm. "Oh my God, there she is. Oh, Hunter, she's even more beautiful in person."

Morgan smiled at the security guard when she set off the buzzer for the third time.

Breaking through his trance of utter surprise, Hunter placed Kylee in Sarah's hands and shoved his way through the crowds, never taking his eyes off of her.

Her lips moved as she spoke, laughing with the man who patted her down. She grabbed her stuff from the bucket, put on her sandals, her jacket, and headed down the long corridor toward her gate.

"Morgan!"

She kept walking.

He stopped at the counter when the security guard placed a hand on his chest, not allowing him any farther. Hunter grabbed for his phone, swearing as he remembered he'd left it in Sarah's car. With no other options, he cupped his hands around his mouth and yelled again. He watched helplessly as she disappeared into the crowd and out of his life again.

✃ CHAPTER THIRTY-NINE ✄

UNABLE TO SLEEP, HUNTER STARED AT THE EIFFEL
Tower illuminating the night sky, thinking of Morgan. In the week since he'd seen her at LAX, he'd
done little but play back their last moments outside the police station. Her eyes brimming with tears monopolized his
mind. She'd fought so hard to keep them from falling, had
battled even harder to appear unaffected by his sudden cruelty. He'd heard her struggles to steady her breathing and
keep her voice from trembling. He'd known he was hurting
her, yet he walked away because it had been easier for him.

He settled his elbows on the balcony, blowing out a long
breath, oblivious to the sights and sounds of Paris far below as his mind wandered back to the airport. Morgan had
looked good—stunning, happy—as if she'd picked up her
life and kept going. Did she think of him? Did she need him
even half as much as he needed her? He clenched his jaw,
fearing she didn't.

Resting his forehead on his palms, he struggled to remember he was on duty, protecting one of Hollywood's
leading ladies on her five-day promotional tour through Europe. His hotel room adjoined Tinseltown's hottest woman,
but he only wanted Morgan.

He pulled his phone from his pocket and pressed a button. He could all but hear Morgan's laughter as he stared at the picture he'd taken while they joked about Mrs. Bester's chicken and dumplings. Her stunning face, frozen in laughter while he grinned at her, illuminated the screen. He pressed the button twice more, until the picture of his lips capturing hers filled the display. He unconsciously rubbed at the ache in his chest as he studied the image in front of him—at the truth glaring back at him, easy to see. Sarah had been right: The man and woman in the pictures were undeniably in love.

God, what had he done?

———◊———

After the twelve-hour flight home from Europe, Hunter walked through the door of his small apartment and flipped on a light as he dropped his bag with a careless thud. Knowing what he needed to do, he picked up the phone and punched in his company code, making his name and number unavailable before he dialed Morgan's cell phone. If her readout came up UNKOWN NAME, UNKOWN NUMBER instead of showing his, she might answer.

Morgan's sexy voice told him if he left a message, she would get back to him. He swore and hung up. After two days of listening to her cell phone go to voicemail, he tried her house line. She could avoid him, but she would have to deal with him eventually. The phone continued to ring, and he jammed a hand through his hair, waiting for her voicemail to pick up.

"Hello?"

Hunter's stomach sank when a man answered. Had she moved on already? "Uh, hello. Is Morgan there?"

"No, she's not. Can I take a message?"

The voice was familiar. "Stanley, is that you? This is Hunter Phillips."

"Hunter, my boy, how are you?"

He didn't miss the way Stanley's tone sharpened. Stanley wasn't a fool. Hunter imagined he knew something had gone on between him and his daughter in Yellowstone. "I can't complain. How about you?"

"I'm pretty good, pretty good. So, you're looking for Morgan."

Hunter ran his tongue along his teeth, imagining the battle light in Stanley's eyes. Stanley could help him or punch him in the balls and make finding Morgan difficult. "Actually, yes. Will she be back soon?"

"No. I haven't seen her much since we got back from Yellowstone. My little Peanut has worked herself ragged for the last nine weeks. She just hasn't been the same since our return from Montana. Ilene's certain Morgan still mourns for her friends, but I almost wonder if it might not be…something else. It concerns a father to see his beautiful daughter's eyes so full of pain and sadness every time he looks at her."

The meaning behind Stanley's words hung heavy on the line. What was he supposed to say to that? "I really need to talk to her."

"Well, Morgan's not here. She was out in your neck of the woods for a good month. Now she's in Maine. They actually tagged one of those damn lynx, if you can believe that."

"That's great, really great." She would be happy about the lynx, but Hunter couldn't get past the fact that Morgan had been in LA for a month and hadn't tried to contact him. He jammed his hand into his pocket as panic slammed into his belly. What if he couldn't fix this? What if he'd ruined the best thing that had ever happened to him? His heart thundered, and he closed his eyes.

"Morgan will be home in a couple of days before she heads out again," Stanley said, offering him a lifeline. "She'll be gone for quite a while on her next journey. If it's urgent, you'll probably want to give her a call at the hotel. She'll check out either tomorrow or the day after. After that, I can't tell you where my little globetrotter will be."

Hunter blew out a breath, relaxing. "Thank you, Stanley."

"You can thank me by making my daughter smile again. Now, here's the number."

Hunter scribbled down the digits. "I really appreciate this."

"I imagine I'll be talking to you again, Hunter, my boy. Bye, now."

"Bye." He hung up and pulled the tarnished o-ring he always carried from his pocket, examining it, flipping it between his fingers. Inhaling deeply, he stuffed the metal back in his pocket and picked up the phone again.

৫৪ CHAPTER FORTY ৪৩

MORGAN SPENT HER LAST AFTERNOON IN MAINE shopping. She stepped from a small boutique, one of the several clapboard shops lining the street, and breathed in the salty scent of the ocean as waves crashed against the rocks across the way. Gray clouds hung low as the wind blew brisk, but that hadn't stopped her from grabbing her brown leather jacket and walking the quarter-mile from her oceanfront hotel.

After a week in hiking boots and grubby clothes, she dressed for comfort in jeans and a creamy white cashmere sweater. Reveling in the luxury of an actual bed and electricity, she'd slept late and curled the ends of her hair, but she hadn't stopped there. She'd also applied her full arsenal of makeup, enjoying the simple pleasures of being back in civilization.

Loaded down with bags, she headed for the hotel as her mind wandered to her purchases. She hoped her mother would love the pretty lighthouse figurine she bought her; hopefully, as much as she adored the seashells and other knick-knacks she'd found for herself. As soon as she'd spotted the starfish and sand dollars arranged in a charming Nantucket basket, a nautical theme for her new apartment materialized—something soothing with touches of blue and white, candles on the bathtub held in place with beach sand in pretty glass vases. It would be perfect.

She sighed, ready for change. She needed it. Tagging the lynx with Jim and Dave had been her last field assignment for the foreseeable future. In two weeks, she was taking over as head researcher for the Los Angeles branch of The Bureau. After Yellowstone, her taste for backcountry tracking vanished. It just hadn't been the same without the team.

Life over the last few months had thrown one cruel punch after another. She'd lost so much—her friends, the man she loved—but tragedy hadn't broken her. She was still standing and determined to move on. Relocating was the first step. When her father offered her the LA position, she'd worried over it, knowing Hunter would be close by. But in a city with millions of people, bumping into him was doubtful. He had his life, and she had her own. If her stomach clutched a bit at the thought, she ignored it.

Chilled by the breeze of the late September day, she stopped at the small bookstore and coffee shop across from the hotel. She grabbed the latest issue of *Celebrity*, along with a cup of green tea with honey. Finding a seat by the cozy fireplace, she sipped at her sweetened drink as heat radiated from the flames, and she relaxed, leafing through the pages.

Morgan shook her head and rolled her eyes as she read about the newest celebrity breakup. She turned the page and froze in shock. Hunter and Tatiana Livingston monopolized an entire glossy page. Decked out in a black suit, Hunter draped an arm around one of Hollywood's most beautiful and popular movie stars. He was so breathtakingly handsome and official looking with an earpiece in place and an expression of fierce determination on his face as he pushed himself and the leading lady through a throng of paparazzi.

Unable to stop herself, she traced a finger over Hunter's striking features as her other hand pressed against her chest and the pain blooming in her heart. God, she *missed* him. She read the caption to the left of the picture. It was dated four days ago. Tatiana had spent five days touring Europe promoting her newest box office sensation.

Several minutes passed while Morgan stared at Hunter's picture. A log snapped, sparking in the grate as her mind floated back to their final night in the Tower Motel. There had been so much emotion, so much fun, so much *heat*, and what she'd foolishly believed to be love. She focused on his cool blue eyes and thought of the police station. His eyes had looked very much the same when he told her it had all been a mistake, that he'd gotten caught up in something that would never work. It still tore her to shreds.

She forced her gaze from the picture and sipped her drink that had gone cold. With a last look at the photograph, Morgan stood and walked away, throwing her paper cup in the trash, and then opened the door.

"Honey, you forgot your magazine," the woman at the counter called.

The wind played with her hair as she gave the lady a small smile. "Thank you, but you can keep it." The pleasure of the day vanished as she left the shop. It stung to know that the wall she'd built around herself could shatter with one look at a picture. It was time to get out of Maine and get on with her life. She was going to change her flight and leave tonight. It was time to get back to DC and get packed up. She no longer wanted the peace and serenity of the ocean. She wanted the mind-numbing chaos a cross-country move would bring.

She let herself into her room, dumped her bags, and peeled off her jacket. She grabbed her suitcase, determined to be on the next plane home. Even if she couldn't get a direct flight, it would be better than staying here.

A knock sounded at the door, and she stopped, frowning. *Who could that be?* She placed her bag down and looked through the peephole, spotting the smiling hotel attendant. Morgan opened the door. "Yes, can I help you?"

"Morgan Taylor?"

"Yes, that's me."

"A message was left for you at the desk." The attendant

handed it over.

She hesitated as she took it. The last time she was given a message in a hotel room, her world had turned upside down. She opened the pink sheet of paper and smiled.

What does a father have to do to get a phone call from his daughter?

Love,
Dad

"Thank you." She shut the door and walked over to pick up her cell phone when another knock sounded. She opened the door again, smiling. "Yes, did you—" Her smile disappeared and her heart pounded as she clutched the doorknob, staring into piercing blue eyes.

Hunter leaned against the doorjamb in jeans and a bomber jacket, looking tough and sinful. "You forgot to ask who it was."

Oh God. She thought she would never see him again, and here he was, standing in front of her, making her feel things she didn't want to feel. Love and pain overwhelmed her. In defense, she slammed the door in his face. Pressing her back against the glossy wood, she covered her face with shaking hands, fighting the need to give in to her watery legs and slide against the door until she sat. Why was he here? What did he want? In a matter of seconds, the life she was rebuilding was blown to pieces.

A knock sounded again. "Morgan, let me in. We need to talk."

She shook her head. He didn't get to do this to her. He didn't get to waltz back into her life almost three months after he'd destroyed it and leave her with nothing again.

"Come on, Morgan."

His voice weakened her, making her want to turn around and do just what he asked. Steeling herself, she crossed to the other side of the room and walked out the sliding glass doors leading to the beach. Eventually he would give up and go away.

The gusts of wind blew her hair, blinding her, and she swiped strands behind her ears. Cold to the bone, she hugged herself tightly, making her way to firmer sand close to the waves. The dull gray water roared, tossing spray. The sky darkened to pewter—a storm was on the way. It fit her mood perfectly.

Tears threatened to fall, but she blinked them back. Hadn't she promised herself there wouldn't be any more for him? Hunter could go back to wherever he came from and leave her the hell alone. She didn't want him anymore, didn't need him. Determined to believe her own lies, she continued down the beach, desperate to find some sort of grasp on the small pieces of happiness she had found over the last couple of months without him.

———◆———

Hunter knocked twice more before he figured Morgan wasn't going to answer. Closing his eyes, he rested his forehead against the frame. Christ, she'd taken his breath away. Her beauty was like a sucker punch to the gut. It had taken everything he had to act casual when she'd opened the door. He'd wanted to yank her into his arms, but the pain had been there, radiating in her eyes, and he'd hesitated for a second too long. Before he knew it, the door slammed with a sharp crack.

He stared at the dark, glossy wood and brushed nickel numbers of room 121 as he pulled the keycard he'd conned from the front desk attendant free from his pocket. His badge and a decent lie had done the trick. Blowing out a weary breath, he knocked, giving her one more chance. "Morgan, if you don't open the door, I'll open it myself. I really have to talk to you."

Still nothing.

His pulse pounded and his nerves stretched tight as he realized she might not give him another chance. He swiped the card, turning the handle as the green light flashed, and stepped into the room, breathing in the dark, sexy scent that was Morgan. Need, hot and bright, clutched in his belly. He had to have her back. He wouldn't leave until she left with him.

"Morgan?" Frowning, he scanned the room and opened the bathroom door. She hadn't answered because she wasn't here. He walked to the only other exit as a cool draft seeped through the sliding glass door Morgan hadn't closed all the way and caught a glimpse of her, slim and beautiful, her hair billowing around her shoulders as she disappeared behind a large grouping of rocks farther down the beach.

He grabbed the soft leather jacket from the bed and followed, walking quickly, afraid she would somehow find a way back to her room and be gone before he could make everything right. The jackhammer of his heart settled a bit when he rounded the rocks, and she stood statue-still with her eyes closed and her face to the wind. A small line creased the skin between her eyebrows, ruining the illusion of peace she projected. Hunter approached quietly, stopping just behind her, and settled the jacket on her shoulders.

She whirled. "Get out of here." Her lips quivered as she spoke. "I don't want you here." Shaking her head, she turned, poised to run.

He caught her arm before she took two steps. "Wait a minute. Wait a minute, Morgan."

"No." She pulled, struggling to free herself. "Just let me go."

In one swift move, he spun her until her back pressed against his chest and his hands held her around the waist.

She stilled instantly, standing rigid.

He pressed his face to her neck, breathing her in, holding on. "Please let me talk to you. I've missed you."

"Stop it." Her voice wavered as she tried to pull free once

more.

He tightened his grip. Whether it was selfish or not, he didn't care. Everything was on the line.

"What are you doing here?"

He turned her to face him, giving her no choice but to look him in the eye. "I came back for you."

"You came back for me?" She let loose a humorless laugh as anger snapped in her eyes, joining the unshed tears. "Should I feel honored?" She shoved him. "Let me go. I won't run."

He didn't want to, but he did as she asked. They both knew he would catch her if she tried.

She turned away, clutching her jacket around her as the waves crashed, pounding against the rocks.

"I needed to see you," he tried again.

"Why? Did the check bounce?"

He clenched his jaw. She wasn't going to make this easy. "This has nothing to do with the check. I shredded the damn thing. We need to talk. There are things I should've said before I left."

She faced him, her eyes still simmering. "I think you said plenty."

He rubbed at his tense jaw. "I was wrong. I screwed everything up."

Her fingers tightened against her folded arms. "On those points I won't argue, but it doesn't matter anymore. You've gone back to your life. So have I. You made everything very clear—there was nothing between us. I don't think we have anything more to say. I've gotta go. I have a plane to catch." She took a step in retreat.

She would walk away. She was finished with him. He grabbed her arm. "Don't go," he pleaded with panic edging his voice. "Please, don't go."

"I can't do this with you." She yanked free again. "I won't. You broke my—" She closed her eyes on a sob.

Her mask of cold indifference vanished, and for the first

time since he'd arrived, hope bloomed. He took advantage of her weakened moment, hugging her close. "Please, Morgan. Please don't walk away from me."

"You hurt me. One minute we were making plans for long weekends, and the next you were finished. No explanations—you were just correcting a mistake."

Guilt ate at him as he rested his cheek against her hair. "I know. After you got shot, it brought stuff back. It—it scared me. I couldn't handle it."

She eased back, looking him in the eye. "After everything we'd been through. I could've helped you if you would've let me, but you don't let anyone in. You have this impenetrable wall around you that no one is allowed to break. You don't need anyone—"

"That's not true. I need you. I want to fix this, Morgan. I have to."

She clutched her hands at the front of his jacket as her breath shuddered out. "Why?"

He ran his hands through her hair and grazed his knuckle against her cheek until she surrendered, dropping her forehead to his chest.

"Why?" she asked again, her voice muffled by the fabric of his shirt.

He placed his fingers under her chin until their gazes met. "Because I woke up one morning and realized you were everything. Because I fell in love with a feisty, hardheaded, sweet, funny woman, and I can't stand the thought of being without her for another second. I love you, Morgan." He brushed his lips against hers as her eyes filled, and he moved his hands, framing her face, desperate for her to believe him. "I love you so much. I'm so sorry I hurt you. It's hard for me to let people into my past, into all of the pain, but I'm working on it. There's no one I want with me more than you. There's no one I'll try harder for than you. Please tell me it's not too late to make everything right."

She took a deep, shaky breath, hesitating as a tear rolled

down her cheek. "No, it's not too late. I love you too."

Relief and happiness bubbled together as he kissed her long and sweet. Her arms came around his waist, pulling him closer as his lips left hers, skimming her neck before he took her hands in his. "A great friend once told me that when you find someone really amazing, you better grab them up before they get away. I'm not letting you get away, Morgan. I want you to marry me." He walked her backwards, pressing her body between his and an enormous boulder. "I want everything, and I want it with you." He pulled a black box from his jacket, flipping open the top. The ugly o-ring rested against the black velvet.

Morgan laughed. "You kept it."

Grinning, he slid the metal on her finger. "I have another ring for you in LA, but I was so nervous I forgot it."

She laughed again, twisting the ugly ring on her finger. "I can't believe you kept it."

"It's the feelings behind the symbol that count, right? Say you'll marry me."

"Oh, yes, Hunter. I'll marry you."

"Thank God." He kissed her and picked her up, carrying her back to the hotel with her head nestled on his shoulder. He set her on her feet in the room.

She took his hand, pulling him away from the glass door, inviting him to take her with her big green eyes. "This would probably be a good time for me to tell you I accepted a new job. I'm moving to LA next week."

His eyebrows rose in surprise as he tried to focus on the thread of their conversation. He had to touch her. "What?"

She removed his jacket, letting it fall to the floor, and slipped her hands under his white t-shirt, skimming her fingers against his skin, making him shiver. "I guess we'll have to bump up that date a bit." Her voice grew thick with desire. "The movers will just have to meet us there."

"Damn right. I'm not leaving here without you. You're coming home with me." He made quick work of her jacket and shirt, groaning as he brushed his hands along the smooth skin of her stomach.

She played her fingers through his hair as her gaze held his. "I'm so happy, Hunter."

He stared at Morgan, at everything he'd ever wanted, and kissed her tenderly as they fell to the bed.

THANK YOU!

Hi there!

Thank you for reading *Morgan's Hunter*. What did you think of Hunter and Morgan's story? Did you love it, like it, or maybe even hate it? I hope you'll share your thoughts by leaving an honest review.

I'll see you again soon when we catch up with another installment of the *Bodyguards of L.A. County* series.

Until next time,

~Cate

Falling For Sarah

Turn the page for a preview of book two in the *Bodyguards of L.A. County Series*.

« CHAPTER ONE »

September 24, 2010

SARAH JOHNSON TURNED THE KEY AND OPENED HER front door. She crossed the threshold, breathing in the familiar scent of fresh-cut flowers and the hint of low tide blowing in from the Pacific. "It's so nice to be home. Welcome home, sweet baby girl." She stared at her sleeping newborn, smiling, and brushed her lips over the soft skin of her baby's forehead.

"Look out, coming through," Ethan Cooke said, loaded down with balloons and vases overflowing with cheerful blooms. "I had no idea bringing a baby home from the hospital required movers."

Sarah stepped aside, chuckling. "I know. Kylee has quite a fan club already. Let me help you with some of this stuff."

"I've got it. You gave birth yesterday, for God's sake. The nurse told you to take it easy." He set the vase on the entryway table and released the balloons to the ceiling as he dropped the diaper bag from his shoulder to the floor. "Besides, Jake would kick my ass if he knew you were hauling things in."

Sarah's smile widened as she thought of her husband. "Yes, you're probably right, but I also know he would be grateful you were able to help me out. My mother wasn't expecting to run her shop today. Dana called in sick, so that was that."

Ethan moved closer to her side, staring at the baby. "I'm happy you called. I wanted to come visit you ladies again last night, but things got a little crazy while I was on duty." He brushed a finger down Kylee's tiny nose. "She really is beautiful, Sarah. She looks just like you."

Sarah's blue eyes twinkled. "Thank you but I definitely see some of Jake in her too." She wrapped her free arm around Ethan's waist. He returned her embrace, and she rested her head against his muscled shoulder. "I'm so happy right now, Ethan, so absolutely happy. Twenty-nine more days and my family will be whole again. I can't wait to hug Jake and watch his face when he holds her for the first time. I could tell he wanted to crawl through the video conferencing equipment yesterday and touch her tiny fingers and toes." She looked down at Kylee. "No more deployments for your daddy. He'll be all ours."

"He'll be mine too." Ethan grinned, wiggling his eyebrows. "I've been waiting just as eagerly for Jake's return. It took me two years to convince him to join my firm. Now I need to get Hunter on board, and the crew will be together again."

"Getting yourselves into as much trouble as ever, I'm sure. You'll have to wait a little longer for your new security expert. He's not leaving my side for at least a week."

"I think I can live with that." He kissed her forehead and started toward the door. "Let me get the rest of the stuff from the truck. Then I'll set up Jake's surprise."

"I can't wait for him to see it. I've nixed the big screen TV idea for so long, I'm pretty sure he's stopped hoping for one."

"It's a beauty, all right. He'll love it. I'll have everything hooked up in no time."

"Great." Brimming with joy, Sarah kissed her daughter again as Ethan went outside. She took the baby to the nursery she'd painstakingly painted on her own. The pale yellow stripes looked wonderful with the touches of pink scattered about the room. She put Kylee to her breast, listening to the door open and slam shut as Ethan brought their items in from his Range Rover. She smiled when she heard him rummaging through the cupboards in the kitchen. If he was anything, it was always hungry.

Kylee's mouth went slack as she fell back to sleep.

Sarah fastened her nursing bra and fixed her shirt. She settled Kylee against her shoulder and walked out to the kitchen while she rubbed her daughter's back, burping her.

Ethan stood in front of the open refrigerator, mumbling his excitement about her stocked shelves. He glanced up, grinning, and she itched for her camera. "Hey, I'm going to make myself a sandwich before I get started on the TV. Want one?"

"No thanks. Do you want me to make it for you?"

"Nah, you don't have to do that."

"Why don't you let me? I have another favor to ask of you." She smiled. "The least I can do is make you something to eat."

He went to the pantry, grabbing a loaf of bread. "Why don't you tell me what you need?" He pulled open a cupboard and took out a plate.

"A shower." She smiled again, nibbling her lip.

His eyes zeroed in on Kylee, and he took a step back. "Geez, I don't know, Sarah. I've never held a baby before. What if I drop her?"

A laugh bubbled in her throat at the sheer horror in his eyes. Even after he'd helped her through hours of labor, watched her deliver Kylee, and cut the cord in Jake's honor, he'd refused to hold her.

She walked to where he stood. "You're not going to drop her. Fold your arm like this." She held out her arm, bending at the elbow.

He cleared his throat, following her lead, and she placed Kylee in the crook of his rigid arm. He grabbed Sarah's hand when Kylee squirmed. "She's moving, she's moving. She's going to fall. Shit, Sarah, I really think this is a bad idea."

"I think it's a great idea. Trust me on this one." She adjusted the baby slightly, moving Ethan's arm closer to his body, making sure his hand held Kylee under her diapered bottom. She backed away from them, grinning at the discomfort and mild panic she read all over Ethan's face. "You're a natural. Look at you two. I need my camera."

He groaned as she moved to the pile of bags outside the kitchen door and grabbed her case, pulling her Nikon D3 from the bag. She held up the camera and looked through the lens. For a test shot, she focused on Ethan's arresting face. Sharp cheekbones and straight black eyebrows accentuated long, thick eyelashes and bold gray eyes. She zoomed in on the clear gray pools surrounded by dark, smoky rings and pressed the shutter closed in rapid succession. His firm, full lips and muscular torso showcased a man perfectly comfortable with his masculinity. She tightened her focus on his big hand holding Kylee's little body and clicked away again, moving in closer, getting lost in her passion for pictures.

"Sarah, do you want that shower or not?"

She pulled the camera back, focusing on Ethan's raised brow and lips pressed firm in annoyance. "Sorry. I got a little carried away. You two make excellent subjects. The camera loves your face."

"So you've told me more times than I can count."

She placed the Nikon back in the bag and zipped it closed. "You're doing a great job with her."

He glanced down at Kylee. "I guess this is okay."

"See? I'll be quick. She just ate so she should sleep. Here's the burp cloth just in case she spits up." Sarah draped the cotton towel over Ethan's shoulder.

As she backed out of the kitchen, Ethan took a step forward. "Wait. Um, what if she starts to cry?"

Amused by his distress, she couldn't help but smile. The man standing before her dealt with the scum of the earth every day, yet a seven-pound infant brought him to his knees. "Just jiggle your arm a little bit. She'll fall right back to sleep."

She turned and walked toward the bathroom, calling over her shoulder, "Oh, and relax. Babies feel tension."

———◆———

Alone and mildly terrified, Ethan stared down at the pretty little bundle snuggled against him. Her serene face, a miniature of Sarah's, was so perfect. She smelled of baby powder and weighed next to nothing.

He began to wiggle his arm just in case. "I guess this isn't so bad. Let's make a deal. If you keep sleeping until your mom comes back, I'll talk her and your dad into a really kick-ass swing set for the backyard. It'll be my present to you."

Kylee's lips made a sucking motion as she continued sleeping.

"Okay, I guess that means we have a deal."

Relaxing with more confidence, he turned back to the counter, attempting to make his sandwich one-handed. He finagled the twist tie from the plastic as Kylee curled closer against him. Startled, he dropped the bread and bent at the knees to pick up the loaf as Kylee grunted. Seconds later, a small, wet explosion sounded in her diaper. Still crouched, he stopped dead.

Kylee nuzzled herself against his chest and slept on.

"That couldn't be good." He stood and walked toward the bathroom, desperately hoping Sarah was finished. The radio played beyond the closed door as water sprayed into the bathtub.

The baby began to stir and fuss. He jiggled his arm from side to side, but Kylee's fussing turned into a lusty cry. Panicked, he almost forgot the rules of friendship and rushed into the bathroom. With his hand on the knob, he stopped himself. *Christ, pull it together, Cooke. You've got this.*

He headed to the pale pink and yellow bedroom, glancing back at the bathroom door wistfully. "Come on, Sarah. Hurry up," he muttered.

Kylee turned a deep pink as she cried harder.

He stared at her mouthful of smooth, toothless gums and her tiny fists curling tight as they moved about. "Okay, kid. I guess we don't have a choice here. Let's get you changed." He glanced around the cheerful room at the stuffed animals piled next to a rocking chair, zeroing in on the pine changing table and the stacks of diapers and wipes lying tidy on the shelf above.

He awkwardly laid Kylee down on the soft white pad, found a package of unopened diapers, and quickly scanned the directions. As Kylee continued to cry, he pulled a diaper off the shelf. "Look at these things. My hand's bigger than this." He located the sides with the tape, putting it down next to her, just like the picture showed. He unbuttoned her sleeper and the white onesie buttoned at her crotch. "How many layers are you wearing?" Blowing out a breath, he pulled the diaper tape next. "Here goes nothing." He eased the diaper away and swore. "Jesus, this isn't *right*. It's black and yellow. I think we need to take you back to the hospital." He focused on the browning raisin protruding from her stomach. "And look at that thing on your belly button. It didn't look like that yesterday." Completely flustered now, he pulled a wad of wipes from the bin and knocked the diaper cream to the floor.

Kylee's short gasping cries shrilled louder.

"Shh, shh, shh, it's okay, kid. I'm trying my best here. You're all right." He moved the wipes over the baby's bottom. "This stuff's like cement. Man, I'd rather be in an alley with three UZIs pointed at my head." With Kylee's tiny baby butt clean, he clumsily placed the new diaper under her and swore again when he realized the tapes faced her stomach. Her legs moved about in her outrage, making it hard to flip the diaper around. "You're not exactly helping me out, kiddo." He adjusted the diaper and fastened the tapes.

"There." He buttoned the onesie, muttering a curse when he mismatched the snaps. "Screw the pink outfit. This will have to do. You're worked up. I'm worked up." He placed his hand under Kylee's neck and head, scooping her bottom up with the other, like he saw Sarah do earlier. Kylee's cheek rested against his heart, and her cries turned to whimpers before they stopped.

"There you go, sweetheart. That was pretty awful, huh? I don't know about you, but I think I'm going to have nightmares for weeks." He walked to the rocking chair with Kylee and sat down, sliding his palm along the peach fuzz on her head as he moved the chair back and forth. "I think I was about to cry myself. Let's keep that between us, okay?"

"Here you are." Sarah peeked in the room with her mass of blonde hair twisted up in a towel on top of her head. Her face was left unframed, showcasing big, exotic eyes, high cheekbones, and a lush Cupid's bow mouth that smiled until she zeroed in on the mess on the changing table. "I see Kylee needed a change."

"Don't even ask. It was exhausting and traumatic for both of us."

She chuckled. "Why don't I take her?"

"Oh yeah, sure, now that the hard work's done."

Sarah reached down and took Kylee, leaving behind the floral scent of her soap.

"Sarah, I don't know how to say this, but I think there's something wrong with her."

Frowning, she pulled the baby back from her shoulder, giving her the once-over. "What is it? What's wrong with her?"

"Her umbilical cord is brown and her poop's all gooey and yellow. Blackish stuff was stuck to her butt. I had a hell of a time getting it off."

Sarah's shoulders relaxed and her grin returned. "The umbilical cord is drying up and will fall off, the black stuff is meconium, and she's breastfed. Everything's perfectly normal."

As if on cue, Kylee began to cry and root around.

"How do you *know* all this stuff? You're so calm. I mean you're always calm, but she's so little and helpless."

"When you grow up with an obstetrician in your house and your mother is obsessed with children in general, you learn. I've been around babies for as long as I can remember."

Kylee whimpered and sucked on her fist.

"Do you mind if I borrow the rocker? I think she's ready to eat again."

"I thought she just did."

"She's establishing her milk supply."

He winced. "Jesus. Let me go take care of the TV for you."

Sarah sat and began to unbutton her shirt. "Thanks."

"No problem."

"Ethan?"

He stepped into the hallway and stopped.

"Your sandwich is on the counter."

He smiled. "Thanks."

———◆———

Ethan brought the sandwich and a bowl of fruit salad to the living room. He took a huge bite of turkey, avocado, and tomato then put the plate on the sturdy oak coffee table. He pulled the tape from the side of the massive box and prepared to set up Jake's new TV. While he leafed through the instructions, Sarah's soft voice cooed to her daughter through the baby monitor. He glanced up from the booklet and around the homey living room, listening to Sarah. A sudden flash of envy for what Jake had snuck up, surprising him. Shaking his head, he looked back at the directions. Marriage and family weren't for him.

He was screwing the plasma screen onto its base when a car pulled up to the curb. "Hey, Sarah, someone's here."

"Hailey, the college girl from down the road, was planning on stopping by. She's desperate to babysit Kylee. You can let her in," she said into the monitor.

He tightened the last screw and stood, walking by the large picture window, expecting to see the short, brown-haired co-ed. Instead, he watched four military men dressed in dark green and khaki step from a black sedan. His heart hammered against his ribs as his stomach sank. "Shit, no. Oh my God, no." He whipped his head around, making sure Sarah wasn't coming and yanked the door open, stepping outside, and closed it behind him.

The men approached and Ethan stood in their path as if that would somehow change the news he knew they were here to bring. "What can I do for you?"

The group stopped in front of him. "Is this the home of Mrs. Sarah Johnson?"

"Yes, it is. Is he dead? Is Jake dead?"

"I'm sorry, sir. We need to speak with Mrs. Johnson."

Ethan saw the apology in the man's eyes, and the sudden grief knocked him back like a heavy blow. Jake had been one of his two best friends for years.

The men tried to move past him, but he blocked their way again. As much as he wanted a moment to catch his breath, he needed to protect Sarah more. "Don't take another step. I get that you can't tell me, but you're going to give me a minute to talk to her first. She just gave birth yesterday morning. This is going to crush her."

"We're here to offer any support we can, sir."

He opened the door and let them in before him. "Please, sit down. I'll go get Sarah." He walked from the room and started down the hall to the nursery. Stopping outside the room, he fisted his hands at his side and took a deep breath. Memories flashed through his mind, one after the other, and he braced his hands on the wall. He took another deep breath, trying to steel himself for what had quickly become the hardest moment of his life. He was about to watch Sarah's life fall apart.

He stepped into Kylee's room and stopped. Sarah had taken her hair from the towel. Wet ropes of smooth gold rested on her shoulders and her eyes were closed while Kylee suckled at her breast. If this were a picture, it would be titled "Beautiful Serenity." He was about to destroy it. He took another breath, walked to Sarah's side, and knelt down, taking her hand.

Her eyes flew open, staring into his. "You startled me." A smile played across her lips and faded. "What's wrong?" She sat up straighter, breaking Kylee's latch with her finger.

He tightened his grip on her hand, willing her to take all the strength he could give. "Sarah, there are some men waiting for you in the living room. They're Marines."

Her fingers clutched his like a vise before they went lax and the bright, bold blue of her eyes dimmed. "Okay," she said dully. She stood, covering her breast and pulled Kylee close, automatically burping her.

He draped his arm around her shoulders, walking with her and the baby to the living room. The men stood as they entered, and the officer stepped forward.

"Mrs. Johnson, I'm Commander Michael Driggs. I'm here to regretfully inform you that your husband, Gunnery Sergeant Jake Johnson, was killed in action today at six thirty-four p.m., Afghanistan time. The United States Marine Corps is truly sorry for your loss and is proud of the service your husband provided our country."

Sarah stared at the commander for several seconds before she slowly sat down on the couch.

Ethan sat beside her.

"Jake's gone?" she asked, her voice barely a whisper. "He can't be. He hasn't held Kylee yet. He's coming home in twenty-nine days to hold Kylee. He watched me give birth yesterday. He said he was coming home in four weeks."

Sarah's face paled with grief. Ethan swore he heard her heart shatter while the commander spoke. Her bubbly vibrancy had been replaced with fragility. He was afraid that if he touched her, she would break into a million pieces.

Ethan glanced at the man who now sat on the other side

of Sarah. "Sir, Gunnery Sergeant Hunter Phillips is in Jake's company. Is there any word on his welfare? He and Jake are—" he closed his eyes on a fresh wave of pain "—were my childhood friends. Hunter is also very close to Sarah."

"Gunnery Sergeant Phillips was wounded in action. He was shot in the shoulder. He's out of surgery and is resting comfortably." Commander Driggs looked at Sarah again. "Sergeant Phillips tried desperately to save your husband, Mrs. Johnson. Is there anyone we can call for you at this time?"

She shook her head. "I don't know. I can't think." She looked at Ethan, lost. "I can't think right now. I don't want to do this. I want to be alone."

He couldn't stand to see her like this. He put his arm around her, pulling her close, pressing his forehead to her hair. "Okay, you don't have to. I'll take care of everything. Go lay down."

The men stood when she took the baby and walked from the room.

"I'm sorry, Commander, gentlemen, but I'm going to have to ask you to leave. Do you have a card or a number I can take from you? I'll have Sarah's father call you as soon as I get ahold of him."

"Of course, sir."

Ethan took the card and walked them to the door, shutting it behind them. He went to the small desk, found Sarah's parents' number programmed into the phone, and called.

———◆———

Sarah lay Kylee in her crib and covered her with a light blanket. Her daughter slept soundly in the center of the mattress, unaware that their lives were forever changed. She stared at the photograph of Jake hanging on the wall above the crib. She had taken the picture the day before he left to finish his deployment, before they were aware they'd made

Kylee. His big, cheesy grin and smiling brown eyes filled the frame. *Oh God, Jake. You're gone. How can you be gone? I need you. I can't do this by myself.*

The dredges of shocked disbelief were melting away, and panicky dread quickly took its place. How was she going to live without him? She glanced down at Kylee again as a thought circled through her mind. It brought such crushing pain, she could hardly breathe. They would never meet. Jake would never touch the daughter he had helped create. Kylee would be robbed of ever knowing her father's love.

Jake's deep, infectious laugh echoed in her head and her legs buckled as her breath shuddered in and out. She would never hear it again.

Ethan's hands rested on her shoulders, and she flinched as he turned her toward him.

She stared into his eyes, saw the grief settled there, and a tear rolled down her cheek. "Tell me this isn't real, Ethan. Please tell me this isn't real," she said on a sob.

He pulled her into his arms, holding her tight. "Come here." He picked her up and sat with her in the rocking chair. Her long legs hung over the side, just skimming the floor as the chair swayed back and forth and Ethan cradled her close to his chest.

Finding comfort in the arms of her friend, she wept as Ethan's hand ran through her damp hair. "He's really gone. I can't believe he's really gone."

He lifted her chin, choking on his own sorrow as he spoke. "I'm making a promise to you right now, Sarah. You'll never be alone through this. I'll be here for you every step of the way, for as long as you need me."

"I'll always need you."

"Then I'll always be here." He cradled her head against his chest as their tears fell, mixing together on their hands they held clutched together.

ABOUT THE AUTHOR

Cate Beauman is the author of the best selling series, The
Bodyguards of L.A. County. She currently lives in Tennes-
see with her husband, two boys, and their St. Bernards, Bear
and Jack.

www.catebeauman.com
www.facebook.com/CateBeauman
www.goodreads.com/catebeauman
Follow Cate on Twitter: @CateBeauman

Morgan's Hunter
Book One: The story of Morgan and Hunter
ISBN: 978-0989569606

Morgan Taylor, D.C. socialite and wildlife biologist, leads a charmed life until everything changes with a phone call. Her research team has been found dead—slaughtered—in backcountry Montana.

As the case grows cold, Morgan is determined to unravel the mystery behind her friends' gruesome deaths. Despite the dangers of a murderer still free, nothing will stand in her way, not even the bodyguard her father hires, L.A.'s top close protection agent, Hunter Phillips.

Sparks fly from the start when no-nonsense Hunter clashes with Morgan's strong-willed independence. Their endless search for answers proves hopeless—until Hunter discovers the truth.

On the run and at the mercy of a madman, Morgan and Hunter must outsmart a killer to save their own lives.

Falling For Sarah
Book Two: The story of Sarah and Ethan
ISBN: 978-0989569613

Widow Sarah Johnson struggled to pick up the pieces after her life was ripped apart. After two years of grieving, she's found contentment in her thriving business as photographer to Hollywood's A-list and in raising her angel-faced daughter, Kylee... until bodyguard and long-time friend Ethan Cooke changes everything with a searing moonlight kiss.

Sarah's world turns upside down as she struggles with her unexpected attraction to Ethan and the guilt of betraying her husband's memory. But when blue roses and disturbing notes start appearing on her doorstep, she has no choice but to lean on Ethan as he fights to save her from a stalker that won't stop until he has what he prizes most.

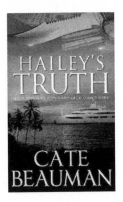

Hailey's Truth
Book Three: The story of Hailey and Austin
ISBN: 978-0989569620

Hailey Roberts has never had it easy. Despite the scars of a tragic childhood, she's made a life for herself. As a part-time student and loving nanny, she yearns for a family of her own and reluctant Austin Casey, Ethan Cooke Security's best close protection agent.

Hailey's past comes back to haunt her when her long lost brother tracks her down, bringing his dangerous secrets with him. At an emotional crossroads, Hailey accepts a humanitarian opportunity that throws her together with Austin, taking her hundreds of miles from her troubles, or so she thinks.

What starts out as a dream come true quickly becomes a nightmare as violence erupts on the island of Cozumel. Young women are disappearing, community members are dying—and the carnage links back to her brother.

As Austin struggles to keep Hailey's past from destroying her future, he's forced to make a decision that could turn her against him, or worse cost them both their lives.

Forever Alexa
Book Four: The story of Alexa and Jackson
ISBN: 978-0989569637

First grade teacher and single mother Alexa Harris is no stranger to struggle, but for once, things are looking up. The school year is over and the lazy days of summer are here. Mini-vacations and relaxing twilight barbeques are on the horizon until Alexa's free-spirited younger sister vanishes.

Ransom calls and death threats force Alexa and her young daughter to flee their quiet home in Maryland. With nowhere else to turn, Alexa seeks the help of Jackson Matthews, Ethan Cooke Security's Risk Assessment Specialist and the man who broke her heart.

With few leads to follow and Abby's case going cold, Alexa must confess a shocking secret if she and Jackson have any hope of saving her sister from a hell neither could have imagined.

Waiting For Wren
Book Five: The story of Wren and Tucker
ISBN: 978-0989569644

Wren Cooke has everything she's ever wanted—a thriving career as one of LA's top interior designers and a home she loves. Business trips, mockups, and her demanding clientele keep her busy, almost too busy to notice Ethan Cooke Security's gorgeous Close Protection Agent, Tucker Campbell.

Jaded by love and relationships in general, Wren wants nothing to do with the hazel-eyed stunner and his heart-stopping grins, but Tucker is always in her way. When Wren suddenly finds herself bombarded by a mysterious man's unwanted affections, she's forced to turn to Tucker for help.

As Wren's case turns from disturbing to deadly, Tucker whisks her away to his mountain home in Utah. Haunted by memories and long-ago tragedies, Tucker soon realizes his past and Wren's present are colliding. With a killer on the loose and time running out, Tucker must discover a madman's motives before Wren becomes his next victim.

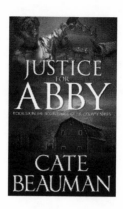

Justice For Abby
Book Six: The story of Abby and Jared
ISBN: 978-0989569651

Fashion designer Abigail Harris has been rescued, but her nightmare is far from over. Determined to put her harrowing ordeal behind her and move on, she struggles to pick up the pieces of her life while eluding the men who want her dead.

The Mid-Atlantic Sex Ring is in ruins after Abby's interviews with the police. The organization is eager to exact their revenge before her testimony dismantles the multi-million dollar operation for good.

Abby's safety rests in the hands of former US Marshal, Jerrod Quinn. Serious-minded and obsessed with protocol, Ethan Cooke Security's newest agent finds himself dealing with more than he bargains for when he agrees to take on his beautiful, free-spirited client.

As the trial date nears, Abby's case takes a dangerous turn. Abby and Jerrod soon discover themselves in a situation neither of them expect while Jerrod fights to stop the ring from silencing Abby once and for all.

Saving Sophie
Book Seven: The story of Sophie and Stone
ISBN: 978-0989569668

Jewelry designer Sophie Burke has fled Maine for the an-onymity of the big city. She's starting over with a job she tol-erates and a grungy motel room she calls home on the wrong side of town, but anything is better than the nightmare she left behind.

Stone McCabe is Ethan Cooke Security's brooding bad boy, more interested in keeping to himself than anything else— until the gorgeous blond with haunted violet eyes catches his attention late one rainy night.

Stone reluctantly gives Sophie a hand only to quickly re-alize that the shy beauty with the soft voice and pretty smile has something to hide. Tangled up in her secrets, Stone offers Sophie a solution that has the potential to free her from her problems once and for all—or jeopardize both of their lives.

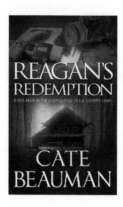

Reagan's Redemption
Book Eight: The story of Reagan and Shane
ISBN: 978-0989569675

Doctor Reagan Rosner loves her fast-paced life of practicing medicine in New York City's busiest trauma center. Kind and confident, she's taking her profession by storm—until a young girl's accidental death leaves her shaken to her core. With her life a mess and her future uncertain, Reagan accepts a position as Head Physician for The Appalachia Project, an outreach program working with some of America's poorest citizens.

Shane Harper, Ethan Cooke Security's newest team member, has been assigned a three-month stint deep in the mountains of Eastern Kentucky, and he's not too happy about it. Guarding a pill safe in the middle of nowhere is boring as hell, but when he gets a look at his new roommate, the gorgeous Doctor Rosner, things start looking up.

Shane and Reagan encounter more than a few mishaps as they struggle to gain the trust of a reluctant community. They're just starting to make headway when a man's routine checkup exposes troubling secrets the town will do anything to keep hidden—even if that means murder.

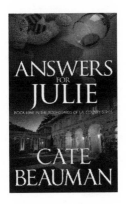

Answers For Julie
Book Nine: The story of Julie and Chase
ISBN: 978-0989569682

Julie Keller relishes the simple things: hot chocolate on winter nights, good friends she calls her family, and her laid-back career as a massage therapist and yoga instructor. Julie is content with her life until Chase Rider returns to Bakersfield.

Bodyguard Chase Rider isn't thrilled to be back in the town where he spent his childhood summers. His beloved grandmother passed away, leaving him a house in need of major repairs. With a three-week timetable and a lot to do, he doesn't have time for distractions. Then he bumps into Julie, the one woman he hoped never to see again. Chase tries to pretend Julie doesn't exist, but ten years hasn't diminished his attraction to the hazel-eyed stunner.

When a stranger grabs Julie's arm at the grocery store—a woman who insists Julie's life isn't what it seems, Chase can't help but get involved. Julie and Chase dig into a twenty-five-year-old mystery, unearthing more questions than answers. But the past is closer than they realize, and the consequences of the truth have the potential to be deadly.

Book Ten Coming Soon!

Finding Lyla
Book Ten: The story of Lyla and Collin
ISBN: 978-0989569699

Made in the USA
Columbia, SC
29 May 2018